John Buchan led a truly extraordinary life: he was a diplomat, soldier, barrister, journalist, historian, politician, publisher, poet and novelist. He was born in Perth in 1875, the eldest son of a Free Church of Scotland minister, and educated at Hutcheson's Grammar School in Glasgow. He graduated from Glasgow University then took a scholarship to Oxford. During his time there – 'spent peacefully in an enclave like a monastery' – he wrote two historical novels.

In 1901 he became a barrister of the Middle Temple and a private secretary to the High Commissioner for South Africa. In 1907 he married Susan Charlotte Grosvenor; they had three sons and a daughter. After spells as a war correspondent, Lloyd George's Director of Information and a Conservative MP, Buchan moved to Canada in 1935 where he became the first Baron Tweedsmuir of Elsfield.

Despite poor health throughout his life, Buchan's literary output was remarkable – thirty novels, over sixty non-fiction books, including biographies of Sir Walter Scott and Oliver Cromwell, and seven collections of short stories. His distinctive thrillers – 'shockers' as he called them – were characterised by suspenseful atmosphere, conspiracy theories and romantic heroes, notably Richard Hannay (based on the real-life military spy William Ironside) and Sir Edward Leithen. Buchan was a favourite writer of Alfred Hitchcock, whose screen adaptation of *The Thirty-Nine Steps* was phenomenally successful.

John Buchan served as Governor-General in Canada from 1935 until his death in 1940, the year his autobiography *Memory Hold-the-door* was published.

STUART KELLY is the Literary Editor of *Scotland on Sunday*. He is the author of *The Book of Lost Books* and has contributed to *The Decadent Handbook*, *Alasdair Gray: Critical Appreciations* and the Scottish Government's *Introducing Scottish Literature*. He is currently writing a book on Sir Walter Scott.

JOHN BUCHAN

Midwinter

Introduced by Stuart Kelly

First published in 1923 by Hodder & Stoughton
This edition published in Great Britain in 2008 by Polygon,
an imprint of Birlinn Ltd

West Newington House
10 Newington Road
Edinburgh
EH9 1QS

www.birlinn.co.uk

ISBN 978 1 84697 070 2

British Library Cataloguing-in-Publication Data
A catalogue record for this book is
available on request from the British Library.

Typeset by Hewer Text UK Ltd, Edinburgh
Printed and bound by CPI Cox & Wyman, Reading, RG1 8EX

to VERNON WATNEY

We two confess twin loyalties—
Wychwood beneath the April skies
Is yours, and many a scented road
That winds in June by Evenlode.
Not less when autumn fires the brake,
Yours the deep heath by Fannich's lake,
The corries where the dun deer roar
And eagles wheel above Sgurr Mór.
So I, who love with equal mind
The southern sun, the northern wind,
The lilied lowland water-mead
And the grey hills that cradle Tweed,
Bring you this tale which haply tries
To intertwine our loyalties.

Contents

Introduction

In his autobiography, *Memory Hold-the-Door*, John Buchan looked back on his writing career, and the difference between his successful 'shockers' and his more literary works. 'These were serious books,' he wrote, 'and they must have puzzled many of the readers who were eager to follow the doings of Richard Hannay and Dickson McCunn. That is the trouble with an author who writes only to please himself; his product is not standardised, and the purchaser is often disappointed. I once had a letter from an Eton boy who, having a taste for a bustling yarn, was indignant at anything of mine that did not conform to their pattern. He earnestly begged me to "pull myself together".' Buchan doesn't specify which of his self-described 'serious books' – *The Free Fishers*, *Witch Wood*, *The Blanket of the Dark* and *Midwinter* – occasioned the irate correspondence. But of all his novels, *Midwinter* is the most curious and unsettling. It is an elegiac thriller, a romance about self-control and an historical novel featuring characters outside of history. It is simultaneously sincere and cheeky.

Buchan started *Midwinter* shortly after moving to Elsfield Manor in Oxfordshire, and it was serialised in the *Daily Telegraph* before being published in 1923. He wanted to 'catch the spell of the great Midland forest and the Old England which lay everywhere beyond the highroads and ploughlands'. In a self-published local history, *Cornbury and the Forest of Wychwood*, by his neighbour Vernon Watney, Buchan learned that many Jacobites, including Lord Mansfield, had found sanctuary and assistance in the area after the failure of Charles Edward Stuart's 1745 campaign. Buchan had previously used a Jacobite setting for *A Lost Lady of Old Years*, and took this hint to revisit the uprising from an unusual new perspective.

The story proper begins with Alastair Maclean, a Highlander in the service of Bonnie Prince Charlie, sent as an advance guard into England to secure the support of the sympathetic gentry. Buchan turns the most famous Jacobite novel, Sir Walter Scott's *Waverley*, systematically inside-out. Instead of an English hero heading north, we have a Scottish hero travel-ling south. The alien landscape – a place of 'tangled forests', 'unfeatured woodland', 'fathomless mud' and 'jungle' – is the rural Cotswolds, not uncultivated Moray. The 'dozen varieties of dialect' and 'slow burring speech' are in the mouths of the English characters (Maclean even becomes Muck Lane in their tongue), while Alastair speaks formal and correct English. As the novel progresses, these inversions and overturned expecta-tions multiply and proliferate. *Waverley's* Jacobite dalliance does not exclude him from a happy ending and a respectable marriage: in contrast, the conclusion of *Midwinter* asserts that 'Clear eyes are for men an honourable possession, but they do not make for happiness'.

Just as the vacillating Edward Waverley meets representatives of the different kinds of Scots, the steadfast Maclean is intro-duced to characters who exemplify Englishness. As well as the fox-hunting and aptly named Squire Thicknesse, Buchan sketches the innkeepers, recruiting sergeants and gamekeepers with deft touches. Part of the charm of *Midwinter* lies in Buchan's inspired idea of having Maclean meet and team up with that acme of 'John Bull' England, Dr Samuel Johnson.

Buchan exploits a lovely loophole in history; the fact that very little is known about Johnson's life in the crucial years 1745–6. His biographer Boswell writes: 'It is somewhat curious, that his literary career appears to have been almost totally suspended in the years 1745 and 1746, those years which were marked by a civil war in Great-Britain, when a rash attempt was made to restore the House of Stuart to the throne. That he had a tenderness for that unfortunate House, is well known; and some may fancifully imagine, that a sympathetick anxiety impeded the exertion of his intellectual powers.' All we do know is that Johnson published in April 1745 *Miscellaneous Observations on the Tragedy of Macbeth*, which included a proposal for Johnson's edition of *The Plays of Shakespeare* (1765). This announcement brought down the wrath of London's premier publisher, Jacob Tonson, who had the copyright for other editions of Shakespeare and threatened Johnson and his publisher with legal action. To compound Johnson's worries, his pamphlet had the embarrassing misprint SHAKESHEAR on the title page.

Buchan has a lot of fun with Johnson's 'missing years', and in the preface wryly suggests that the events of *Midwinter* explain the Great Cham's notorious antipathy to the Scots. Time and again, the most quotable quotes of Johnson spring to his lips: 'A man may be tired of the country, but when he is tired of London he is tired of life', 'With you, sir, patriotism is the last refuge of the scoundrel' and even 'The end was a proof, if proof were wanted, of the vanity of human wishes'. It's done with such a light and unobtrusive hand that you have to remember the clunky modern historical novels, usually featuring a famous figure as a detective, to appreciate the gracefulness. In a neat and knowing touch, Buchan even has Johnson contemplating the idea that he will 'change his name to MacIan, and be as fierce as any Highlander'.

The other representative of Englishness is the eponymous and mysterious Amos Midwinter, a gentleman who has forsaken his inheritance to live with the gipsies, charcoal-burners, and 'spoonbills' of Old England. He describes it as an England that 'has outlived Roman and Saxon and Dane and Norman and will outlast the Hanoverian. It has seen priest turn to presbyter and presbyter to parson and has only smiled. It is the land of the edge of the moorlands and the rim of the forests and the twilight before dawn.'

Midwinter's secret league, the 'Naked Men', assists Maclean in moments of peril, but remains aloof from the political

machinations. He symbolises a pagan continuity in England,
the kind of magical harmony with nature that can be seen in
Wayland Smith in Scott's *Kenilworth* and Herne the Hunter in
John Masefield's *The Box of Delights*. Oddly, when Buchan
returned to the theme of persisting, pre-Christian attitudes in
The Dancing Floor (1926) and *Witch Wood* (1927), it was in far
darker tones: yet in *Midwinter*, the pagan is wholly healthy and
beneficent. Midwinter may have foregone civilisation, but not
chivalry. The Roman altar that is the focus for black magic in
Witch Wood is a convivial gathering place in *Midwinter*.

But the England of Buchan's novel is changing, regardless of
the futility of the Pretender's campaign. It is no coincidence that
the villain of the piece – one of Buchan's most engaging and
understandable villains – is motivated by mercantile and bour-
geois love of money rather than by ideology or commitment.
The curious gothic section when the wicked gypsy Ben threa-
tens to plunge Alastair into a deep pothole he calls 'Journeyman
John' has overtones of the coming Industrial Revolution. The
pothole makes 'a sound like millstones working under a full
press of water'. It grinds away, and nothing comes out but
'threads and buttons'.

The changing nature of England is handled most thoroughly in
the wonderful debate between Alastair and his honourable opponent, General Oglethorpe. 'But, sir, there is a new temper in the
lands. You may have heard of the people they call Methodists,' he
says. 'They preach a hope for the vilest. With them is the key of the
new England, for they bring healing to the souls of the people . . .
What can your fairy Prince say to the poor and the hungry?'; thus
succinctly damning the whole Jacobite enterprise.

Oglethorpe also is given Buchan's most articulate summary
of his conservative and high Tory principles: 'I hold this
mongering of novelties an invention of the Devil . . . I plead
for the English people and I want no change, least of all the
violent change of revolution.' In his denunciations of profiteers
and time-servers, it's hard not to discern Buchan's own inter-
war anxieties about the sacrifices of the First World War.

There is a chilly, melancholy tone to the whole novel. From the outset, where the Duchess counsels Alastair – 'You have before you two worlds – the enclosed garden and the wild beyond. The wild is yours, by birthright and training and choice. Beyond the pale is Robin Hood's land, where men adventure. Inside is a quiet domain where they make verses and read books and cherish possessions – my brother's land' – it is clear that the days of derring-do are over. At the beginning, Alastair wonders, 'What did a kestrel in the home of peacocks?', a sentiment which returns at the end, subtly and sadly changed as he predicts the rout at Culloden – 'as hopeless as a battle of a single kestrel against a mob of ravens'.

Even Midwinter's romantic 'Naked Men' must be foregone. Midwinter admits that although 'a naked man travels fast and light, for he has nothing that he can lose', nevertheless 'he is also defenceless and the shod feet of the world can hurt him'. The final offer, of joining the Old England 'which is the refuge of battered men', is tempting, but insufficient. For Buchan, life always has to go on, and escape is an impossibility. If there is a moral to *Midwinter* it may well be the admonition of the Eton schoolboy to Buchan: 'Pull yourself together.'

Reviewing *Midwinter*, the *New York Times* said that 'it is a story that has many merits and few faults, the greatest of which is that it tells too little of Midwinter. Can it be that the author is reserving him for another tale?' Buchan never did return to the mysterious Midwinter, and, in a way, I rather prefer that he remains an enigmatic and haunting presence, glimpsed through blackthorn hedges and disappearing into holloways.

Midwinter may move with the pace and vigour of one of Buchan's shockers, but it is a more mature and sophisticated novel, both morally astute and emotionally complicated. The reader knows the outcome in advance – rather than the 'if' of the thrillers, Buchan explores the 'how' and 'why' of the historical novel. It also lends a quiet irony to many of the characters' aspirations and exchanges: Alastair's final epiphany is of 'the ironic pattern of life spread out beneath, as a man views a campaign from a mountain, and he came near to laughter – laughter with an undertone of tears'. J.B. Priestley once complained that Buchan's steady stream of popular fiction distracted him from writing a truly great novel: *Midwinter* shows exactly what he was capable of as a novelist. But most of all, *Midwinter* is the finest tribute to English landscape, English customs and English character ever penned by a Scotsman.

Stuart Kelly
July 2008

Preface
by the Editor

Last year my friend, Mr Sebastian Derwent, on becoming senior partner of the reputable firm of solicitors which bears his name, instituted a very drastic clearing out of cupboards and shelves in the old house in Lincoln's Inn Fields. Among a mass of derelict papers – cancelled deeds, mouldy files of correspondence, copies of pleadings in cases long ago forgotten – there was one little bundle which mystified him, since it had no apparent relation to the practice of the law. He summoned me to dinner, and, with our chairs drawn up to a bright fire and a decanter of his famous brown sherry between us, we discussed its antecedents.

First there was a document of three quarto pages, which appeared to be a fair copy in a scrivener's hand. It started and finished abruptly, so we judged it to be a portion of a larger work. Then came a long ill-written manuscript, partly in a little volume of which the clasp and lock had been broken, and partly on loose paper which seemed to have been torn from the beginnings and ends of printed books. The paper had no watermark that we could discover, but its quality suggested the eighteenth century. Last there was a bundle of letters in various hands, all neatly docketed and dated. Mr Derwent entrusted me with the papers, for certain words and phrases in the quarto sheets had stirred my interest. After considerable study I discovered that the packet contained a story, obscure in parts, but capable of being told with some pretence of continuity.

First for the matter copied by the amanuensis. It was clearly a fragment, intended by the compiler to form part of an intro-

duction to the work. On first reading it I rubbed my eyes and
tasted the joy of the discoverer, for I believed that I had
stumbled upon an unknown manuscript of Mr James Boswell,
written apparently after the publication of his *Life of Johnson*, and
designed for a supplementary volume, which, Dr Johnson being
dead, he felt at liberty to compile. On reflection I grew less
certain. The thing was undoubtedly the work of an intimate
friend of the Great Lexicographer, but, though there were
mannerisms of style and thought which suggested Mr Boswell,
I did not feel able to claim his authorship with any confidence. It
might be the production of one or other of the Wartons, or of Sir
Robert Chambers, or of some Oxford friend of Johnson whose
name has not come down to us. Mr Derwent at my request
explored the records of his firm, which extended back for the
better part of a century, but could find no evidence that it had
ever done business for any member of the family of Auchinleck.
Nevertheless I incline to attribute the thing to Mr Boswell, for he
alone of Johnson's circle was likely to have the eager interest in
Scotland which the manuscript reveals, and the dates do not
conflict with what we know of his movements.

Here, at all events, is the text of it:

In the last week of June in the year 1763 Johnson was in
Oxford, and I had the honour to accompany him one
afternoon to the village of Elsfield, some four miles from
the city, on a visit to Mr Francis Wise, one of the fellows of
Trinity College and Radcliffe's librarian. As I have already
mentioned, there were certain episodes in the past life of
my illustrious friend as to which I knew nothing, and
certain views, nay, I venture to say prejudices, in his mind,
for the origin of which I was at a loss to account. In
particular I could never receive from him any narrative of
his life during the years 1745 and 1746, the years of our
last civil war, during which his literary career seems to
have been almost totally suspended. When I endeavoured
to probe the matter, he answered me with some asperity,

so that I feared to embarrass him with further questions. 'Sir, I was very poor,' he once said, 'and misery has no chronicles.' His reticence on the point was the more vexatious to me, since, though a loyal supporter of the present Monarchy and Constitution, he always revealed a peculiar tenderness towards the unfortunate House of Stuart, and I could not but think that in some episode in his past lay the key to a sentiment which was at variance with his philosophy of government. I was also puzzled to explain to my own mind the reason for his attitude towards Scotland and the Scotch nation, which afforded him matter for constant sarcasms and frequent explosions of wrath. As the world knows, he had a lively interest in the primitive life of the Highlands, and an apparent affection for those parts, but towards the rest of Scotland he maintained a demeanour so critical as to be liable to the reproach of harshness. These prejudices, cherished so habitually that they could not be attributed to mere fits of spleen, surprised me in a man of such pre-eminent justice and wisdom, and I was driven to think that some early incident in his career must have given them birth; but my curiosity remained unsatisfied, for when I interrogated him, I was met with a sullen silence, if we were alone, and, if company were present, a tempestuous ridicule which covered me with blushes.

On this occasion at Elsfield that happened which whetted my curiosity, but the riddle remained unread till at this late stage of my life, when my revered Master has long been dead, fortune has given the key into my hand. Mr Francis Wise dwelt in a small ancient manor of Lord North's, situated on the summit of a hill with a great prospect over the Cherwell valley and beyond it to the Cotswold uplands. We walked thither, and spent the hour before dinner very pleasantly in a fine library, admiring our host's collection of antiquities and turning the pages of a noble folio wherein he had catalogued the coins in the

Bodleian collection. Johnson was in a cheerful humour, the exercise of walking had purified his blood, and at dinner he ate heartily of veal sweetbreads, and drank three or four glasses of Madeira wine. I remember that he commended especially a great ham. 'Sir,' he said, 'the flesh of the pig is most suitable for Englishmen and Christians. Foreigners love it little, Jews and infidels abhor it.'

When the meal was over we walked in the garden, which was curiously beautified with flowering bushes and lawns adorned with statues and fountains. We assembled for tea in an arbour, constructed after the fashion of a Roman temple, on the edge of a clear pool. Beyond the water there was a sharp declivity, which had been utilised to make a cascade from the pool's overflow. This descended to a stone tank like an ancient bath, and on each side of the small ravine lines of beeches had been planted. Through the avenue of the trees there was a long vista of meadows in the valley below, extending to the wooded eminence of the Duke of Marlborough's palace of Blenheim, and beyond to the Cotswold hills. The sun was declining over these hills, and, since the arbour looked to the west, the pool and the cascade were dappled with gold, and pleasant beams escaped through the shade to our refuge.

Johnson was regaled with tea, while Mr Wise and I discussed a fresh bottle of wine. It was now that my eminent friend's demeanour, which had been most genial during dinner, suffered a sudden change. The servant who waited upon us was an honest Oxfordshire rustic with an open countenance and a merry eye. To my surprise I observed Johnson regarding him with extreme disfavour. 'Who is that fellow?' he asked when the man had left us. Mr Wise mentioned his name, and that he was of a family in the village. 'His face reminds me of a very evil scoundrel,' was the reply. 'A Scotchman,' he added.

'But no nation has the monopoly of rogues.'

After that my friend's brow remained cloudy, and he stirred restlessly in his chair, as if eager to be gone. Our host talked of the antiquities in the neighbourhood, notably of the White Horse in Berkshire and of a similar primitive relic in Buckinghamshire, but he could elicit no response, though the subject was one to which I knew Johnson's interest to be deeply pledged. He remained with his chin sunk on his breast, and his eyes moody as if occupied with painful memories. I made anxious inquiries as to his health, but he waved me aside. Once he raised his head, and remained for some time staring across the valley at the declining sun.

'What are these hills?' he asked.

Mr Wise repeated names – Woodstock, Ditchley, Enstone. 'The trees on the extreme horizon,' he said, 'belong to Wychwood Forest.'

The words seemed to add to Johnson's depression. 'Is it so?' he murmured. 'Verily a strange coincidence. Sir, among these hills, which I now regard, were spent some of the bitterest moments of my life.'

He said no more, and I durst not question him, nor did I ever succeed at any later date in drawing him back to the subject. I have a strong recollection of the discomfort of that occasion, for Johnson relapsed into glumness and presently we rose to leave. Mr Wise, who loved talking and displayed his treasures with the zest of the owner of a raree show, would have us visit, before going, a Roman altar which, he said, had lately been unearthed on his estate. Johnson viewed it peevishly, and pointed out certain letters in the inscription which seemed fresher than the rest. Mr Wise confessed that he had himself recut these letters, in conformity, as he believed, with the purpose of the original. This threw Johnson into a transport of wrath. 'Sir,' he said, 'the man who would tamper with an ancient monument, with whatever intentions, is

capable of defiling his father's tomb.' There was no word
uttered between us on the walk back to Oxford. Johnson
strode at such a pace that I could scarcely keep abreast of
him, and I would fain have done as he did on an earlier
occasion, and cried *Sufflamina.*[1]

The incident which I have recorded has always remained vivid in my memory, but I despaired of unravelling the puzzle, and believed that the clue was buried for
ever in the grave of the illustrious dead. But, by what I
prefer to call Providence rather than Chance, certain
papers have lately come into my possession, which enable
me to clear up the mystery of that summer evening, to add
a new chapter to the life of one of the greatest of mankind,
and to portray my dear and revered friend in a part which
cannot fail to heighten our conception of the sterling
worth of his character.

Thus far the quarto pages. Their author – Mr Boswell or some
other – no doubt intended to explain how he received the further
papers, and to cast them into some publishable form. Neither
task was performed. The rest of the manuscript, as I have said,
was orderly enough, but no editorial care had been given it. I
have discovered nothing further about Alastair Maclean save
what the narrative records, and my research among the archives
of Oxfordshire families has not enabled me to add much to the
history of the other figures. But I have put such materials as I
had into the form of a tale, which seems of sufficient interest to
present to the world. I could wish that Mr Boswell had lived to
perform the task, for I am confident that he would have made a
better job of it.

---

1 See Boswell's *Life of Johnson*, anno 1754.

ONE

In which a Highland Gentleman Misses His Way

The road which had begun as a rutted cart-track sank presently to a grassy footpath among scrub oaks, and as the boughs whipped his face the young man cried out impatiently and pulled up his horse to consider. He was on a journey where secrecy was not less vital than speed, and he was finding the two incompatible. That morning he had avoided Banbury and the high road which followed the crown of Cotswold to the young streams of Thames, for that way lay Beaufort's country, and at such a time there would be jealous tongues to question passengers. For the same reason he had left the main Oxford road on his right, since the channel between Oxford and the North might well be troublesome, even for a respectable traveller who called himself Mr Andrew Watson, and was ready with a legend of a sea-coal business in Newcastle. But his circumspection seemed to have taken him too far on an easterly course into a land of tangled forests. He pulled out his chart of the journey and studied it with puzzled eyes. My Lord Cornbury's house could not be twenty miles distant, but what if the twenty miles were pathless? An October gale was tossing the boughs and whirling the dead bracken, and a cold rain was beginning. Ill weather was nothing to one nourished among Hebridean north-westers, but he cursed a land in which there were no landmarks. A hill-top, a glimpse of sea or loch, even a stone on a ridge, were things a man could steer by, but what was he to do in this unfeatured woodland? These soft south-country folk stuck to their roads, and the roads were forbidden him.

A little further and the track died away in a thicket of hazels. He drove his horse through the scrub and came out on a glade, where the ground sloped steeply to a jungle of willows, beyond which he had a glimpse through the drizzle of a grey-green fen. Clearly that was not his direction, and he turned sharply to the right along the edge of the declivity. Once more he was in the covert, and his ill-temper grew with every briar that whipped his face. Suddenly he halted, for he heard the sound of speech.

It came from just in front of him – a voice speaking loud and angry, and now and then a squeal like a scared animal's. An affair between some forester and a poaching hind, he concluded, and would fain have turned aside. But the thicket on each hand was impenetrable, and, moreover, he earnestly desired advice about the road. He was hesitating in his mind, when the cries broke out again, so sharp with pain that instinctively he pushed forward. The undergrowth blocked his horse, so he dismounted and, with a hand fending his eyes, made a halter of the bridle and dragged the animal after him. He came out into a little dell down which a path ran, and confronted two human beings.

They did not see him, being intent on their own business. One was a burly fellow in a bottle-green coat, a red waistcoat and corduroy small clothes, from whose gap-toothed mouth issued volleys of abuse. In his clutches was a slim boy in his early teens, a dark sallow slip of a lad, clad in nothing but a shirt and short leather breeches. The man had laid his gun on the ground, and had his knee in the small of the child's back, while he was viciously twisting one arm so that his victim cried like a rabbit in the grip of a weasel. The barbarity of it undid the traveller's discretion.

'Hold there,' he cried, and took a pace forward.

The man turned his face, saw a figure which he recognised as a gentleman, and took his knee from the boy's back, though he still kept a clutch on his arm.

'Sarvant, sir,' he said, touching his hat with his free hand. 'What might 'ee be wanting o' Tom Heather?' His voice was civil, but his face was ugly.

'Let the lad go.'

'Sir Edward's orders, sir – that's Sir Edward Turner, Baronet, of Ambrosden House in this 'ere shire, 'im I 'as the honour to serve. Sir Edward 'e says, "Tom," 'e says, "if 'ee finds a poacher in the New Woods 'ee knows what to do with 'im without troubling me"; and I reckon I does know. Them moor-men is the worst varmints in the country, and the youngest is the black-heartedest, like foxes.'

The grip had relaxed and the boy gave a twist which freed him. Instantly he dived into the scrub. The keeper made a bound after him, thought better of it and stood sullenly regarding the traveller.

'I've been a-laying for the misbegotten slip them five weeks, and now I loses him, and all along of 'ee, sir.' His tones suggested that silver might be a reasonable compensation.

But the young man, disliking his looks, was in no mood for almsgiving, and forgot the need of discretion. Also he came from a land where coin of the realm was scarce.

'If it's your master's orders to torture babes, then you and he can go to the devil. But show me the way out of this infernal wood and you shall have a shilling for your pains.'

At first the keeper seemed disposed to obey, for he turned and made a sign for the traveller to follow. But he swung round again, and, resting the gun which he had picked up in the crook of his arm, he looked the young man over with a dawning insolence in his eyes. He was beginning to see a more profitable turn in the business. The horseman was soberly but reputably dressed, and his beast was good, but what did he in this outlandish place?

'Making so bold,' said the keeper, 'how come 'ee a-wandering 'ere, sir? Where might 'ee be a-making for?'

'Charlbury,' was the answer.

The man whistled. 'Charlbury,' he repeated. 'Again begging pardon, sir, it's a place known for a nest of Papishes. I'd rather ha' heerd 'ee was going to Hell. And where might 'ee come from last, sir?'

The traveller checked his rising temper. 'Banbury,' he said
shortly.

The keeper whistled again. ''Ee've fetched a mighty round-
about way, sir, and the good turnpike running straight for any
Christian to see. But I've heard tell of folks that fought shy of
turnpikes.'

'Confound you, man,' the traveller cried; 'show me the road
or I will find it myself and you'll forfeit your shilling.'

The keeper did not move. 'A shilling's no price for a man's
honesty. I reckon 'ee mun come up with me to Sir Edward, sir.
He says to me only this morning – '' 'Ee watch the Forest, Tom,
and if 'ee finds any that can't give good account of themselves,
'ee fetch them up to me, and it'll maybe mean a golden guinea
in your pocket.'' Sir Edward 'e's a Parliament man, and a
Justice, and 'e's hot for King and country. There's soldiers at
Islip bridge-end asking questions of all as is journeying west,
and there's questions Sir Edward is going to ask of a gentleman
as travels from Banbury to Charlbury by the edges of Otmoor.'

The servility had gone from the man's voice, and in its place
were insolence and greed. A guinea might have placated him,
but the traveller was not accustomed to bribe. A hot flush had
darkened his face, and his eyes were bright.

'Get out of my way, you rogue,' he cried.

The keeper stood his ground. ''Ee will come to Sir Edward
with me if 'ee be an honest man.'

'And if not?'

'It's my duty to constrain 'ee in the name of our Lord the
King.'

The man had raised his gun, but before he could bring the
barrel forward he was looking at a pistol held in a very steady
hand. He was no coward, but he had little love for needless
risks, when he could find a better way. He turned and ran up the
steep path at a surprising pace for one of his build, and as he ran
he blew shrilly on a whistle.

The traveller left alone in the dell bit his lips with vexation. He
had made a pretty mess of a journey which above all things

should have been inconspicuous, and had raised a hue and cry after him on the domain of some arrogant Whig. He heard the keeper's steps and the note of his whistle grow fainter; he seemed to be crying to others and answers came back faintly. In a few minutes he would be in a brawl with lackeys. . . . In that jungle there was no way of escape for a mounted man, so he must needs stand and fight.

And then suddenly he was aware of a face in the hazels.

It was the slim boy whom his intervention had saved from a beating. The lad darted from his cover and seized the horse's bridle. Speaking no word, he made signs to the other to follow, and the traveller, glad of any port in a storm, complied. They slithered at a great pace down the steep bank to the thicket of willows, which proved to be the brink of a deep ditch. A little way along it they crossed by a ford of hurdles, where the water was not over a man's riding boots. They were now in a morass, which they threaded by a track which showed dimly among the reeds, and, as the whistling and cries were still audible behind them, they did not relax their pace. But after two more deep runnels had been passed, and a mere thick with water-lilies crossed by a chain of hard tussocks like stepping-stones, the guide seemed to consider the danger gone. He slowed down, laughing, and cocked snooks in the direction of the pursuit. Then he signed to the traveller to remount his horse, but when the latter would have questioned him, he shook his head and put a finger on his lips. He was either dumb, or a miracle of prudence.

The young man found himself in a great green fenland, but the falling night and the rain limited his view to a narrow circle. There was a constant crying of snipe and plover around him, and the noise of wild fowl rose like the croaking of frogs in the Campagna. Acres of rank pasture were threaded with lagoons where the brown water winked and bubbled above fathomless mud. The traveller sniffed the air with a sense of something foreign and menacing. The honest bitter smell of peat-bogs he loved, but the odour of this marsh was heavy and sweet and

rotten. As his horse's hooves squelched in the sodden herbage
he shivered a little and glanced suspiciously at his guide. Where
was this gypsy halfling leading him? It looked as if he had found
an ill-boding sanctuary.

With every yard that he advanced into the dank green wilderness his oppression increased. The laden air, the mist, the
clamour of wild birds, the knowledge that his horse was no
advantage since a step aside would set it wallowing to the girths,
all combined to make the place a prison-house, hateful to one on
an urgent mission. . . . Suddenly he was above the fen on a hard
causeway, where hooves made a solid echo. His spirits recovered, for he recognised Roman work, and a Roman road did not
end in sloughs. On one side, below the level of the causeway,
was a jungle of blackthorn and elder, and a whiff of wood-smoke
reached his nostrils. The guide halted and three times gave a call
like that of a nesting redshank. It was answered, and from an
alley in the scrub a man appeared.

He was a roughly dressed countryman, wearing huge
leathern boots muddied to the knee. Apparently the guide
was not wholly dumb, for he spoke to him in an odd voice
that croaked from the back of his throat, and the man nodded
and bent his brows. Then he lifted his eyes and solemnly
regarded the horseman for the space of some seconds.

'You be welcome, sir,' he said. 'If you can make shift with
poor fare there be supper and lodging waiting for you.'

The boy made signs for him to dismount, and led off the
horse, while the man beckoned him to follow into the tunnel in
the scrub. In less than fifty yards he found himself in a clearing
where a knuckle of gravel made a patch of hard ground. In the
centre stood a small ancient obelisk, like an overgrown mile-
stone. A big fire of logs and brushwood was burning, and round
it sat half a dozen men, engaged in cooking. They turned slow
eyes on the newcomer, and made room for him in their circle.

'Tom Heather's been giving trouble. He cotched Zerry and
was a-basting him when this gentleman rides up. Then he turns
on the gentleman, and, being feared o' him as man to man, goes

whistling for Red Tosspot and Brother Mark. So Zerry brings the gentleman into the Moor, and here he be. I tell him he's kindly welcome, and snug enough with us moor-men, though the King's soldiers was sitting in all the Seven Towns.'

'He'd be safe,' said one, 'though Lord Abingdon and his moor-drivers was prancing up at Beckley.'

There was a laugh at this, and the new-comer, cheered by the blaze and the smell of food, made suitable reply. He had not quite understood their slow burring speech, nor did they altogether follow his words, for he spoke English in the formal clipped fashion of one to whom it was an acquired tongue. But the goodwill on both sides was manifest, and food was pressed on him – wild duck roasted on stakes, hunks of brown bread, and beer out of leather jacks. The men had been fowling, for great heaps of mallard and teal and widgeon were piled beyond the fire.

The traveller ate heartily, for he had had no meal since breakfast, and as he ate, he studied his companions in the firelight. They were rough-looking fellows, dressed pretty much alike in frieze and leather, and they had the sallowish skin and yellow-tinged eyes which he remembered to have seen among dwellers in the Ravenna marshes. But they were no gipsies or outlaws, but had the assured and forthright air of men with some stake in the land. Excellent were their manners, for the presence of a stranger in no way incommoded them; they attended to his wants, and with easy good-breeding talked their own talk. Understanding little of that talk, he occupied himself in observing their faces and gestures with the interest of a traveller in a new country. These folk were at once slower and speedier than his own kind – more deliberate in speech and movement, but quicker to show emotion in their open counte-nances. He speculated on their merits as soldiers, for against such as these he and his friends must presently fight.

''Morrow we'd best take Mercot Fleet,' said one. 'Mas'r Midwinter reckons as the floods will be down come Sunday.'

'Right, neighbour Basson,' said another. 'He knows times and seasons better'n Parson and near as well as Almighty God.'

'What be this tale of bloody wars?' asked a third. 'The Spoonbills be out, and that means that the land is troubled. They was saying down at Noke that Long Giles was seen last week at Banbury fair and the Spayniard was travelling the Lunnon road. All dressed up he were like a fine gentleman, and at Wheatley Green Man he was snuffing out o' Squire Norreys' box.'

'Who speaks of the Spoonbills?' said the man who had first welcomed the traveller. 'We bain't no ale-house prattlers. What Mas'r Midwinter wants us to know I reckon he'll tell us open and neighbourly. Think you he'll make music the night?'

'He's had his supper the best part of an hour, and then he'll take tobacco. After that happen he'll gie us a tune.'

The speaker had looked over his shoulder, and the traveller, following his glance, became aware that close on the edge of the thicket a small tent was pitched. The night had fallen thick and moonless, but the firelight, wavering in the wind, showed it as a grey patch against the gloom of the covert. As the conversation droned on, that patch held his eyes like a magnet. There was a man there, someone with the strange name of Midwinter, someone whom these moor-men held in reverence. The young man had the appetite of his race for mysteries, and his errand had keyed him to a mood of eager inquiry. He looked at the blur which was the tent as a terrier watches a badger's earth.

The talk round the fire had grown boisterous, for someone had told a tale which woke deep rumbling laughter. Suddenly it was hushed, for the thin high note of a violin cleft the air like an arrow.

The sound was muffled by the tent-cloth, but none the less it dominated and filled that lonely place. The traveller had a receptive ear for music and had heard many varieties in his recent wanderings, from the operas of Rome and Paris to gypsy dances in wild glens of Apennine and Pyrenees. But this fiddling was a new experience, for it obeyed no law, but jigged and wailed and chuckled like a gale in an old house. It seemed to be a symphony of the noises of the moor, where unearthly birds sang duets with winds from the back of beyond. It stirred him strangely. His own bagpipes could bring tears to his eyes with memory of things dear and familiar; but this quickened his blood, like a voice from a far world.

The group by the fire listened stolidly with their heads sunk, but the young man kept his eyes on the tent. Presently the music ceased, and from the flap a figure emerged with the fiddle in its hand. The others rose to their feet, and remained standing till the musician had taken a seat at the other side of the fire from the traveller. 'Welcome, Mas'r Midwinter,' was the general greeting, and one of them told him the story of Tom Heather and their guest.

The young man by craning his neck could see the new figure clear in the glow of the embers. He made out a short man of an immense breadth of shoulder, whose long arms must have reached well below his knees. He had a large square face, tanned to the colour of bark, and of a most surprising ugliness, for his nose was broken in the middle, and one cheek and the corner of one eye were puckered with an old scar. Chin and lips were shaven, and the wide mouth showed white regular teeth. His garments seemed to be of leather like the others, but he wore a cravat, and his hair, though unpowdered, was neatly tied.

He was looking at the traveller and, catching his eye, he bowed and smiled pleasantly.

'You have found but a rough lodging, Mr—' he said, with the lift of interrogation in his voice.

'Andrew Watson they call me. A merchant of Newcastle, sir, journeying Bristol-wards on a matter of business.' The formula, which had sounded well enough hitherto, now seemed inept, and he spoke it with less assurance.

The fiddler laughed. 'That is for change-houses. Among friends you will doubtless tell another tale. For how comes a merchant of the North country to be so far from a high road? Shall I read the riddle, sir?'

He took up his violin and played very low and sweetly a Border lilt called 'The Waukin' o' the Fauld'. The young man listened with interest, but his face did not reveal what the musician sought. The latter tried again, this time the tune called 'Colin's Cattle', which was made by the fairies and was hummed everywhere north of Forth. Bright eyes read the young man's face. 'I touch you,' the fiddler said, 'but not closely.'

For a moment he seemed to consider, and then drew from his instrument a slow dirge, with the rain in it and the west wind and the surge of forlorn seas. It was that lament which in all the country from Mull to Moidart is the begetter of long thoughts. He played it like a master, making his fiddle weep and brood and exult in turn, and he ended with a fantastic variation so bitter with pain that the young man, hearing his ancestral melody in this foreign land, cried out in amazement.

The musician lowered his violin, smiling. 'This time,' he said, 'I touch you at the heart. Now I know you. You have nothing to fear among the moor-men of the Seven Towns. Take your ease, Alastair Maclean, among friends.'

The traveller, thus unexpectedly unveiled, could find no words for his astonishment.

'Are you of the honest party?' he stammered, more in awe than in anxiety.

'I am of no party. Ask the moor-men if the Spoonbills trouble their heads with Governments?'

The answer from the circle was a laugh.

'Who are you, then, that watches thus the comings and goings of travellers?'

'I am nothing – a will-o'-the-wisp at your service – a clod of vivified dust whom its progenitors christened Amos Midwinter. I have no possession but my name, and no calling but that of philosopher. Naked I came from the earth, and naked I will return to it.'

He plucked with a finger at the fiddle-strings, and evoked an odd lilt. Then he crooned:

'Three naked men I saw,
One to hang and one to draw,
One to feed the corbie's maw.'

The men by the fire shivered, and one spoke. 'Let be, Mas'r Midwinter. Them words makes my innards cold.'

'I will try others,' and he sang:

'Three naked men we be,
Stark aneath the blackthorn tree.
Christ ha' mercy on such as we!'

The young man found his apprehensions yielding place to a lively curiosity. From this madman, whoever he might be, he ran no risk of betrayal. The thought flashed over his mind that here was one who might further the cause he served.

'I take it you are not alone in your calling?' he said.

'There are others – few but choice. There are no secrets among us who camp by Jacob's Stone.' He pointed to the rude obelisk which was just within the glow of the fire. 'Once that was an altar where the Romans sacrificed to fierce gods and pretty goddesses. It is a thousand years and more since it felt their flame, but it has always been a trysting place. We Christian men have forsworn Apollo, but maybe he still lingers, and the savour of our little cooking fires may please him. I am one that takes no chances with the old gods. . . . Here there is safety for the honest law-breaker, and confidence for the friend, for we are reverent souls. How does it go? – *Fides et Pax et Honos Pudorque priscus.*'

'Then tell me of your brotherhood?'

The man laughed. 'That no man can know unless he be sealed of it. From the Channel to the Tyne they call us the Spoonbills, and on Cumbrian moors they know us as the Bog-blitters. But our titles are as many as the by-names of Jupiter. Up in your country I have heard that men talk of us as the Left-Handed.'

He spoke the last word in Gaelic – *ciotach* – and the young man at the sound of his own tongue almost leapt to his feet.

'Have you the speech?' he cried in the same language.

The man shook his head. 'I have nothing. For our true name is that I have sung to you. We are the Naked Men.' And he crooned again the strange catch.

For an instant Alastair felt his soul clouded by an eeriness which his bustling life had not known since as a little boy he had wandered alone into the corries of Sgurr Dubh. The moonless night was black about him, and it had fallen silent except for the sputter of logs. He seemed cut off from all things familiar by infinite miles of midnight, and in the heart of the darkness was this madman who knew all things and made a mock of knowledge. The situation so far transcended his experience that his orderly world seemed to melt into shadows. The tangible bounds of life dislimned and he looked into outer space. But the fiddler dispelled the atmosphere of awe, for he pulled out a pipe and filled and lit it.

'I can offer you better hospitality, sir, than a bed by the fire. A share of my tent is at your service. These moor-men are hardened to it, but if you press the ground this October night you will most surely get a touch of the moor-evil, and that is ill to cure save by a week's drinking of Oddington Well. So by your grace we will leave our honest friends to their talk of latimer and autumn markets.'

Accompanied by deep-voiced 'Good-nights' Alastair followed the fiddler to the tent, which proved to be larger and more pretentious than it had appeared from the fire. Midwinter lit a small lamp which he fastened to the pole, and closed the flap. The traveller's mails had been laid on the floor, and two couches had been made up of skins of fox and deer and badger heaped on dry rushes.

'You do not use tobacco?' Midwinter asked. 'Then I will administer a cordial against the marsh fever.' From a leathern case he took a silver-mounted bottle, and poured a draught into a horn cup. It was a kind of spiced brandy which Alastair had drunk in Southern France, and it ran through his blood like a mild and kindly fire, driving out the fatigue of the day but disposing to a pleasant drowsiness. He removed his boots and coat and cravat, loosened the points of his breeches, replaced his wig with a kerchief, and flung himself gratefully on the couch.

Meantime the other had stripped almost to the buff, revealing a mighty chest furred like a pelt. Alastair noted that the underclothes which remained were of silk; he noticed, too, that the man had long fine hands at the end of his brawny arms, and that his skin, where the weather had not burned it, was as delicately white as a lady's. Midwinter finished his pipe, sitting hunched among the furs, with his eyes fixed steadily on the young man. There was a mesmerism in those eyes which postponed sleep, and drove Alastair to speak. Besides, the lilt sung by the fire still hummed in his ears.

'Who told you my name?' he asked.

'That were too long a tale. Suffice it to say that I knew of your coming, and that long before Banbury you entered the orbit of my knowledge. Nay, sir, I can tell you also your errand, and I warn you that you will fail. You are about to beat at a barred and bolted door.'

'I must think you mistaken.'

'For your youth's sake, I would that I were. Consider, sir. You come from the North to bid a great man risk his all on a wild hazard. What can you, who have all your days been an adventurer, know of the dragging weight of an ordered life and broad lands and a noble house? The rich man of old turned away sorrowful from Christ because he had great possessions! Think you that the rich man nowadays will be inclined to follow your boyish piping?'

Alastair, eager to hear more but mindful of caution, finessed.

'I had heard better reports of his Grace of Beaufort,' he said.

The brown eyes regarded him quizzically. 'I did not speak of the Duke, but of Lord Cornbury.'

The young man exclaimed. 'But I summon him in the name of loyalty and religion.'

'Gallant words. But I would remind you that loyalty and religion have many meanings, and self-interest is a skilled interpreter.'

'Our Prince has already done enough to convince even self-interest.'

'Not so. You have for a moment conquered Scotland, but you will not hold it, for it is written in nature that Highlands will never for long control Lowlands. England you have not touched and will never move. The great men have too much to lose and the plain folk are careless about the whole quarrel. They know nothing of your young Prince except that he is half foreigner and whole Papist, and has for his army a mob of breechless mountainers. You can win only by enlisting Old England, and Old England has forgotten you.'

'Let her but remain neutral, and we will beat the Hanoverian's soldiers.'

'Maybe. But to clinch victory you must persuade the grandees of this realm, and in that I think you will fail. You are Johnnie Armstrong and the King. "To seek het water beneath cauld ice, surely it is a great follie." And, like Johnnie, the time will come for you to say good-night.'

'What manner of man are you, who speak like an oracle? You are gentle born?'

'I am gentle born, but I have long since forfeited my heritage. Call me Ulysses, who has seen all the world's cities and men, and has at length returned to Ithaca. I am a dweller in Old England.'

'That explains little.'

'Nay, it explains all. There is an Old England which has outlived Roman and Saxon and Dane and Norman and will outlast the Hanoverian. It has seen priest turn to presbyter and presbyter to parson and has only smiled. It is the land of the edge of moorlands and the rims of forests and the twilight before dawn, and strange knowledge still dwells in it. Lords and Parliament-men bustle about, but the dust of their coaches stops at the roadside hedges, and they do not see the quiet eyes watching them at the fords. Those eyes are their masters, young sir. I am gentle born, as you guess, and have been in my day scholar and soldier, but now my companions are the moor-men and the purley-men and the hill-shepherds and the raggle-taggle gypsies. And I am wholly content, for my calling is philosophy. I stand aside in life, and strike no blows and make no bargain, but I learn that which is hid from others.'

Alastair stirred impatiently.

'You are not above forty,' he said. 'You have health and wits and spirit. Great God, man, have you no cause or leader to fight for? Have you no honest ambition to fulfil before you vanish into the dark?'

'None. You and I are at opposite poles of mind. You are drunken with youth and ardent to strike a blow for a dozen loves. You value life, but you will surrender it joyfully for a whimsy of honour. You travel with a huge baggage of ambitions and loyalties. For me, I make it my business to travel light, caring nothing for King or party or church. As I told you, I and my like are the Naked Men.'

Alastair's eyes were drooping.

'Have you no loyalties?' he asked sleepily.

The answer wove itself into his first dream. 'I have the loyalties of Old England.'

When Alastair awoke he found his boots cleaned from the mud of yesterday, and his coat well brushed and folded. The moor-men had gone off to their fowling, and the two were alone in the clearing, on which had closed down a dense October fog. They breakfasted off a flagon of beer and a broiled wild-duck, which Midwinter cooked on a little fire. He had resumed his coarse leather garments, and looked like some giant gnome as he squatted at his task. But daytime had taken from him the odd glamour of the past night. He now seemed only a thick-set countryman – a horse-doctor or a small yeoman.

The boy Zerry appeared with the horse, which had been skilfully groomed, and Midwinter led the young man to the Roman causeway.

'It is a clear road to Oddington,' he told him, 'where you can cross the river by the hurdle bridge. Keep the bells of Woodea-ton that we call the Flageolets on your left hand – they will be ringing for St Luke's morn. Presently you will come to the Stratford road, which will bring you to Enstone and the fringe of Wychwood forest. You will be at Cornbury long before the dinner-hour.'

When Alastair was in the saddle, the other held out his hand.

'I have a liking for you, and would fain serve you. You will not be advised by me but will go your own proud road. God prosper you, young sir. But if it so be that you should lose your fine baggage and need a helper, then I have this word for you. Find an ale-house which, whatever its sign, has an open eye painted beneath it, or a cross-roads with a tuft of broom tied to the signpost. Whistle there the catch I taught you last night, and maybe the Naked Men will come to your aid.'

TWO

In which a Nobleman is Perplexed

By midday Alastair, riding at leisure, had crossed the first downs of Cotswold and dropped upon the little town of Charlbury, drowsing by Evenlode in a warm October noon. He had left the fog of morning behind in the Cherwell valley, the gale of the previous day had died, and the second summer of St Luke lay soft on the countryside. In the benign weather the events of the night before seemed a fantastic dream. No mystery could lurk in this land of hedgerows and fat pastures; and the figure of Midwinter grew as absurd in his recollection as the trolls that trouble an indifferent sleeper. But a vague irritation remained. The fellow had preached a cowardly apathy towards all that a gentleman held dear. In the rebound the young man's ardour flamed high; he would carve with his sword and his wits a road to power, and make a surly world acknowledge him. Unselfish aims likewise filled his mind – a throne for his Prince, power for Clan Gillian, pride for his land, and for his friends riches and love.

In Charlbury he selected his inn, the Wheatsheaf, had his horse fed and rubbed down, drank a tankard of ale, rid himself of the dust of the roads, and deposited his baggage. A decorous and inconspicuous figure, in his chocolate coat and green velvet waistcoat with a plain dark hat of three cocks, the servants of the inn were at once civil and incurious. He questioned the landlord about the Forest of Wychwood, as if his errand lay with one of the rangers, and was given a medley of information in a speech which had the slurred 's's' and the burred 'r's' of Gloucestershire. There was the Honourable Mr Baptist Leveson-Gower, at the Rangers' Lodge, and Robert Lee at the Burford Lawn Lodge, and Jack Blackstone, him they called Chuffle Jack, at the Thatched Lodge, and likewise the Verderers, Peg Lee and Bob Jenkinson. He assumed that his guest's business lay with Mr Leveson-Gower, and Alastair did not undeceive him, but asked casually where lay Cornbury. The landlord took him by the arm, and pointed beyond the stream to the tree-clad hills. 'Over the river, sir, by the road that turns right-handed at the foot of the street. You passes the gate on your way to Rangers' Lodge. His Lordship be in residence, and entertains high quality. His lady sister, the Scotch Duchess, arrived two days back, and there's been post-chaises and coaches going to and fro all week.'

Alastair remounted his horse in some disquiet, for a houseful of great folks seemed to make but a poor setting for urgent and secret conclaves. By a stone bridge he crossed the Evenlode which foamed in spate, the first free-running stream he had seen since he left the North, and passed through massive iron gates between white lodges built in Charles the Second's day. He found himself in an avenue of chestnuts and young limes, flanked by the boles of great beeches, which stretched magnificently up the slopes of a hill. In the centre was a gravelled road for coaches, but on either side lay broad belts of turf strewn with nuts and fallen leaves. . . . His assurance began to fail, for he remembered Midwinter's words on the Moor. The place was a vast embattled fortress of ease, and how would a messenger fare here who brought a summons to hazard all? In his own country a gentleman's house was a bare stone tower, looking out on moor or sea, with a huddle of hovels round the door. To such dwellings men sat loose, as to a tent in a campaign. But the ordered amenities of such a mansion as this – the decent town at the gates richer than a city of Scotland, the acres of policies that warded the house from the vulgar eye, the secular trees, the air of long-descended peace – struck a chill to his hopes. What did a kestrel in the home of peacocks?

At the summit of the hill the road passed beneath an archway into a courtyard; but here masons were at work and Alastair turned to the left, in doubt about the proper entrance. Fifty yards brought him in sight of a corner of the house and into a pleasance bright with late flowers, from which a park fell away into a shallow vale. There in front of him was a group of people walking on the stone of the terrace.

He was observed, and from the party a gentleman came forward, while the others turned their backs and continued their stroll. The gentleman was in the thirties, a slim figure a little bent in the shoulders, wearing his own hair, which was of a rich brown, and dressed very plainly in a country suit of green. He advanced with friendly peering eyes, and Alastair, who had dismounted, recognised the master of the house from a miniature he had seen in M. de Tremouille's hands.

'Have I the honour to address Lord Cornbury?' he asked.

The other bowed, smiling, and his short-sighted eyes looked past the young man, and appraised his horse.

'My lord, I have a letter from M. de Tremouille.'

Lord Cornbury took the letter, and, walking a few paces to a clump of trees, read it carefully twice. He turned to Alastair with a face in which embarrassment strove with his natural kindliness.

'Any friend of M. de Tremouille's is friend of mine, Captain Maclean. Show me how I can serve you. Your baggage is at the inn? It shall be brought here at once, for I would not forgive myself if one recommended to me by so old a friend slept at a public hostelry.'

The young man bowed. 'I will not refuse your hospitality, my lord, for I am here to beg an hour of most private conversation. I come not from France, but from the North.'

A curious embarrassment twisted the other's face.

'You have the word?' he asked in a low voice.

'I am *Alcinous*, of whom I think you have been notified.'

Lord Cornbury strode off a few steps and then came back. 'Yes,' he said simply, 'I have been notified. I expected you a month back. But let me tell you, sir, you have arrived in a curst inconvenient hour. This house is full of Whiggish company.

There is my sister Queensberry, and there is Mr Murray, His Majesty's Solicitor. . . . Nay, perhaps the company is the better cloak for you. I will give you your private hour after supper. Meantime you are Captain Maclean – of Lee's Regiment. I think, in King Louis' service – and you have come from Paris from Paul de Tremouille on a matter of certain gems in my collection that he would purchase for the Duc de Bouillon. You are satisfied you can play that part, sir? Not a word of politics. You do not happen to be interested in statecraft, and you have been long an exile from your native country, though you have a natural sentiment for the old line of Kings. Is that clear, sir? Have you sufficient of the arts to pose as a virtuoso?'

Alastair hoped that he had.

'Then let us get the first plunge over. Suffer me to introduce you to the company.'

The sound of their steps on the terrace halted the strollers. A lady turned, and at the sight of the young man her eyebrows lifted. She was a slight figure about the middle size, whose walking clothes followed the new *bergère* fashion. Save for her huge hooped petticoats, she was the dainty milkmaid, in her flowered chintz, her sleeveless coat, her flat straw hat tied with ribbons of cherry velvet, her cambric apron. A long staff, with ribbons at the crook, proclaimed the shepherdess. She came toward them with a tripping walk, and Alastair marked the delicate bloom of her cheeks, unspoiled by rouge, the flash of white teeth as she smiled, the limpid depth of her great childlike eyes. His memory told him that the Duchess had passed her fortieth year, but his eyes saw a girl in her teens, a Flora of spring whose summer had not begun.

'Kitty, I present to you Captain Maclean, a gentleman in the service of His Majesty of France. He has come to me on a mission from Paul de Tremouille – a mission of the arts.'

The lady held out a hand. 'Are you by any happy chance a poet, sir?'

'I have made verses, madam, as young men do, but I halt far short of poetry.'

'The inspiration may come. I had hoped that Harry would provide me with a new poet. For you must know, sir, that I have lost all my poets. Mr Prior, Mr Gay, Mr Pope – they have all been gathered to the shades. I have no one now to make me verses.'

'If your Grace will pardon me, your charms can never lack a singer.'

'La, la! The singers are as dry as a ditch in midsummer. They sigh and gloom and write doleful letters in prose. I have to fly to Paris to find a well-turned sonnet. . . . Here we are so sage and dutiful and civically minded. Mary thinks only of her lovers, and Mr Murray of his law-suits, and Mr Kyd of his mortgage deeds, and Kit Lacy of fat cattle – nay, I do not think that Kit's mind soars even to that height.'

'I protest, madam,' began a handsome sheepish young gentleman behind her, but the Duchess cut him short.

'Harry!' she cried, 'we are all Scotch here – all but you and Kit, and to be Scotch nowadays is to be suspect. Let us plot treason. The King's Solicitor cannot pursue us, for he will be *criminis particeps*.'

Mr Murray, a small man with a noble head and features so exquisitely moulded that at first sight most men distrusted him, pointed to an inscription cut on the entablature of the house.

'*Deus haec nobis otia fecit*,' he read, in a voice whose every tone was clear as the note of a bell. 'We dare not offend the *genius loci*, and outrage that plain commandment.'

'But treason is not business.'

'It is apt to be the most troublous kind of business, madam.'

'Then Kit shall show me the grottos.' She put an arm in the young man's, the other in the young girl's, and forced them to a pace which was ill suited to his high new hunting boots. Alastair was formally introduced to the two men remaining, and had the chance of observing the one whom the Duchess had called Mr Kyd. He had the look of a country squire, tall, heavily built and deeply tanned by the sun. He had brown eyes, which regarded the world with a curious steadiness, and a mouth the corners of which were lifted in a perpetual readiness for laughter. Rarely had Alastair seen a more jovial and kindly face, which was yet redeemed from the commonplace by the straight thoughtful brows and the square cleft jaw. When the man spoke it was in the broad accents of the Scotch lowlands, though his words and phrases were those of the South. Lord Cornbury walked with Mr Murray, and the other ranged himself beside Alastair.

'A pleasant habitation, you will doubtless be observing, sir. Since you're from France you may have seen houses as grand, but there's not the like of it in our poor kingdom of Scotland. In the Merse, which is my countryside, they stick the kitchen-midden up against the dining-room window, and their notion of a pleasance is a wheen grosart bushes and gillyflowers sore scarted by hens.'

Alastair looked round the flowery quincunx and the trim borders where a peacock was strutting amid late roses.

'I think I would tire of it. Give me a sea loch and the heather and a burn among birchwoods.'

'True, true, a man's heart is in his calf-country. We Scots are like Ulysses, and not truly at home in Phaeacia.' He spoke the last word with the slightest lift of his eyebrows, as if signalling to the other that he was aware of his position. 'For myself,' he continued, 'I'm aye remembering sweet Argos, which in my case is the inconsiderable dwelling of Greyhouses in a Lammermoor glen. My business takes me up and down this land of England, and I tell you, sir, I wouldn't change my crow-step gables for all the mansions ever biggit. It's a queer quirk in us mercantile folk.'

'You travel much?'

'I needs must, when I'm the principal doer of the Duke of Queensberry. My father was man of business to auld Duke James, and I heired the job with Duke Charles. If you serve a mighty prince, who is a duke and marquis in two kingdoms and has lands and messuages to conform, you're not much off the road. Horses' iron and shoe-leather are cheap in that service. But my pleasure is at home, where I can read my Horace and crack with my friends and catch trout in the Whitader.'

Mr Kyd's honest countenance and frank geniality might have led to confidences on Alastair's part, but at the moment Lord Cornbury rejoined them with word that dinner would be served in half an hour. As they entered the house, Alastair found himself beside his host and well behind the others.

'Who is this Mr Kyd?' he whispered. 'He mentioned Phaeacia, as if he knew my character.'

Lord Cornbury's face wore an anxious look. 'He is my brother Queensberry's agent. But he is also one of you. You must know of him. He is *Menelaus*.'

Alastair shook his head. 'I landed from France only three weeks back, and know little of Mr Secretary Murray's plans.'

'Well, you will hear more of him. He is now on his way to Badminton, for he is said to have Beaufort's ear. His connection with my brother is a good shield. Lord! how I hate all this business of go-betweens and midnight conclaves!' He looked at his companion with a face so full of a quaint perplexity that Alastair could not forbear to laugh.

'We must creep before we can fly, my lord, in the most honest cause. But our wings are fledging well.'

A footman led him to his room, which was in the old part of the house called the Leicester Wing, allotted to him, he guessed, because of its remoteness. His baggage had been brought from the inn, and a porcelain bath filled with hot water stood on the floor. He shaved, but otherwise made no more than a traveller's toilet, changing his boots for silk stockings and buckled shoes, and his bob for an ample tie-wig. The mirror showed a man not yet thirty, with small sharp features, high cheek bones, and a reddish tinge in skin and eyebrows. The eyes were of a clear, choleric blue, and the face, which was almost feminine in its contours, was made manly by a certain ruggedness and fire in its regard. His hands and feet were curiously small for one with so deep a chest and sinewy limbs. He was neat and precise in person and movement, a little finical at first sight, till the observer caught his quick ardent gaze. A passionate friend, that observer would have pronounced him, and a most mischievous and restless enemy.

His Highland boyhood and foreign journeyings had not prepared him for the suave perfection of an English house. The hall, paved with squares of black and white marble, was hung with full-length pictures of the Hyde and Danvers families, and the great figures of the Civil War. The party assembled beneath them was a motley of gay colours – the Duchess in a gown of sky-blue above rose-pink petticoats; the young girl, whose name was Lady Mary Capell, all in green like a dryad; Mr Murray wore black velvet with a fuller wig than was the fashion of the moment; while Sir Christopher Lacy had donned the blue velvet and ermine collar of the Duke of Beaufort's Hunt, a garb in which its members were popularly believed to sleep. Mr Kyd had contented himself with a flowered waistcoat, a plum-coloured coat and saffron stockings. Only the host was in sad colours, and, as he alone wore his natural hair, he presented a meagre and dejected figure in the flamboyant company.

The Duchess talked like a brook.

'Harry must show you the Vandykes,' she told Mr Murray. 'He knows the age and tale of everyone as I know my boys' birthdays. I wish he would sell them, for they make me feel small and dingy. Look at them! We are no better than valets-de-chambre in their presence.'

The major-domo conducted them to dinner, which was served in the new Indian Room. On the walls was a Chinese paper of birds and flowers and flower-hung pagodas; no pictures adorned them, but a number of delicately carved mirrors; and at intervals tall lacquer cabinets glowed on their gilt pedestals. The servants wore purple ('like bishops,' Mr. Kyd whispered), and, since the room looked west, the declining October sun brought out the colours of wall and fabric and set the glasses and decanters shimmering on the polished table. Through the open windows the green slopes of the park lay bathed in light, and a pool of water sparkled in the hollow.

To Alastair, absorbed in his errand, the scene was purely phantasmal. He looked on as at a pretty pageant, heard the ladies' tinkling laughter, discussed the *manège* in France at long range with Lord Cornbury, who was a noted horsemaster, answered Lady Mary's inquiries about French modes as best he could, took wine with the men, had the honour to toast the Duchess Kitty – but did it all in a kind of waking dream. This daintiness and ease were not of that grim world from which he had come, or of that grimmer world which was soon to be. . . . He noticed that no word of politics was breathed; even the Duchess's chatter was discreet on that point. The ice was clearly too thin, and the most heedless felt the need of wary walking. Here sat the King's Solicitor, and the wife of a Whig Duke cheek by jowl with two secret messengers bearing names out of Homer, and at the head of the table was one for whom both parties angled. The last seemed to feel the irony, for behind his hospitable gaiety was a sharp edge of care. He would sigh now and then, and pass a thin hand over his forehead. But the others – Mr Solicitor was discussing Mr Pope's 'Characters of Women' and quoting unpublished variants. No hint of embarrassment was to be detected in that mellow voice. Was he perhaps, thought Alastair, cognisant of the strange mixture at table, and not disapproving? He was an officer of the Government, but he came of Jacobite stock. Was he not Stormont's brother? . . . And Mr Kyd was deep in a discussion about horses with the gentleman in the Beaufort uniform. With every glass of claret the even rosiness of his face deepened, till he bloomed like the God of Wine himself – a Bacchus strictly sober, with very wide-awake eyes.

Then to complete the comedy the catch he had heard on Otmoor began to run in Alastair's head. *Three naked men we be* – a far cry from this bedecked and cosseted assemblage. He had a moment of suffocation, until he regained his humour. They were all naked under their fine clothes, and for one of them it was his business to do the stripping. He caught Lord Cornbury's eye and marked its gentle sadness. Was such a man content? Had he the assurance in his soul to listen to one who brought to him not peace but swords?

The late autumn afternoon was bright and mild, with a thin mist rising from the distant stream. The company moved out-of-doors, where on a gravelled walk stood a low carriage drawn by a pair of cream-coloured ponies. A maid brought the Duchess a wide straw hat and driving gloves, and, while the others loitered at the garden door, the lady chose her companion. '*Sa singularité*,' Mr Murray whispered. 'It is young Mr Walpole's name for her. But how prettily she plays the rustic!'

'Who takes the air with me?' she cried. 'I choose Captain Maclean. He is the newest of you, and can tell me the latest scandal of Versailles.'

It was like an equipage fashioned out of Chelsea porcelain, and as Alastair took his place beside her, with his knees under a driving cloth of embroidered silk, he felt more than ever the sense of taking part in a play. She whipped up the ponies and they trotted out of the wrought-iron gates, which bounded the pleasance, into the wide spaces of the park. Her talk, which at first had been the agreeable prattle of dinner, to which he responded with sufficient ease, changed gradually to interrogatories. With some disquiet he realised that she was drifting towards politics.

'What do they think in France of the young man's taste in womankind?' she asked.

He raised his eyebrows.

'The Prince – Charles Stuart – the Chevalier. What of Jenny Cameron?'

'We heard nothing of her in Paris, madam. You should be the better informed, for he has been some months on British soil.'

'Tush, we hear no truth from the North. But they say that she never leaves him, that she shares his travelling carriage. Is she pretty, I wonder? Dark or fair?'

'That I cannot tell, but, whatever they be, her charms must be mature. I have heard on good authority that she is over forty years old.'

It did not need the Duchess's merry laughter to tell him that he had been guilty of a *bêtise*. He blushed furiously.

'La, sir,' she cried, 'you are ungallant. That is very much my own age, and the world does not call me matronly. I had thought you a courtier, but I fear – I gravely fear – you are an honest man.'

They were now on the west side of the park, where a road led downhill past what had once been a quarry, but was now carved into a modish wilderness. The scarps of stone had been fashioned into grottos and towers and fantastic pinnacles; shrubs had been planted to make shapely thickets; springs had been turned to cascades or caught in miniature lakes. The path wound through midget Alps, which were of the same scale and quality as the chaise and the cream ponies and the shepherdess Duchess.

'We call this spot Eden,' she said. 'There are many things I would fain ask you, sir, but I remember the consequence of Eve's inquisitiveness and forbear. The old Eden had a door and beyond that door lay the desert. It is so here.'

They turned a corner by the edge of a small lake and came on a stout palisade which separated the park from Wychwood Forest. Through the high deer-gate Alastair looked on a country the extreme opposite of the enclosed paradise. The stream, which in the park was regulated like a canal, now flowed in rough shallows or spread into morasses. Scrub clothed the slopes, scrub of thorn and hazel and holly, with now and then an ancient oak flinging gnarled arms against the sky. In the bottom were bracken and the withered blooms of heather, where bees still hummed. The eye looked up little glens towards distant ridges to which the blue October haze gave the air of high hills.

As Alastair gazed at the scene he saw again his own countryside. These were like the wild woods that cloaked Loch Sunart side, the wind brought him the same fragrance of heath and fern, he heard the croak of a raven, a knot of hinds pushed from the coppice and plashed through a marshy shallow. For a second his eyes filled with tears.

He found the Duchess's hand on his. It was a new Duchess, with grave kind face and no hint of petulance at her lips or artifice in her voice.

'I brought you here for a purpose, sir,' she said. 'You have before you two worlds – the enclosed garden and the wild beyond. The wild is yours, by birthright and training and choice. Beyond the pale is Robin Hood's land, where men adventure. Inside is a quiet domain where they make verses and read books and cherish possessions – my brother's land. Does my parable touch you?'

'The two worlds are one, madam – one in God's sight.'

'In God's sight, maybe, but not in man's. I will be plainer still with you. I do not know your business, nor do I ask it, for you are my brother's friend. But he is my darling and I fear a threat to his peace as a mother-partridge fears the coming of a hawk. Somehow – I ask no questions – you would persuade him to break bounds and leave his sanctuary for the wilds. It may be the manlier choice, but oh, sir, it is not for him. He is meant for the garden. His health is weak, his spirit is most noble but too fine for the clash of the rough world. In a year he would be in his grave.'

Alastair, deeply perplexed, made no answer. He could not lie to this woman, nor could he make a confidante of the wife of Queensberry.

'Pardon me if I embarrass you,' she went on. 'I do not ask a reply. Your secrets would be safe with me, but if you told me them I should stop my ears. For politics I care nothing, I know nothing. I speak on a brother's behalf, and my love for him makes me importunate. I tell you that he is made for the pleasance, not for the wilderness. Will you weigh my words?'

'I will weigh them most scrupulously. Lord Cornbury is blessed in his sister.'

'I am all he has, for he never could find a wife to his taste.' She whipped up the ponies and her voice changed to its old lightness. 'La, sir, we must hasten. The gentlemen will be clamouring for tea.'

In the great gallery, among more Vandykes and Knellers and Lelys and panels of Mortlake tapestry, the company sipped tea and chocolate. The Duchess made tea with her own hands, and the bright clothes and jewels gleaming in the dusk against dim pictures had once more the airy unreality of a dream. But Alastair's mood had changed. He no longer felt imprisoned among potent shadows, for the glimpse he had had of his own familiar country had steadied his balance. He saw the life he had chosen in fairer colours, the life of toil and hazard and enterprise, in contrast with this airless ease. The blood ran quicker in his veins for the sight of a drugged and sleeping world. Ancient possessions, the beauty of women, the joy of the senses were things to be forsworn before they could be truly admired. Now he looked graciously upon what an hour ago had irked him.

When the candles were lit and the curtains drawn the scene grew livelier. The pretty Lady Mary, sitting under the Kneller portrait of her mother, was a proof of the changelessness of beauty. A pool was made at commerce, in which all joined, and the Duchess's childlike laughter rippled through the talk like a trout-stream. She was in her wildest mood, the incomparable Kitty whom for thirty years every poet had sung. The thing became a nursery party, where discretion was meaningless, and her irreverent tongue did not refrain from politics. She talked of the Stuarts.

'They intermarried with us,' she cried, 'so I can speak as a kinswoman. A grave dutiful race – they were, tragically misunderstood. If their passions were fierce, they never permitted them to bias their statecraft.'

A portrait of Mary of Scots hung above her as she spoke. Mr Murray cast a quizzical eye upon it.

'Does your summary embrace that ill-fated lady?' he asked.

'She above all. Her frailties were not Stuart but Tudor. Consider Harry the Eighth. He had passions like other monarchs, but instead of keeping mistresses he must marry each successive love, and as a consequence cut off the head of the last one. His craze was not for amours but for matrimony. So, too, with his sister Margaret. So, too, with his great-niece Mary. She might have had a hundred lovers and none would have gainsaid

her, but the mischief came when she insisted on wedding them.
No! No! What ruined the fortunes of my kinsfolk was not the
Stuart blood but the Tudor – the itch for lawful wedlock which
came in with the Welsh bourgeoisie.'

'Your Grace must rewrite the histories,' said Mr Murray,
laughing.

'I have a mind to. But my Harry will bear me witness. The
Stuart stock is sad and dutiful. Is not that the character of him
who now calls himself the rightful King of England?'

'So I have heard it said,' Lord Cornbury answered, but the
eyes which looked at his sister were disapproving.

The ladies went early to bed, after nibbling a sweet biscuit and
sipping a glass of negus. Supper was laid for the gentlemen in
the dining-room, and presently Mr Murray, Mr Kyd and Sir
Christopher Lacy were seated at a board which they seemed to
have no intention of leaving. Alastair excused himself on the
plea of fatigue, and lit a bedroom candle. 'I will come to your
room,' his host whispered as they crossed the hall. 'Do not
undress. We will talk in my little cabinet.'

The young man flung himself into a chair, and collected his
thoughts. He had been chosen for this mission, partly because
of his address and education, but mainly because of the fierce
ardour which he had hitherto shown in the Prince's cause. He
knew that much hung on his success, for Cornbury, though
nothing of a soldier and in politics no more than Member of
Parliament for the University of Oxford, was so beloved that
his adherence would be worth a regiment. He knew his
repute. Such a man could not quibble in matters of principle;
the task was rather to transform apathy into action. He
remembered the Duchess's words – honest words, doubtless,
but not weighty. Surely in so great a test of honour a man
could not hesitate because his health was weak or his home
dear to him.

There was a knock at the door and Lord Cornbury entered
with a silk dressing-gown worn over his clothes. He looked
round the room with his sad restless eyes.

'Here Lord Leicester died – Elizabeth's favourite. They say that when the day of his death comes round his spirit may be heard tapping at the walls. It is a commentary on mortal ambition, Captain Maclean. Come with me to my cabinet. Mr Solicitor is gone to bed, for he is ready enough for an all-night sitting at St James's among the wits, but has no notion of spoiling his sleep by potations among bumpkins. Kit Lacy and Mr Kyd will keep it up till morning, but happily they are at the other end of the house.'

He led the way down a narrow staircase to a little room on the ground floor, which had for its other entrance a door giving on a tiny paved garden. It was lined with books and a small fire had been lit on the hearth.

'Here we shall be secure, for I alone have the keys,' Lord Cornbury said, taking a seat by a bureau where the single lamp was behind his head. 'You have something private for my ear? I must tell you, sir, I have been plagued for many months by portentous secret emissaries. There was my lord Clancarty, a Cyclops with one eye and a shocking perruque, who seemed to me not wholly in possession of his wits. There was a Scotch gentleman – Bahaldy – Bohaldy – whom I suspected of being a liar. There was Traquair, whose speech rang false in every stutter. They and their kind were full of swelling words, but they were most indisputably fools. You are not of their breed, sir. From you I look for candour and good sense. What have you to say to me?'

'One thing only, my lord. From me you will get no boasts or promises. I bring you a summons.'

Alastair took from his breast a letter. Lord Cornbury broke the seal and revealed a page of sprawling irregular handwriting, signed at the foot with the words 'Charles P.' He read it with attention, read it again, and then looked at the messenger.

'His Royal Highness informs me that I will be "inexcusable before God and men" if I fail him. For him that is a natural opinion. Now, sir, before answering this appeal, I have certain questions to ask you. You come from the Prince's army, and you

are in the secrets of his Cabinet. You are also a soldier. I would
hear from you the Prince's strength.'

'He can cross the Border with not less than five thousand
horse and foot.'

'Highlanders?'

'In the main, which means the best natural fighting stock in
this land. They have already shown their prowess against Cope's
regulars. There are bodies of Lowland horse with Elcho and
Pitsligo.'

'And your hopes of increment?'

'More than half the clans are still to raise. Of them we are
certain. There are accessions to be looked for from the Lowlands. In England we have promises from every quarter – from
Barrymore, Molyneux, Grosvenor, Fenwick, Petre, Cholmonde-
ley, Leigh, Curzon in the North; from the Duke of Beaufort and
Sir Watkin Wynn in the West. Likewise large sums of money
are warranted from the city of London.'

'You speak not of sympathy only, but of troops? Many are no
doubt willing to drink His Royal Highness's health.'

'I speak of troops. There is also the certain aid from France.
In this paper, my lord, you will find set down the numbers and
dates of troops to be dispatched before Christmas. Some are
already on the way – Lord John Drummond with his regiment of
Royal Ecossais and certain Irish companies from the French
service.'

'And you have against you?'

'In Scotland – nothing. In England at present not ten
thousand men. Doubtless they will make haste to bring back
troops from abroad, but before that we hope to conquer. His
Royal Highness's plan is clear. He seeks as soon as possible
to win a victory in England. In his view the land is for the first
comer. The nation is indifferent and will yield to boldness. I
will be honest with you, my lord. He hopes also to confirm
the loyalty of France, for it is certain that if his arms triumph
but once on English soil, the troops of King Louis will take the
sea.'

The other mused. 'It is a bold policy, but it may be a wise one. I would raise one difficulty. You have omitted from your calculation the British Fleet.'

Alastair shrugged his shoulders. 'It is our prime danger, but we hope with speed and secrecy to outwit it.'

'I have another objection. You are proposing to conquer England with a foreign army. I say not a word against the valour of your Highland countrymen, but to English eyes they are barbarous strangers. And France is the ancient enemy.'

'Then, my lord, it is a strife of foreigner against foreigner. Are King George's Dutch and Danes and Hessians better Englishmen than the Prince's men? Let England abide the issue, and join the victor.'

'You speak reasonably, I do not deny it. Let me ask further. Has any man of note joined your standard?'

'Many Scots nobles, though not the greatest. But Hamilton favours us, and there are grounds for thinking that even the Whig dukes, Argyll and Montrose and Queensberry, are soured with the Government. It is so in England, my lord. Bedford . . .'

'I know, I know. All are waiting on the tide. But meantime His Royal Highness's Cabinet is a rabble of Irishmen. Is it not so? I do not like to have Teague in the business, sir, and England does not like it.'

'Then come yourself, my lord.'

Lord Cornbury smiled. 'I have not finished my questions. What of His Royal Highness's religion? I take it that it is the same as your own.'

'He has already given solemn pledges for liberty and toleration. Many Presbyterians of the straitest sect are in his camp. Be sure, my lord, that he will not be guilty of his grandfather's blunder.'

Lord Cornbury rose and stood with his back to the fire.

'You are still in the military stage, where your first duty is a victory in the field. What does His Royal Highness wish me to do? I am no soldier, I could not raise a dozen grooms and foresters. I do not live in Sir Watkin's county, where you can blow a horn and summon a hundred rascals. Here in Oxford-shire we are peaceable folk.'

'He wants you in his Council. I am no lover of the Irish, and there is sore need of statesmanship among us.'

'Say you want me for an example.'

'That is the truth, my lord.'

'And, you would add, for statecraft. Then let us look at the matter with a statesman's eye. You say truly that England does not love her Government. She is weary of foreign wars, and an alien Royal house, and gross taxes, and corruption in high places. She is weary, I say, but she will not stir to shift the burden. You are right; she is for the first comer. You bring a foreign army and it will fight what in the main is a foreign army, so patriotic feeling is engaged on neither side. If you win, the malcontents, who are the great majority, will join you, and His Royal Highness will sit on the throne of his fathers. If you fail, there is no loss except to yourselves, for the others are not pledged. Statesmanship, sir, is an inglorious thing, for it must consider first the fortunes of the common people. No states-man has a right to risk these fortunes unless he be reasonably assured of success. Therefore I say to you that England must wait, and statesmen must wait with England, till the issue is decided. That issue still lies with the soldiers. I cannot join His Royal Highness at this juncture, for I could bring no aid to his cause and I might bring needless ruin to those who depend on me. My answer might have been otherwise had I been a soldier.'

A certain quiet obstinacy had entered the face which was revealed in profile by the lamp on the bureau. The voice had lost its gentle indeterminateness and rang crisp and clear. Alastair had knowledge enough of men to recognise finality. He made his last effort.

'Are considerations of policy the only ones? You and I share the same creeds, my lord. Our loyalty is owed to the House which has the rightful succession, and we cannot in our obedience to God serve what He has not ordained. Is it not your duty to fling prudence to the winds and make your election before the world, for right is right whether we win or lose.'

'For some men maybe,' said the other sadly, 'but not for me. I am in that position that many eyes are turned on me and in my decision I must consider them. If your venture fails, I desire that as few Englishmen as possible suffer for it, it being premised that for the moment only armed men can help it to success. Therefore I wait, and will counsel waiting to all in like position. Beaufort can bring troops, and in God's name I would urge him on, and from the bottom of my heart I pray for the Prince's welfare.'

'What will decide you, then?'

'A victory on English soil. Nay, I will go farther. So soon as His Royal Highness is in the way of that victory, I will fly to his side.'

'What proof will you require?'

'Ten thousand men south of Derby on the road to London, and the first French contingent landed.'

'That is your answer, my lord?'

'That is the answer which I would have you convey with my most humble and affectionate duty to His Royal Highness. . . . And now, sir, will you join me in a turn on the terrace, as the night is fine. It is my habit before retiring.'

The night was mild and very dark, and from the lake rose the honk of wild fowl and from the woods the fitful hooting of owls. To Alastair his failure was scarcely a disappointment, for he realised that all day he had lived in expectation of it. Nay, inasmuch as it placed so solemn a duty upon the soldiers of the Cause, it strung his nerves like a challenge. Lord Cornbury put an arm in his, and the sign of friendship moved the young man's affection. It was for youth and ardour such as his to make clear the path for gentler souls.

They left the stones of the terrace and passed the lit window of the dining-room, where it appeared that merriment had advanced, for Sir Christopher Lacy was attempting a hunting-song.

'Such are the squires of England,' whispered Cornbury. 'They will drink and dice and wench for the Prince, but not fight for him.'

'Not yet,' Alastair corrected. 'But when your lordship joins us he will not be unattended.'

They reached the corner of the house from which in daylight the great avenue could be seen, the spot where that morning Alastair had delivered his credentials.

'I hear hooves,' said Cornbury, with a hand to his ear. 'Nay, it is only the night wind.'

'It is a horse,' said the other. 'I have heard it for the last minute. Now it is entering the courtyard. See, there is a stable lantern.'

A light swayed, and there was the sound of human speech.

'That is Kyd's Scotch servant,' Cornbury said. 'Let us inquire into the errand of this night-rider.'

As they moved towards the lantern a commotion began, and the light wavered like a ship's lamp in a heavy sea.

'Haud up, sir,' cried a voice. 'Losh, the beast's foundered, and the man's in a dwam.'

THREE

In which Private Matters Cut Across Affairs of State

In the circle of the lantern's light the horseman, a big shambling fellow, stood swaying as if in extreme fatigue, now steadying himself by a hand on the animal's neck, now using the support of the groom's shoulder. His weak eyes peered and blinked, and at the sight of the gentlemen he made an attempt at a bow.

'My lord!' he gasped with a dry mouth. 'Do I address my lord Cornbury?'

He did not wait for an answer. 'I am from Chastlecote, my lord. I beg – I supplicate – a word with your lordship.'

'Now?'

'Now, if it please you. My business is most urgent. It is life or death, my lord, the happiness or despair of an immortal soul.'

'You are the tutor from Chastlecote, I think. You appear to have been trying your beast high.'

'I have ridden to Weston and to Heythrop since midday.'

'Have you eaten?'

'Not since breakfast, my lord.' The man's eyes were wolfish with hunger and weariness.

'Then you shall eat, for there can be no business between a full man and a fasting. The groom will see to your horse. Follow me.'

Lord Cornbury led the way past the angle of the house to where the lit windows of the dining-room made a glow in the dark.

''Tis a night of queer doings,' he whispered to Alastair, as they heard the heavy feet of the stranger stumbling behind

them. 'We will surprise Kit Lacy in his cups, but there will be
some remnants of supper for this fellow. 'Pon my soul, I am
curious to know what has shifted such a gravity out of bed.'

He unlocked the garden-door and led the way through the
great hall to the dining-room. Sir Christopher, mellow but still
sober, was interrupted in a song, and, with admirable presence
of mind, cut it short in a view holloa. Mr Kyd, rosy as the dawn,
hastened to place chairs.

'Your pardon, gentlemen, but I bring you a famished traveller. Sit down, sir, and have at that pie. There is claret at your
elbow.'

The newcomer muttered thanks and dropped heavily into a
chair. Under the bright candelabrum, among crystal and silver
and shining fruit and the gay clothes of the others, he cut an
outrageous figure. He might have been in years about the age of
Lord Cornbury, but disease and rough usage had wiped every
sign of youth from his face. That face was large, heavily-featured
and pitted deep with the scars of scrofula. The skin was puffy
and grey, the eyes beneath the prominent forehead were pale
and weak, the mouth was cast in hard lines as if from suffering.
His immense frame was incredibly lean and bony, and yet from
his slouch seemed unwholesomely weighted with flesh. He
wore his own hair, straight and lank and tied with a dusty
ribbon. His clothes were of some coarse grey stuff and much
worn, and, though on a journey, he had no boots, but instead
clumsy unbuckled shoes and black worsted stockings. His cuffs
and neckband were soiled, and overcrowded pockets made his
coat hang on him like a sack. Such an apparition could not but
affect the best-bred gentleman. Kit Lacy's mouth was drawn into
a whistle, Mr Kyd sat in smiling contemplation. Alastair thought
of Simon Lovat as he had last seen that vast wallowing chieftain,
and then reflected that Simon carried off his oddity by his air of
arrogant command. This fellow looked as harassed as a mongrel
that boys have chivvied into a corner. He cut himself a wedge of
pie and ate gobblingly. He poured out a tankard of claret and
swallowed most of it at a gulp. Then he grew nervous, choked on

a crumb, gulped more claret and coughed till his pale face grew crimson.

The worst pangs of hunger allayed, he seemed to recollect his errand. His lips began to mutter as if he were preparing a speech. His tired eyes rested in turn on each member of the company, on Lacy and Kyd lounging at the other side of the table, on Cornbury's decorous figure at the head, on Alastair wrapped in his own thoughts at the foot. This was not the private conference he had asked for, but it would appear that the urgency of his need must override discretion. A spasm of pain distorted the huge face, and he brought his left hand down violently on the table, so that the glasses shivered.

'My lord,' he said, 'she is gone.'

The company stared, and Sir Christopher tittered.

'Who is your "she," sir?' he asked as he helped himself to wine.

'Miss Grevel . . . Miss Claudia.'

The young baronet's face changed.

'The devil! Gone! Explain yourself, sir.'

The man had swung round so that he faced Lord Cornbury, with his head screwed oddly over his right shoulder. As he spoke it bobbed in a kind of palsied eagerness.

'You know her, my lord. Miss Claudia Grevel; the cousin and housemate of the young heir of Chastlecote, who has been committed to my charge. Three days ago she was of age and the controller of her fortune. This morning the maids found her bed unslept in, and the lady flown.'

Lord Cornbury exclaimed. 'Did she leave no word?' he asked.

'Only a letter to her cousin, bidding him farewell.'

'Nothing to you?'

'To me nothing. She was a high lady and to her I was only the boy's instructor. But I had marked for some weeks a restlessness in her deportment and, fearing some rash step, I had kept an eye on her doings.'

'You spied on her?' said Kyd sweetly. 'Is that part of an usher's duties?'

The man was too earnest to feel the rudeness of the question.

'She was but a child, sir,' he said. 'She had neither father nor mother, and she was about to be sole mistress of a rich estate. I pitied her, and, though she in no way condescended to me, I loved her youth and beauty.'

'You did right,' Lord Cornbury said. 'Have your observations given you no clue to the secret of her flight?'

'In some measure, my lord. You must know that Miss Grevel is ardent in politics, and, like many gentlewomen, has a strong sentiment for the young Prince now in Scotland. She has often declared that if she had been a man she would long ago have hastened to his standard, and she was wont to rage against the apathy of the Oxfordshire squires. A scrap of news from the North would put her into a fury or an exaltation. There was one gentleman of the neighbourhood who was not apathetic and who was accordingly most welcome at Chastlecote. From him she had her news of the Prince, and it was clear by his manner towards her that he valued her person as well as shared her opinions. I have been this day to that gentleman's house and found that at an early hour he started on a journey. I was ill received there and told little, but I ascertained that he had departed with a coach and led horses. My lord, I am convinced that the unhappy girl is his companion.'

'The man's name?' Lord Cornbury asked sharply.

'Sir John Norreys of Weston.'

The name told nothing to two of the company, but it had a surprising effect on Sir Christopher Lacy. He sprang to his feet, and began to stride up and down the room, his chin on his breast.

'I knew his father,' said Lord Cornbury, 'but the young man I have rarely seen. 'Tis a runaway match doubtless; but such marriages are not always tragical. Miss Grevel is too highly placed and well dowered for misadventure. Let us hope for the best, sir. She will return presently a sober bride.'

'I am of your lordship's opinion,' Mr Kyd observed with a jolly laugh. 'Let a romantic maid indulge her fancy and choose her own way of wedlock, for if she get not romance at the start she will not find it in the dreich business of matrimony. But you and me, my lord, are bachelors and speak only from hearsay.'

The tutor from Chastlecote seemed to be astounded at the reception of his news.

'You do not know the man,' he cried. 'It is no case of a youthful escapade. I have made inquiries, and learned that he is no better than a knave. If he is a Jacobite it is for gain, if he weds Miss Grevel it is for her estate.'

'Now what the devil should a dominie like you know about the character of a gentleman of family?'

The words were harsh, but, as delivered by Mr Kyd with a merry voice and a twinkle of the eye, they might have passed as a robust pleasantry. But the tutor was not in the mood for them. Anger flushed his face, and he blew out his breath like a bull about to charge. Before he could reply, however, he found an ally in Sir Christopher. The baronet flung himself again into his chair and stuck both elbows on the table.

'The fellow is right all the same,' he said. 'Jack Norreys is a low hound, and I'll take my oath on it. No scamp is Jack, for his head is always cool and he has a heart like a codfish. He has a mighty good gift for liquor – I say that for him – but the damnable fellow profits by the generous frailties of his betters. He is mad for play, but he loves the cards like an attorney, not like a gentleman, and he makes a fat thing out of them. No, damme! Jack's no true man. If he wants the girl 'tis for her fortune, and if he sings Jacobite, 'tis because he sees some scoundrelly profit for himself. I hate the long nose and the mean eyes of him.'

'You hear?' cried the tutor who had half risen from his seat in his excitement. 'You hear the verdict of an honest man!'

'You seem to know him well, Kit,' said Lord Cornbury, smiling.

'Know him! Gad, I have had some chances. We were birched together at Eton, and dwelt in the same stairway at Christ Church. I once rode a match with him on the Port Meadow and bled him for a hundred guineas, but he has avenged himself a thousandfold since then at the Bibury meetings. He may be Lord High Chancellor when I am in the Fleet, but the Devil will get him safe enough at the end.'

Lord Cornbury looked grave, Mr Kyd wagged a moralising head.

'The thing has gone too far to stop,' said the former. Then to the tutor: 'What would you have me do?'

The visitor's uncouth hands were twisting themselves in a frenzy of appeal.

'My mistress at Chastlecote is old and bedridden, my charge is but a boy, and Miss Grevel has no relatives nearer than Dorset. I come to you as the leading gentleman in this shire and an upright and public-spirited nobleman, and I implore you to save that poor pretty child from her folly. They have gone north, so let us follow. It may not be too late to prevent the marriage.'

'Ah, but it will be,' said Mr Kyd. 'They can find a hedge-parson any hour of the day to do the job for a guinea and a pot of ale.'

'There is a chance, a hope, and, oh sir, I beseech you to pursue it.'

'Would you have me mount and ride on the track of the fugitives?' Lord Cornbury asked.

'Yes, my lord, and without delay. Grant me a chair to sleep an hour in, and I am ready for any labour. We can take the road before daybreak. It would facilitate our task if your lordship would lend me a horse better fitted for my weight.'

The naiveness of the request made a momentary silence. Then in spite of himself Alastair laughed. This importunate usher was on the same mission as himself, that mission which an hour earlier had conclusively failed. To force their host into activity was the aim of both, but one whom a summons from a Prince had not moved was not likely to yield to an invitation to pursue a brace of green lovers. Yet he respected the man's ardour, though he had set him down from his looks as a boor and an oddity; and regretted his laugh, when a distraught face

was turned towards him, solemn and reproachful like a perse-
cuted dog's.

Lord Cornbury's eyes were troubled and his hands fidgeted
with a dish of filberts. He seemed divided between irritation at a
preposterous demand and his natural kindliness.

'You are a faithful if importunate friend, sir. By the way, I
have not your name.'

'Johnson, my lord – Samuel Johnson. But my name matters
nothing.'

'I have heard it before. . . . Nay, I remember. . . . Was it Mr
Murray who spoke of it? Tell me, sir, have you not published
certain writings?'

'Sir, I have made a living by scribbling.'

'Poetry, I think. Was there not a piece on the morals of Town
– in the manner of Juvenal?'

'Bawdy, I'll be bound,' put in Mr Kyd. He seemed suddenly to
have grown rather drunk and spoke with a hiccough.

The tutor looked so uncouth a figure for a poet that Alastair
laughed again. But the poor man's mind was far from humour,
for his earnestness increased with his hearers' cynicism.

'Oh, my lord,' he cried, 'what does it matter what I am or what
wretched books I have fathered? I urge you to a most instant
duty – to save a noble young lady from a degrading marriage. I
press for your decision, for the need is desperate.'

'But what can I do, Mr Johnson? She is of age, and they
have broken no law. I cannot issue a warrant and hale them
back to Oxfordshire. If they are not yet wed I have no authority
to dissuade, for I am not a kinsman, not even a friend. I
cannot forbid the banns, for I have no certain knowledge of
any misdeeds of this Sir John. I have no *locus*, as the lawyers
say, for my meddling. But in any case the errand must be
futile, for if you are right and she has fled with him, they will
be married long ere we can overtake them. What you ask from
me is folly.'

The tutor's face changed from lumpish eagerness to a lumpish gloom.

'There is a chance,' he muttered. 'And in the matter of saving souls a chance is enough for a Christian.'

'Then my Christianity falls short of yours, sir,' replied Lord Cornbury sharply.

The tutor let his dismal eyes dwell on the others. They soon left Mr Kyd's face, stayed longer on Alastair's and came to rest on Sir Christopher's, which was little less gloomy than his own.

'You, sir,' he said, 'you know the would-be bridegroom. Will you assist me to rescue the bride?'

The baronet for a moment did not reply and hope flickered in the other's eyes. Then it died, for the young man brought down his fist on the table with an oath.

'No, by God. If my lord thinks the business not for him, 'tis a million times too delicate for me. You're an honest man, Mr usher, and shall hear my reason. I loved Miss Grevel, and for two years I dared to hope. Last April she dismissed me and I had the wit to see that 'twas final. What kind of figure would I cut galloping the shires after a scornful mistress who has chosen another? I'd ride a hundred miles to see Jack Norreys' neck wrung, but you will not catch me fluttering near the honeypot of his lady.'

'You think only of your pride, sir, and not of the poor girl.'

The tutor, realising the futility of his mission, rose to his feet, upsetting a decanter with an awkward elbow. The misadventure, which at an earlier stage would have acutely embarrassed him, now passed unnoticed. He seemed absorbed in his own reflections, and had suddenly won a kind of rude dignity. As he stood among them Alastair was amazed alike at his shabbiness and his self-possession.

'You will stay the night here, sir? The hour is late and a bed is at your disposal.'

'I thank you, my lord, but my duties do not permit of sleep. I return to Chastlecote, and if I can get no helpers I must e'en seek for the lady alone. I am debtor to your lordship for a hospitality upon which I will not further encroach. May I beg the favour of a light to the stable?'

Alastair picked up a branched candlestick and preceded the tutor into the windless night. The latter stumbled often, for he seemed purblind, but the other had no impulse to laugh, for toward this grotesque he had conceived a curious respect. The man, like himself, was struggling against fatted ease, striving to break a fence of prudence on behalf of an honourable hazard.

Kyd's servant brought the horse, refreshed by a supper of oats, and it was Alastair's arm which helped the unwieldy horseman to the saddle.

'God prosper you!' Alastair said, as he fitted a clumsy foot into a stirrup.

The man woke to the consciousness of the other's presence.

'You wish me well, sir? Will you come with me? I desire a colleague, for I am a sedentary man with no skill in travel.'

'I only rest here for a night. I am a soldier on a mission which does not permit of delay.'

'Then God speed us both!' The strange fellow pulled off his hat like a parson pronouncing benediction, before he lumbered into the dark of the avenue.

Alastair turned to find Kyd behind him. He was exchanging jocularities with his servant.

'Saw ye ever such a physiog, Edom?' he cried. 'Dominies are getting crouse, for the body was wanting my lord to up and ride with him like a post-boy after some quean that's ta'en the jee. He's about as blate as a Cameronian preacher. My lord was uncommon patient with him. D'you not think so, Captain Maclean?'

'The man may be uncouth, but he has a stout heart and a very noble spirit. I take off my hat to his fidelity.'

The reply changed Mr Kyd's mood from scorn to a melting sentiment.

'Ay, but you're right. I hadn't thought of that. It's a noble-hearted creature, and we would all be better if we were liker him. Courage, did you say? The man with that habit of body, that jogs all day on a horse for the sake of a woman that has done nothing but clout his lugs, is a hero. I wish I had drunk his health.'

FOUR

Mr Kyd of Greyhouses

Next morning Alastair rode west, and for the better part of a fortnight was beyond Severn. He met Sir Watkin at Wynnstay and Mr Savage in Lanthony vale, and then penetrated to the Pembroke coast where he conferred with fisherfolk and shy cloaked men who gave appointments by the tide at nightfall. His task was no longer diplomacy, but the ordinary intelligence service of war, and he was the happier inasmuch as he the better understood it. If fortune favoured elsewhere, he had made plans for a French landing in a friendly countryside to kindle the West and take in flank the defences of London. Now, that errand done, his duty was with all speed to get him back to the North.

On a sharp noon in the first week of November he recrossed Severn and came into Worcestershire, having slept at Ludlow the night before. His plan was to return as he had come, by the midlands and Northumberland, for he knew the road and which inns were safe to lie at. Of the doings of his Prince he had heard nothing, and he fretted every hour at the lack of news. As a trained soldier with some experience of war, he distrusted profoundly the military wisdom of Charles's advisers, and feared daily to hear of some blunder which would cancel all that had already been won.

He rode hard, hoping to sleep in Staffordshire and next day join the road which he had travelled south three weeks before. An unobtrusive passenger known to none, knowing none, he took little pains to scan the visages of those he met. It was therefore with some surprise that, as he sat in the tap-room of an ale-house at Chifney, he saw a face which woke some recollection.

It was that of a tall, thin and very swarthy man who was engaged in grating a nutmeg into a pot of mulled ale. His clothes had the shabby finery of a broken-down gentleman, but the air of a minor stage-player which they suggested was sharply contradicted by his face. That was grave, strong almost to hardness, and with eyes that would have dictated if they had not brooded. He gave Alastair good-day as he entered, and then continued his occupation in such a way that the light from the window fell very clearly upon his features. The purpose, which involved a change of position, was so evident that Alastair's attention was engaged, and he regarded him over the edge of his tankard.

The memory was baffling. France, London, Rome – he fitted nowhere. It seemed a far-back recollection, and not a coincidence of his present journey. Then the man raised his head, and his sad eyes looked for a moment at the window. The gesture Alastair had seen before – very long before – in Morvern. Into the picture swam other details: a ketch anchored, a sea-loch, a seafarer who sang so that the heart broke, a cluster of boys huddled on hot sand listening to a stranger's tales.

'The Spainneach!' he exclaimed.

The man looked up with a smile on his dark face and spoke in Gaelic. 'Welcome, heart's darling,' he said – the endearment used long ago to the child who swam out to the foreign ship for a prize of raisins. 'I have followed you for three days, and this morning was told of your inquiries, divined your route, and took a short cut to meet you here.'

The picture had filled out. Alastair remembered the swarthy foreigner who came yearly at the tail of the harvest to enlist young men for the armies of Spain or France or the Emperor – who did not brag or bribe or unduly gild the prospect, but who, less by his tongue than by his eyes, drew the Morvern youth to wars from which few returned. An honest man, his father had named this Spainneach, but as secret in his ways as the woodcock blown shoreward by the October gales.

'You have a message for me?' he asked, thinking of Cornbury.

'A message – but from a quarter no weightier than my own head. You have been over long in the South, Sir Sandy.' The name had been the title given by his boyish comrades to their leader, and its use by this grave man brought to the chance meeting something of the intimacy of home.

'That's my own notion,' he replied. 'But I am now by way of curing the fault.'

'Then ride fast, and ride by the shortest road. There's sore need of you up beyond.'

'You have news,' Alastair cried eagerly. 'Has His Highness marched yet?'

'This very day he has passed the Border.'

'How – by what route – in what strength?'

'No great increase. He looks for that on the road.'

'Then he goes by Carlisle?'

The Spaniard nodded. 'And Wade lies at Newcastle,' he said.

Alastair brought down his fist on the board so hard that the ale lipped from the other's tankard.

'The Devil take such blundering! Now he has the enemy on his unprotected flank, when he might have destroyed him and won that victory on English soil which is the key to all things. Wade is old and doited, but he will soon have Cumberland behind him. Who counselled this foolishness? Not His Highness, I'll warrant.'

The Spaniard shrugged his shoulders. 'No. His Highness would have made a bee-line for Newcastle. But his captains put their faith in Lancashire, and would have the honest men of North England in their ranks before they risked a battle. They picture them as waiting, each with a thousand armed followers, till the first tartans are south of Shap, and then rushing to the standard.'

Alastair, his brows dark with irritation, strode up and down the floor.

'The fools have it the wrong way round. England will not rise to fight a battle, but only when a battle has been won. Wade at Newcastle was a sovran chance – and we have missed it. Blind!

Blind! You are right, my friend. Not a second must I lose in pushing north to join my Prince. There are no trained soldiers with him save Lord George, and he had no more than a boyish year in the Royals. . . . You say he travels by Shap?'

The Spaniard nodded. 'And your course, Sir Sandy, must be through West England. Ride for Preston, which all Scots invasions must pass. Whitchurch – Tarporley – Warrington are your stages. See, I will make you a plan.'

On the dust of a barrel he traced the route, while Alastair did up the straps of his coat and drew on his riding gloves. His horse was brought, the lawing paid, and as the young man mounted the other stood by his stirrup.

'Where do you go?' Alastair asked.

'Northward, like swallows in spring. But not yet awhile. I have still errands in these parts.'

An ostler inspected the horse's shoes, and Alastair sat whistling impatiently through his teeth. The tune which came to him was Midwinter's catch of 'The Naked Men'. The Spaniard started at the sound, and long after Alastair had moved off stood staring after him down the road. Then he turned to the house, his own lips shaping the same air, and cast a glance at the signboard. It showed a red dragon marvellously rampant on a field of green, and beneath was painted a rude device of an open eye.

The chill misty noontide changed presently to a chillier drizzle, and then to a persistent downfall. Alastair's eagerness was perforce checked by the weather, for he had much ado to grope his way in the maze of grassy lanes and woodland paths. Scarcely a soul was about – only a dripping labourer at a gate, and a cadger with pack-horses struggling towards the next change-house. He felt the solitude and languor of the rainy world, and at the same time his bones were on fire to make better speed, for suddenly the space between him and the North seemed to have lengthened intolerably. The flat meadows were hideously foreign; he longed for a sight of hill or heath to tell him that he was nearing the North and the army of his Prince.

He cursed the errand that had brought him to this friendless land, far from his proper trade of war.

The November dusk fell soon, and wet greyness gave place to wet mirk. There was no moon, and to continue was to risk a lost road and a foundered horse. So, curbing his impatience, he resolved to lie the night at the first hostelry, and be on the move next day before the dawn.

The mist thickened, and it seemed an interminable time before he found a halting-place. The patch of road appeared to be uninhabited, without the shabbiest beerhouse to cheer it. Alastair's patience was wearing very thin, and his appetite had waxed to hunger, before the sound of hooves and the speech of men told him that he was not left solitary on the globe. A tiny twinkle of light shone ahead, rayed by the falling rain, and, shrouded and deadened by the fog, came human voices.

He appeared to be at a cross-roads, where the lane he had been following intersected a more considerable highway, for he blundered against a tall signpost. Then, steering for the light, he all but collided with a traveller on horseback, who was engaged in talk with someone on foot. The horseman was on the point of starting, and the light, which was a lantern in the hand of a man on foot, gave Alastair a faint hurried impression of a tall young man muffled in a fawn-coloured riding-coat, with a sharp nose and a harsh drawling voice. The colloquy was interrupted by his advent, the horseman moved into the rain, and the man with the lantern swung it up in some confusion. Alastair saw what he took for an ostler – a short fellow with a comically ugly face and teeth that projected like the eaves of a house.

'Is this an inn, friend?' he asked.

The voice which replied was familiar.

'It's a kind of a public, but the yill's sma' and wersh, and there's mair mice than aits in the mangers. Still and on, it's better than outbye this nicht. Is your honour to lie here?'

The man took two steps back and pushed open the inn door, so that a flood of light emerged, and made a half-moon on the cobbles. Now Alastair recognised the lantern-bearer.

'You are Mr Kyd's servant?' he said.

'E'en so. And my maister's in bye, waitin' on his supper. He'll be blithe to see ye, sir. See and I'll tak your horse and bed him weel. Awa in wi' ye and get warm, and I'll bring your mails.'

Alastair pushed open the first door he saw and found a room smoky with a new-lit fire, and by a table, which had been spread with the rudiments of a meal, the massive figure of Mr Nicholas Kyd.

Mr Kyd's first look was one of suspicion and his second of resentment; then, as the sun clears away storm clouds, benevolence and good fellowship beamed from his face.

'God, but I'm in luck the day. Here's an old friend arrived in time to share my supper. Come in by the fire, sir, and no a word till you're warmed and fed. You behold me labouring to make up for the defeeciencies of this hostler wife with some contrivances of my own. An old campaigner like Nicol Kyd doesna travel the roads without sundry small delicacies in his saddlebags, for in some of these English hedge-inns a merciful man wouldna kennel his dog.'

He was enjoying himself hugely. A gallon measure full of ale was before him, and this he was assiduously doctoring with various packets taken from a travellingcase that stood on a chair. 'Small and sour,' he muttered as he tasted it with a ladle. 'But here's a pinch of soda to correct its acidity, and a nieve-full of powdered ginger-root to prevent colic. Drunk hot with a toast and that yill will no ken itself.'

He poured the stuff into a mulling pot, and turned his attention to the edibles. 'Here's a wersh cheese,' he cried, 'but a spice of anchovy will give it kitchen. I never travel without these tasty wee fishes, Captain Maclean. I've set the wife to make kail, for she had no meat in the house but a shank-end of beef. But I've the better part of a ham here, and a string of pig's sausages, which I take it is the English equivalent of a haggis. Faith, you and me will no fare that ill. Sit you down, sir, if your legs are dry, for I hear the kail coming. There's no wine in the place, but I'll contrive a brew of punch to make up for it.'

The hostess, her round face afire from her labours in the kitchen, flung open the door, and a slatternly wench brought in a steaming tureen of broth. More candles were lit, logs were laid on the fire, and the mean room took on an air of rough comfort. After the sombre afternoon Alastair surrendered himself gladly to his good fortune, and filled a tankard of the doctored ale, which he found very palatable. The soup warmed his blood and, having eaten nothing since morning, he showed himself a good trencherman. Mr Kyd in the intervals of satisfying his own appetite beamed upon his companion, hospitably happy at being able to provide such entertainment.

'It's a thing I love,' he said, 'to pass a night in an inn with a friend and a bottle. Coming out of the darkness to a warm fire and a good meal fair ravishes my heart, and the more if it's unexpected. That's your case at this moment, Captain Maclean, and you may thank the Almighty that you're not supping off fat bacon and stinking beer. A lucky meeting for you. Now I wonder at what hostel *Menelaus* and *Alcinous* could have foregathered. Maybe, the pair of them went to visit Ulysses in Ithaca and shoot his paitricks. But it's no likely.'

'How did *Menelaus* prosper at Badminton?' Alastair asked.

'Wheesht, man! We'll get in the condiments for the punch and steek the door before we talk.'

The landlady brought coarse sugar in a canister and half a dozen lemons, and placed a bubbling kettle on the hob. Mr Kyd carefully closed the door behind her and turned the key. With immense care and a gusto which now and then revealed itself in a verse of song, he poured the sugar into a great blue bowl, squeezed the lemons over it with his strong fingers, and added boiling water, with the quantities of each most nicely calculated. Then from a silver-mounted case-bottle he poured the approved modicum of whisky ('the real thing, Captain Maclean, that you'll no find south of the Highland line') and sniffed affectionately at the fragrant steam. He tasted the brew, gave it his benediction, and filled Alastair's rummer. Then he lit one of the church-

wardens which the landlady had supplied, stretched his legs to
the blaze, and heaved a prodigious sigh.

'If I shut my eyes I could believe I was at Greyhouses. That's
my but-and-ben in the Lammermuirs, sir. It's a queer thing, but
I can never stir from home without the sorest kind of homesickness. I was never meant for this gangrel job. . . . But if I
open that window it will no be a burn in the howe and the
peesweeps that I'll hear, but just the weariful soughing of
English trees. . . . There's a lot of the bairn in me, Captain
Maclean.'

The pleasant apathy induced by food and warmth was passing
from Alastair's mind, and he felt anew the restlessness which
the Spaniard's news had kindled. He was not in a mood for Mr
Kyd's sentiment.

'You will soon enough be in the North, I take it,' he said.

'Not till the New Year, for my sins. I'm the Duke's doer, and I
must be back at Amesbury to see to the plantings.'

'And the mission of *Menelaus*?'

'Over for a time. My report went north a week syne by a sure
hand.'

'Successful?'

Mr Kyd pursed his lips. 'So-so.' He looked sharply towards door
and window. 'Beaufort is with us – on conditions. And you?'

'I am inclined to be cheerful. We shall not lack the English
grandees, provided we in the North play the game right.'

'Ay. That's gospel. You mean a victory in England.'

Alastair nodded. 'Therefore *Alcinous* has done with Phaeacia
and returns to the Prince as fast as horse will carry him. But
what does *Menelaus* in these parts? You are far away from
Badminton and farther from Amesbury.'

'I had a kind of bye-errand up this way. Now I'm on my road
south again.'

'Has the Cause friends hereabouts? I saw a horseman at the
door in talk with your servant.'

Mr Kyd looked up quickly. 'I heard tell of none. What was he
like?'

'I saw only a face in the mist – a high collar and a very sharp nose.'

The other shook his head. 'It beats me, unless it was some forwandered traveller that speired the road from Edom. I've seen no kenned face for a week, except' – and he broke into a loud guffaw – 'except yon daft dominie we met at Cornbury – the man that wanted us all to mount and chase a runaway lassie. I passed him on the road yestereen mounted like a cadger and groaning like an auld wife.'

Mr Kyd's scornful reference to the tutor of Chastlecote slightly weakened in Alastair the friendliness which his geniality had inspired.

'It will be well for us if we are as eager in our duties as that poor creature,' he said dryly. 'I must be off early to-morrow and not spare horseflesh till I see the Standard.'

'Ay, you maun lose no time. See, and I'll make you a list of post-houses, where you can command decent cattle. It is the fruit of an uncommon ripe experience. Keep well to the east, for there's poor roads and worse beasts this side of the Peak.'

'That was the road I came, but now I must take a different airt. I had news to-day – disquieting news. The Prince is over the Border.'

Mr Kyd was on his feet, his chair scraping hard on the stone floor, and the glasses rattling on the shaken table.

'I've heard nothing of it. Man, what kind of news reaches you and not me?'

'It is true all the same. I had it from one who came long ago to Morvern and knows my clan. This day His Highness crossed Liddel.'

'Liddel!' Mr Kyd almost screamed. 'Then he goes by Carlisle. But Wade's at Newcastle.'

'That is precisely the damnable folly of it. He is forgoing his chance of an immediate victory over a dotard – and a victory in England. God, sir, His Highness has been ill advised. You see now why I ride north hell-for-leather. I am a soldier of some

experience and few of the Prince's advisers have seen a campaign. My presence may prevent a more fatal error.'

Mr Kyd's face was a strange study. Officially it was drawn into
lines of tragic melancholy, but there seemed to be satisfaction,
even jubilation, behind the despair, and the voice could not
escape a tremor of pleased excitement. Alastair, whose life at the
French court had made him quick to judge the *nuances* of
feeling, noted this apparent contradiction, and set it down to the
eagerness of loyalty which hears at last that the Rubicon is
crossed.

'They will march through Lancashire,' said Mr Kyd, 'and look
to recruit the gentry. If so, they're a sturdier breed up yonder
than on the Welsh Marches –' He hesitated. 'I wonder if you're
right in posting off to the North? Does this news not make a
differ? What about Cornbury and Sir Watkin? Will the casting of
the die not make up their minds for them? Faith, I think I'll take
another look in at Badminton.'

Alastair saw in the other's face only an earnest friendliness.

'No, no,' he cried. 'Nothing avails but the English victory. We
must make certain of that. But do you, Mr Kyd, press the
grandees of the Marches, while I prevent fools and schoolboys
from over-riding the natural good sense of our Prince.'

Mr Kyd had recovered his composure, and insisted on filling
the rummer again for a toast to fortune. The lines about his eyes
were grave, but jollity lurked in the corners of his mouth.

'Then you'll take the west side of England and make for
Warrington? Ay, that's your quickest road. I'll draw you an
itinerarium, for I whiles travel that gait.' He scribbled a list on a
leaf from a pocket-book and flung it to Alastair. 'The morn's
night you lie at Flambury, and the third night you'll be in
Chester.'

'Flambury,' Alastair exclaimed. 'That takes me too far east-
ward.'

'No, no. In this country the straight road's apt to be the long
road. There's good going to Flambury, and the turnpike on to
Whitchurch. You'll lie there at the Dog and Gun, and if you

speak my name to the landlord you'll get the best in his house.
. . . Man, I envy you, for you'll be among our own folk in a week.
My heart goes with you, and here's to a quick journey.'

Alastair was staring into the fire, and turned more suddenly
than the other anticipated. Mr Kyd's face was in an instant all
rosy goodwill, but for just that one second he was taken by
surprise, and something furtive and haggard looked from his
eyes. This something Alastair caught, and, as he snuggled
between the inn blankets, the memory of it faintly clouded
his thoughts, like a breath on a mirror.

FIVE

Chance-Medley

In his dreams Alastair was persistently conscious of Mr Kyd's face, which hung like a great sun in that dim landscape. Fresh-coloured and smiling at one moment, it would change suddenly to a thing peaked and hunted, with aversion and fear looking out of narrow eyes. And it mixed itself oddly with another face, a pale face framed in a high coat collar, and adorned with a very sharp nose. It may have been the supper or it may have been the exceeding hardness of the bed, but his sleep was troubled, and he woke with that sense of having toiled furiously which is the consequence of nightmare. He had forgotten the details of his dreams, but one legacy remained from them – a picture of that sharp-nosed face, and the memory of Mr Kyd's open countenance as he had surprised it for one second the night before. As he dressed the recollection paled, and presently he laughed at it, for the Mr Kyd who now presented himself to his memory was so honest and generous and steadfast that the other picture seemed too grotesque even for a caricature.

On descending to breakfast he found, though the day was yet early, that his companion had been up and gone a good hour before. Had he left a message? The landlady said no. What road had he taken? The answer was a reference to a dozen unknown place names, for countryfolk identify a road by the nearest villages it serves. Mr Kyd's energy roused his emulation. He breakfasted hastily, and twenty minutes later was on the road.

The mist had cleared, and a still November morn opened mild and grey over a flat landscape. The road ran through acres of unkempt woodlands where spindlewood and briars glowed above russet bracken, and then over long ridges of lea and fallow, where glimpses were to be had of many miles of smoky-brown forest, with now and then a slender wedge of church steeple cutting the low soft skies. Alastair hoped to get a fresh horse at Flambury which would carry him to Chester, and as his present beast had come far, he could not press it for all his impatience. So as he jogged through the morning his thoughts had leisure to wander, and to his surprise he found his mind enjoying an unexpected peace. He was very near the brink of the torrent; let him make the most of these last yards of solid land. The stormy October had hastened the coming of winter, and the autumn scents had in most places yielded to the strong clean fragrance of a bare world. It was the smell he loved, whether he met it in Morvern among the December mosses, or on the downs of Picardy, or in English fields. At other times one smelled herbage and flowers and trees; in winter one savoured the essential elements of water and earth.

In this mood of content he came after midday to a large village on the borders of Stafford and Shropshire, where he halted for a crust and a jug of ale. The place was so crowded that he judged it was market day, and the one inn had a press about its door like the visiting hours at a debtors' prison. He despaired of forcing an entrance, so commissioned an obliging loafer to fetch him a tankard, while he dismounted, hitched his bridle to the signpost, and seated himself at the end of a bench which ran along the inn's frontage.

The ale was long in coming, and Alastair had leisure to observe his neighbours. They were a remarkable crowd. Not villagers clearly, for the orthodox inhabitants might be observed going about their avocations, with many curious glances at the strangers. They were all sizes and shapes, and in every variety of dress from fustian to camlet, but all were youngish and sturdily built, and most a trifle dilapidated. The four men who sat on the bench beside him seemed like gamekeepers out of employ, and were obviously a little drunk. In the throng at the door there were horse-boys and labourers and better-clad hobbledehoys who might have been the sons of yeomen. A raffish young

gentleman with a greyhound and with a cock of his hat broken
was engaged in an altercation with an elderly fellow who had a
sheaf of papers and had mounted a pair of horn spectacles to
read them. Through the open window of the tap-room floated
scraps of argument in a dozen varieties of dialect.

Alastair rubbed his eyes. Something in the sight was familiar.
He had seen it in Morvern, in the Isles, in a dozen parts of
France and Spain, when country fellows were recruited for
foreign armies. But such things could not be in England, where
the foreign recruiter was forbidden. Nor could it be enlistment
for the English regiments, for where were the bright uniforms
and the tuck of drums? The elderly man with the papers was
beyond doubt a soldier, but he had the dress of an attorney's
clerk. There was some queer business afoot here, and Alastair
set himself to probe it.

His neighbour on the bench did not understand his question.
But the raffish young man with the greyhound heard it, and
turned sharply to the speaker. A glance at Alastair made his
voice civil.

'Matter!' he exclaimed. 'The matter, sir, is that I and some
two-score honest men have been grossly deceived. We are of
Oglethorpe's, enlisted to fight the Spaniard in the Americas.
And now there is word that we are to be drafted to General
Wade, as if we were not gentleman-venturers but so many ham-
handed common soldiers. Hark, sir!'

From within the inn came a clatter of falling dishes and high
voices.

'That will be Black Benjamin warming to work,' said the
young man, proffering a pewter snuff-box in which there
remained a few grains of rappee. 'He is striving in there with
the Quartermaster-Sergeant while I seek to convince Methody
Sam here of the deceitfulness of his ways.'

The elderly man, referred to as Methody Sam, put his
spectacles in his pocket, and revealed a mahogany face lit by
two bloodshot blue eyes. At the sight of Alastair he held himself
at attention, for some instinct in him discerned the soldier.

'I ain't denyin' it's a melancholy business, sir,' he said, 'and vexatious to them poor fellows. They was recruited by Gen'ral Oglethorpe under special permission from His Majesty, God bless 'im, for the dooty of keeping the Spaniards out of His Majesty's territory of Georgia in Ameriky, for which purpose they 'as signed on for two years, journeys there and back included, at the pay of one shilling per lawful day, and all vittles and clothing provided 'andsome. But now 'Is Majesty thinks better on it, and is minded to let Georgia slip and send them lads to General Wade to fight the Scotch. It's a 'ard pill to swallow, I ain't denyin' it, but orders is orders, and I 'ave them express this morning from Gen'ral Oglethorpe, who is a-breakin' the news to the Shropshire Companies.'

One of the drunkards on the bench broke into a flood of oaths which caused Methody Sam to box his ears. 'Ye was enlisted for a pious and honourable dooty, and though that dooty may be changed the terms of enlistment is the same. No foul mouth is permitted 'ere, my lad.'

The young gentleman with the greyhound was listening eagerly to what was going on indoors. 'Benjamin's getting his dander up,' he observed. 'Soon there will be bloody combs going. Hi! Benjy!' he shouted. 'Come out and let's do the job fair and foursquare in the open. It's a high and holy mutiny.'

There was no answer, but presently the throng at the door began to fan outward under pressure from within. A crowd of rough fellows tumbled out, and at their tail a gypsy-looking youth with a green bandana round his head, dragging a small man, who had the air of having once been in authority. Alastair recognised the second of the two non-commissioned officers, but while one had protested against oaths the other was filling the air with a lurid assortment. This other had his hands tied with a kerchief, and a cord fastening the joined palms to his knees, so that he presented a ridiculous appearance of a man at his prayers.

'Why hain't ye trussed up Methody?' the gypsy shouted to the owner of the greyhound.

The sergeant cast an appealing eye on Alastair. There seemed to be no arms in the crowd, except a cudgel or two and the gypsy's whinger. It was an appeal which the young man's tradition could not refuse.

'Have patience, gentlemen,' he cried. 'I cannot have you prejudging the case. Forward with your prisoner, but first untie these bonds. Quick.'

The gypsy opened his mouth in an insolent refusal, when he saw something in the horseman's eye which changed his mind. Also he noted his pistols, and his light travelling sword.

'That's maybe fair,' he grunted, and with his knife slit his prisoner's bonds.

'Now, out with your grievances.'

The gypsy could talk, and a very damning indictment he made of it. 'We was 'listed for overseas, with good chance of prize money, and a nobleman's freedom. And now we're bidden stop at home as if we was lousy lobsters that took the King's money to trick the gallows. Is that fair and English, my sweet pretty gentleman? We're to march to-morrow against the naked Highlanders that cut out a man's bowels with scythes, and feed their dogs with his meat. Is that the kind of fighting you was dreaming of, my precious boys? No, says you, and we'll be damned, says you, if we'll be diddled. Back we goes to our pretty homes, but with a luckpenny in our pocket for our wasted time and our sad disappointment. Them sergeants has the money, and we'll hold them upside down by the heels till we shake it out of them.'

Methody Sam replied, looking at Alastair. 'It's crool 'ard, but orders is orders. Them folks enlisted to do the King's commands and if 'Is Majesty 'appens to change 'is mind, it's no business o' theirs or mine. The money me and Bill 'as is Government money, and if they force it from us they'll be apprehended and 'anged as common robbers. I want to save their poor innocent souls from 'anging felony.'

The crowd showed no desire for salvation. There was a surge towards the two men and the gypsy's hand would have been on the throat of Methody Sam had not Alastair struck it up. The smaller of the two non-commissioned officers was chafing his wrists, which his recent bonds had abraded, and lamenting that he had left his pistols at home.

'What made you come here with money and nothing to guard it?' Alastair asked.

'The General's orders, sir. But it was different when we was temptin' them with Ameriky and the Spaniards' gold. Now we'll need a file o' loaded muskets to get 'em a step on the road. Ay, sir, we'll be fort'nate if by supper time they've not all scattered like a wisp o' snipes, takin' with 'em 'Is Majesty's guineas.'

'Keep beside me!' Alastair whispered. A sudden rush would have swept the little man off, had not Methody Sam plucked him back.

'Better yield quiet,' said the gypsy. 'We don't want no blood-lettin', but we're boys as is not to be played with. Out with the guineas, tear up the rolls, and the two of ye may go to Hell for all we care.'

'What are you going to do?' Alastair asked his neighbours.

The little man looked bleakly at the crowd. 'There don't seem much of a chance, but we're bound to put up a fight, seein' we're in charge of 'Is Majesty's property. That your notion, Sam?'

The Methody signified his assent by a cheerful groan.

'Then I'm with you,' said Alastair. 'To the inn wall? We must get our backs protected.'

The suddenness of the movement and the glint of Alastair's sword opened a way for the three to a re-entrant angle of the inn, where their flanks and rear were safe from attack. Alastair raised his voice.

'Gentlemen,' he said, 'as a soldier I cannot permit mutiny. You will not touch a penny of His Majesty's money, and you will wait here on General Oglethorpe's orders. If he sees fit to disband you, good and well; if not, you march as he commands.'

Even as he spoke inward laughter consumed him. He, a follower of the Prince, was taking pains that certain troops should reach Wade, the Prince's enemy. Yet he could not act otherwise, for the camaraderie of his profession constrained him.

The power of the armed over the unarmed was in that moment notably exemplified. There was grumbling, a curse or two, and sullen faces, but no attempt was made to rush that corner where stood an active young man with an ugly sword. The mob swayed and muttered, the gypsy went off on an errand behind the inn, one of the drunkards lurched forward as if to attack and fell prone. A stone or two was thrown, but Alastair showed his pistols, and that form of assault was dropped. The crowd became stagnant, but it did not disperse.

'I must get on to Flambury,' Alastair told his neighbours. 'I cannot wait all day here. There is nothing for it but that you go with me. My pistols will get us a passage to my horse yonder, and we can ride and tie.'

The plan was never put into action. For at the moment from a window over their heads descended a shower of red-hot embers. All three leaped forward to avoid a scorching and so moved outside the protecting side wall. Then, neatly and suddenly, the little man called Bill was plucked up and hustled into the crowd. Alastair could not fire or draw upon a circle of gaping faces. He looked furiously to his right, when a cry on his left warned him that the Methody also had gone.

But him he could follow, for he saw the boots of him being dragged inside the inn door. Clearing his way with his sword, he rushed thither, stumbling over the greyhound and with a kick sending it flying. There were three steps to the door, and as he mounted them he obtained a view over the heads of the mob and down the village street. He saw his horse still peacefully tethered to the signpost, and beyond it there came into view a mounted troop clattering up the cobbles.

The door yielded to his foot and he received in his arms the Methody, who seemed to have made his escape from his captors. 'They've got Bill in the cellar,' he gasped. 'It's that Gypsy Ben.' And then he was stricken dumb at something which he saw below Alastair's armpits.

The crowd had scattered and its soberer members now clustered in small knots with a desperate effort at nonchalance. Opposite the inn door horsemen had halted, and the leader, a tall man with the black military cockade in his hat, was looking sternly at the group, till his eye caught the Methody. 'Ha! Sewell,' he cried, and the Methody, stricken into a ramrod, stood erect before him.

'These are recruits of ours?' he asked. 'You have explained to them the new orders?'

'Sir,' said the ramrod, raising his voice so that all could hear, 'I have explained, as in dooty bound, and I 'ave to report that, though naturally disappointed, they bows to orders, all but a gypsy rapscallion, of whom we be well quit. I 'ave likewise to report that Bill and me 'as been much assisted by this gentleman you sees before you, without whom things might 'ave gone ugly.'

The tall soldier's eyes turned towards Alastair and he bowed.

'I am in your debt, sir. General Oglethorpe is much beholden to you.'

'Nay, sir, as a soldier who chanced upon a difficult situation I had no choice but to lend my poor aid.'

The General proffered his snuff-box. 'Of which regiment?'

'Of none English. My service has been outside my country, on the continent of Europe. I am born a poor Scottish gentleman, sir, whose sword is his livelihood. They call me Maclean.'

General Oglethorpe looked up quickly. 'A most honourable livelihood. I too have carried my sword abroad – to the Americas, as you may have heard. I was returning thither, but I have been intercepted for service in the North. Will you dine with me, sir? I should esteem your company.'

'Nay, I must be on the road,' said Alastair. 'Already I have delayed too long. I admire your raw material, sir, but I do not covet your task of shaping it to the purposes of war.'

The General smiled sourly. 'In Georgia they would have been good soldiers in a fortnight. Here in England they will be still raw after a year's campaigning.'

They parted with elaborate courtesies, and looking back, Alastair saw what had five minutes before been an angry mob falling into rank under General Oglethorpe's eye. He wondered what had become of Ben the Gypsy.

Flambury proved but a short two-hours' journey. It was a large village with a broad street studded with ancient elm trees, and, as Alastair entered it, that street was thronged like a hiring fair. The noise of human voices, of fiddles and tabrets and of excited dogs, had greeted him half a mile off, like the rumour of a battlefield. Wondering at the cause of the din, he wondered more when he approached the houses and saw the transformation of the place. There were booths below the elm trees, protected from possible rain by awnings of sacking, where ribands and crockery and cheap knives were being vended. Men and women, clothed like mummers, danced under the November sky as if it had been May-day. Games of chance were in progress, fortunes were being spae'd, fairings of gingerbread bought, and, not least, horses sold to the accompaniment of shrill cries from stable boys and the whinnyings of startled colts and fillies. The sight gave Alastair a sense of security, for in such an assemblage a stranger would not be questioned. He asked a woman what the stir signified. 'Lawk a mussy, where be you borned,' she said, 'not to know 'tis Flambury Feast-Day?'

The Dog and Gun was easy to find. Already the darkness was falling, and while the street was lit with tarry staves, the interior of the hostelry glowed with a hundred candles. The sign was undecipherable in the half light, but the name in irregular letters was inscribed above the ancient door. Alastair rode into a courtyard filled with chaises and farmers' carts, and having with some difficulty found an ostler, stood over him while his horse was groomed, fed and watered. Then he turned to the house, remembering Mr Kyd's recommendation to the landlord. If that recommendation could procure him some privacy in this visit, fortunate would have been his meeting with the Laird of Greyhouses.

The landlord, discovered not without difficulty, was a lusty florid fellow, with a loud voice and a beery eye. He summoned the traveller into his own parlour, behind the tap-room, from which all day his bustling wife directed the affairs of the house. The place was a shrine of comfort, with a bright fire reflected in polished brass and in bottles of cordials and essences which shone like jewels. The wife at a long table was mixing bowl after bowl of spiced liquors, her face glowing like a moon, and her nose perpetually wrinkled in the task of sniffing odours to detect the moment when the brew was right. The husband placed a red-cushioned chair for Alastair, and played nervously with the strings of his apron. It occurred to the traveller that the man had greeted him as if he had been expected, and at this he wondered.

The name of Mr Kyd was a talisman that wrought mightily upon the host's goodwill, but that goodwill was greater than his powers.

'Another time and the whole house would have been at your honour's service,' he protested. 'But to-day—' and he shrugged his shoulders. 'Oh, you shall have a bed, though I have to lie myself on bare boards, but a private room is out of my power. We've but the three of them, and they're all as throng as a bee-hive. There's Tom Briggs in the Blue Room, celebrating the sale of his string of young horses – an ancient engagement, sir; and there's the Codgers' Supper in the Gents' Attic, and in Shrews-bury there's five pig dealers sleeping on chairs. That's so, mother?'

'Six in Shrewsbury,' said the lady, 'and there's five waiting on the Attic, as soon as the Codgers have supped.'

'You see, sir, how I'm situated. You'll have a good bed to yourself, but I fear I must ask you to sup in the bar parlour with the other gentry that's here to-day. Unless your honour would prefer the kitchen?' he added hopefully.

Alastair, who had a vision of a company of drunken squirel-ings of an inquisitive turn, announced that he would greatly prefer the kitchen. The decision seemed to please the landlord.

'There's a good fire and not above half a dozen for company at present. Warm yourself there, sir, and your supper will be ready before your feet are comforted. A dish of pullets and eggs, mutton chops, a prime ham, a good cut of beef, and the best of double Gloucester. What say you to that now? And for liquor a bowl of mother's spiced October, with a bottle of old port to go with the cheese.'

Alastair was hungry enough to approve of the lot, and tired and cold enough to welcome the chance of a roaring kitchen hearth. In the great shadowy place, the rafters loaded with hams and the walls bright with warming-pans, there was only a handful of topers, since the business out-of-doors was still too engrossing. The landlord was as good as his word, and within half an hour the traveller was sitting down to a most substantial meal at the massive board. The hostess's spiced October was delicate yet potent, the port thereafter – of which the host had a couple of glasses – a generous vintage. The young man at length drew his chair from the table to the fireside and stretched his legs to the blaze, replete and comfortable in body, and placid, if a little hazy, in mind. . . . Presently the leaping flames of the logs took odd shapes; the drone of voices from the corner became surf on a shore: he saw a fire on a beach and dark hills behind it, and heard the soft Gaelic of his kin. . . . His head nodded on his breast and he was sound asleep.

He woke to find an unpleasant warmth below his nose and to hear a cackle as of a thousand geese in his ears. Something bright and burning was close to his face. He shrank from it and at once sprawled on his back, his head bumping hard on the stone floor.

The shock thoroughly awakened him. As he sprang to his feet he saw a knot of flushed giggling faces. One of the group had been holding a red-hot poker to his face, while another had drawn away the chair from beneath him.

His first impulse was to buffet their heads, for no man is angrier than a sleeper rudely awakened. The kitchen was now crowded, and the company seemed to appreciate the efforts of the practical jokers, for there was a roar of applause and shouts of merriment. The jokers, who from their dress were hobbledehoy yeomen or small squires, were thus encouraged to continue, and, being apparently well on the way to drunkenness, were not disposed to consider risks. Two of them wore swords, but it was clear that the sword was not their weapon.

Alastair in a flaming passion had his hand on his blade, when his arm was touched from behind and a voice spoke. 'Control your temper, sir, I beseech you. This business is premeditated. They seek to fasten a quarrel on you. Don't look round. Smile and laugh with them.'

The voice was familiar though he could not put a name to it. A second glance at the company convinced him that the advice was sound and he forced himself to urbanity. He took his hand from his sword, rubbed his eyes like one newly awakened, and forced a parody of a smile.

'I have been asleep,' he stammered. 'Forgive my inattention, gentlemen. You were saying . . . Ha ha! I see! A devilish good joke, sir. I dreamed I was a blacksmith and woke to believe I had fallen in the fire.'

The hobbledehoys were sober enough to be a little non-plussed at this reception of their pleasantry. They stood staring sheepishly, all but one who wore a mask and a nightcap, as if he had just come from a mumming show. To judge by his voice he seemed older than the rest.

'Tell us your dreams,' he said rudely. 'From your talk in your sleep they should have been full of treason. Who may you be, sir?'

Alastair, at sight of a drawer's face round the corner of the tap-room door, called for a bowl of punch.

'Who am I?' he said quietly. 'A traveller who has acquired a noble thirst, which he would fain share with other good fellows.'

'Your name, my thirsty friend?'

'Why, they call me Watson – Andrew Watson, and my business is to serve his Grace of Queensberry, that most patriotic nobleman.' He spoke from a sudden fancy, rather than from any purpose; it was not likely that he could be controverted, for Mr Kyd was now posting into Wiltshire.

His questioner looked puzzled, but it was obvious that the name of a duke, and Queensberry at that, had made an impression upon the company. The man spoke aside with a friend, and then left the kitchen. This was so clear a proof that there had been purpose in his baiting that Alastair could have found it in him to laugh at such clumsy conspirators. Somehow word had been sent of his coming, and there had been orders to entangle him; but the word had not been clear and his ill-wishers were still in doubt about his identity. It was his business in no way to enlighten them, but he would have given much to discover the informant.

He had forgotten about the mentor at his elbow. Turning suddenly, he was confronted with the queer figure of the tutor of Chastlecote, who was finishing a modest supper of bread and cheese at the main table. The man's clothes were shabbier than ever, but his face and figure were more wholesome than at Cornbury. His cheeks had a faint weathering, his neck was less flaccid, and he held himself more squarely. As Alastair turned, he also swung round, his left hand playing a tattoo upon his knee. His eye was charged with confidences.

'We meet again,' he whispered. 'Ever since we parted I have had a premonition of this encounter. I have much for your private ear.'

But it was not told, for the leader of the hobbledehoys, the fellow with the mask and nightcap, was again in the kitchen. It looked as if he had been given instructions by someone, for he shouted, as a man does when he is uncertain of himself and would keep up his courage.

'Gentlefolk all, there are vipers among us tonight. This man who calls himself a duke's agent, and the hedge schoolmaster at his elbow. They are naught but lousy Jacobites and 'tis our business as good Englishmen to strip and search them.'

The others of his party cried out in assent, and there was a measure of support from the company at large. But before a man could stir the tutor spoke.

'Bad law!' he said. 'I and, for all I know, the other gentleman are inoffensive travellers moving on our lawful business. You cannot lay hand on us without a warrant from a justice. But, sirs, I am not one to quibble about legality. This fellow has insulted me grossly and shall here and now be brought to repentance. Put up your hands, you rogue.'

The tutor had suddenly become a fearsome figure. He had risen from his chair, struggled out of his coat, and, blowing like a bull, was advancing across the floor on his adversary, his great doubled fists held up close to his eyes. The other gave ground.

'I do not fight with scum,' he growled. But as the tutor pressed on him, his hand went to his sword.

He was not permitted to draw it. 'You will fight with the natural weapon of Englishmen,' his assailant cried, and caught the sword strap and broke it, so that the weapon clattered into a corner and its wearer spun round like a top. The big man seemed to have the strength of a bull. 'Put up your hands,' he cried again, 'or take a coward's drubbing.'

The company was now in high excitement, and its sympathies were mainly against the challenged. Seeing this, he made a virtue of necessity, doubled his fists, ducked and got in a blow on the tutor's brisket. The latter had no skill, but immense reach and strength and the uttermost resolution. He simply beat down the other's guard, reckless of the blows he received, and presently dealt him such a clout that he measured his length on the floor, whence he rose sick and limping and departed on the arm of a friend. The victor, his cheeks mottled red and grey and his breath whistling like the wind in a chimney, returned amid acclamation to the fireside, where he accepted a glass of Alastair's punch.

For a moment the haggardness was wiped from the man's face, and it shone with complacence. His eyes shot jovial but martial glances at the company.

'We have proved our innocence,' he whispered to Alastair. 'Had you used sword or pistol you would have been deemed spy and foreigner, but a bout of fisticuffs is the warrant of the true-born Englishman.'

SIX

Introduces the Runaway Lady

Alastair stole a glance at his neighbour's face and found it changed from their first meeting. It had lost its dumb misery and – for the moment – its grey pallor. Now it was flushed, ardent, curiously formidable, and, joined with the heavy broad shoulders, gave an impression of truculent strength.

'I love to bandy such civilities,' said the combatant. 'I was taught to use my hands by my uncle Andrew, who used to keep the ring at Smithfields. We praise the arts of peace, but the keenest pleasure of mankind is in battles. You, sir, follow the profession of arms. Every man thinks meanly of himself for not having been a soldier.'

He helped himself to the remainder of the bowl of punch, which he gulped down noisily. Alastair was in two minds about his new acquaintance. The man's simplicity and courage and honest friendliness went to his heart, but he was at a loss in which rank of society to place him. Mr Johnson spoke with a queer provincial accent – to him friend was 'freend' and a shire a 'sheer' – and his manners were those of a yokel, save that they seemed to spring from a natural singularity rather than from a narrow experience, for at moments he had a fine dignity, and his diction was metropolitan if his pronunciation was rustic. The more the young man looked at the weak heavy-lidded eyes and the massive face, the more he fell under their spell. The appearance was like a Moorish palace – outside, a bleak wall which had yet a promise of a treasure-house within.

'What of your errand?' he asked. 'When we last parted you were in quest of a runaway lady.'

'My quest has prospered, though I have foundered a good horse over it, and when I have paid for this night's lodging, shall have only a quarter-guinea to take me back to Chastlecote. Why, sir, since you are kind enough to interest yourself in this affair, you shall be told of it. Miss Grevel is duly and lawfully wed and is now my lady Norreys. Sir John has gone north on what he considers to be his duty. He is, as you are aware, a partisan of the young Prince. My lady stays behind; indeed she is lodged not a mile from this inn in the house of her mother's brother, Mr Thicknesse.'

'Then you are easier in mind about the business?'

'I am easier in mind. The marriage was performed as decently as was possible for a thing so hastily contrived. He has behaved to the lady in all respects with courtesy and consideration, and he has shown the strength of his principles by departing at once to the camp of his Prince. I am disposed to think better of his character than I had been encouraged to by rumour. And, sir, there is one thing that admits of no shadow of doubt. The lady is most deeply in love.'

'You have seen her?'

'This very day. She carries her head as if she wore a crown on it, and her eyes are as happy as a child's. I did not venture to present myself, for if she guessed that I had followed her she would have laid a whip over my back.' He stopped to laugh, with affection in his eyes. 'She has done it before, sir, for 'tis a high-spirited lady. So I bribed a keeper with sixpence to allow me to watch from a covert, as she took her midday walk. She moved like Flora, and she sang as she moved. That is happiness, said I to myself, and whatever the faults of the man who is its cause, 'twould be sacrilege to mar it. So I slipped off, thanking my Maker that out of seeming ill the dear child had won this blessedness.'

Mr Johnson ceased to drum on the table or waggle his foot, and fell into an abstraction, his body at peace, his eyes fixed on the fire in a pleasant dream. The company in the kitchen had thinned to half a dozen, and out-of-doors the din of the fair seemed to be dying down. Alastair was growing drowsy, and he too fell to staring at the flames and seeing pictures in their depths. Suddenly a hand was laid on his elbow and, turning with a start, he found a lean little man on the form behind him.

'Be 'ee the Dook's man?' a cracked voice whispered.

Alastair puzzled, till he remembered that an hour back he had claimed to be Queensberry's agent. So he nodded.

The little man thrust a packet into his hands.

'This be for 'ee,' he said, and was departing, when Alastair plucked his arm.

'From whom?' he asked.

'I worn't to say, but 'ee knows.' Then he thrust forward a toothless mouth to the other's ear. 'From Brother Gilly,' he whispered.

'And to whom were you sent?'

'To 'ee. To the Dook's man at the Dog and Gun. I wor to ask at the landlord, but 'e ain't forthcoming, and one I knows and trusts points me to 'ee.'

Alastair realised that he was mistaken for Mr Nicholas Kyd, now posting south; and, since the two were on the same business, he felt justified in acting as Mr Kyd's deputy. He pocketed the package and gave the messenger a shilling. At that moment Mr Johnson came out of his reverie. His brow was clouded.

'At my lord Cornbury's house there was a tall man with a florid face. He treated me with little politeness and laughed out of season. He had a servant, too, a rough Scot who attended to my horse. I have seen that servant in these parts.'

Alastair woke to a lively interest. Then he remembered that Mr Kyd had told him of a glimpse he had had of the tutor of Chastlecote. Johnson had seen the man Edom before he had started south.

His thoughts turned to the packet. There could be no chance of overtaking Mr Kyd, whose correspondent was so culpably in arrears. The thing might be the common business of the Queensberry estates, in which case it would be forwarded when he found an occasion. But on the other hand it might be business of *Menelaus*, business of urgent import to which Alastair could attend. . . . He debated the matter with himself for a little, and then broke the seal.

The packet had several inclosures. One was in a cypher to which he had not the key. Another was a long list of names, much contracted, with figures in three columns set against each. The third riveted his eyes, so that he had no ear for the noises of the inn or the occasional remarks of his companion.

It was a statement, signed by the word *Tekel* and indorsed with the name of *Mene* – a statement of forces guaranteed from Wales and the Welsh Marches. There could be no doubt about its purport. There was Sir Watkin's levy and the day and the hour it would be ready to march; that was a test case which proved the document authentic, for Alastair himself had discussed provisionally these very details a week ago at Wynnstay. There were other levies in money and men against the names of Cotton, Herbert, Savage, Wynne, Lloyd, Powell. Some of the figures were queried, some explicit and certified. There was a note about Beaufort, promising an exact account within two days, which would be sent to Oxford. Apparently the correspondent called Gilly, whoever he might be, knew of Kyd's journey southward, but assumed that he had not yet started. At the end were three lines of gibberish – a cypher obviously.

As his mind grasped the gist of the thing, a flush crept over his face and he felt the beat of his heart quicken. Here was news, tremendous news. The West was rising, careless of a preliminary English victory, and waiting only the arrival of the Prince at some convenient rendezvous. There were ten thousand men and half a million of money in these lists, and they were not all. Beaufort was still to come, and Oxfordshire and Gloucestershire, and the Welsh south-west. The young man's eyes kindled, and then grew a little dim. He saw the triumph of his Prince, and the fulfilment of his dreams, for the war would no longer be a foreign invasion but a rising of Englishmen. He remembered Midwinter's words, 'You can win only by enlisting Old England.' It looked as if it had been done. . . . He saw now why Kyd must linger in the south. He was the conduit pipe of a vital intelligence which must go to the Prince by the swiftest means, for on it all his strategy depended. He himself would carry this budget, and for the others Kyd had doubtless made his own plans. Even now Lancashire would be up, and Cheshire stirring. . . .

The kitchen door was flung open with a violence which startled three topers left by the table. A lantern wavered in the doorway, and in front of it a square-set man in fustian stumped into the place. He carried a constable's stave in one hand and in the other a paper. Behind him a crowd followed, among which might be recognised the mummers of the evening, notably the one whose bandaged face bore witness to the strength of Mr Samuel Johnson's fist.

The constable marched up to the hearth.

'By these 'ere presents I lays 'old on the bodies of two suspected pussons, to wit one Muck Lane, a Scotchman, and one Johnson, a schoolmaster, they being pussons whose doings and goings and comings are contrairy to the well-bein' of this 'ere realm and a danger to the peace of our Lord the King.'

The mention of himself by name showed Alastair that this was no affair of village spy-hunters, but a major peril. In his hand he still held the packet addressed to Kyd. Were he searched it might be damning evidence; moreover he had already the best part of the intelligence therein contained in his head. Mr Johnson, who was chilly, had just flung on more logs and the fire blazed high. Into the red heart of it went the paper and, since the tutor's bulky figure was between him and the door, the act was not noticed by the constable and his followers.

'What whim of rascality is this?' asked Mr Johnson, reaching for a stout oak stick which he had propped in a corner.

'A very troublesome whim for you,' said a voice. 'The constable holds a warrant issued by Squire Thicknesse for the arrest of two Jacobite emissaries traced into this village.'

'Ay,' said the constable, ''ee'd better come quiet, for Squire 'ave sent a brave lot o' keepers and stable lads to manhandle 'ee if 'ee don't. My orders is to carry 'ee to the Manor and lock 'ee up there till such time as 'ee can be sent to Brumming'am.'

'Arrant nonsense,' cried Johnson. 'I'm a better subject of His Majesty than any rascal among you, and so, I doubt not, is my friend. Yet so great is our veneration for the laws of England, that we will obey this preposterous summons. Take me to your Squire, but be warned, every jack of you, that if a man lays his hand on me I will fell him to the earth.'

'And I say likewise,' said Alastair, laying a significant hand on his sword.

The constable, who had no great stomach for his duty, was relieved by his prisoners' complaisance, and after some discussion with his friend announced that no gyves should be used if they consented to walk with the Squire's men on both sides of them. Alastair insisted on having his baggage brought with him, which was duly delivered to one of the Manor's grooms by a silent landlady; Mr Johnson carried his slender outfit in his pockets. The landlord did not show himself. But at the inn door, before the Manor men closed up, a figure pressed forward from the knot of drunken onlookers, and Alastair found his sleeve plucked and the face of Brother Gilly's messenger beside him.

'I've been mistook, maister. 'Ee bain't the Dook's man, not the one I reckoned. Gimme back the letter.'

'It's ashes now. Tell that to him that sent you. Say the letter's gone, but the news travels forward in a man's head.'

The messenger blinked uncomprehendingly and then made as if to repeat his request, but a sudden rush of merrymakers, hungry for a fresh spectacle, swept him down the street. Presently the escort was clear of the village and tramping through a black aisle of trees. Someone lit a lantern, which showed the mattress of chestnut leaves underfoot and the bare branches above. The keepers and stable-boys whistled, and Mr Johnson chanted aloud what sounded like Latin hexameters. For him there was no discomfort in the adventure save that on a raw night it removed him from a warm fireside.

But for Alastair the outlook was grave. Here was he arrested by a booby constable on the warrant of some Justice Shallow, but arrested under his own name. He had passed secretly from Scotland to Cornbury, and but for the party at the latter place and one strange fellow on Otmoor, no one had known that name. Could the news have leaked out from the Cornbury servants? But, even then, he was not among the familiar figures of Jacobitism, and he had but just come from France. Only Lord Cornbury knew his true character, and Lord Cornbury did not talk. Yet someone with full knowledge of his past and present had tracked him to this village, a place far from any main highway to the North.

What he feared especially was delay. Unless Cornbury bore witness against him, or the man from Otmoor, the law had no evidence worth a farthing. Hearsay and suspicion could not hang him. He would play the part of the honest traveller now returning from an Oxfordshire visit, and if needs be he would refer to Queensberry's business. But hearsay and suspicion could delay. He was suddenly maddened by the thought that some bumbling Justice might detain him in these rotting midlands when the Prince was crossing Ribble. And he had to get north with the news of the Welsh recruiting! At the thought he bit his lips in a sharp vexation.

They passed through gates into a park where the trees fell back from the road, and presently were in a flagged courtyard with a crack of light showing from a door ajar. It opened and a portly butler filled it.

'You will await his honour in the Justice Room,' he announced, and the prisoners swung to the right under an archway into another quadrangle.

The Justice Room proved to be a bare apartment, smelling strongly of apples, with a raised platform at one end and on the floor a number of wooden forms arranged like the pens at a sheep fair. On the platform stood a large handsome armchair covered in Spanish leather, and before it a small table. The butler entered by a door giving on the platform, and on the table placed a leather-bound book and on the chair a red velvet cushion.

'Exit the clerk, enter the preacher,' said Johnson.

The servant, bowing profoundly, ushered in a tall gentleman in a suit of dark-blue velvet, with a fine lace cravat falling over a waistcoat of satin and silver. The gentleman might have been fifty years of age by the lines round his mouth, but his cherubic countenance was infantine in contour, and coloured, by hunting or the bottle, to an even pink. He had clearly been dining well, for he plumped down heavily in the chair and his eye was as blue and vacant as a frosty sky. When he spoke it was with the careful enunciation of one who is not in a condition to take liberties with the English tongue.

'Makin' so bold, your honour,' said the constable, 'them 'ere's the prisoners as is named in your honour's worshipful warrant.'

His honour nodded. 'What the devil do you want me to do, Perks?' he asked.

The mummer with the broken head, who had become mysteriously one of the party, answered.

'Lock 'em up for to-night, Squire Thicknesse, and to-morrow send 'em to Birmingham with a mounted escort. It's political business, and no matter of poaching or petty thieving.'

'I require that the charge be read,' said Johnson.

Squire Thicknesse took up a paper, looked at it with aversion, and gazed round him helplessly. 'Where the devil is my clerk?' he lamented. 'Gone feasting to Flambury, I'll warrant. I cannot read this damned crabbed hand.'

'Let me be your clerk, Nunkie dear.'

A girl had slipped through the door, and now stood by the chair looking over the Squire's shoulder. She was clearly very young, for her lips had the pouting fullness and her figure the straight lines of a child's, and her plain white gown and narrow petticoats had a nursery simplicity. The light was bad, and Alastair could not note the details, seeing only a glory of russet hair and below it a dimness of pearl and rose. On that much he was clear, and on the bird-like charm of her voice.

The effect of the vision on Johnson was to make him drive an elbow into Alastair's ribs and to murmur in what was meant for a whisper: 'That is my lady. That is the dear child.'

The sharp young eyes had penetrated the gloom below the platform.

'Why, Nunkie, there is a face I know. Heavens! It is our tutor from Chastlecote. Old Puffin we called him, for he puffs like my spaniel. A faithful soul, Nunkie, but at times oppressive. What can he want so far from home?'

The mummer, who seemed to have assumed the duties of prosecution, answered:

'The man Johnson is accused of being act and part with the other in conspiracy against His Majesty's throne.'

The girl's laughter trilled through the place. 'Oh, what delectable folly! Mr Samuel a conspirator! He is too large and noisy, Nunkie, and far, far too much of a sobersides. But give me the paper and I will be your clerk.'

With disquiet and amazement Alastair listened to the record. His full name was set down and his rank in King Louis' service. His journey into Oxfordshire was retailed, and its purpose, but the name of Cornbury was omitted. Then followed his expedition into Wales, with special mention of Wynnstay, and last his urgent reasons for returning north. Whoever had compiled the indictment was most intimately informed of all his doings. His head swam, for the thing seemed starkly incredible, and the sense of having lived unwittingly close to a deadly foe affected him with something not far from fear.

'What do you say to that?' Squire Thicknesse asked.

'That it is some foolish blunder. You have laid hold on the wrong man, sir, and I admit no part of it except the name, which is mine, and, with deference, as ancient and unsmirched as your honour's. No single fact can be adduced to substantiate these charges.'

'They will be abundantly proven.' The mummer's voice croaked ominous as a raven's.

The charge against Johnson proved to be much flimsier, and was derided by the girl. 'I insist that you straightly discharge my Mr Samuel,' she cried. 'I will go bail for his good behaviour, and to-morrow a servant shall take him back to Chastlecote. He is too innocent to be left alone. The other—'

'He says he is an agent of the Duke of Queensberry,' said the relentless mummer. 'I can prove him to be a liar.'

The girl was apparently not listening. Her eyes had caught Alastair's and some intelligence seemed to pass from them to his. She spoke a word in the Squire's ear and then looked beyond the prisoners to the mummer.

'My uncle, who is known for his loyalty to the present Majesty, will take charge of the younger prisoner and send him safe to-morrow to Birmingham. The other he will discharge. . . . That is your will, Nunkie?'

The Squire nodded. He was feeling very sleepy and at the same time very thirsty, and his mind hovered between bed and a fresh bottle.

'You may go home now, friends,' she said, 'and sweet dreams to you. You, constable, bring the two men to the Great Hall.' Then she slipped an arm inside her uncle's. 'My Mr Sam shall sup in the buttery and have a bed from Giles. Tomorrow we will find him a horse. You are a wise judge, Nunkie, and do not waste your wisdom on innocents. The other man looks dangerous and must be well guarded. Put him in the Tower garret, and give Giles the key. But first let the poor creature have bite and sup, if he wants it. He has the air of a gentleman.'

As Alastair walked before the staff of the constable, who wielded it like an ox-goad, his mind was furiously busy at guessing the source of the revelations in the warrant. Not till they stood in the glow of the hall lights did the notion of Kyd's servant come to him by the process of exhausting other possibilities. But the man had set off with Kyd early that morning for the South from a place forty miles distant. It was a naked absurdity, but nevertheless he asked Johnson the question, 'Where did you see the serving man who took your horse at Cornbury?'

The answer staggered him. 'This very day at the gate of this place about an hour after noon.'

As his perturbed gaze roamed round the hall he caught again the eye of the girl, looking back with her foot on the staircase. This time there could be no mistake. Her face was bright with confidential friendliness.

SEVEN

How a Man May Hunt with the Hounds and yet Run with the Hare

The butler Giles conducted him through long corridors to the door which separated the manor proper from its ancient Edwardian tower, and then up stone stairways to a room under the roof which had once been the sleeping apartment of the lord of the castle. The walls were two yards thick, the windows mere slits for arrows, the oaken floor as wavy as a ploughland. He had refused supper and asked only peace to collect his wits. Giles set a candle down on an oak table, and nodded to a cavernous canopied bed. 'There's blankets enow to keep you warm, since the night be mild for the time o' year. Good sleep to ye and easy dreams.' The key turned in the lock, and the shuffle of heelless shoes died on the stair.

Alastair flung himself on the bed, and lay staring at the roof of the canopy, fitfully illuminated by the dancing candle. A light wind must have crept into the room from some cranny of the windows, for the flame flickered and queer shadows chased each other over the dark walls. He was in a torment of disquietude since hearing the warrant – not for his own safety, for he did not despair of giving these chawbacons the slip, but for the prospects of the Cause. There was black treason somewhere in its innermost councils. The man who had betrayed every danger-point in his own career could do the same thing for others. The rogue – Kyd's servant or whoever he might be – was in the way of knowing the heart of every secret. Kyd, charged with a most vital service on which the future of England hung, had this Judas always at his elbow to frustrate or falsify any message to the North, to play the devil with the Prince's recruiting, and at the end to sell his master's head for gold. The thought made the young man dig his nails into his palms. God's pity that in an affair so gossamer-fine there should be this rude treachery to rend the web. . . . But if the miscreant was Kyd's servant, how came he in this neighbourhood? Had he been dismissed Kyd's service? Or was Kyd himself at hand and the journey into Wiltshire relinquished? His mind was in utter confusion.

Nevertheless the discovery had quickened his spirit, which of late he thought had been growing languid. He was a campaigner, and made his plans quick. His immediate duty was to escape, his next to reach the Prince and concert measures to meet the case of West England. Fortunate for him that the letter of Brother Gilly had fallen into his hand, for now he knew the magnitude of the business. But first he must sleep, for all evening he had been nodding. He had the soldier's trick of snatching odd hours of slumber, so, drawing a blanket round him and resolutely shutting off all thoughts, he was soon unconscious.

He slept lightly, and woke to see the candle, which he had left burning, guttering over the edge of the iron candlestick. A swift shadow ran across the wall before him, and a sudden waft of air caused the candle-end to flare like a torch. He glanced at the door, and it seemed to move. Then the place was quiet again, but it was brighter, for a new light had come into it. He scrambled from the bed to see the glow of a shaded lantern, and a slim cloaked figure slipping the key from the door.

The lantern was set beside the candle on the table. The figure wore a furred bed-gown and a nightcap of lace and pink satin, and its brown eyes in the shadow were bright as a squirrel's and very merry.

'La, la, such a commotion ere I could come to you, sir,' she said. 'Giles must carry Nunkie to bed and hoist Squire Bretherton and Sir Ambrose on their horses, and get a message from me to Black Ben, and pass a word to Stable Bill about Moonbeam. You have slept, wise man that you are? But it is time to be about your business of escaping, for in three hours it will be daylight.'

She was like a pixie in the half darkness, a tall pixie, that had a delicious small stammer in its speech. Alastair was on his feet now, bowing awkwardly.

'Tell me,' she whispered. 'The warrant is true? You are Alastair Maclean, a captain in Lee's Regiment of France, and a messenger from the Prince in Scotland. Oh, have no fear of me, for I am soul and body for the Cause.'

'The warrant spoke truly,' he said.

'And you will join the Prince at the first possible moment? How go things in the North? Have you any news, sir?'

'The Prince crossed the Border yesterday. He marches to Lancashire.'

She twined her fingers in excitement. 'You dare not delay an hour. And you shall not. I have made everything ready. Sir, you will find I have made everything ready. See, you shall follow me downstairs and Giles will be waiting. The lock of your door fits badly, for the wood around is worm-eaten. To-morrow it will be lying on the floor, to show my uncle how you escaped. Giles will take you by a private way to the Yew Avenue, and there Bill from the stables will await you with Moonbeam saddled and ready – my uncle's favourite, no less. You will ride down the avenue very carefully, keeping on the grass and making no sound, till you reach the white gate which leads to Wakehurst Common. There Ben will meet you and guide you out of this county so that by the evening you may be in Cheshire.'

'Ben the Gypsy?' he asked.

'The same. Do you know him? He is on our side and does many an errand for me.'

'But, madam, what of yourself? What will your uncle say when he finds his horse gone?'

'Stolen by the gypsies – I have the story pat. There will be a pretty hue and cry, but Ben will know of its coming and take precautions. I am grieved to tell fibs, but needs must in the day of war.'

'But I leave you alone to face the consequences.'

'Oh, do not concern yourself for me. My dear uncle is indulgent and, though a Whig, is no bigot. He will not grieve for your absence at breakfast to-morrow. But I fear the loss of Moonbeam will put him terribly out, and I should be obliged if you could find some way of restoring his horse when his purpose is served. As for myself, I propose leaving this hospitable house no later than to-morrow and journeying north into Derbyshire. I will take Mr Johnson with me as company and protector, and I have also my servants from Weston.'

She spoke with the air of a commander-in-chief, an air so mature and mistressly that it betrayed her utter youth.

'I am most deeply beholden to you, my lady,' said Alastair. 'You know something of me, and I will beg in return some news of my benefactress. You are my lady Norreys?'

The matronly airs fled and she was a shy child again.

'I am m-my lady,' she stammered, 'this week back. How did you know, sir? The faithful Puffin? My dear Sir John has gone north to join his Prince, by whose side you will doubtless meet him. Tell him I too have done my humble mite of service to the Cause, and that I am well, and happy in all things but his absence. . . . See, I have written him a little letter which will serve equally to present you to him and to assure him of my love. He is one of you – one of the trusted inner circle, I mean.' She lowered her voice. 'He bears the name of *Achilles*.'

The hazel eyes had ceased to sparkle and become modest and dim.

'Tell me one thing, my lady, before I go. My mission to the South was profoundly secret, and not four men in the Prince's army knew of it. Yet I find myself and my doings set forth in a justice's warrant as if I had cried them in the streets. There is a traitor abroad and if he goes undetected he spells ruin to our Cause. Can you help me to unearth him?'

She wrinkled her brows and narrowed her startled eyes.

'I cannot guess. Save you and Sir John I have seen no professor of our faith. Stay, who was the mummer last night in the Justice Room?'

'Some common jackal of Hanover. No, the danger is not there. But, madam, you have a quick brain and a bold heart. If you can lay your finger on this fount of treason, you will do a noble work for our Prince. Have you the means to send a message to the North?'

She nodded. 'Assuredly – by way of Sir John. . . . But you must start forthwith, sir. I will take your mails into Derbyshire in my charge, for you must ride fast and light. Now, follow me, and tread softly when I lift my hand.'

Down the long stone stairs the lantern fluttered, and at a corner the man who followed caught a glimpse of bare rosy ankles above the furred slippers. In the manor galleries, where oaken flooring creaked, a hand was now and then raised to advise caution. Once there came the slamming of a door, and the lantern-bearer froze into stillness behind an armoire, while Alastair, crouched beside her, felt the beating of her heart. But without mishap they reached the Great Hall, where the last red embers crackled fitfully and a cricket ticked on the hearthstone. Through a massive door they entered another corridor and the girl whistled long and soft. The answer was a crack of light from a side door, and Giles appeared, cloaked like a conspirator and carrying a pewter candlestick. Gone was the decorum of the butler who had set the stage in the Justice Room, and it was a nervous furtive old serving-man who received the girl's instructions.

'Oh, my lady, I'm doing this for your mother's sake, her as I used to make posies for when I was no more'n buttery lad. But my knees do knock together cruel, for what Squire would say if he knew makes my blood freeze to think on.'

'Now, don't be a fool, Giles. I can manage your master, and you have nothing to do but lead this gentleman to the Yew Avenue, and then back to your bed with a clear conscience.'

She laid a hand on the young man's arm – the gesture with which a boy encourages a friend.

'Adieu, sir, and I pray God that He lead you swift and straight to your journey's end. I will be in Derbyshire – at Brightwell

under the Peak, waiting to bid you welcome when you come
south to the liberation of England.' He took her hand, kissed it,
and, with a memory of wistful eyes and little curls that strayed
from her cap's lace and satin, he followed the butler through the
kitchen postern into the gloom of the night.

A short and stealthy journey among shrubberies brought
them to a deeper blackness which proved to be a grove of yews.
Something scraped and rustled close ahead, and the hoarse
whisper of Giles received a hoarse answer. The night was not so
dark as to hide objects outside the shade of the trees, and on a
patch of grass Alastair made out a horse with a man beside it.
Bill the stableman put the bridle into his hand, after making
certain by a word with Giles that he was the person awaited.
Alastair found a guinea for each, and before their muttered
thanks were done was in the saddle, moving, as he had been
instructed, into the blackness of the great avenue.

The light mouth, the easy paces, the smooth ripple of
muscle under his knees told him that he was mounted on
no common horse, but his head was still too full of his late
experience to be very observant about the present. The nut-
brown girl, the melodious voice with a stammer like a break in
a nightingale's song, seemed too delicious and strange for
reality. And yet she was flesh and blood; he had felt her body
warm against his when they sheltered behind the armoire: it
was her doing that he was now at liberty and posting northward. Now he understood Mr Johnson's devotion. To serve
such a lady he would himself scale the blue air and plough the
high hills, as the bards sang.

The bemusement took him down the avenue till the trees
thinned out and on the right came the ghostly glimmer of a
white gate. He turned and found it open, and by it another
horseman.

'The gentleman from Miss Claudy – beg y'r pardon – from
m'lady?' a voice asked.

'The same,' Alastair replied. The speech was that of the gypsy
he had met the day before.

The man shut the gate with his whip. 'Then follow me close and not a cheep o' talk. We've some cunning and fast journeying to do before the day breaks.'

They swept at a canter down a long lane, deeply rutted, and patched here and there with clumps of blackberries. Then they were on a heath, where the sky was lighter and the road had to be carefully picked round sandpits and quarry-holes. Alastair had no guess at direction, for the sky showed never a star, and though the dark was not impenetrable it was hopeless to look for landmarks. A strange madcap progress they made over every kind of country, now on road, now in woodland, now breasting slopes of heath with the bracken rubbing on the stirrups. Oftenest they were in forest land, where sometimes there was no path and Alastair found it best to give his horse its head and suffer it to do the steering. He had forgotten that England could be so wild, for these immense old boles and the miles of thicket and mere belonged surely to a primeval world. Again the course would be over fallow and new plough, and again in lanes and parish roads and now and then on the turnpike. The pace was easy – a light canter, but there were no halts, and always ahead over hedge and through gap went the slim figure of the gypsy.

The air was chilly but not cold, and soon the grey cloth of darkness began to thin till it was a fine veil dimming but not hiding objects, and the light wind blew which even on the stillest night heralds the dawn. The earth began to awake, lights kindled in farms and cottages, lanterns flickered around steadings. Movement through this world just struggling out of sleep was a joy and an exhilaration. It reminded Alastair of a winter journey from Paris to Beauvais – part of a Prince's wager – when with relays of horses he had ridden down the night, through woods and hamlets dumb with snow, intoxicated with his youth, and seeing mystery in every light that glimmered out of the dark. Now he was in the same mood. His spirits rose at the signs of awaking humanity. That lantern by a brook was a shepherd pulling hay for the tups now huddled in the sheepcote. The light at that window was the goodwife grilling bacon for the farmer's breakfast, or Blowselinda of the Inn sweeping the parlour after the night's drinking. And through that homely ritual of morn he was riding north to the Wars which should upturn thrones and make nobles of plain captains. Youth! Romance! And somewhere in the background of his brain a voice sounded like a trill of music. 'Adieu, sir. I pray God . . . I go to B-Brightwell under the P-Peak . . .'

The light had grown and he had his first view of Black Ben, and Ben of him. They jostled at a gate and stared at each other.

'We meet again,' he said.

'Happy meeting, my dear good gentleman. But you were on a different errand yesterday when my duty drove me the way of hot ashes. No offence took along of a poor man's honesty, kind sir?'

'None,' said Alastair. He saw now the reason for the gypsy's presence with the recruits. He was in Jacobite pay, hired to scatter Oglethorpe's levies and so reduce Wade's command. But none the less he disliked the man – his soft sneering voice, and the shifty eyes which he remembered from yesterday.

It was now almost broad day, about eight in the morning, and Alastair reckoned that they must have travelled twenty miles and be close on the Cheshire border. The country was featureless – much woodland interspersed with broad pastures, and far to the east a lift of ground towards a range of hills. The weather was soft and clear, a fine scenting morning for the hunt, and far borne on the morning air came the sound of a horn.

The gypsy seemed to be at fault. He stopped and considered for a matter of five minutes with his ear cocked. Then he plunged into a copse and emerged in a rushy bottom between high woods. Here the sound of the horn was heard again, apparently from the slopes at the end of the bottom.

'The turnpike runs yonder at the back of the oak clump,' he said. 'Best get to it by the brook there and the turf bridge. I must leave you, pretty gentleman. You take the left turn and hold on, and this night you will sleep in Warrington.'

They were jogging towards the brook when Alastair took a fancy to look back, and saw between the two woods a tiny landscape neatly framed in the trees. There was a church tower in it, and an oddly shaped clump of ashes. Surely it was familiar.

Across the brook the hunting horn sounded again, this time from beyond a spinney at the top of the slope.

'There lies your road, pretty sir,' and the gypsy pointed to the left of the spinney and wheeled his horse to depart.

But Alastair was looking back again. The higher ground of the slope gave him a wider prospect, and he saw across one of the enclosing woods the tall chimneys of a great house. That did not detain his eye, which was caught by something beyond. There on a low ridge was sprawled a big village with square-towered church and a blur of smoke above the line of houses. England must be a monotonous land, for this village of Cheshire was the very image of Flambury, and the adjacent mansion might have been Squire Thicknesse's manor.

At the same moment the music of hounds crashed from the spinney ahead, and a horn was violently blown. Round the edge of the spinney came the hunt, and the pack was spilled out of its shade like curds from a broken dish. The sight, novel in his experience, held him motionless. He saw the huntsman struggling with outrunners, and the field, urged on by the slope, crowding on the line. In the rear he saw a figure which was uncommonly like the magistrate who had presided last night in the Justice Room. As he observed these things he realised that his twenty miles of the morning had been a circuit, and that he was back now at the starting-point, mounted on a stolen horse, and within a hundred yards of the horse's owner. The gypsy had set spurs to his beast and was disappearing round the other end of the spinney, and even in the hubbub of the hunt he thought he detected the man's mocking laugh.

To hesitate was to be lost, and there was but the one course open. A tawny streak had slid before the hounds towards the brook. That must be the fox, and if he were not to become the quarry in its stead he must join in the chase. The huntsman was soon twenty yards from him, immediately behind the hounds, and fifty yards at his back came the van of the field. In that van he could see Squire Thicknesse mounted on a powerful grey, and he seemed to have eyes only for the hounds. Alastair cut in well behind him, in the hope that he would be taken for a straggler at covert-side, and in three seconds was sweeping forward in the second flight.

The morning's ride had been for Moonbeam no more than a journey to the meet, and the beautiful animal now laid back his ears and settled down to his share in that game which he understood as well as any two-legged mortal. But in the very perfection of the horse lay the rider's peril. Moonbeam was accustomed to top the hunt, for Squire Thicknesse was famed over three shires as a good goer. He would not be content to travel a field or two behind hounds; he must keep them company. Alastair found that no checking could restrain his mount. The animal was lightly bitted and he had not the skill or the strength to hold him back. True, he could have swerved and fetched a wide circuit, but in that first rush these tactics did not suggest themselves, and he set himself to a frantic effort at reining in, in which he was worsted. Moonbeam crossed the brook like a swallow; in a boggy place he took off badly, topped an ox-bar in the hedge, and all but fell on his nose in the next meadow. But after that he made no mistake, and in five minutes Alastair found himself looking from ten yards' distance at the broad back of the huntsman, with no rider near him except Squire Thicknesse on the grey.

The going was good over old pasture, and the young man had leisure to recover his breath and consider his position. He had hunted buck in France – stately promenades in the forests of Fontainebleau and Chantilly, varied by mad gallops along grassy rides where the only risk was the cannoning with other cavaliers. But this chase of the fox was a very different matter, the glory of it went to his head like strong wine, and he would not have cried off if he could. So far he was undiscovered. Were the fumes of last night's revel still in the Squire's head, or had he never meant to ride Moonbeam that day and his groom kept the loss from him? Crossing a thickset hedge neck by neck, Alastair stole a glance at him, and decided that the former explanation was the true one. His late host was still in the process of growing sober. . . . It could not last for ever. Sooner or later must come a check or a kill, when he would have a chance to look at his neighbour and his neighbour's horse. . . . Then he must ride for it, become himself the fox, and trust to Moonbeam. Pray God that the run took them to the north and ended many miles from Flambury.

For the better part of an hour hounds ran without a check – away from the enclosed fields and the woodlands to a country of furzy downs and bracken-filled hollows, and then once more into a land of tangled thickets. It took about twenty minutes to clear Squire Thicknesse's brain. Alastair heard a sudden roar behind him and looked over his shoulder to see a furious blue eye fixed on him, and to hear a bellow of – 'Damme, it's my horse. It's my little Moonbeam!' He saw a whip raised, and felt it swish a foot from his leg. There was nothing for it but to keep his distance from the wrathful gentleman, and so gallantly did Moonbeam respond that he was presently at the huntsman's elbow.

Had he known it, the grey was the faster of the two, though lacking Moonbeam's sweet paces and lionlike heart. His enemy was up on him at once, and it looked as if there was nothing before him but to override hounds. But the discipline of the sport was stronger than a just wrath. The Squire took a pull on the grey and drew back. He was biding his time.

Alastair seized the first chance, which came when hounds were engulfed in a wide wood of oaks on the edge of a heath. Taking advantage of a piece of thick cover, he caught Moonbeam by the head and swung him down a side glade. Unfortunately he was observed. An oath from Squire Thicknesse warned him that that sportsman had forgone the pleasure of being in at the death for the satisfaction of doing justice on a horse-thief.

Now there was no hunt etiquette to be respected. The grey's hooves spurned the rotten woodland turf, and pursuer and pursued crashed into a jungle of dry bulrushes and sallows. Alastair was saved by the superior agility of his horse, which could swerve and pivot where the heavier grey stumbled. He gained a yard or two, then a little more by a scramble through a gap, and a crazy scurry down a rabbit track. . . . He saw that his only chance was to slip off, for Moonbeam had the madness of the chase on him, and if left riderless would rejoin the hounds. So when he had gained some forty yards and was for the moment out of the Squire's sight, he took his toes from the stirrups and flung himself into a bed of bracken. He rolled over and over into a dell, and when he came to a halt and could look up he saw the grey's stern disappearing round the corner, and heard far off the swish and crash of Moonbeam's flight.

Not a second was to be lost, for the Squire would soon see that the rider had gone and turn back in the search for him. Alastair forced his stiff legs to a run, and turned in the direction which he thought the opposite of that taken by hounds. Up a small path he ran, among a scrub of hazels and down into a desert of red bracken and sparse oak trees. The noises in the wood grew fainter, and soon his steps were the loudest sound, his steps and the heavy flight of an occasional scared pigeon. He ran till he had put at least a mile of rough land behind him, and had crossed several tracks, which would serve to mislead the pursuit. Lacking a bloodhound, it would not be easy to follow his trail. Then in a broader glade he came upon a thatched hovel, such as foresters and charcoal-burners use when they have business abroad in the night hours.

Alastair crept up to it cautiously, and through a crack surveyed the interior. His face hardened and an odd light came into his eye. He strode to the door and pushed the crazy thing open.

Within, breakfasting on a hunch of bread and cheese, sat the man Edom, Mr Kyd's servant.

EIGHT

Broom at the Cross-Roads

The face before him had the tightened look of a sudden surprise: then it relaxed into recognition; but it showed no fear, though the young man's visage was grim enough.

'You are Mr Kyd's servant?'

'Your honour has it. I'm Edom Lowrie at your honour's service.'

'Your master started yesterday for Wiltshire. Why are you not with him?'

The man looked puzzled.

'Ye're mista'en, sir. My master came here yestereen. I left him at skreigh o' day this morning.'

It was Alastair's turn to stare. Kyd had lied to him, thinking it necessary to deceive him about his road – scurvy conduct, surely, between servants of the same cause. Or perhaps this fellow Edom was lying. He looked at him and saw no hint of double-dealing in the plain ugly face. His sandy eyebrows were indistinguishable from his freckled forehead and gave him an air of bald innocence, his pale eyes were candid and good-humoured, the eaves of his great teeth were comedy itself. The more Alastair gazed the harder he found it to believe that this rustic zany had betrayed him. But what on earth was Kyd about?

'Where is your master now?' he asked.

The other took off his hat and scratched his head. 'I wadna like to say, sir. You see he telled me little, forbye sayin' that he wadna see me again for the best pairt o' a month. I jalouse mysel' that he's gone south, but he micht be for Wales.'

'Were you in Flambury last night?'

The man looked puzzled till Alastair explained. 'Na, na, I was in nae village. I had a cauld damp bed in a bit public. My maister wasna there, but he appeared afore I was out o' the blankets, a' ticht and trim for the road, and gied me my marching-orders. I was to traivel the woods on foot, and no get mysel' a horse till I won to a place they ca' Camley.'

'Are you for Scotland?'

'Nae sic fortune. I'm for the Derbyshire muirs wi' letters.' He hesitated. 'Your honour's no gaun that road yoursel'? I wad be blithe o' company.'

The light in the hut was too dim to see clearly, for there was no window, the door was narrow and the day was sullen.

'Step outside, Mr Lowrie, till I cast an eye over you,' said Alastair.

The man pocketed the remains of his bread and cheese and shambled into the open. He wore a long horseman's coat and boots, a plain hat without cocks, and carried a stout hazel riding-switch. He looked less like a lackey than some small yeoman of the Borders, habited for a journey to Carlisle or St Boswell's Fair.

'You know who I am,' said Alastair. 'You are aware that like your master I am in a certain service, and that between him and me there are no secrets.'

'Aye, sir. I ken that ye're Captain Maclean, and a gude Scot, though ower far north o' Forth for my ain taste, if your honour will forgie me.'

'You carry papers? I must know more of your journey. What is your goal?'

'A bit the name o' Brightwell near a hill they ca' the Peak.'

Alastair had not been prepared for this, had had no glimmering of a suspicion of it, and the news decided him.

'It is of the utmost importance that I see your papers. Your master, if he were here now, would consent.'

The man's face flushed. 'I kenna how that can be. Your honour wadna have me false to my trust.'

'You will not be false. You travel on a matter of the Prince's interest, as I do, and I must know your errand fully in order to shape my own course. Your master and I have equal rank in His Highness's councils.'

The other shook his head, as if perplexed. 'Nae doot – nae doot. But, ye see, sir, I've my orders, and I maun abide by them. "Pit thae letters," my maister says, "intil the hand of him ye ken o' and let naebody else get a glisk o' them."'

'Then it is my duty to take them by force,' said Alastair, showing the hilt of his sword and the butt of a pistol under his coat.

Edom's face cleared.

'That is a wiser-like way o' speakin'. If ye compel me I maun e'en submit, for ye're a gentleman wi' a sword and I'm a landward body wi' nocht but a hazel wand. It's no that I mistrust your honour, but we maun a' preserve the decencies.'

He unbuttoned his coat, foraged in the recesses of his person, and from some innermost receptacle extracted a packet tied with a dozen folds of cobbler's twine. There was no seal to break, and Alastair slit the knots with his sword. Within was a bunch of papers of the same type as those he had received from Brother Gilly, and burned in the fire of the Dog and Gun. These he put in his pocket for further study. 'I must read them carefully, for they contain that which must go straight to the Prince's ear,' he told the perplexed messenger.

But there was a further missive, which seemed to be a short personal note from Mr Kyd to the recipient of the papers.

'*Dear Achilles,*' it ran. '*Affairs march smoothly and the tide SETS well to bring you to Troy town, where presently I design to crack a bottle and exchange tales. The Lady Briseis purposes to join you and will not be dissuaded by her kinsman. A friendly word: mix caution with your ardour her-ward, for she has got a political enthusiasm and is devilish strong-headed. The news of the Marches and the West will travel to you with all expedition, but I must linger behind to encourage my correspondents. Menelaus greets you – a Menelaus that never owned a Helen.*'

The full sense of the document did not at first reach Alastair's brain. But he caught the word '*Achilles*', and remembered a girl's whispered confidence the night before. A second phrase arrested him – 'Briseis' – he remembered enough of Father Dominic's teaching to identify the reference. This Norreys, this husband of the russet lady, was far deeper in the secrets of the Cause than he had dreamed, if he were thus made the channel of vital intelligence. He was bidden act cautiously towards his new wife, and Mr Kyd, who had heard Johnson's accusations at Cornbury and said nothing, had all the time been in league with him. A sudden sense of a vast insecurity overcame the young man. The ground he trod on seemed shifting sand, and nowhere was there a firm and abiding landmark. And the girl too was walking in dark ways, and when she thought that she tripped over marble and cedar was in truth skimming the crust of quicksands. He grew hot with anger.

'Do you know the man to whom these are addressed?' he asked with stern brows.

Edom grinned.

'I ken how to find him. I'm to speir in certain quarters for ane Achilles, and I mind eneuch o' what the Lauder dominie lickit intil me to ken that Achilles was a braw sodger.'

'You do not know his name? You never saw him?'

The man shook his head. 'I wad like the letters back, sir,' he volunteered warily, for he was intimidated by Alastair's dark forehead.

The latter handed back the *Achilles* letter, and began to read more carefully the other papers. Suddenly he raised his head and listened. The forest hitherto had been still with the strange dead quiet of a November noon. But now the noise of hounds was heard again, not half a mile off, as if they were hunting a line in the brushwood. He awoke with a start to the fact of his danger. What better sport for the patrons of the Flambury Hunt than to ride down a Jacobite horse-thief? A vague fury possessed him against that foolish squire with the cherubic face and the vacant blue eye.

'The hunt is cried after me,' he told Edom, 'and I take it you too have no desire to advertise your whereabouts. For God's sake let's get out of this place. Where does this road lead?'

Edom's answer was drowned in a hubbub of hounds which seemed to be approaching down the ride from the east. Alastair led the way from the hut up a steepish hill, sparsely wooded with scrub oak, in the hope of finding a view-point. Unfortunately at the top the thicket was densest, so the young man swung himself into a tree and as quickly as riding-boots would permit sought a coign of vantage in its upper branches. There he had the prospect he wanted – a great circle of rolling country, most of it woodland, but patched with large heaths where gorse-fires were smouldering. The piece of forest in which he sat stretched far to east and west, but to the north was replaced in less than a mile by pasture and small enclosures. As he looked he saw various things to disquiet him. The grassy road they had left was visible for half a mile, and down it came horsemen, while at the other end there seemed to be a picket placed. Worse still, to the north, which was the way of escape he had thought of, there were mounted men at intervals along the fringe of the trees. The hounds could be heard drawing near in the scrub east of the hut, and men's voices accompanied them. He remembered that they would find the hut door open, see the crumbs of Edom's bread and cheese, and no doubt discover the track which led up the hill.

He scrambled to the ground, his heart filled with forebodings and a deep disgust. He, who should long ago have been in the battle-field among the leaders, was befogged in this remote countryside, pursued by yokels, clogged and hampered at every step, and yet with the most desperate urgency of haste to goad him forward. His pride was outraged by such squalid ill-fortune. He must get his head from the net which was entangling and choking him. But for the moment there was nothing for it but to cower like a hare, and somewhere in the deep scrub find a hiding-place. Happily a fox-hound was not a bloodhound.

Down the other side of the hill they went, Edom panting heavily and slipping every second yard. At the bottom they came on another road running parallel with the first, and were about to cross it when a sound from in front gave them pause. There were men there, keepers perhaps, beating the under-growth and whistling. The two turned to the west and ran down the track, keeping as far as possible in the shadow of the adjacent coppice. A fine rain was beginning, which brought with it a mist that lowered the range of vision to a few hundred yards. In that lay Alastair's one hope. Let the weather thicken and he would undertake to elude all the foresters and fox-hunters in England. He cursed the unfamiliar land, which had no hills where fleetness of foot availed or crags where a bold man could laugh at pursuit.

The place seemed terribly full of folk, as if whole parishes had emptied their population to beat the covers. Now he realised that the mist had its drawbacks as well as its merits, for he might stumble suddenly into a posse of searchers, and, though he himself might escape, the clumsier Edom would be taken. He bade the latter choose a line of his own and save himself, as he was not the object of the hunt, and owed his chief danger to his company, but this the man steadfastly refused to do. He ploughed stubbornly along in Alastair's wake, wheezing like a bellows.

Then the noises seemed to die down, and the two continued in a dripping quiet. It was idle to think of leaving the forest, and the best that could be done was to find a hiding-place when they were certain that the pursuit was outdistanced. But this meant delay, and these slow rustics might keep up their watch for a week. . . .

Presently they came to a cross-roads, where a broader path cut their ride, and in the centre stood an old rotting stake, where long ago some outlaw may have swung. They halted, for Edom had his breath to get. He flung himself on the ground, and at that moment Alastair caught sight of something tied to the post. Going nearer, he saw that it was a bunch of broom.

Had his wits not been sharpened by danger and disgust it might have had no meaning for him. But, as it was, Midwinter's parting words on Otmoor came back to him, and with it the catch which he had almost forgotten. As Edom lay panting, he shaped his lips to whistle the air. In the quiet the tune rang out clear and shrill, and as he finished there was silence again. Then the bushes parted, and a man came out.

He was a charcoal-burner, with a face like an Ethiopian, and red sore eyes curiously ringed about with clean white skin.

'Ye have the tune, master,' he said. 'What be your commands for the Spoonbills? Folks be huntin' these woods, and maybe it's you as they're seekin'.'

'The place is surrounded,' said Alastair, 'and they are beating the covers between the rides. Get us out, or show us how we can be hid.'

The man did not hesitate. 'Escape's better'n hidin',' he said. 'Follow me, sirs, and I'll do my best for ye.'

He led them at a great pace some two hundred yards into a tiny dell. There a glaze hung in the dull air from a charcoal-oven, which glowed under a mound of sods. Neat piles of oak and birch billets stood around, and the shafts of a cart stuck up out of the long bracken. On one side an outcrop of rock made a fine wind-shelter, and, pushing aside the creepers which veiled it, the charcoal-burner revealed a small cave.

'Off with your clothes, sirs,' he said. 'They'll be safe enough in that hidy-hole till I gets a chance to return 'em. Them rags is my mates', and in this pickle are better'n fine silks.'

Two filthy old smocks were unearthed, and two pairs of wooden-soled clogs which replaced their boots. The change was effected swiftly under the constant urging of the charcoal-burner, who kept his ears cocked and his head extended like a dog. In five minutes Alastair was outwardly a figure differing only in complexion from the master of the dingle. Then the latter set to work, and with a handful of hot charcoal smeared hands and faces, rubbing the dirt into the eye-sockets so that the eyes smarted and watered. Hats and cravats were left in the cave, and Alastair's trim hair was roughly clubbed, and dusted with soot for powder. There was no looking-glass to show him the result, but the charcoal-burner seemed satisfied. The transformation was simpler for Edom, who soon to Alastair's eyes looked as if he had done nothing all his days but tend a smoky furnace.

'I'll do the talking if we happen to meet inquiring folk,' the charcoal-burner admonished them. 'Look sullen and keep your eyes on the ground, and spit – above all, spit. Ours is a dry trade.'

He led them back to the main ride, and then boldly along the road which pointed north. The forest had woke up, and there were sounds of life on every side. The hounds had come out of covert and were being coaxed in again by a vociferous huntsman. Echoes of 'Sweetlip', 'Rover', 'True-man', mingled with sundry oaths, came gustily down the wind. Someone far off blew a horn incessantly, and in a near thicket there was a clamour of voices like those of beaters after roebuck. The three men tramped stolidly along, the two novices imitating as best they could the angular gait, as of one who rarely stretched his legs, and the blindish carriage of the charcoal-burner.

A knot of riders swept down on them. Alastair ventured to lift his eyes for one second, and saw the scarlet and plum colour of Squire Thicknesse and noted the grey's hocks. The legs finicking and waltzing near them he thought belonged to Moonbeam, and was glad that the horse had been duly caught and restored. The Squire asked a question of the charcoal-burner and was answered in a dialect of gutturals. Off surged the riders, and presently the three were at the edge of the trees where a forester's cottage smoked in the rain. Beyond, wrapped in a white mist, stretched ploughland and pasture.

Alastair saw that his tree-top survey had been right. This edge of the wood was all picketed, and as the three emerged a keeper in buckskin breeches came towards them, and a man on horseback turned at his cry and cantered back.

The keeper did not waste time on them, once he had a near view.

'Yah!' he said, 'it's them salvages o' coalies. They ain't got eyes to obsarve nothin', pore souls! 'Ere, Billy,' he cried, 'seen any strange gen'elmen a-wanderin' the woods this morning?'

The charcoal-burner stopped, and the two others formed up sullenly behind him.

'There wor a fallow-buck a routin' round my foorness,' he grumbled in a voice as thick as clay. 'Happen it come to some 'urt, don't blame me, gossip. Likewise there's a badger as is makin' an earth where my birch-faggots should lie. That's all the strange gen'elmen I seen this marnin', barrin' a pack o' red-coats a-gallopin' 'orses and blowin' 'orns.'

The rider had now arrived and was looking curiously at the three. The keeper in corduroy breeches turned laughing to him. 'Them coalies is pure salvages, Mr Gervase, sir. Brocks and bucks, indeed, when I'm inquirin' for gen'elmen. Gawd A'mighty made their 'eads as weak as their eyes.'

What answer the rider gave is not known, for the charcoal-burners had already moved forward. They crossed a piece of plough and reached a shallow vale seamed by a narrow stagnant brook. Here they were in shelter, and to Alastair's surprise their leader began to run. He took them at a good pace up the water till it was crossed by a high-road, then along a by-path, past a farm-steading, to a strip of woodland, which presently opened out into a wide health. Here in deference to Edom's heaving chest he slackened pace. The rain was changing from a drizzle to a heavy downpour and the faces of the two amateurs were becoming a ghastly piebald with the lashing of the weather.

The charcoal-burner turned suddenly to Alastair and spoke in a voice which had no trace of dialect.

'You have escaped one danger, sir. I do not know who you may be or what your desires are, but I am bound to serve you as far as it may lie in my power. Do you wish me to take you to my master?'

'I could answer that better, if I knew who he was.'

'We do not speak his name at large, but in a month's time the festival of his name-day will return.'

Alastair nodded. The thought of Midwinter came suddenly to him with an immense comfort. He, if anyone could, would help him out of this miasmic jungle in which his feet were entangled and set him again upon the highway. His head was still confused with the puzzle of Kyd's behaviour. – Edom's errand, the exact part played by Sir John Norreys, above all the presence of a subtle treason. He remembered the deep eyes and the wise brow of the fiddler of Otmoor, and had he not that very day seen a proof of his power?

The heath billowed and sank into ridges and troughs, waterless and furze-clad, and in one of the latter they came suddenly upon a house. It was a small place, built with its back to a steep ridge all overgrown with blackberries and heather – two stories high, and flanked by low thatched outbuildings, and a pretence at a walled garden. On the turf before the door, beside an ancient well, a sign on a pole proclaimed it the inn of the Merry Woman, but suns and frosts had long since obliterated all trace of the rejoicing lady, though below it and more freshly painted was something which might have resembled a human eye.

The three men lounged into the kitchen, which was an appanage to the main building, and called for ale. It was brought by a little old woman in a mutch, who to Alastair's surprise curtseyed to the grimy figure of the charcoal-burner.

'He's alone, sir,' she said, 'and your own room's waiting if you're ready for it.'

'Will you go up to him?' the charcoal-burner asked, and Alastair followed the old woman. She led the way up a narrow staircase with a neat sheep-skin rug on each tread, to a tiny corridor from which two rooms opened. The one on the left they entered and found an empty bedroom, cleanly and plainly furnished. A door in the wall at the other end, concealed by a hanging cupboard, gave access to a pitch-dark passage. The woman took Alastair's hand and led him a yard or two till she found a door-handle. It opened and showed a large chamber with daylight coming through windows apparently half cloaked with creepers. Alastair realised that the room had been hollowed out of the steep behind the house, and that the windows opened in the briars and heath of the face.

A fire was burning and a man sat beside it reading in a book. He was the fiddler of Otmoor, and in the same garb, save that he had discarded his coat and wore instead a long *robe de chambre*. A keen eye scanned the visitor, and then followed a smile and an outstretched hand.

'Welcome, Alastair Maclean,' he said. 'I heard of you in these parts and hoped for a meeting.'

'From whom?'

'One whom you call the Spainneach. He left me this morning to go into Derbyshire.'

The name stirred a question.

'Had he news?' Alastair asked. 'When I last saw you you prophesied failure. Are you still of that mind?'

'I do not prophesy, but this I say – that since I saw you your chances and your perils have grown alike. Your Cause is on the razor-edge and you yourself may have the deciding.'

NINE

Old England

'Yesterday morning your Prince was encamped outside Carlisle. By now the place may have fallen.'

'Who told you?' Alastair asked.

'I have my own messengers who journey in Old England,' said Midwinter. 'Consider, Captain Maclean. As a bird flies, the place is not a hundred and fifty miles distant, and no mile is without its people. A word cried to a traveller is taken up by another and another till the man who rubs down a horse at night in a Chester inn-yard will have news of what befell at dawn on the Scotch Border. My way is quicker than post-horses. . . . But the name of inn reminds me. You have the look of a fasting man.'

Food was brought, and the November brume having fallen thick in the hollow, the windows were curtained, a lamp lit, and fresh fuel laid on the fire. Alastair kicked the boots from his weary legs, and as soon as his hunger was stayed fell to questioning his host; for he felt that till he could point a finger to the spy who had dogged him he had failed in his duty to the Cause. He poured out his tale without reserve.

Midwinter bent his brows and stared into the fire.

'You are satisfied that this servant Edom is honest?' he asked.

'I have observed him for half a day and the man is as much in the dark as myself. If he is a rogue he is a master in dissimulation. But I do not think so.'

'*Imprimis*, you are insulted in the Flambury inn by those who would fasten a quarrel on you. *Item*, you are arrested and carried before this man Thicknesse, and one dressed like a mummer presses the accusation. *Item*, in a warrant you and your purposes are described with ominous accuracy. You are likewise this very day tricked by your gypsy guide, but that concerns rather my lady Norreys. These misfortunes came upon you after you had supped with Kyd, and therefore you suspected his servant, for these two alone in this countryside knew who you were. A fairly argued case, I concede, and to buttress it Kyd appears to have been near Flambury last night, when he professed to be on the road for Wiltshire. But you have ceased to suspect the servant. What of the master?'

Alastair started. 'No, no. That is madness. The man is in the very heart of the Prince's counsels. He is honest, I swear – he is too deep committed.'

Midwinter nodded. 'If he were false, it would indeed go ill with you; for on him, I take it, depends the rising of Wales and the Marches. He holds your Prince in the hollow of his hand. And if all tales be true the omens there are happy.'

Alastair told of the message from Brother Gilly, and, suddenly remembering Edom's papers, drew them from his pocket, and read them again by the firelight. Here at last was news from Badminton and from Monmouth and Hereford: and at the foot, in the cypher which was that most commonly used among the Jacobites, was a further note dealing with Sir Watkin Wynn. The writer had concerted with him a plan, by which the Welsh levies should march straight through Gloucester and Oxfordshire to cut in between Cumberland and the capital. To Alastair, the thing was proved authentic beyond doubt, for it bore the pass-word which had been agreed between himself and Sir Watkin a week before at Wynnstay.

He fell into a muse from which he was roused by Midwinter's voice.

'Kyd receives messages and forwards them northward, while he himself remains in the South. By what channel?'

'It would appear by Sir John Norreys, who is now, or soon will be, at Brightwell under the Peak.'

As he spoke the words his suspicions took a new course. Johnson had thought the man a time-server, though he had yesterday recanted that view. Sir Christopher Lacy at Cornbury had been positive that he was a rogue. The only evidence to the contrary was that his wife believed in him, and that he had declared his colours by forsaking his bride for the Prince's camp. But he had not gone to the army, and it would seem that he had no immediate intention of going there, for according to Edom he would be at Brightwell during the month; and as for his wife's testimony, she was only a romantic child. Yet this man was the repository of Kyd's secret information, the use of which meant for the Prince a kingdom or a beggar's exile. If Kyd were mistaken in him, then the Cause was sold in very truth. But how came Kyd to be linked with him? How came a young Oxfordshire baronet, of no great family, and no record of service, to be *Achilles* of the innermost circle?

He told his companion of his doubts, unravelling each coil carefully, while the other marked his points with jerks of his pipe-bowl. When he had finished Midwinter kept silent for a little. Then 'You swear by Kyd's fidelity?' he asked.

'God in Heaven, but I must,' cried Alastair. 'If he is false, I may return overseas to-morrow.'

'It is well to test all links in a chain,' was the dry answer. 'But for the sake of argument we will assume him honest. Sir John Norreys is the next link to be tried. If he is rotten, then the Prince had better bide north of Ribble, for the Western auxiliaries will never move. But even if the whole hive be false, there is still hope if you act at once. This is my counsel to you, Captain Maclean. Write straightway to the Army – choose the man about the Prince who loves you most – and tell him of the great things to be hoped for from the West. Name no names, but promise before a certain date to arrive with full proof, and bid them hasten south without delay. An invasion needs heartening, and if the worst should be true no word from Kyd is likely to reach the Prince. Hearten him, therefore, so that he marches to meet you. That is the first thing. The second is that you go yourself into Derbyshire to see this Sir John Norreys. If he be true man you will find a friend; if not you may be in time to undo his treason.'

The advice was what had dimly been shaping itself in
Alastair's own mind. His ardour to be back with the Army,
which for days had been a fever in his bones, had now changed
to an equal ardour to solve the riddle which oppressed him.
Midwinter was right; the Cause was on a razor edge and with
him might lie the deciding. . . . There was black treachery
somewhere, and far more vital for the Prince than any victory
in Scotland was the keeping the road open for West England to
join him. Shadows of many reasons flitted across his mind and
gave strength to his resolve. He would see this man Norreys
who had won so adorable a lady. He would see the lady again,
and at the thought something rose in his heart which surprised
him, for it was almost joy.

'Have you paper and ink?' he asked, and from a cupboard
Midwinter produced them and set them before him.

He wrote to Lochiel, who was his kinsman, for though he
knew Lord George Murray there was a certain jealousy between
them. Very roughly he gave the figures which he had gleaned
from Brother Gilly's letter and that taken from Edom. He
begged him to move the Prince to march without hesitation
for the capital, and promised to reach his camp with full
information before the month ended. 'And the camp will, I
trust, be by that time no further from St James's than —' He
asked Midwinter for a suitable place, and was told 'Derby.' He
subscribed himself with the affection of a kinsman and old
playmate of Morvern and Lochaber.

'I will see that it reaches its destination,' said Midwinter.
'And now for the second task. The man Edom is not suspect
and can travel by the high road. I will send him with one who
will direct him to my lady Norreys' party, which this day, as
you tell me, sets out for Derbyshire. For yourself I counsel a
discreeter part. Mark you, sir, you are sought by sundry
gentlemen in Flambury as a Jacobite, and by Squire Thicknesse and his Hunt as a horse-thief. In this land suspicion is
slow to waken, but in the end it runs fast and dies hard.
Rumour of your figure, face, clothes, manner and bloodthirsty

spirit will have already flown fifty miles. If you would be safe you must sink into Old England.'

'I will sink into Acheron if it will better my purpose.'

Midwinter regarded him critically. 'Your modish clothes are in Kit's locker, and will duly be sent after you. Now you are the born charcoal-burner, save that your eyes are too clear and your finger nails unscorched. The disguise has served your purpose to-day, but it is too kenspeckle except in great woodlands. Mother Jonnet will find you a better. For the rest I will guide you, for I have the key.'

'Where is this magic country?'

'All around you – behind the brake, across the hedgerow, under the branches. Some can stretch a hand and touch it – to others it is a million miles away.'

'As a child I knew it,' said Alastair, laughing. 'I called it Fairyland.'

Midwinter nodded. 'Children are free of it, but their elders must earn admission. It is a safe land – at any rate it is secure from common perils.'

'But it has its own dangers?'

'It makes a man look into his heart, and he may find that in it which destroys him. Also it is ambition's mortal foe. But if you walk in it you will come to Brightwell without obstruction, for the King's writ does not run in the greenwood.'

'Whose is the law, then?' Alastair asked.

For answer Midwinter went to the window and flung it open. 'My fiddle cannot speak except with free air about it,' he said. 'If any drunken rustic is on the heath he will think the pixies are abroad.'

He picked up the violin which had been lying on the table behind him, and drew forth a slow broken music, which presently changed into a rhythmical air. At first it was like the twanging of fine wires in a wind, mingled with an echo of organ music heard over a valley full of tree-tops. It was tame and homely, yet with a childish inconsequence in it. Then it grew wilder, and though the organ notes remained it was an organ

that had never sounded within church walls. The tune went with
a steady rhythm, the rhythm of growing things in spring, of
seasonal changes; but always ran the under-current of a leaping
bacchanal madness, of long wild dances in bare places. The
fiddle ceased on a soft note, and the fiddler fell to singing in a
voice so low that the words and air only just rose above the pitch
of silence. 'Diana and her darling crew,' he sang.

> 'Diana and her darling crew
>   Will pluck your fingers fine,
> And lead you forth right pleasantly
>   To drink the honey wine, –
> To drink the honey wine, my dear,
>   And sup celestial air,
> And dance as the young angels dance,
>   Ah, God, that I were there!'

'Hers is the law,' he said. 'Diana, or as some say, Proserpina.
Old folk call her the Queen of Elfhame. But over you and me, as
baptized souls, she has no spell but persuasion. You can hear
her weeping at midnight because her power is gone.'

Then his mood changed. He laid down the fiddle and shouted
on Mother Jonnet to bring supper. Edom, too, was sent for, and
during the meal was closely catechised. He bore it well, professing no undue honesty beyond a good servant's, but stiff on his
few modest scruples. When he heard Midwinter's plans for
him, he welcomed them, and begged that in the choice of a
horse his precarious balance and round thighs might be chari-
tably considered. Alastair returned him the letter and watched
him fold it up with the others and shove it inside his waistcoat.
A prolonged study of that mild, concerned, faintly humorous
face convinced him that Edom Lowrie was neither fox nor
goose. He retired to bed to dream of Mr Kyd's jolly countenance,
which had mysteriously acquired a very sharp nose.

Edom went off in the early morning in company with the man
called Kit and mounted on an ambling forest cob whose paces

he whole-heartedly approved. Alastair washed himself like a Brahmin in a tub of hot water in the back-kitchen, and dressed himself in the garments provided by Mother Jonnet – frieze and leather and coarse woollen stockings and square-toed country shoes. The haze of yesterday had gone, and the sky was a frosty blue, with a sharp wind out of the north-east. He breakfasted with Midwinter off cold beef and beer and a dish of grilled ham, and then stood before the door breathing deep of the fresh chilly morning. The change of garb or the prospect before him had rid him of all the languor of the past week. He felt extraordinarily lithe and supple of limb, as in the old days when he had driven deer on the hills before the autumn dawn. Had he but had the free swing of a kilt at his thighs and the screes of Ben Aripol before him he would have recaptured his boyhood.

Midwinter looked at him with approval.

'You are clad as a man should be for Old England, and you have the legs for the road we travel. We do not ride, for we go where no horse can go. Put not your trust in horses, saith the Scriptures, which I take to mean that a man in the last resort should depend on his own shanks. Boot and spur must stick to the paths, and the paths are but a tiny bit of England. How sits the wind? North by east? There is snow coming, but not in the next thirty hours, and if it comes, it will not stay us. *En avant, mon capitaine.*'

At a pace which was marvellous for one of his figure, Midwinter led the way over the heath, and then plunged into a tangled wood of oaks. He walked like a mountaineer, swinging from the hips, the body a little bent forward, and his long even strides devoured the ground. Even so, Alastair reminded himself, had the hunters at Glentarnit breasted the hill, while his boyish steps had toiled in their rear. Sometimes on level ground he would break into a run, as if his body's vigour needed an occasional burst of speed to chasten it. The young man exulted in the crisp air and the swift motion. The stiffness of body and mind which had beset him ever since he left Scotland vanished under this cordial, he lost his doubts and misgivings, and felt again that lifting ardour of the heart which is the glory of youth. His feet were tireless, his limbs were as elastic as a sword-blade, his breath as deep as a greyhound's. Two days before, jogging in miry lanes, he had seemed caught and stifled in a net; now he was on a hill-top, and free as the wind that plucked at his hair.

It is probable that Midwinter had for one of his purposes the creation of this happy mood, for he kept up the pace till after midday, when they came to a high deer-fence, beyond which stretched a ferny park. Here they slackened speed, their faces glowing like coals, and, skirting the park, reached a thatched hut which smoked in a dell. A woman stood at the door, who at the sight of the two would have retired inside, had not Midwinter whistled sharply on his fingers. She blinked and shaded her eyes with her hand against the frosty sunshine; then to Alastair's amazement she curtseyed deep.

Midwinter did not halt, but asked if Jeremy were at the stone pit.

'He be, Master,' was her answer. 'Will ye stop to break bread?'

'Nay, Jeremy shall feed us,' he cried, and led the way up the dingle where a brook flowed in reedy pools. Presently there was a sound of axe-blows, and, rounding a corner, they came on a man cutting poles from a thicket of saplings. Again Midwinter whistled, and the woodcutter dropped his tool and turned with a grinning face, pulling at his forelock Midwinter sat down on a tree-trunk.

'Jeremy, lad, you behold two hungry men waiting to sample the art of the best cook in the Borton Hundreds. Have you the wherewithal, or must we go back to your wife?'

'I has, I surely has,' was the answer. 'Be pleased to be seated, kind sirs, and Jerry Tusser will have your meat ready before ye have rightly eased your legs. This way, Master, this way.'

He led them to a pit where a fire burned between three stones and a kettle bubbled. Plates of coarse earthenware were brought from some hiding-place, and in five minutes Alastair was supping with an iron spoon as savoury a stew as he had ever eaten. The fruits of Jeremy's snares were in it, and the fruits of

Jeremy's old fowling piece, and it was flavoured with herbs whose merits the world has forgotten. The hot meal quickened his vigour, and he was on his feet before Midwinter had done, like a dog eager to be on the road again.

He heard the man speak low to Midwinter. 'Dook o' Kingston's horse,' he heard and a hand was jerked northward.

In the afternoon the way lay across more open country, which Midwinter seemed to know like the palm of his hand, for he made points for some ridge or tree-top, and yet was never held up by brook or fence or dwelling. The air had grown sharper, clouds were banking in the east, and a wind was moaning in the tops of the high trees. Alastair seemed to have been restored to the clean world of his youth, after long absence among courts and cities. He noted the woodcock fitting between the bracken and the leafless boughs, and the mallards silently flighting from mere to stubble. A wedge of geese moving south made him turn his face skyward, and a little later he heard a wild whistle, and saw far up in the heavens a line of swans. His bodily strength was great as ever, but he had ceased to exult in it, and was ready to observe and meditate.

A highway cut the forest, and the two behind a bush of box watched a company of riders jingle down it. They were rustic fellows, poor horsemen most of them, mounted on every variety of beast, and at the head rode a smarter youth, with brand-new holsters out of which peeped the butts of ancient pistols.

'Recruits for the Duke of Kingston,' Midwinter whispered. 'They rendezvous at Nottingham, I hear. Think you they will make a good match of it with your Highland claymores?'

Night fell when they were still in the open, and Midwinter, after halting for a second to take his bearings, led the way to a wood which seemed to flow in and out of a shallow vale.

'The night will be cold, Captain Maclean, and a wise man takes comfort when he can find it. I could find you twenty lodgings, but we will take the warmest.'

The woodland path ended in a road which seemed to be the avenue to a great house. It was soon very dark, and Alastair heard the rustling of animals which revived some ancestral knowledge, for he could distinguish the different noises which were rabbit, badger, stoat and deer. Down the avenue Midwinter led unconcernedly, and then turned off to a group of buildings which might have been stables. He bade Alastair wait while he went forward, and after some delay returned with a man who carried a lantern. The fellow, seen in the dim light, was from his dress an upper servant, and his bearing was in the extreme respectful. He bowed to Alastair, and led them through a gate into a garden, where their feet rang on flagged stones and rustled against box borders. A mass loomed up on the left which proved to be a great mansion.

The servant admitted them by a side door, and led them to a room, where he lit a dozen candles from his lantern, and revealed a panelled octagonal chamber hung with full-length portraits of forbidding gentlemen. There he left them, and when he returned it was with an elderly butler in undress, who bowed with the same deferent decorum.

'His lordship has gone since yesterday into Yorkshire, sir,' he informed Midwinter. 'I will have the usual rooms made ready for you at once, and you can sup in my lord's cabinet which is adjacent.'

The two travellers soon found themselves warming their feet before a bright fire, while some thousands of volumes in calf and vellum looked down on them from the walls. They supped royally, but Alastair was too drowsy for talk, and his body had scarcely touched the sheets of his bed before he was asleep. He was woke before dawn, shaved and dressed by the butler, and given breakfast – with China tea in place of beer – in the same cabinet. It was still dark when the first servant of the night before conducted them out of the house by the same side door, led them across the shadowy park, and through a gate in the wall ushered them out to a dusky common, where trees in the creeping light stood up like gibbets. Midwinter led off at a trot, and at a trot they crossed the common and put more than one little valley behind them, so that when day dawned fully there was no sign in all the landscape of their night's lodging.

'Whose was the house?' Alastair asked, and was told – 'We name no names in Old England.'

The second day was to Alastair like the first for joy in the movement of travel, but the weather had grown bitterly cold and unfallen snow was heavy in the leaden sky. The distances were still clear, and though all the morning the road seemed to lie in hollows and dales, yet he had glimpses in the north of high blue ridges. Other signs told him that he was nearing the hills. The streams ceased to be links of sluggish pools, and chattered in rapids. He saw a water ouzel with its white cravat flash from the cover of a stone bridge. A flock of plovers which circled over one heath proved to be not green but golden. He told this to Midwinter, who nodded and pointed to a speck in the sky.

'There is better proof,' he said.

The bird dropped closer to earth, and showed itself as neither sparrow-hawk nor kestrel, but merlin.

'We are nearing the hills,' he said, 'but Brightwell is far up the long valleys. We will not reach it before to-morrow night.'

Just at the darkening the first snow fell. They were descending a steep boulder-strewn ridge to a stream of some size, which swirled in icy grey pools. Above them hung a tree-crowned hill now dim with night, and ere they reached the cover on its crest the flakes were thick about them. Midwinter grunted, and broke into a trot along the ridge. 'Ill weather,' he croaked, 'and a harder bed than yestereen. We'll have to make shift with tinkler's fare. They told me at Harrowden that Job Lee's pack were in the Quarters Wood, and Job has some notion of hospitality. Job it must be, for the snow is fairly come.'

In a broad coombe on the sheltered side of the ridge they came presently on a roaring fire of roots with three tents beside it, so placed that they were free alike from wind and smoke. The snow was falling hard, and beginning to drift, when Midwinter strode into the glow, and the man he called Job Lee – a long man with untied hair brushing his shoulders and a waistcoat of dyed

deerskin – took his right hand between both of his and carried it
to his lips. The newcomers shook themselves like dogs and were
allotted one of the tents, thereby ousting two sleeping children
who staggered to the hospitality of their father's bed. They
supped off roast hare and strong ale, and slept till the wintry sun
had climbed the Derbyshire hills and lit a world all virgin-white.

'The Almighty has sent a skid for our legs,' Midwinter
muttered as he watched the wet logs hiss in Job Lee's morning
fire. "We can travel slow, for the roads will be heavy for my lady.'
So they did not start till the forenoon was well advanced, and as
soon as possible exchanged the clogged and slippery hillside for
a valley road. A wayside inn gave them a scrag of boiled mutton
for dinner, and thereafter they took a short cut over a ridge of
hill to reach the dale at whose head lay the house of Brightwell.
On the summit they halted to reconnoitre, for the highway was
visible there for many miles.

Just below them at the road side, where a tributary way
branched off, stood an inn of some pretensions, whose sign
was deciphered by Alastair's hawk eyes as a couchant stag.
Fresh snow was massing on the horizon, but for the moment
the air was diamond clear. There had been little traffic on the
road since morning and that only foot passengers, with one
horse's tracks coming down the valley. These tracks did not pass
the door, therefore the horseman must be within. There were
no signs of a coach's wheels, so Lady Norreys had not yet
arrived. He lifted his eyes and looked down the stream. There, a
mile or so distant, moved a dark cluster, a coach apparently and
attendant riders.

The snow was on them again and Alastair bowed his head to
the blast. 'They will lie at that inn,' said Midwinter. 'Brightwell is
half a dozen miles on, and the road is dangerous. You will, of
course, join them. I will accompany you to the door and leave
you, for I have business in Sherwood that cannot wait.'

Again Alastair peered through the snow. He saw a man come
out of the inn door as in a great hurry, mount a waiting horse,
and clatter off up the vale – a tall man in a horseman's cloak with

a high collar. Then a little later came the vanguard of the approaching party to bespeak quarters. The two men watched till the coach came abreast the door, and a slender hooded figure stepped from it. Then they began to make their way down the hillside.

TEN

Snowbound at the Sleeping Deer

The whole staff of the Sleeping Deer were around the door when my lady Norreys, making dainty grimaces at the weather, tripped over the yards of snow-powdered cobbles between the step of her coach and the comfortable warmth of the inn. The landlord, ill-favoured and old, was there with his bow, and the landlady, handsome and not yet forty, with her curtsey, and in the gallery which ran round the stone-flagged hall the chamber-maid tribe of Dollys and Peggys clustered to regard the new-comer, for pretty young ladies of quality did not lie every night at a moorland hostelry. But the lady would not tarry to warm her toes by the great fire or to taste the landlady's cordials. A fire had been bespoke in her bedchamber and there she retired to drink tea, which her woman, Mrs Peckover, made with the secret airs of a plotter in the sanctum beside the bar. The two servants from Weston attended the coach in the inn-yard. Mr Edom Lowrie comforted himself with a pot of warm ale, while Mr Samuel Johnson, finding a good fire in the parlour, removed his shoes, and toasted at the ribs his great worsted stocking soles.

Twenty minutes later, when the bustle had subsided, two unassuming travellers appeared below the signboard on which might be seen the fresh-painted gaudy lineaments of a couching fallow deer. The snow was now falling thick, and the wind had risen so that the air was one wild scurry and smother. Midwinter marched straight for the sanctum, and finding it empty but for Mrs Peckover, continued down a narrow passage, smelling of onions, to a little room which he entered unbidden. There sat the landlord with horn spectacles on his nose, making a splice of a trout rod. At the sight of Midwinter he stood to attention, letting all his paraphernalia of twine and wax and tweezers slip to the floor.

'I have brought a friend,' said Midwinter. 'See that you entreat him well and do his biddings as if they were my own. For myself I want a horse, friend Tappet, for snow or no I must sleep in the next shire.'

So as Alastair was changing into this own clothes, which the landlord fetched for him from Edom, he saw from his window in the last faint daylight a square cloakless figure swing from the yard at a canter and turn south with the gale behind it.

The young man had now secured all his belongings, some having come with Edom by grace of the charcoal-burner and the rest from Squire Thicknesse's manor in the lady's charge. As he dressed, his mind was busy on his old problem, and he had sadly to confess that though he had covered much country in recent days he had got little new light. More than once he had tried to set Midwinter's mind to work on it, but, beyond his advice to come to Brightwell, he had shown no interest. Why should he, Alastair reflected, since his creed forswore all common loyalties? But as he had plodded up and down the foothills that day his thoughts had been running chiefly on the lady's husband whom she believed to be now with the Prince, but who most certainly was, or was about to be, in the vicinity of Brightwell. For what purpose? To receive a letter from Edom – a continuing correspondence, sent by Kyd, and charged with the most desperate import to the Prince – a correspondence which should be without delay in the Prince's hands. What did Sir John Norreys in the business? Why did Kyd send the letters by Brightwell, which was not the nearest road to Lancashire?

As he came downstairs he noticed a map hanging on a panel between prints of the new gardens at Chatsworth and the old Marquis of Granby. It was a Dutch thing, drawn by Timothy Hooge a hundred years before, and it showed all the southern part of the Peak country, with fragments of Yorkshire, Notts and Staffordshire adjoining. It was hard to read, for it had been pasted on a wooden board and then highly varnished, but the main roads were strongly marked in a purplish red. He saw the road from the north-west descend the valleys to Derby and so to London, the road from Manchester and Lancashire which the Prince's army would travel. With some trouble he found Brightwell and to his surprise saw the road which passed it marked with equal vigour, as if it vied with the other in importance. A moment's reflection told him the reason. It was the main way from the West. By this road must come the levies from Wales if they were to join the Prince before he reached Derby and the flat country. By this road, too, must all messages come from West England as soon as the army left Manchester. More, the Hanoverian forces were gathering in Nottinghamshire. If they sought to cut in the Prince's rear they would march this way. . . . Brightwell was suddenly revealed as a point of strategy, a ganglion; if treachery were abroad, here it would roost.

He walked into the kitchen, for he had an odd fancy about the horseman whom he had seen ride away a little before Lady Norreys' arrival – an incredible suspicion which he wished to lay. A kitchen wench was busy at the fire, and on a settle a stableman sat drinking beer while a second stamped the snow from his boots at the back door. The appearance of a dapper gentleman in buckled shoes and a well-powdered wig so startled the beer-drinker that he spilled half his mug on the floor. Alastair ordered fresh supplies for all three and drank his on the seat beside the others. Had they been in the yard all afternoon? They had, and had prophesied snow since before breakfast, though Master wouldn't have it so and had sent the waggons to Marlock, where they would be storm-stayed. . . . Yes. A rider had come down the valley and had put up his horse for the better part of an hour. He had been indoors most of the time – couldn't say why. A tall fellow, Bill said. No, not very powerful – lean shoulders – pale face – big nose. Young, too – Tom reckoned not more than twenty-five. . . . Alastair left them with an easier mind, for the worst of his suspicions had been disproved. The back he had seen from the ridge-top posting up the dale had had a disquieting resemblance to Kyd's.

In the parlour he found Mr Johnson stretching his great bulk before a leaping fire and expanding in the warmth of it. The windows had not been shuttered, so the wild night was in visible contrast to the snug hearth. A small girl of five or six years, the landlady's child, had strayed into the room, and, fascinated by a strange gentleman, had remained to talk. She now sat on one of Johnson's bony knees, while he told her a fairy tale in a portentous hollow voice. He told of a dragon, a virtuous dragon in reality a prince, who lived in a Derbyshire cave, and of how the little girl stumbled on the cave, found the dragon, realised his true character, and lived with him for a year and a day, which was the prescribed magical time if he were to be a prince again. He was just describing the tiny bed she had in the rock opposite the dragon's lair, which lair was like a dry mill-pond, and the child was punctuating the narrative with squeals of excitement, when Alastair entered. Thereupon the narrator became self-conscious, the story hastened to a lame conclusion, and the small girl climbed from his knee and with many backward glances sidled out of the room.

'You find me childishly employed, sir,' said Johnson, 'but I dearly love a little miss and I think my company has charms for them. I rejoiced to hear from the Scotch serving-man, who by the way is a worthy fellow, that you were expected to meet us at this place. We are fortunate in winning here thus early, for presently the snow will so conglobulate that the road will be impossible for coach and horses. . . . You have not yet dined, sir? No more have I or the Scotchman, and my lady has retired to her chamber. Our hostess promised that the meal should not be long delayed, and I have bidden the Scotchman to share it, for though his condition is humble he has becoming manners and a just mind. I do not defend the sitting down of servants and masters as a quotidian occurrence, but customs abate their rigidity on a journey.'

To Johnson's delight a maid entered at that moment for the purpose of laying the table. She lit a half-dozen of candles, and closed and barred the heavy shutters so that the only evidence of the storm that remained was the shaking of the window frames, the rumbling in the chimney and the constant fine hissing at the back of the fire where the snow descended. This distant reminder gave an edge to the delicate comfort of the place, and as fragrant odours were wafted from the kitchen through the open door Johnson's spirits rose and his dull eyes brightened like children's at the sight of sweets.

'Of all the good gifts of a beneficent Providence to men,' he cried, 'I think that none excels a well-appointed appointed inn, and I call it a gift, for our fallible mortal nature is not capable unaided of devising so rare a thing. Behold me, Captain Maclean. My wealth is less than a crown and, unless I beg my way, I see not how I can return to Chastlecote. I am dependent upon my dear young lady for the expense of this journey, which she chose to command. Therefore I do not feel justified in ordering what my fancy dictates. Yet so strongly am I delighted by this place that I propose to spend this my last crown on a bowl of bishop to supplement the coming meal, which from its odour should be worthy of it. Like Ariadne in her desertion I find help in Bacchus.'

'Nay, sir, I am the host,' said Alastair. 'Last night I slept by a tinkler's fire and dined off a tinkler's stew. To-night we shall have the best the house affords. The food, I take it, is at the discretion of the landlady, but the wine shall be at yours.'

'Oh brave we!' cried Johnson. 'Let us have in the landlord forthwith for, Captain Maclean, sir, I would be indeed a churl if I scrupled to assent to your good fellowship.'

He rang the bell violently and, when the landlord was fetched, entered upon a learned disquisition on wines, with the well-thumbed cellar-book of the inn as his text. 'Claret we shall not drink, though our host recommends his binns and it is the favourite drink of gentlemen in your country, sir. In winter weather it is too thin, and, even when well warmed, too cold. Nay, at its best it is but a liquor for boys.'

'And for men?' Alastair asked.

'For men port, and for heroes brandy.'

'Then brandy be it.'

'Nay, sir,' he said solemnly. 'Brandy on the unheroic, such as I confess myself to be, produces too soon and certainly the effect of drunkenness. Drunkenness I love not, for I am a man accustomed to self-examination, and I am conscious when I am drunk, and that consciousness is painful. Others know not when they are drunk or sober. I know a man, a very worthy bookseller, who is so habitually and equally drunk that even his intimates cannot perceive that he is more sober at one time than another. Besides, my dear lady may summon us to a hand at cartes or to drink tea with her.'

Eventually he ordered a bottle of port, one of old madeira and one of brown sherry, that he might try all three before deciding by which he should abide. Presently Edom was summoned, and on his heels came dinner. It proved to be an excellent meal to which Mr Johnson applied himself with a serious resolution. There was thick hare soup, with all the woods and pastures in its fragrance, and a big dressed pike, caught that morning in the inn stewpond. This the two Scots did not touch, but Mr Johnson ate of it largely, using his fingers, because, as he said, he was short-sighted and afraid of bones. Then came roast hill mutton, which he highly commended. 'Yesterday,' he declared, 'we also dined upon mutton – mutton ill-fed, ill-killed, ill-kept and ill-dressed. This is as nutty as venison.' But he reserved his highest commendations for a veal pie, made with plums, which he averred was his favourite delicacy. With the cheese and wheaten cakes which followed he sampled the three bottles and decided for the port. Alastair and Edom were by comparison spare eaters, and had watched with admiration the gallant trencher-work of their companion. For liquor they drank a light rum punch of Alastair's compounding, while Mr Johnson consumed, in addition to divers glasses of sherry and Madeira, two bottles of rich dark port, dropping a lump of sugar into each glass and stirring it with the butt of a fork.

And all the while he talked, wisely, shrewdly, truculently, and with a gusto comparable to that which he displayed in the business of eating.

'You slept hard last night?' he asked of Alastair. 'How came you here?'

'On foot. For ten days I have been in an older world with a man who is a kind of king there.' He spoke for a little of Midwinter, but Johnson was unimpressed.

'I think I have heard these boasts before, sir. When a man decries civility and exalts barbarism, it is because he is ill fitted to excel in good society. So when one praises rusticity it is because he is denied the joys of town. A man may be tired of the country, but when he is tired of London he is tired of life.'

'Yet the taste can be defended,' said Alastair. 'A lover of natural beauty will be impatient of too long a sojourn in town, and if he would indulge his fancy he must leave the highway.'

Mr Johnson raised his head and puffed out his cheeks.

'No, sir, I do not assent to this fashionable cant of natural beauty, nor will I rave like a green girl over scenery. One part of the earth is very much as another to me, provided it support life. The most beautiful garden is that which produces most fruits, and the fairest stream that which is fullest of fish. As for mountains—'

The food and the wine had flushed Mr Johnson's face, and his uncouth gestures had become more violent. Now with a wheel of his right hand he swept two glasses to the floor and narrowly missed Edom's head.

'Mountains!' he cried, 'I deny any grandeur in the spectacle. There is more emotion for me in a furlong of Cheapside than in the contemplation of mere elevated bodies.'

Edom, with an eye on the port, was whispering to Alastair that they would soon be contemplating another elevated body, when there came a knocking and the landlady entered.

'Her ladyship's services to you, sirs,' she announced, 'and she expects Mr Johnson to wait upon her after the next half-hour, and she begs him to bring also the gentleman recently arrived with whom she believes she has the honour of an acquaintance.'

The landlady, having got the message by heart, delivered it with the speed and monotony of a bell-man. Mr Johnson rose to his feet and bowed.

'Our service to my lady,' he said, 'and we will obey her commands. *Our* service, mark you,' and he inclined towards Alastair. The summons seemed to have turned his thoughts from wine, for he refused the bottle when it was passed to him.

'The dear child is refreshed, it would seem,' he said. 'She found this morning's journey irksome, for she has little patience. Reading she cannot abide, and besides the light was poor.'

'Is madam possessed of many accomplishments?' Alastair asked, because it was clear that the other expected him to speak on the subject.

'Why no, sir. It is not right for a gentlewoman to be trained like a performing ape. Adventitious accomplishments may be possessed by any rank, but one can always distinguish the born gentlewoman.'

Then he repented.

'But I would not have you think that she is of dull wits. Nay, she is the most qualitied lady I have ever seen. She has an admirable quick mind which she puts honestly to yours. I have had rare discussions with her. Reflect, sir; she has lived always in the broad sunshine of life, and has had no spur to form her wits save her own fancy. A good mind in such a one is a greater credit than with those who are witty for a livelihood. 'Twill serve her well in matrimony, for no woman is the worse for sense and knowledge. For the present, being not three weeks married, her mind is in a happy confusion.'

He smiled tenderly as he spoke, like a father speaking of a child.

'She is happy, I think,' he said, and repeated the phrase three times. 'You have seen her,' he turned to Alastair. 'You can confirm my belief that she is happy?'

'She is most deeply in love,' was the reply.

'And transmutes it into happiness,' said Johnson, and repeated with a rolling voice some lines of poetry, beating time with his hand,

> 'Love various minds does variously inspire;
> It stirs in gentle bosoms gentle fire
> Like that of incense on the altar laid.'

'There,' said he, 'Dryden drew from a profundity which Pope could not reach. But it is time for us to be waiting on my lady.' He hoisted himself from his chair, brushed the crumbs from his waistcoat, straightened his rusty cravat, and opened the door with a bow to the others. He was in the best of spirits.

The landlady was waiting to show the two upstairs, Edom having meantime retired to smoke a pipe in the bar. As they ascended, the gale was still pounding on the roof and an unshuttered lattice showed a thick drift of snow on the outer sill, but over the tumult came the echo of a clear voice singing. To Alastair's surprise it was a song he knew, the very song that Midwinter had played two nights before. 'Diana and her darling crew' sang the voice, and as the door opened it was Diana herself that seemed to the young man to be walking to meet him. *Vera incessu patuit Dea.*

Mrs Peckover had dressed her hair, which the coach journey had disarranged, but to Alastair's eye her air was childlike, as contrasted with the hooped and furbelowed ladies of the French court. Her skirts were straight and unmodish, so that her limbs moved freely, and the slim young neck was encircled with her only jewel – a string of pearls. The homely inn chamber, which till a few hours before had been but the Brown Room, was now to him a hall in a palace, a glade in the greenwood, or wherever else walk princesses and nymphs.

She gave him her hand and then dropped into a chair, looking at him earnestly from under her long eyelashes.

'I thought that b-by this time you would be in L-Lancashire, Captain Maclean.'

'So also did I,' and he told her the story of Gypsy Ben and his morning's hunt. 'There is business I have had news of in these parts, a riddle I must unravel before I can ride north with a quiet mind. The enemy musters in Nottinghamshire, and I must carry word of his dispositions.'

Her brown eyes had kindled. 'Ben is a rogue then! By Heaven, sir, I will have him stript and whipt from Thames to Severn. Never fear but my vengeance shall reach him. Oh, I am heartily glad to know the truth, for though I have used him much I have had my misgivings. He carried letters for me to my dear Sir John.' She stopped suddenly. 'That is why the replies are delayed. Oh, the faithless scoundrel! I can love a foe but I do abhor all traitors. . . . Do you say the enemy musters in Nottingham?' The anger in her voice had been replaced by eagerness at this new thought.

'So it is reported, and, as I read it, he may march by this very road if he hopes to take the Prince's flank. You at Brightwell may have the war in your garden.'

Her eyes glistened. 'If only Sir John were here! There is the chance of a famous exploit. You are a soldier, sir. Show me, for I love the gossip of war.'

On the hearthstone with a charred stick he drew roughly the two roads from the north. 'Here or hereabouts will lie the decision,' he said. 'Cumberland cannot suffer the Prince to approach nearer London without a battle. If you hear of us south of Derby undefeated, then you may know, my lady, that honesty has won.'

She cried out, twining her hands.

'Tell me more, sir. I had thought to pass the evening playing Pope Joan with my Puffin, but you are here to teach me a better pastime. Instruct me, for I am desperate ignorant.'

Alastair repeated once again his creed in which during the past days he had come the more firmly to believe. There must be a victory in England, but in the then condition of Wales and the West a very little victory would suffice to turn the scale. The danger lay in doubting counsels in the Prince's own circle. Boldness, and still boldness, was the only wisdom. To be cautious was to be rash; to creep soberly south with a careful eye to communications was to run a deadly peril; to cut loose and march incontinent for London was safe and prudent. 'Therefore I must get quickly to the Prince's side,' he said, 'for he has many doubting Thomases around him, and few with experience of war.'

'He has my Sir John,' she said proudly. 'Sir John is young, and has not seen such service as you, but he is of the same bold spirit. I know his views, for he has told them me, and they are yours.'

'There are too many half-hearted, and there is also rank treason about. Your Gypsy Ben is the type of thousands.'

She clenched her hands and held them high. 'How I l-loathe it! Oh, if I thought I could betray the Cause I should hang myself. If I thought that one I loved could be a traitor I should d-die.' There was such emotion in her voice that the echo of it alarmed her and she changed her tone.

'Puffin,' she cried, 'are you honest on our side? I have sometimes doubted you.'

'Madam,' Mr Johnson replied in the same bantering voice, 'I can promise that at any rate I will not betray you. Being neither soldier nor statesman, I am not yet called to play an overt part in the quarrel, but I am a Prince's man inasmuch as I believe in the divine origin of the Christian state and therefore in the divine right of monarchs to govern. I am no grey rat from Hanover.'

'Yet,' she said, with a chiding finger, 'I have heard you say that a Tory was a creature generated between a non-juring parson and one's grandmother.'

'Nay, my dear lady,' he cried, 'such heresy was never mine. I only quoted it as a pernicious opinion of another, and I quoted too my answer that "the Devil, as the first foe to constituted authority, was the first Whig".'

At this juncture Mrs Peckover appeared with a kettle of boiling water and the rest of the equipment of tea, which the girl dispensed out of the coarse inn earthenware and sweetened with the coarse sugar which Mr Johnson had used for his port.

While the latter drank his dish noisily, she looked curiously at Alastair.

'You are no politician, Captain Maclean, and doubtless have no concern with the arguments with which our gentleman soothe their consciences. You do not seek wealth or power – of that I am certain. What are the bonds that join you to the Prince?'

'I am a plain soldier,' he said, 'and but fulfil my orders.'

'Nay, but you do not answer me. You do more than obey your orders; you are an enthusiast, as Sir John is – as I am – as that dull Puffin is not. I am curious to know the reason of your faith.'

Alastair, looking into the fire, found himself constrained to reply.

'I am of the old religion,' he said, 'and loyalty to my king is one of its articles.'

She nodded. 'I am a daughter of another church, which has also that teaching.'

'Also I am of the Highlands, and I love the ancient ways. My clan has fought for them and lost, and it is in my blood to fight still and risk the losing.'

Her eyes encouraged him, and he found himself telling the tale of Clan Gillian – the centuries-long feud with Clan Diarmaid, the shrinking of its lands in Mull and Morvern, the forays with Montrose and Dundee, the sounding record of its sons in the wars of Europe. He told of the old tower of Glentarnit, with the loch lapping about it, and his father who had no other child but him; of the dreams of his youth in the hot heather; of that little ragged clan which looked to him as leader and provider; and into his voice there came the pathos and passion of long memories.

'I fight for that,' he said; 'for the old things.'

It seemed that he had touched her. Her eyes were misty and with a child's gesture she laid a hand on his sleeve and stroked it. The spell which had fallen on them was broken by Mr Johnson.

'I conceive,' he said, 'that the power of the Scottish chief is no less than Homeric, and his position more desirable than that of any grandee in England. He may be poor, but he has high duties and exacts a fine reverence. When I was a child my father put into my hands Martin's book on the Western Isles, and ever since I have desired to visit them and behold the patriarchal life with my own eyes.'

'Your Highlanders are good soldiers?' she asked.

'They are the spear-point of the Prince's strength,' said Alastair.

'It is a strange time,' said Johnson, 'which sees enlisted on the same side many superfine gentlemen of France, certain sophisticated politicians of England, and these simple, brave, ignorant clansmen.'

'There is one bond which unites them all,' she cried with enthusiasm, 'which places my Sir John and the humblest Scotch peasant on an equality. They have the honesty to see their duty and the courage to follow it. What can stand against loyalty? It is the faith that moves mountains.'

'Amen, my dear lady,' said Johnson, and Alastair with a sudden impulse seized her hand and carried it to his lips.

The next morning dawned as silent as midnight. The wind had died, the snowfall had ceased, and the world lay choked, six-foot drifts in the road, twenty foot in the dells, and, with it all, patches of hill-top as bare as a man's hand. The shepherds were out with the first light digging sheep from the wreaths, and the cows after milking never left the byres. No traveller appeared on the road, for a coach was a manifest impossibility, and a horse little better. Alastair and Johnson breakfasted at leisure, and presently the elder of the Weston servants brought word of the condition of the highway. This was borne by Mrs Peckover to her mistress, who summoned Mr Johnson to her to discuss the situation. The landlord was unhopeful. Unless he could put six horses to it the coach would not get to Brightwell, though a squad of men went ahead to clear the drifts. The extra four horses he could not provide since his waggons were all at Marlock and the two riding horses were useless for coach work.

The best plan would be to send to Brightwell for the requisite horses, and this should be done later in the day, if no further snow fell. The lady pouted, but settled herself comfortably at cartes with her maid.

She inquired after Alastair's plans, and was told that he would make a shift to travel, since his errand brooked no delay. Thereafter he found the landlord and drew him aside. 'You were bidden by our friend to take orders from me,' he said. 'I have but the one. I stay on here, but you will let it be known that I have gone – this day after noon. You will give me a retired room with a key, forbid it to chambermaids, serve me with your own hand, and show me some way of private entry. It is important that I be thought to have left the countryside.'

The man did as he was told and Alastair spent the morning with Mr Johnson, who suffered from a grievous melancholy after the exhilaration of the night before. At first he had turned the pages of the only book in the inn, an ancient devotional work entitled 'A Shove for a Heavy-sterned Christian.' But presently he flung it from him and sat sidelong in a chair with his shoulders humped, his eye dull and languid, and his left leg twitching like a man with the palsy. His voice was sharp-pitched, as if it came from a body in pain.

'I am subject to such fits,' he told Alastair. 'They come when my mind is unemployed and when I have pampered my body with over-rich food. Now I suffer from both causes. Nay, sir, do not commiserate me. Each of us must live his life on the terms on which it is given him. Others have some perpetual weakness of mind or some agonising pain. I have these black moods when I see only the littleness of life and the terrors of death.'

Lady Norreys had written a letter to her husband's great-uncle at Brightwell, and armed with it Alastair set out a little before midday. He had dressed himself in the frieze and leather with which Midwinter had provided him, for it was as good a garb as a kilt for winter snows. The direction was simple. He had but to follow the valley, for Brightwell was at its head, before the road began to climb to the watershed.

To one who had shot hinds on steeper hills in wilder winter the
journey was child's play. He made his road by the barer ridges,
and circumvented the hollows or crossed them where matted
furze or hazel made a foundation. He found that the higher he
moved up the vale the less deep became the fall, and the shallower
the wreaths, as if the force of the wind had been abated by the
loftier mountains. Brightwell lay in a circle of woods on whose
darkness the snow had left only a powder; before it ran the upper
streams of a little river; behind it the dale became a ravine and
high round-shouldered hills crowded in on it.

A thin column of smoke rose from a chimney into the bitter
windless noon, so the place was inhabited. But the gates of the
main entrance were shut – massive gates flanked by stone
pillars bearing a cognisance of three mullets on a chief – and
the snow of the avenue was a virgin sheet of white. Alastair
entered the park by a gap in the wall, crossed the snow-filled
river, and came by way of a hornbeam avenue to the back parts
of the house. There he found signs of humanity. The courtyard
was trampled into slush, and tracks led out from it to the woody
hills. But nevertheless an air of death sat on the place, as if this
life it bore witness to was only a sudden start in a long slumber.
With his spirits heavily depressed he made his way to what
seemed to be the door, and entered a lesser courtyard, where he
was at once attacked by two noisy dogs.

As he drove them off, half thankful for their cheerful violence,
an old man, dressed in black like a butler, appeared. He had a
thin peevish face, and eyes that squinted so terribly that it was
impossible to guess the direction of his gaze. He received the
letter without a word and disappeared. After a considerable
lapse of time he returned and bade Alastair follow him through
a labyrinth of passages, till they reached a high old panelled hall,
darkened by lozenged heraldic windows, and most feebly
warmed by a little fire of damp faggots. There he was left alone
a second time, while he had leisure to observe the immense
dusty groining and the antlers and horns, black as bog oak, on
the walls. Then suddenly a woman stood before him.

She was tall as a grenadier and beaked like a falcon, and to defend her against the morning cold she wore what seemed to be a military coat and a turban. Her voice was surprisingly deep and large.

'You are the messenger from the Sleeping Deer? My lady Norreys lies there storm-stayed, because of the snow and asks for horses? You travelled that road yourself. Would six horses bring a coach through?'

Alastair, coarsening his accent as best he could, replied that with care six horses could get a coach to Brightwell.

'Then return at once and say that the horses will be there an hour before sunset.'

A new voice joined in, which came from an older woman, fat as the other was lean, who had waddled to her side.

'But, sister, bethink you we have not the animals.'

The first speaker turned fiercely. 'The animals must and shall be found. We cannot have our new cousin moping in a public hostel on her first visit to us. For shame, Caroline.'

'Back with you,' she turned to Alastair. 'Bennet will give you a glass of ale, but see you do not dally over it.'

The buttery ale was not such as to invite dalliance, and like the whole place smacked either of narrow means or narrow souls. Even the kitchen, of which he had a glimpse, was comfortless. To warm his blood Alastair trotted across the park, and as he ran with his head low almost butted into a horseman who was riding on one of the paths that converged on the back courtyard. He pulled himself up in time, warned by the rider's cry, and saw pass him a gentleman in a heavy fawn riding-coat, whose hat was pulled down over his brows and showed little of his face. Two sharp eyes flashed on him and then lifted, and a sharp nose, red with the weather, projected over the high coat collar.

Alastair stared after him and reached certain conclusions. That was the nose he had seen by the light of Edom's lantern the night he spent with Kyd at the inn. That was the back he had observed yesterday afternoon riding away from the Sleeping

Deer. Thirdly and most important – and though his evidence was scanty he had no doubt on the matter – the gentleman was Sir John Norreys. My lady when she reached Brightwell would find her husband.

ELEVEN

Night at the Same: Two Visitors

Four nights later Alastair was in his little bedroom at the Sleeping Deer, dressing by the light of two home-made candles. He had been taken to this inn by Midwinter because of the honesty of the landlord, who lived only for trout-fishing, and the facilities of the rambling old house for a discreet retirement. He was given an attic at the back where the dwelling part of the building merged in a disused watermill and granary. There was an entrance to it from the first floor, by way of a store cupboard; another from the kitchen regions, and still a third from the mill-house. Accordingly he was able to enter unobtrusively at any hour of the day or night, and had the further advantage that the mill-house road led directly to a covert of elders and so to the hillside. His meals, when he was at home to partake of them, were brought him by the landlord himself, who also would ascend to smoke his pipe of an evening, and discuss the habits of Derbyshire trout as compared with their northern kin.

Clad in his leather and frieze he had spent the days among the valleys and along the great road. The snow had not melted, but it was bound in the stricture of a mild frost, and all day a winter sun shone on the soft white curves of the hills. It was weather to kindle the blood and lift the heart, and Alastair found his journeys pleasant enough, though so far fruitless. He had haunted Brightwell like a cattle-lifting Macgregor looking down on a Lennox byre, and since few could teach him woodcraft in hilly places, he had easily evaded the race of keepers and foresters. Twice he had met the man whom he took to be Sir John Norreys. The first time he had watched him from cover, setting out on horseback by a track which ran from Brightwell to

Dovedale – a man in a furious hurry, with a twitching bridle-hand and a nervous eye. The second time he met him full face on the high road, and seemed to be recognised. Sir John half pulled up, thought better of it, and rode on with one glance behind him. He had made certain inquiries in the neighbourhood and learned that the tall gentleman in the fawn coat was a new-comer and beyond doubt sojourned in Brightwell: but he had a notion that in that vast decaying pile a man might lodge unbeknown to the other dwellers. He was curious to discover if Sir John had yet greeted his lady.

Four days ago she had departed in her coach, fresh horsed from Brightwell, attended by Mr Johnson and Edom Lowrie. Since then he had seen no sign of the party. The old house had swallowed them up, and neither taking the air in the park nor riding on the highway had any one of them emerged to the outer world. The mystery of the place grew upon him, till he came to look on the bleak house lying in the sparkling amphitheatre of hill as the enchanted castle of a fairy tale. It held a princess and it held a secret – *the* secret, he was convinced, most vital to his Prince's cause. He need not scour the country; in that one dwelling he could read the riddle.

On this, the fourth night of his reconnaissance, he returned to the inn assured that the first part of his task was over. He must find some way of entering Brightwell and growing familiar with the household, and his head was busy with plans as he slipped into the mill-house in the early dark, and climbed the dusty wooden ladder to the loft which gave on his attic. In his bedroom stood the landlord.

'I heard ye come in by the mill,' he said, 'and I'm here because I've news ye may like to hear. There's a famous gentleman coming here to-night. Ye'll have heard o' General Oglethorpe, him that's been fighting in Ameriky? He's coming to his supper, no less. His regiment is lying down the vale, and an officer rides here this afternoon and says the General will be to sup sharp at seven o'clock. After that he's to meet a friend here and wants to be left quiet. He needs no bed, for he's riding back to his camp when he's done his business. Now, what d'ye make of that, sir?'

'Where does he sup?' Alastair asked.

'In the Brown Room, the one my lady had.'

'When he arrives pray give him a message from me. Say that one who had the happiness to oblige him a week back is in the house, and will do himself the honour of waiting on him if he will name the hour. Is that clear? Now fetch me some hot water, for I must make a toilet.'

He got rid of his soaked clothes and assumed his old habit – chocolate coat and green velvet waistcoat, stockings and buckled shoes, and a tie-wig new dressed by the landlord. The exposure of the past days had darkened his skin, and it was a hard-bitten face that looked back at him from the cracked mirror. Before completing his toilet he lay down on the truckle bed and stared at the ceiling. Oglethorpe was friendly to him, and might give him news of moment – he had the name himself of a Jacobite or at any rate of a lukewarm Hanoverian. But the man the General was to meet? He had no doubt it was Sir John and he chuckled at the chance which Fortune had offered him.

As he lay his thoughts roamed wide but always returned to one centre, the Brown Room at the inn. But it was not Oglethorpe or Sir John that he saw there, but a slim girl with eyes now ardent, now laughing, now misty, and a voice that stammered adorably and sang 'Diana' like a linnet. Sometimes he saw Brightwell and its chilly hall, but he saw no human personage other than the girl, a little forlorn and lost now, but still happy and dreaming. . . . He pulled himself up sharply. For the first time in his life a woman's face was filling the eye of his mind – he, the scorner of trivialities whose whole being was dedicate to a manly ambition! He felt irritated and a little ashamed, and began laboriously to examine himself to prove his resolution. Now in the very crisis of his fate he could least afford a whimsy.

The landlord disturbed him when he had become drowsy.

'The gentleman is here – General Oglethorpe. I give him your message, and he says, pleasant-like, "I can guess who the gentleman is. Tell him that my gratitude is not exhausted and that I will be happy if he will add to his obligations by giving me his company at supper." Ye'd better hasten, sir, for supper is being dished up.'

Alastair followed the landlord through the cobwebby back regions of the store-room and out to the gallery at the head of the stairs whence the Brown Room opened. He noticed that the dusky corridor was brightly lit just opposite the room door because of the lamps in the hall below which shone up a side passage. This glow also revealed in full detail the map which he had studied on his first night there. As he glanced at it, the two great roads from the north seemed to stand out like blood, and Brightwell, a blood-red name, to be the toll-house to shut or open them.

The Brown Room was bright with candles and firelight, and warming his back at the hearth stood a tall man in military undress. He was of a strong harsh aquiline cast of countenance; his skin was somewhat sallow from the hot countries he had dwelt in, but he carried his forty-odd years lightly, and, to Alastair's soldier eye, would be a serious antagonist with whatever weapon of hand or brain. His face relaxed at the sight of the young man and he held out his hand.

'I am overjoyed to see you again, Mr Maclean. . . . Nay, I never forget a name or a face . . . I do not ask your business here, nor will I permit you to ask mine, save in so far as all the world knows it. I have my regiment billeted at Marlock, and am on my way across England to Hull, there to join General Wade. In that there is no secret, for every old woman on Trent side proclaims it. . . . Let us fall to, sir, for I am plaguily hungry with the frosty air, and this house has a name for cookery.'

General Oglethorpe proved himself a trencherman of the calibre of Mr Samuel Johnson; that is to say, he ate heartily of everything – beefsteak pie, roast sirloin, sheep's tongues, cranberry tarts and a London bag-pudding – and drank a bottle of claret, a quart of ale, and the better part of a bottle of Madeira. But unlike Mr Johnson he did not become garrulous, nor did the iron restraint of his demeanour relax. The board was cleared and he proceeded to brew a dish of punch, mixing the several ingredients of limes, rum, white sugar and hot water with the meticulosity of an alchemist. Then he produced from a flat silver box which he carried in his waistcoat pocket a number of thin brown sticks, which he offered to his companion.

'Will you try my cigarros, sir? It is a habit which I contracted in Georgia, and I find them mighty comforting to a campaigner. . . . You journey northward, Mr Maclean, but you make slow progress.' He smiled with a quizzical kindliness which stripped the martinet's cloak from him and left only benevolence.

Alastair smiled back. 'I journey slowly for I have had mischances. But I must mend my pace, for I am still far from my home, and my time of leave passes quick.'

'From the French King's service?'

'From the French King's service.'

'You are aware that there are certain rumours of war in this land?'

'I heard gossip to that effect in Paris.'

General Oglethorpe laughed. 'I can guess where your sympathies lie, Mr Maclean. Your name, your birthplace and your profession are signposts to them.'

'I too have heard tales from which I could hazard a guess at General Oglethorpe's sentiments,' said Alastair.

'Tut, tut, sir. I bear His Majesty's commission and am embarked in His Majesty's service.'

'I could name some in the same case – and with the same sympathies.'

The other's brows had descended and he was staring in the fire like a perplexed bird of prey.

'I do not altogether deny it. I have been a Member of Parliament for years and I have never concealed my views on politics, sir. I regret that England ever lost her natural and rightful line of kings. I have no love for Ministers with their

courting of this neighbour, and baiting of that, and bleeding the
commonalty of England for their crazy foreign wars. I detest
and abhor the cabal of greedy bloodsuckers that call themselves
Whigs. I am a Tory, sir, I serve the ancient constitution of this
realm, I love and reverence its Church, and I hold this mongering of novelties an invention of the Devil. But – and it is a
potent *but* – I cannot wish that this attempt of the Chevalier
should succeed. I must with all my soul hope that it fail and do
my best to ensure that failure.'

'Your conclusion scarcely accords with your premises, sir.'

'More than may at first sight appear. What has a young man
bred abroad in a vapid Court, and suckled into Papistry, to say to
the people of England?'

'His church is the same as mine, sir. But he is no bigot, and
has sworn to grant to all beliefs that full tolerance which
England has denied to his.'

'It is not enough. He is the young gallant, a figure from an old
chivalrous world. Oh, I do not deny his attraction; I do not doubt
that he can charm men's hearts. But, sir, there is a new temper in
the land. You have heard of the people they call Methodists –
humble folk, humble servants of Almighty God, who carry the
Gospel to dark places at the expense of revilings and buffetings
and persecutions. I have had them with me in Georgia, and they
fight like Cromwell's Ironsides, they are tender and merciful and
brave, and they preach a hope for the vilest. With them is the key of
the new England, for they bring healing to the souls of the people.
. . . What can your fairy Prince say to the poor and the hungry?'

General Oglethorpe's eye was lit with a fervour which sof-
tened the rigour of his face into something infinitely gentle.
Alastair had no words to answer so strange a plea.

'But – but King George is no more of that way of thinking
than my Prince,' he stammered.

The other nodded. 'I am not arguing on behalf of his present
Majesty. I plead for the English people and I want no change,
least of all the violent change of revolution, unless it be to their
benefit. A mere transfer of monarchs will do small good to

them, and it will bring needless suffering to the innocent. Therefore, I, James Oglethorpe, who am reputed a Jacobite, will do my utmost to nip this rising in the bud and confine it to the barbarous parts of the North. In the service of my country I will pretermit no effort to keep England neutral in the quarrel, for it is in England's participation that the danger lies.'

Alastair deemed it wise not to answer, but, as he regarded this man who was now his declared opponent, he felt the satisfaction of a fighter who faces an honourable foe. Here was one whose hand he could clasp before he crossed swords.

'I am no Englishman,' he said, 'and therefore I am remote from this particular controversy.'

The other's eye burned with a fanatic's heat. 'I will fight like a tiger for England against all who would do her hurt. God forgive them, but there are many on my side whose hearts are like rotten eggs. They are carrion crows who flock wherever there is blood and pain. In times of civil strife, sir, the base can make money. Had you travelled north by Chester you would have passed through a land of fat pastures and spreading parks and snug manors, and had you asked the name of the fortunate owner you would have been told Sir Robert Grosvenor. You know the name? A worthy gentleman and somewhat of your way of thinking. Now Sir Robert's mother was an heiress and all the faubourgs of London between St James' and Kensington village were her fortune. Whence came that fortune, think you, to enrich the honest knights of Cheshire? 'Twas the fortune of an ancient scrivener who bought up forfeited lands from Cromwell's Government, bought cheap, and sold most profitably at his leisure. There are other fortunes to-day waiting for the skilled broker of fines and attainders. But to make the profit there must be a forfeiture, and for the forfeiture there must be first the treason. Therefore it is in the interest of base men to manufacture rebels, to encourage simple folk to take blindly some irrevocable and fatal step. Do you follow me?'

Alastair nodded automatically. He saw as in a long vista a chain of infamies and the name to them was Sir John Norreys.

'The scoundrels must be in the confidence of both sides,' Oglethorpe went on. 'With their victims they are honest Jacobites, but next day they are closeted with Mr Pelham in Whitehall. They will draw a poor innocent so far that he will lose his estate, but they will prevent his loss being of service to the Prince.'

The man had risen and strode about the room, a formidable figure of wrath, with his jaw set sternly and his eyes hard.

'Do you know my purpose, Mr Maclean? So far as the Almighty permits me, I will save the pigeon from the crow. The pigeon will be hindered from meddling in matters of Government, his estate will be saved to him, and the crow, please God, will be plucked. Do you commend my policy?'

'It is the conduct of an honest gentleman, sir, and though I may not share your politics I would hope to share your friendship.'

Oglethorpe's face relaxed into the convivial kindliness it had shown at supper.

'Then two friends and honourable opponents will shake hands and bid farewell. You will be for bed, sir, and I must return presently to my regiment.'

But as the young man left the room the General seemed in no hurry to call for his horse. He flung another log on the fire, and stood by the hearth with his brows knit in meditation.

Alastair retired to his bedroom but did not undress. His brain was dazzled with new light, and he saw all the events of the past weeks in a new and awful perspective. This man Norreys was the traitor, the *agent provocateur* who lured honest clodpoles to their doom and pocketed his commission on their ruin. That was what Sir Christopher Lacy had said at Cornbury – the man cared only for gain. But he must be a rogue of vast accomplishments, for he had deceived a proud lady, and he had won the confidence of a shrewd Scots lawyer. It was Kyd's beguilement that staggered him. He, a sagacious man of affairs, had used a traitor as an agent for the most precious news – news which instead of going straight to the Prince would be transferred to the enemy and used for honest men's undoing. General Oglethorpe would prevent the fellow from making his foul profit; it was the business of Alastair Maclean to stamp the breath from him, to rid the Prince's cause of a menace and the world of a villain.

He mused on this strange thing, England, which was like a spell on sober minds. Midwinter had told of Old England like a lover of his mistress, and here was this battered traveller, this Oglethorpe, thrilling to the same fervour. That was something he had not met before. He had been trained to love his family and clan and the hills of his home, and a Prince who summed up centuries of wandering loyalty. But his devotion had been for the little, intimate things, and not for matters large and impersonal like a country or a people. He felt himself suddenly and in very truth a stranger and alone. The Prince, the chiefs, the army – they were all of them strangers here. How could they ask for loyalty from what they so little understood?

The reflection pained him and he put it from him and turned to his immediate business. Kicking off his shoes, he tiptoed back through the store-cupboard and into the long corridor, at the end of which he saw the bright reflection from the hall lamp falling on the map and the Brown Room door. He listened, but there was no sound except a faint clatter from far away in the direction of the kitchen, where presumably the General's servant waited on his master's orders. He stole to the door of the Brown Room for a second, and played the eavesdropper. Yes, there were voices within, a low voice speaking fast, and another replying in monosyllables. He had no wish to overhear them, so he crept back to the store-room door, where he was securely hid. Thence he could see all that he wanted, in the patch of light by the map.

He did not wait long. The door opened, and a figure was illumined for one instant in profile before it turned to descend the stairs. It was a tall man in a long riding-coat which he had unbuttoned in the warmth of the room. He bowed his head a little as one does when one walks stealthily, and his lips were tightly pursed. But where was the sharp nose like a pen, and the pale complexion of Sir John? This man had a skin like red sandstone, a short blunt nose and a jovial mouth. He cast one glance at the map, and then went softly down the staircase.

With a queer flutter of the heart Alastair recognised Mr Nicholas Kyd.

TWELVE

The Hut in the Oak Shaw

The sinking at the heart disappeared long before Alastair reached his attic, and was replaced by a violent heat of anger. He lit a candle, for the dark irked him, and sat on his bed with his face as scarlet as if it had been buffeted. He felt his temples throb and a hot dryness at the back of his throat. For the moment thoughts of the dire peril to the Cause were swallowed up in natural fury at a rogue.

Blind fool that he had been! All the steps were now bitterly clear in his bedraggled Odyssey. At Cornbury Kyd had been sowing tares in my lord's mind – not in partnership with the Duchess Kitty, of that he was assured – he did not believe that that vivacious lady, Whig as she might be, was a partner of his villainy. From the first encounter at the roadside inn the man had dogged him; perhaps that meeting had been premeditated. The scene at Flambury, the accusing mummer in Squire Thicknesse's Justice Room, the well-informed warrant, Ben the Gypsy and his treachery – all were the doing of the pawky Lammermuir laird. General Oglethorpe would use his services but prevent his getting his reward; but there were others less scrupulous, and anyhow these services spelled death to the Prince's fortunes. . . . A second Grosvenor fortune would be achieved! No, by God, it should not, if Alastair Maclean were left another six months alive!

Sir John Norreys was the man's tool, and the news from the West passed through him to Kingston and Wade, and Ligonier and Cumberland, and Mr Pelham in London. Mr Pelham doubtless had taken steps. He would arrest the levy in the West before it had grown dangerous; and the fines and forfeitures of

broken loyalists would go to enrich the Exchequer and Mr
Nicholas Kyd of Greyhouses. . . . He had lost his dislike of
Sir John. That huckstering baronet was only an instrument in
the hand of a cleverer knave.

But why was Kyd here, when he had sent Edom to Brightwell
with the news that he was not to be looked for before the close of
the month? He did not believe that Edom had lied, so either
there was a deeper game afoot, or Kyd had changed his plans.
He thought the latter, for even rogues were the sport of
circumstance. Some news had reached him of surpassing
importance and he had posted all that way to see Oglethorpe,
who, as a former Jacobite, would be the more readily believed by
the Government when he acted against his former friends.

It stood to reason that Kyd would visit Brightwell, to see
Norreys, to instruct his servant – some errand or other, even if
he returned next day to the South. Brightwell was the Philippi of
the campaign, the place of meetings, or why had Norreys been
sent there? Even now the laird's ruddy visage and the baronet's
lean jaw might be close together in some damnable machina-
tion. . . . And the lady, the poor lady. At the thought of her
Alastair clenched his hands, and shut his eyes tight to kill the
pain in them. That poor nymph, that dainty innocence in such a
den of satyrs!

And then, oddly enough, his mood changed to a happier one
as the picture of Claudia Norreys brightened on the screen of his
memory. Please God, she was cut off now for ever from the man
she called husband. Her eyes must soon be opened, and he
pictured her loathing, her horror of disgust. There were other
thoughts at the back of his mind, which he choked down, for
this was no time for pretty fancies. But it comforted him to think
that he was fighting for the happiness of the girl who sang
'Diana.'

He slept little and at dawn was up and dressed in his frieze
and leather, his coarse stockings and his hob-nailed shoes. The
frost was passing, and a mild south wind blew up the vale,
softening the snow crust and sending runnels of water down the

hollows and eaves of the great drifts. Alastair found the landlord breakfasting in the dog-kennel he called his room.

'I am going to Brightwell,' he told him, 'and may be absent for days. Expect me back when you see me. Keep my room locked, and leave the key as before in the crack below the broken axle-hole of the mill.' Then he stepped out-of-doors, where the milkers were just opening the byres, and soon was on the hillside with his face to the High Peak.

He crossed the high road and looked at the tracks. There was one fresh and clear, that of a man in heavy boots plodding towards the inn. There were faint hoof marks also, but they seemed to be old. He reflected that the thaw could not have begun till after midnight, and that if Kyd had ridden this road his horse's track would have shown no more than the others of yesterday.

The sun was well above the horizon when he reached the park wall of Brightwell and entered the demesne by his usual gap. It was a morning like early spring, when the whole world was full of melting snows, running waters and light breezes. His plan was to go to the wood which overhung the kitchen yard and gave a prospect of the house and all its environs. There he would watch till noon, in the hope that either Kyd would appear or one of Lady Norreys' party. If the former, he would follow him and have the interview for which his soul longed; if the latter, then he would find a way of getting speech and learning the nature of the household. If nothing happened by noon, he would contrive to make his way into the kitchen as before, and trust to his wits to find an errand.

He saw no one as he forded the now turbulent stream and climbed the farther slope to the wood of hazels and ashes which clung like an eyebrow to the edge of a bare grey bluff, beneath which were the roofs of the rearmost outbuildings. But as he entered the wood he received a shock. Suddenly he had the consciousness that he was being observed, which comes as from a special sense to those who have lived much in peril of their lives in lonely places. He cowered like a rabbit, and seemed to detect very faint and far-off movements in the undergrowth which were too harsh and sudden for a wild animal. Then they ceased, and the oppression passed. He threaded his way through the undergrowth to his old lair beside a stone, where a tangle of fern hid his head, and there he sat him down to wait.

It was a very wet anchorage. The frozen ground beneath him was melting into slush, rivulets descended from the branches, vagrant winds blew avalanches of melting snow like hail in his face. He grew cold and stiff, and there was no such drama on the stage before him as might have caused him to forget his icy stall. He saw in every detail the morning awakening of a Derbyshire manor. A man with his head tied up in a stocking wheeled barrowloads of chopped logs from the wood-hovel; another brought milk pails from the byres; while two stable-boys led out to water various horses, among which Alastair recognised those once ridden by Mr Johnson and Edom. The butler Bennet, wearing a kind of dingy smock, shuffled out-of-doors and cried shrilly for someone who failed to appear. Then came a long spell of quiet – breakfast, thought Alastair. It was broken by a stout fellow in boots, whom he had not seen before, coming from the direction of the kitchen, shouting the name of 'Peter'. Peter proved to be one of the stable-boys, who, having been goaded by a flight of oaths into activity, produced in a space of five minutes a horse saddled and bridled and tolerably well groomed. This the man in boots led round to the front of the house, and presently, out from the shelter of the leafless avenue, appeared Sir John Norreys, in a hurry as usual and heading for the bridle-path to Dovedale.

This told Alastair two things. First, that in all likelihood Mr Kyd had never been to Brightwell, or had left earlier, otherwise Sir John would scarcely have fled his company. Second, that the said Sir John had been restored to his lady and was living openly in the house, and not, as he had half suspected, hidden in some priest-hole in the back parts.

The morning passed on leaden wings, for the thought that Kyd was not there had dashed Alastair's spirits. Once he seemed to hear the sound of breathing close at hand, and after some search traced it to a deep bed of leaves under which a hedgehog was snoring in its winter sleep. Once the pied snout of a badger, returning late to his earth, parted the thicket. Just before noon he saw that which set his mind off on a new tack. Down the valley, a matter of half a mile from the house, a brook entered the stream from the west, and, since the hills there overhung the water, flowed for the last part of its course in a miniature ravine. Both sides of the dell were thickly covered with scrub oak, but glades had been cut, and at the intersection of two on the near bank stood a thatched hut. Alastair had noticed it before, and from his present eyrie it was clearly visible.

Below him in the courtyard the butler suddenly appeared and, shading his eyes, looked down the valley. Then he took from his pocket a handkerchief and waved it three times, staring hard after each wave. Alastair followed his gaze and saw that he was looking towards the oak wood. Presently from the hut there a figure emerged, waved a white rag three times, and disappeared in the scrub. The butler seemed satisfied, and turned back to the house, from which he emerged again with a covered basket. A boy rose from a bench, took the basket and set off at a boy's trot. Alastair watched his progress and noted that he did not take the direct road, but kept unobtrusively in the shade of thickets. He avoided the glades and reached the hut by an overland route through the scrub. He seemed to stay about a minute within, and then hurried back by the way he had gone. The butler was waiting for him in the yard, and the two talked for a little, after which the boy went off whistling.

There was someone in the hut in the oak scrub – someone who was being fed, and who did not wish to reveal himself to the house. It could only be Kyd. At the notion Alastair's face flushed and he forgot his cold vigil. The road was open for that meeting with Kyd, alone and secure, which was his main desire. Having satisfied himself that the coast was clear, he began to worm his way along the hillside.

At the edge of the covert he reconnoitred again. A figure had revealed itself in the pleasance which skirted one side of the house – a large figure which took the air on a green walk and appeared to be reading, with a book held very near its eyes. It was Mr Samuel Johnson, and for one moment he hesitated as to whether he should not first have speech with him. There was ample cover to reach him by way of a sunk fence. It was a critical decision, had he known it, but he took it lightly. His duty and his pleasure was first to settle with Kyd.

He reached the oak shaw without difficulty, and, like the boy, shunned the glades and squeezed through the thick under-growth. He stopped once, for he thought he heard a faint whistle, but decided that it was only a bird. There were no windows in the hut, which, as he neared it, proved to be a far solider thing than he had imagined, being built of stout logs, jointed between stouter uprights, and roofed in with thatch as carefully woven as that of a dwelling-house. He listened, but all was quiet within.

The door yielded and he stepped inside with a quick motion, drawing it behind him, for the place was in sight of the house. . . . Then something smote him in the dark. He felt himself falling, and threw out his hand, which gripped only on vacancy and blackness. . . .

The first pin-prick of consciousness found him climbing. There was a sound of sea water in his ears, and the salt tingled in his eyes and nostrils, for he had been diving from the Frenchman's Rock and was still breathless with it. Now he was going up and up steeps of bracken and granite to the flat top where the ripe blackberries were. He was on Eilean a Fhraoich, had crossed over that morning in Angus Og's coble – a common Saturday's ploy. . . . But he found it very hard to get up the ledges, for they were always slipping from beneath him, and only wild clutches at the bracken kept him from slithering down to the beach. Also his head sang abominably, and there was a queer smell in his nose, more than salt, a smell like burning – burning lime. He wished he had not dived so deep. . . . Then his eyes suddenly stabbed him with pain and the beach of Eilean a Fhraoich disappeared, and the sun and the sky and the dancing sea. All was black now, with a pin-point of light which was not the sun.

'Ye struck him over hard, Ben,' a voice said.

'Never you fear,' came the answer. 'I know the stout pretty heads of these Scotchmen.' He waved the light over his face. 'See, he is coming round already.'

Alastair would have liked to speak, for he was worried about Eilean a Fhraoich and the smell in his nose was overpowering. But as his voice struggled to emerge it woke a deadly nausea, and he seemed to sink again down, down through cottony worlds of utter feebleness. . . .

His next conscious moment found him lying with his head propped up, while someone tried to open his lips with a spoon and pour hot liquid between them. The stuff burned his throat but did not sicken him. He moved himself to take it better and discovered that the slightest motion shot a flight of arrows through his head, arrows of an intolerable pain. So he kept very still, only opening his eyes by slow degrees. It was very dark, but there was a tiny light somewhere which showed a hand and arm moving from a bowl to his mouth and back again. . . . He began to piece his surroundings together. He was indoors somewhere and someone was feeding him, but beyond that he could tell nothing, so he slipped back into sleep.

After that he began to come again more frequently to the world, and the pain in his head and eyes bothered him less. He knew when meal-time came, for it was preceded by a dazzling brightness (which was daylight through the open door) and attended by a lesser light, which was a stable lantern. Slowly he began to reason and observe, and work his way back till he saw suddenly in his mind's eye the outside of the hut, and could remember the last waking moment. Then he heard a man's voice which woke a chord in his memory, and further bits of the past emerged. Soon he reached a stage when in a flood the whole story of his journeys and perplexities rolled back into his mind, and he grew sick again with a worse kind of nausea. Still he could not quite recapture the link; he saw everything up to a certain noon, and realised the dim world which now enveloped him, but he could not find the archway between the two. Then one day the hand that brought his food left the door wide open, and in the light of it he saw a dark gypsy-looking fellow who smiled impishly but not malevolently.

'No ill will, dear pretty gentleman,' he whined. 'You knew too much and were proving too inquisitive, so them as I obeys bade me put you to sleep for a tidy bit. No harm is meant you, so eat your pretty dinner and say your pretty prayers and go beddie-bye like a good little master. You're picking up strength like a cub fox.'

Alastair saw again the dim door of the hut, felt the musty darkness, and the fiery pain that seemed to rend his skull. Now he had the tale complete.

The gypsy left him to feed himself, which was achieved at the expense of spilling a third of the soup. He sat on a pile of ash poles, swinging his legs, and preening himself like a jay.

'Ben was too clever for you, my dainty gentleman. He was a-watching for you days back, and when you was a-creeping belly-flat Ben was never a dozen yards behind you. He was in the wood above the stable that morning when you arrived, and 'twas him as arranged the play about the Shaw Hut with old Bennet. Not but what you had a pretty notion of travelling, my dear, and nimble legs to you. I owed you one for the day with Oglethorpe's soldiers and I paid it that morning at the Flambury meet. Now you owes me one for this device, and I'm waiting to pay it. All for a bit of sport is Ben.'

Alastair let him brag and asked him but the one question. 'How long have I been here?'

'Nineteen days,' said the gypsy. 'This is now the second day of December.'

The news would have put the young man into a fever had his wits been strong enough to grasp its full meaning. As it was, he only felt hazily that things had gone very ill with him, without any impulse to take the wheel from Destiny's hand and turn it back.

All morning he drowsed. He was not uncomfortable, for he had a bed of bracken and rushes and sufficient blankets for the mild winter weather. An old woman, the wife of the butler, brought water and bathed his head daily, and the food, which was soup or stew of game, was good and sufficient. That day for the first time he felt his strength returning, and as the hours passed restlessness grew on him. It was increased by an incident which happened in the afternoon. He was awakened from a doze by the sound of steps and voices without. Two people were walking there, and since there were interstices between the logs of the wall it was possible to overhear their conversation.

Said one, a female voice, 'He left Manchester two days ago?'

'Two days ago, St Andrew's Day,' was the reply, 'and therefore a day of happy omen for a Scot.'

'So in two days he will be in D-derby.'

That stammer he would have known in the babble of a thousand tongues. The other – who could he be but her husband, and the man they spoke of but the Prince?

A hand was laid on the latch and the door shook. Then a key was inserted and the lock turned. Alastair lay very quiet, but below his eyelids he saw the oblong of light blocked by a figure. That figure turned in profile the better to look at him, and he saw a sharp nose.

'He is asleep,' said the man to his companion without. 'He has been sick, for there was a sharp scuffle before he was taken, but now he is mending. Better for him, poor devil, had he died!'

'Oh, Jack, what will they do with him?'

'That is for His Highness to decide. A traitor's death, at any rate. He may get the benefit of his French commission and be shot, or he may swing like better men in hemp.'

The other voice was quivering and anxious. 'I cannot credit it. Oh, Jack, I am convinced that there is error somewhere. He may yet clear himself.'

'Tut, the man was caught in open treason, intercepting messages from the West and handing them to the Government.

His lies to you prove his guilt. He professed to be hastening to the Prince, and he is taken here crouching in a wood fifty miles from his road, but conveniently near General Ligonier and the Duke of Kingston.'

The door was shut and the key turned, but not before Alastair heard what he took for a sigh.

There was no sleep for him that night. His head had cleared, his blood ran easily again, the strength had come back to his limbs, and every nerve in him was strung to a passion of anger. His fury was so great that it kept him calm. Most desperately had things miscarried. The Prince was on the threshold of the English Midlands, and all these weeks Kyd and Norreys had been at their rogueries unchecked. Where were the western levies now? What devil's noose awaited the northern army, marching into snares laid by its own professed allies? Worse, if worse were possible, the blame would be laid on him; Norreys and Kyd had so arranged it that he would pass as traitor; doubtless they had their cooked evidence in waiting. And in the dear eyes of the lady he was guilty, her gentle heart wept for his shame. At the memory of her voice, as it had made its last protest, he could have beaten his head on the ground.

His bonds had always been light – a long chain with a padlock clasping his left ankle and fastened to a joist of the hut – for his captors trusted to the strength of the walls and his frail condition. During the night he worked at this and managed so to weaken one of the links that he thought he could break it at will. But the morning brought him a bitter disappointment. Some fresh orders must have been issued, for Gypsy Ben produced new fetters of a more formidable type, which bound Alastair to a narrow radius of movement. As a make-weight he did not lock the door, but left it ajar. 'You're like me, gentleman dear,' he said; 'you like the sky over you and to hear birds talking round about. I can humour you in that, if you don't mind a shorter tether.'

It was a fine morning, the third of December, with a loud frolicking wind and clouds that sailed in convoys. In black depression of heart Alastair watched the tiny half-moon of landscape vouchsafed to him, three yards of glade, a clump of hazels, the scarred grey bole of an ancient oak. He had toiled at his bonds till every muscle was wrung, and he had not moved a link or coupling one fraction of an inch. Breathless, furious, despairing, he watched a pert robin approaching the door in jerks, when the bird rose startled at someone's approach. Alastair, lifting dreary eyes, saw the homely countenance of Edom.

The man cried out, and stood staring.

'Guid sake, sir, is this the way of it? I heard that something ill had happened to ye, but I never jaloused this.'

Hungry eyes read the speaker's face, and saw nothing there but honest perplexity.

'They have invented a lie,' Alastair said, 'and call me a traitor. Do you believe it?'

'Havers,' said Edom cheerfully. 'They never telled me that, or they'd have got the lee in their chafts. Whae said it? Yon lang wersh lad they ca' Sir John?'

'Is your master here?'

'He's comin' the morn and I'm michty glad o't. For three weeks I've been like a coo in an unco loan. But, Captain Maclean, sir, I'm wae for you, sittin' sae gash and waefu' in this auld bourock.'

Alastair's eyes had never left Edom's face, and suddenly his mind was made up. He resolved to trust everything to this man's honesty.

'You can help me if you will. Can I count on you?'

'If it's onything reasonably possible,' said the cautious Edom.

'I need friends. I want you to summon them.'

'I'll be blithe to do that.'

'You know the country round and the inns?'

'I've traivelled the feck o't on my twae feet and sampled the maist o' the publics.'

'Then find a cross-roads which has broom on the signpost or an inn with an open eye painted under the sign. Whistle this air,' and he hummed Midwinter's ditty.

Edom made a tolerable attempt at it. 'I mind ye whustled that when we were huntit i' the big wud. And after that?'

'Someone will come to you and ask your errand. Tell him of my plight and direct him or guide him here.'

Edom nodded, and without more ado turned and swung out for the river-bridge and the high road.

THIRTEEN

Journeyman John

The hours passed slowly, for Alastair was in a ferment of hope and fear, into which like lightning-flashes in a dark sky shot now and then a passion of fury, as he remembered Claudia Norreys. He had not seen her as she stood outside the hut, but he could picture the sad disillusionment of her eyes, and the quiver of her mouth as she protested against a damning truth which she yet needs must believe. Her gentle voice sounded maddeningly in his ears. He could not forecast what his fate might be, he could not think settled thoughts, he could not plan; his mind was in that helplessness in which man falls back upon prayer.

The afternoon drew to a quiet sunset. The door of the hut remained open, and through it he saw the leafless knotted limbs of the oaks, which had before been a grey tracery against the smoky brown of the scrub, fire with gold and russet. There was no sign of Edom or his friends, but that at the best he could hardly hope for till late, there was no sign of his gaoler or of any living thing – he was left alone with the open door before him, and the strict fetters on his limbs. The sun sank, the oaks grew grey again, a shiver went through the earth as the night cold descended. The open space in the door had turned to ebony dark before there was a sound of steps.

It was Ben the Gypsy, and he had two others with him, whom Alastair could not see clearly in the light of the single lantern. The man seemed in high excitement.

' 'Tis time to be stirring, pretty gentleman,' he chirruped. 'Hey for the high road and the hills in the dark o' the moon, says I. No time for supper, neither, but there'll be a long feast and a fine feast where you're going. Up with him, Dick lad and Tony

lad. I'm running no risks with the bonds of such a fiery fearless
gentleman.'

Two stalwart followers swung him in their arms, and
marched down one of the glades, the gypsy with the lantern
dancing before, like a will-o'-the-wisp. At the foot of the slope
were horses, and on one of them – a ragged shelty – they set
him, undoing his leg bonds, and fastening them again under
the animal's belly. The seat was not uncomfortable, for he had
his feet in stirrups of a sort, but it was impossible for him to
escape. His hands they tied, and one of the party took the
shelty's bridle.

The road ran up-hill, first through woods and then in a waste
of bracken and heather and scree. Black despair was Alastair's
portion. His enemies had triumphed, for even if Edom discovered some of Midwinter's folk, they would find the hut
empty, and how could they trace him by night over such
trackless country? His body as well as his heart was broken,
for the sudden change from the inertia of the hut made every
limb ache and set his head swimming. Soon he was so weary
that he lost all count of the way. Dimly he was conscious that
they descended into glens and climbed again to ridges, but the
growing chill and greater force of the wind told him that they
were steadily rising. Presently the wrack was blown off the face
of the sky, the winter regiment of stars shone out, and in their
faint radiance he saw all about him the dark fields of the hills.
Often he thought himself fainting. Repeatedly he would have
fallen, but for the belly girth, and more than once he bowed over
his horse's neck in deep weariness. Ben the Gypsy spoke to him,
but as he did not answer rode ahead, with his lantern bobbing
like a ship's riding light in a gusty harbour.

Then Alastair fell asleep, and was tortured by nightmares.
Indeed all the latter part of the journey was a nightmare,
sleeping and waking, for it was a steady anguish, half muffled
by a sense of crazy unreality. When the party stopped at last, he
came back from caverns of confused misery, and when the
belly-girth was cut fell leadenly to the ground. The ride in an

unnatural position had given him a violent cramp in his right leg, and the sharp pain woke him to clear consciousness. He was picked up and carried inside some building, and as he crossed the threshold had a vision of steep walls of cliff all about him.

After that he must have slept, for when he next remembered he was lying on a settle before a fire of peat and heather-roots, and, watching him through the smoke, sat Gypsy Ben, whittling a stick with a long, fine shagreen-handled knife.

'Feeling happier now?' the gypsy asked. 'Soon it will be supper time and after that the soft bed and the long sleep, my darling dear. Ben's are the kind hands.'

Something in the voice made Alastair shake off his torpor. The gypsy, as he first remembered him, had been a mischievous sneering fellow, and he had longed to wring his neck when he rode off grinning that day at the Flambury Hunt. In the hut he had been almost friendly, protesting that he bore no malice but only obeyed orders. But now – there was something bright and mad about those dark dancing eyes, something ghoulish in the soft gloating voice. Had his orders been changed? What plan of his foes was served by bringing him thus into this no-man's-land of the hills?

'Why am I here?' he asked, and his tongue so stumbled between his dry lips that the gypsy passed him a jug of ale that was being kept warm by the fire.

'Orders, kind precious sir. Them that I obeys has changed their mind about you, and thinks you are too dear and good for this wicked, wicked world. Therefore they hands you over to Gypsy Ben, who brings you the straight way to Journeyman John.'

The other looked puzzled, and the gypsy rose and, dancing to a far end of the room, opened a large rough door like a partition in a cowshed. Instantly a great gust swept the place, driving clouds of fine dust from the hearth. A noise came from that darkness beyond the door, a steady rumbling and grinding which had been a mere undercurrent of sound when the door

was shut, but now dominated the place – a sound like millstones working under a full press of water, joined with a curious
shuddering like wind in an old garret. The gypsy stood en-
tranced, one hand to his ear, his eyes glittering.

'That's him we call Journeyman John. Hark to him grinding
his old teeth! Ah, John, hungry again! But cheer up, there's a
fine supper a-coming.'

He shut the door as a showman shuts a cage. The light died
out of his eyes, leaving only smouldering fires.

'That's the deepest pot-hole in all the land,' he said, 'and John
like a scaly serpent lies coiled at the foot of it. Nothing that goes
in there comes out – leastways only in threads and buttons by
way of Eldingill, and that long after. There's your bed made for
you, master, and it's Ben's duty to tuck you in. Oh, Ben's a kind
mammy.'

The young man's brain had been slow to grasp the fate
prepared for him, but the crazy leer which accompanied the
last words brought a hideous illumination, and at the same time
the faintest ray of hope. The man was clearly a madman, and
therefore incalculable. With a great effort Alastair steeled his
heart and composed his voice.

'What of supper?' he asked. 'That comes before bed in a
hospitable house.'

The gypsy laughed like a magpie, high and harsh. 'Supper be
it!' he cried, 'and a good one, for John is a generous host. Hey,
Bobadilla!'

An old woman answered his cry and proceeded to lay on the
table plates and glasses, a platter of bread and the end of a
cheese. Presently she came back with a great dish of frizzling
eggs and fried ham. The gypsy lifted the jug of ale from the
fireside, and drew in a chair to the board.

'Mammy will feed her pretty chick,' he said, 'for the chick's
claws are too dangerous to loose.'

Alastair's heart had ceased fluttering, and an immense composure had settled upon him. He had even an appetite, and was
able to swallow the portion of eggs and ham which the gypsy

conveyed to his mouth on the end of his knife. The ale was most welcome, for his thirst was fierce, and the warmth and the spice of it recalled his bodily strength. By now he was recovering a manlier resolution. He was a soldier and had faced death often, though never in so gruesome a form. If it were the end, so let it be, but he would not abandon hope while breath was in his body. He even forced himself to a laugh.

'Tell me of this Journeyman John,' he asked. 'What house is this that he lurks behind?'

'A poor farm called Pennycross, with no neighbour nearer than six miles. Goody Lugg is the farmer, a worthy widow who looks after a cow and a dozen wethers and leaves the care of John to Ben and his friends. Mighty convenient fellow is John to keep in a neighbourhood. If a girl would be quit of a love-child or a wife of a stepson they come to Ben to do their business. Ay, pretty sir, and John has had dainty meat. Listen,' and he thrust his face close to Alastair. 'I have done a job or two for Lord Dash and Lord Mash – naming no names, as being against my sworn oath – when they were in trouble with petticoats no longer wanted. And before my time there was the young heir of Crokover – you've heard that tale. Ay, ay, the Journeyman does his work swift and clean and lasting and keeps mum!'

'Who paid you to bring me here?'

The gypsy grinned cunningly. 'Since I swore no oaths and you'll never live to peach, you shall hear. Down in Brightwell live two grey she-corbies. 'Twas them gave Ben the office.'

'No other?'

'No other except a red-faced Scot that rides the roads like a packman. Him I have not seen for weeks, but the corbies in Brightwell work to his bidding. All three love the bright yellow gold.'

'Sir John Norreys had a part in it?'

'Nay, nay, pretty sir. Sir John, brave gentleman, was privy to your capture and imprisonment, but he knows nothing of this night's work. He is too young and raw for so rare a thing as my John.'

'You are paid well, I fancy. What if I were to pay you better to let me go?'

'What you have is already mine,' said the gypsy.

'A large sum will be brought you in twelve hours if you will let me send a message, and as proof of good faith I will remain here in your power till it is paid.'

The gypsy's eye glittered with what was not greed.

'Though you filled my hat with guineas, my darling, I would not let you go. John is hungry, for it is long since he tasted proper meat, and I have promised him that to-night he shall sup. I have whispered it in his great ear, and he has purred happily like a cat. Think you I would disappoint John? Do not fear, pretty sir. It is midwinter and the world is cold, and full of hard folks and wan cheeks and pinched bellies. But down with John there is deep sleep and it is sunny and warm, for the fires of Hell burn next door. Nay, nay, John is not the Devil, but only a cousin on the spindle side.'

In spite of his resolution Alastair felt his blood chilling as the gypsy babbled. Hope had grown very faint, for what could he do, manacled as he was, in a struggle against a lithe and powerful madman, who could call in the other companions of the night to help him? The undercurrent of sound seemed to be growing louder, and the wooden partition shook a little with the reverberation. How many minutes would pass before he was falling into that pit of echoing darkness!

'When does John sup?' he asked.

'When he calls for supper,' was the answer. 'At a certain hour each night the noise of his grinding becomes louder. Hark, it is beginning now. In less than half an hour he will speak. . . . You have a ring on your finger, a pretty ring – give it to Ben that it may remind him of a happy night and a sweet gentleman.'

'Why do you ask for it when I am in your power, and it is yours for the taking?'

'Because a thing gifted is better than a thing taken. Plunder a man must sell, but a gift he can wear. If I had a dead man's hat on my head took from his body, it would be crying out in my ears, but if he had kindly given it me, it would fit well and hold its peace. I want that ring that I may wear it and kiss it and call to mind my darling dear.'

The gypsy seized the hand and peered at the ring, a heavy jasper cut with the crest of Morvern, a tower embattled.

'Set free my hands, then, and I will give it you,' said Alastair.

The gypsy grinned cunningly. 'And risk your strong fingers at my throat, my pretty one. Nay, nay. Just say the words, "I gift my ring freely and lovingly to Gypsy Ben", and hark to the service I will do you. With my own hand I will cut your pretty throat, and save you the cruel fall down, down into the darkness. Most gentlemen fear that more than death. 'Tis unfair to the Journeyman, for he's no raven that can put up with dead carrion, but a peregrine who kills what he eats. But for this once he will pardon his servant Ben. Say the words, gentleman dear. See, it is getting very close on supper time and John is crying out.'

He lifted his hand, an eldritch and evil figure, and sure enough the noise of the grinding had risen till it was like a storm in the night. The wooden partition and the windows at the far side of the room rattled violently and the whole place, roof, walls and rafters, shuddered. In a tumult a small sound pitched in a different key will sometimes make itself heard, and on Alastair's ear there fell something like a human voice. It may have been fancy, but, though he had abandoned hope, it encouraged him to play for time.

'I do not fear the darkness,' he said, 'or death in the darkness. But it is a notion of my family to die in the daylight. I will gladly speak the words which gift you the ring if you will let me live till dawn. It cannot be far distant.'

The gypsy took from his fob a vast old silver watch. 'Nay, sir, not till daybreak, which is still four hours distant. But John shall wait for one half-hour on his supper, and he cannot complain, for he will have the killing of it himself. Take your pleasure, then, for thirty minutes by this clock which Ben had of the Miller of Bryston before he was hanged at Derby. What shall we do to make the moments go merrily? Shall Ben sing to you, who soon will be singing with angels?'

The gypsy was on his feet now, his face twitching with excitement and his eyes like two coals. He skipped on the table and cut a step.

'You shall see the Gallows Jig, darling mine, which goes to the tune of "Fairladies".'

With grace and skill he threaded his way among the dishes on the stout oaken board, showing a lightness of foot amazing in one wearing heavy ridingboots.

'Bravo,' cried Alastair. 'If I were unshackled I would give you the sword-dance as we dance it in the Highlands.' If the maniac could be absorbed in dance and song he might forget the passage of time. Somehow the young man believed that with daylight he would have a chance of salvation.

The gypsy leaped from the table, and took a long pull at the ale jug.

'Sing in turn or sing in chorus,' he cried. 'Raise a ditty, precious gentleman.'

Alastair's dry throat produced a stave of Desportes – a love song which he had last heard at a *fête champêtre* at Fontaine-bleau. The gypsy approved and bellowed a drinking catch. Then to Alastair's surprise he lowered his voice and sang very sweetly and truly the song of 'Diana'. The delicate air, with the fragrance of the wildwood in it, pierced Alastair like a sword. He remembered it as Midwinter had sung it – as Claudia Norreys had crooned it, one foot beating time by the hearth and the glow of firelight on her slim body. It roused in him a new daring and a passionate desire to live. He saw, by a glance at the watch which lay on the table, that the half-hour had already been exceeded.

'Nobly sung,' he cried. 'Where got you that song?'

'Once I heard a pretty lady chant it as she walked in a garden. And I have heard children sing it far away from here – and long, long ago.'

The man's craziness had ebbed a little, and he was staring into the fire. Alastair, determined that he should not look at the watch, coaxed him to sing again, and praised his music, and, when he did not respond, himself sang – for this new mood had brought back his voice – a gypsy lay of his own land, a catch of the wandering Macadams that trail up and down the sea-coast. Gentle and soothing it was, with fairy music in it, which the Good Folk pipe round the sheilings on the July eves. Ben beat time to it with his hand, and after it sang 'Colin on a summer day' with a chorus that imitated very prettily a tabor accompaniment. . . . Alastair's glance at the watch told him that more than an hour had passed, and he realised, too, that the noise of the Journeyman was dying down.

'Your turn,' said the gypsy, who had let his legs sprawl toward the fire, and seemed like one about to go to sleep.

An unlucky inspiration came to the young man. He broke into the song of 'The Naked Men' and he let his voice ring out so that the thing might have been heard outside the dwelling. For a moment the gypsy did not seem to hear; then he frowned, as if an unpleasant memory were aroused; then suddenly he woke to full consciousness.

'Hell and damnation!' he cried. 'What warlock taught you that? Stop the cursed thing,' and he struck the singer in the face.

Then his eye saw the watch, and his ear caught the cessation of the Journeyman's grinding. His madness flared up again, he forgot all about the ring, and he leaped upon the prisoner like a wild-cat. He dragged him, helpless as he was, from the settle and flung him across the table, sending the remains of supper crashing to the floor. Then he left him, rushed to the wooden partition, and tore it apart. From the black pit thus revealed a thin grey vapour seemed to ascend, and the noise was like the snarling of hounds in kennel.

'John is hungry,' he cried. 'I have kept you waiting, my darling, but your meat is ready,' and he was back clutching his prisoner's middle.

The despair and apathy of the earlier hours had gone, and Alastair steeled himself to fight for his life. The gypsy's strength was always respectable and now his mania made it prepotent.

The young man managed to get his manacled ankles crooked in a leg of the table, but they were plucked away with a dislocating wrench. His head grated on the floor as he was dragged towards the pit. And then he saw a chance, for the rope that bound his wrists caught in a staple fixed in the floor, apparently to make an anchorage for a chain that had worked an ancient windlass. The gypsy pulled savagely, but the good hemp held, and he was forced to drop the body and examine the obstacle. Alastair noted that beyond the pit was a naked dripping wall of cliff, and that the space between the edge and the walls of the shed inclined downward, so that anything that once reached that slope would be easily rolled into the abyss. Death was very near him and yet he could not despair. He lifted up his voice in a great shout for help. A thousand echoes rang in the pit, and following on them came the gypsy's crazy cackle.

'Do not fear, pretty darling. John's arms are soft bedding,' and he dragged him over the lip of stone beyond which the slope ran to the darkness.

Once again by a miracle his foot caught. This time it was only a snag of rock, but it had a rough edge to it, and by the mercy of God, the bonds at his ankles had been already frayed. The gypsy, who had him by the shoulders and arms, tugged frantically, and the friction of the stone's edge severed the last strands. Suddenly Alastair found his ankles free, and with a desperate scramble tried to rise. But his feet were cramped and numb and he could not find a stand. A tug from the gypsy brought him to the very edge of the abyss. But the incident had wakened hope, and once again he made the vault ring with a cry for help.

It was answered. The dim place suddenly blazed with light, and there was a sound of men's voices. For an instant the gypsy loosed his hold to stare, and then with a scream resumed his efforts. But in that instant Alastair's feet had found on the very brink a crack of stone, which enabled him to brace his legs and resist. The thing was trivial and he could not hold out long, but the purchase was sufficient to prevent that last heave from hurling him into the void.

The gypsy seemed suddenly to change his mind. He let the young man's shoulders drop, so that he fell huddled by the edge, plucked the long shagreen-handled knife from his belt and struck at his neck. But the blow never fell. For in the same fraction of time something bright quivered through the air, and struck deep in his throat. The man gurgled, then grew limp like a sack, and dropped back on the ground. Then with a feeble clawing at the air he rolled over the brink, struck the side twice, and dropped till the noise of his fall was lost in the moaning of the measureless deep.

Alastair lay sick and trembling, not daring to move, for his heels were overhanging the void. A hand seized him, a strong hand; and though he cried out in terror it dragged him up the slope and into the room. . . . The intense glare stabbed his eyes and he had the same choking nausea as when he had been felled in the hut. Then he came suddenly out of the fit of horror and saw himself on the settle, ready to weep from weariness, but sane again and master of himself.

A dark friendly face was looking down at him.

'You may travel the world's roads for a hundred years,' said the Spainneach, 'and never be nearer death. I warned you, Sir Sandy. You have been overlong in the South.'

FOURTEEN

Duchess Kitty on the Road

Five hours' sleep were not enough to rest his body, but they were all that his unquiet mind would permit. He woke to a sense of great weariness combined with a feverish impulse to drive himself to the last limits of his strength. His limbs were desperately stiff, and at his first attempt to rise he rolled over. A bed had been made for him in the attic of the farm, and the view from the window showed only the benty shoulder of a hill. Slowly the doings of the night came back to him; from the bowels of the earth he seemed to hear the mutterings of Journeyman John, and he crawled down the trap-ladder in a fret to escape from the place of horror.

In the kitchen the Spainneach was cooking eggs in a pan, smiling and crooning to himself as if the morning and the world were good. He put Alastair in a chair and fed him tenderly, beating up an egg in a cup with French brandy.

'Have that for your morning's draught, Sir Sandy,' he said. 'You are with your friends now, so let your anxieties sleep.'

'They cannot,' said the young man. 'I have lost weeks of precious time. My grief! but I have been the broken reed to lean on! And the Prince is in this very shire.'

'To-night he will lie in Derby. Lord George Murray has led a column in advance to Congleton and the Duke of Kingston has fled back to Lichfield. His Grace of Newcastle has sent offers to the Prince. All goes well, heart's darling. Your friends have given Cumberland the slip and are on the straight road to London.'

The news stirred his languid blood.

'But the West,' he cried. 'What news of the West – of Barrymore and Sir Watkin and Beaufort? There is the rub.'

And with the speaking of the words the whole story of the past weeks unrolled itself clear and he dropped his head into his hands and groaned. Then he staggered to his feet.

'There is a man reaches Brightwell this day. He must be seized – him and his papers.' Swiftly he told the story of Kyd. 'Let me lay hands on him and I will extort the truth though I have to roast him naked, and that truth the Prince must have before a man of us sleep. It is the magic key that will unlock St James's. Have you men to lend me?'

The Spainneach smiled. 'Last night they tracked you, as few men in England could, and they were here to overpower the rascaldom that held the door. Now they are scattered, but I have a call to pipe them back like curlews. The Spoonbills are at your back, Sir Sandy.'

'Then for God's sake let us be going,' Alastair cried. 'Have you a horse for me, for my legs are like broomshanks?'

'Two are saddled and waiting outbye. But first I have a little errand to fulfil, which the Master charged on me.'

From a shed he brought armfuls of hay and straw and piled them in a corner where the joists of the roof came low and the thatch could be reached by a man's hand. Into the dry mass he flung a smouldering sod from the fire. As Alastair, stiffly feeling his stirrups, passed between the dry-stone gateposts, he heard a roaring behind him, and, turning, saw flames licking the roof.

'Presently Journeyman John will lie bare to the heavens,' said the Spainneach, 'and the wayfaring man, though a fool, will understand. Brightwell is your goal, Sir Sandy? 'Tis fifteen moorland miles.'

'First let us go to the Sleeping Deer,' was the answer. 'I have a beard weeks old, and my costume is not my own. Please God, this day I am going into good society and have a high duty to perform, so I would be decently attired.'

The Spainneach laughed. 'Still your old self. You were always for the thing done in order. But for this Kyd of yours – he comes to Brightwell to-day, and may depart again, before you take order with him. It is desirable that he be detained?'

'By God, he shall never go,' cried Alastair.

'The Spoonbills do not fight, but they can make a hedge about a man, and they can bring us news of him.'

So at a grey cottage in the winding of a glen the Spainneach turned aside, telling Alastair that he would overtake him, and when he caught him up his face was content. 'Mr Kyd will not enter Brightwell unknown to us,' he said, 'and he will assuredly not leave it.'

The day had been bright in the morning, but ere they descended from the high moors to the wider valleys the wind had veered to the north, and a cold mist had blown up, which seemed a precursor of storm. Rain fell heavily and then cleared, leaving a windy sky patched with blue and ruffled with sleet blasts. The tonic weather did much to refresh Alastair's body, and to add fuel, if that were possible, to the fire in his brain. He knew that he was living and moving solely on the passion in his spirit, for his limbs were fit only for blankets and sleep. When his horse stumbled or leaned on the bit he realised that the strength had gone out of his arms. But his mind amazed him by its ardour of resolution, as if all the anxieties of the past week had been fused into one white-hot fury. . . . So far the Prince had not failed, and these forced marches which would place him between Cumberland and the capital were surely proof of undivided counsels. Perhaps he had news of the West after all. There was his own letter to Lochiel – but in that he had promised proofs at Derby, and this day the Prince would be in Derby and would not find him.

'You have seen His Highness?' he asked the Spainneach.

'At Manchester, for a brief minute, surrounded by white cockades.'

'How did he look?'

'Sad and reflective – like a man who has staked much against odds and does not greatly hope.'

It was the picture he had made in his own mind. But by Heaven he would change it, and bring a sparkle again to those eyes and the flush of hope to that noble brow. . . . For weeks no news could have reached the camp from the West, for Kyd would have passed it to Norreys and Norreys to one of the Whig Dukes in Nottinghamshire, and if the levies had marched from Wales the Government had had ample warning to intercept them. . . . Probably they had not started, for Kyd could no doubt counterfeit orders from the Prince. But the point was that they were there – men, armed men, and money – ready and eager for the field. His thoughts were drawing to a point now, and he realised what had been the vague fear that so long had tormented him. It was that the Prince would lose heart – nay, not he, but his Council, and instead of striking for St James's, fall back to a defensive war inside the Scottish Border. That way lay destruction, slow or speedy – with England unconverted and France uncommitted. But the bold road, the true road, would bring France and England to their side, and strike terror to the heart of their already perplexed enemy. Tower Hill or St James's! Would to God he was now by the Prince's side, instead of Lord George with his slow Atholl drawl, or the Secretary Murray, fussy and spluttering and chicken-hearted, or the Teagues, whose boldness was that of kerns and only made the others more cautious. At the thought of his Prince's haggard face he groaned aloud.

But, please God, it was still in his power to find the remedy, and by evening the peril might be past. He spurred his horse at the thought, and, since the beasts were fresh and they were now on the good turf of the vales, the miles flew fast, and they rode out of sleet showers into sun. To his surprise he found that his attitude to Kyd had changed. He loathed the man and longed to crush him, but it was as a vile creeping thing and not as a personal enemy. But against Sir John Norreys he felt a furious hatred. The thing was illogical – to hate a tool rather than the principal, the more as Norreys had done him no personal ill, while Kyd had connived at his death. But had the two been on the sward before him with drawn swords he could have left the Laird of Greyhouses to the Spainneach and taken the baronet for himself. Why? His heart inexorably gave the answer. The man was the husband of the russet lady; to her ears he had lied, and with his lies drawn a moan of pity from her gentle lips. For Sir John Norreys, Alastair reserved a peculiar vengeance. Kyd might fall to a file of the Prince's muskets, but Norreys must die before the cold point of his own steel. And then . . . ? Claudia would be a free woman – sorrowful, disillusioned, shamefaced, but still a child with the world before her, a white page on which love could yet write a happy tale.

They skirted the little hill on which Alastair had stood with Midwinter, and came to the high road and the door of the Sleeping Deer. There was now no need of back stairs, and Alastair, giving up his horse to an ostler, boldly entered the hall and made for the landlord's sanctum. But an elegant travelling trunk caught his eye, its leather bearing the blazon of a crowned heart, and by the fire a lackey in a red-and-blue livery was warming himself. A glance through the open door of the stable-yard revealed more red and blue, and a fine coach which three stable-boys were washing. The landlord was not in his room, but in the kitchen, superintending the slicing of hams, the plucking of pullets and the spicing of great tankards of ale. At the sight of Alastair he started, called another to take his place at the table and beckoned him out-of-doors.

'I'm joyful to see ye again, for I feared ye had come by foul play. That Scotch serving-man was here seeking ye more than once, and' – lowering his voice – 'word came from the Spoonbills, and you not here to answer, and me not knowing where in hell or Derbyshire ye had got to. Ye've happened on a rare to-do at the Sleeping Deer. Her right honourable Grace, the Duchess of Queensberry, has come here to lie the night, before journeying down into the West country. She has been at Chatsworth, but the gentles is all a-fleeing south now, for fear of the wild Highlandmen. Duke William himself escorted her here, and that pretty lad, his eldest son, the Lord Hartington, and dinner is ordered for three, and my wife's like to fire the roof with perplexity. Ye'll be for your old room, doubtless. It's been kept tidy against your return, and I'll see that a bite of dinner is sent up to ye, when Her Grace is served.'

The Spainneach had disappeared, so Alastair mounted to his attic and set about the long process of his toilet. His cramped fingers made a slow business of shaving, but at last his chin and cheeks were smooth, and the mirror showed a face he recognised, albeit a face hollow in the cheeks and dark about the eyes. As his dressing proceeded his self-respect stole back; the fresh-starched shirt, the well-ironed cravat, were an assurance that he had returned from savagery. By the time he had finished he felt his bodily health improved, and knew the rudiments of an appetite. The meal and the glass of brandy which the landlord brought him assisted his transformation, and he seemed to breathe again without a burden on his chest. He had bidden the landlord look out for the Spainneach, and meantime he had an errand to do on his own account; for it occurred to him that the arrival of the Duchess Kitty was the solution of one perplexity.

He walked through the store-closet to the landing above the staircase. At the half-opened door of the Brown Room stood a footman in the Queensberry colours, one who had been with his mistress at Cornbury and recognised Alastair. He bowed and let him pass; indeed he would have pushed the door wide for him had not the young man halted on the threshold. There were voices inside the room, and one of them had a familiar sound.

The sight which greeted his eyes made him shut the door firmly behind him. Duchess Kitty, still wearing the cloak of grey fur and the velvet mittens which had kept her warm in the coach, sat in the chair which Claudia had once sat in, one little foot on the hearth-stone, the other tapping impatiently on the hearth-rug. On a table lay the remains of a meal, and beside it, balancing himself with one large hand among the platters, stood Mr Samuel Johnson. It was not the Mr Johnson to whom he had bade farewell three weeks ago, but rather the distraught usher who had made the midnight raid on Cornbury. His dress was the extreme of shabbiness, his hair was in disorder, his rusty small clothes and coarse stockings were splashed with mud; and he seemed to be famished, too, for his cheeks were hollow, and for all his distress, he could not keep his eyes from straying towards the table.

'I beseech your Grace to remember your common woman-hood,' he was saying when Alastair's entrance diverted the Duchess's attention.

She recognised him, and a look which was almost alarm crossed her face.

'Here enters the first of the conquerors,' she cried, and swept him a curtsey. 'What is the latest news from the seat of war? My woman tells me that the Prince is already in Bedfordshire and that London is ablaze and King George fled to Holland. Your news, Captain Maclean?'

'I have none, madam. I have been no nearer the Prince's camp than I am at this moment.'

Her eyes opened wide. 'Faith, you have dallied long in the South. Have you been sick, or is Beaufort's conscience a tender plant? Or did you return to Cornbury?' Her face had grown stern.

'I left Cornbury on the day you remember, and I have not since seen my lord, your brother.'

'That is well,' she said, with an air of relief. 'I ask no further questions lest they embarrass you. But you are come opportunely, for you can give me counsel. This gentleman,' and she turned to Johnson, 'has forced his company upon me, and, when you arrived, had embarked upon a monstrous tale. He bespeaks my pity, so I have composed myself to listen.'

'The gentleman and I are acquainted, and I can vouch for his honesty. Nay, madam, I have a fancy that his errand is also mine.'

She looked curiously from one to the other, as Johnson, rolling his head like a marionette, seized Alastair's hand. 'It is the mercy of God, sir, that you have returned,' the tutor cried. 'I have missed you sorely, for that house of Brightwell is no better than a prison. Its master is aged and bedridden and demented, and it is governed by two malevolent spinsters. Brightwell! Bridewell is its true name. I myself have eaten little and slept bare, but that matters nothing. It is my poor lady I grieve for. 'Tis true, she has her husband, but he is little at home, and is

much engrossed with affairs. Soon, too, he will ride south with
his Prince, and Miss Claudia cannot travel with him nor can she
be left behind in that ill-omened den. She must have a woman to
befriend her in these rough days, and conduct her to Chastlecote or Weston, but she has few female friends of her rank and I
knew not where to turn. But to-day, walking on the high road, I
saw an equipage and learned that it was Her Grace travelling
south, and that she would lie at this inn. So I ran hither like a
Covent-garden porter, and have been admitted to her presence,
though my appearance is not so polite as I could have desired.'
He bowed to the Duchess, and in his clumsiness swept her
travelling-mask from the table to the floor.

She looked at him for a little without speaking, and then fixed
her eyes on Alastair, those large childlike eyes which were rarely
without a spark of impish humour.

'Your friend,' she said, 'has already opened his tale to me, but
his manner of telling it is not of the clearest. Since you say that
his errand may be yours, I pray you expound it. But be seated,
gentlemen both. I have already a crick in my neck from looking
up to such enormities.'

Mr Johnson, as if glad of the permission, dropped into a
chair, but Alastair remained standing. His legs no longer felt
crazy, but they were amazingly stiff, and once in a chair he
distrusted his ability to rise. He stood at the opposite side of the
hearth to the Duchess, looking down on the elfin figure, as
pretty as porcelain in the glow of firelight.

'I do not ask your politics,' he said, 'which I take to be your
husband's. But you are an honourable lady, by the consent of all,
and, I can add of my own knowledge, a kind one. To you a traitor
must be doubly repulsive.'

Her answer was what Claudia Norreys's had been in that very
room.

'You judge rightly, sir. If I thought I could betray a friend or a
cause I should hang myself forthwith to avert the calamity.'

Alastair bowed. 'Mr Johnson has told you of this girl, my lady
Norreys. She is own sister to you, tender and brave and

infinitely faithful. Her husband is otherwise. Her husband is a black traitor, but she does not know it.'

Mr Johnson cried out. 'I had thought better of him, sir. Have you got new evidence?'

'I have full evidence. News of desperate import is sent to him here by another in the South, that other being one of the foremost agents of our Cause. That news should go forthwith to the Prince's camp. It goes forthwith to the enemy's.'

'For what reward?' the Duchess asked.

'For that reward which is usual to traitors in times of civil strife. They induce honest but weak-kneed souls to take a bold step, and then betray them to the Government, receiving a share of the fines and penalties that ensue. Great fortunes have been built that way.'

'But if the rebellion wins?'

'Then they are lost, unless indeed they are skilful enough to make provision with both sides and to bury whichever of the two villainies is unprofitable.'

'He is a young man,' she said. 'He shows a shocking precocity in guile. And the poor child his wife dreams nothing of this?'

'Ah, madam,' cried Johnson. 'She is the very soul and flower of loyalty. If she suspected but a tithe of it, her heart would break.'

'His precocity is remarkable,' said Alastair, 'but he is not the principal in the business. The principal is that other I have mentioned who is in the very centre of the Prince's counsels.'

She put her hands to her ears. 'Do not tell me,' she cried. 'I will be burdened with no secrets that do not concern me. I take it that this other has not a wife whom you would have me befriend.'

'Nevertheless I fear that I must outrage your ears, madam. This other is known to you – closely allied with you.'

Her eyes were suddenly bright with anxiety.

'His name is Mr Nicholas Kyd.'

Her face showed relief; also incredulity.

'You are certain? You have proof?'

'I have long been certain. Before night I will have full proof.'

She fell into a muse. 'Kyd – the bluff honest *bon enfant*! The man of the sad old songs and ready pathos, who almost makes a Jacobite of me – Kyd to play the rogue! Faith, His Grace had better look into his accounts. What do you want of me, Captain Maclean?'

'Two things, madam. My purpose is to do justice on rogues, but justice is a cruel thing, and I would spare the lady. I want you to carry her southward with you, and leave her at Chastlecote or Weston, which you please, or carry her to Amesbury. She shall never know her husband's infamy – only that he has gone to the Prince, and when he does not return will think him honourably dead.'

The Duchess nodded. 'And the other?'

'I beg your presence when Mr Kyd is confounded. He is on his way to Brightwell and this night will sleep there. His errand in the West is now done, and to-morrow, as I read it, he descends into Nottinghamshire to the Government headquarters to receive his reward. Therefore he will have papers with him, and in those papers I look for my proof. If they fail, I have other sources.'

'And if he is found guilty, what punishment?'

Alastair shrugged his shoulders. 'That is not for me. Both he and Norreys go bound to the Prince.'

She brooded with her chin on her hand. Then she stood up, laughing.

'I consent. 'Twill be better than a play. But how will you set the stage?'

'I go to Brightwell presently, and shall force admission. My lady Norreys will keep her chamber, while in another part of the house we deal with grimmer business. I nominate you of our court of justice. See, we will fix an hour. Order your coach for six, and you will be at Brightwell by seven. By that time the house will be ours, and we shall be waiting to receive you. You will bring Mr Johnson with you, and after that you can comfort the lady.'

She nodded. 'I will come masked,' said she, 'and I do swear that I will not fail you or betray you – by the graves of Durrisdeer I swear it, the ancient Douglas oath. Have you men enough? I can lend you two stout fellows.'

'Your Grace has forgotten that you are a Whig,' said Alastair, laughing.

'I have forgotten all save that I am trysted to a merry evening,' she cried.

When Alastair returned to his attic he found the Spainneach.

'Your Kyd is nearing port,' he said. 'I have word that he slept at Blakeley and dined early at Little Laning. In two hours or less he will be at Brightwell.'

'And the Spoonbills?'

'Await us there. Haste you, Sir Sandy, if you would arrive before your guest.'

FIFTEEN

Bids Farewell to a Scots Laird

The night was mild and dark, and the high road which the two men followed was defined only by the faint glimmer of the rain-pools that lay in every rut. The smell of wet earth was in their nostrils, and the noise of brimming streams in their ears, and to Alastair, with a sword at his side again, the world was trans-formed. All might yet be saved for the Cause, and in twelve hours he should see the Prince; the thought comforted him, but it was not the main tenant of his mind. For a woman's face had lodged there like an obsession in sleep; he saw Claudia's eyes change from laughter to tragedy and back again to laughter, he heard her tongue stumble musically among greetings, he fancied he saw – nay, it was beyond doubt – her face some day light up for him, as a girl's lights up for her lover. . . . Across the pleasant dream passed the shadow of a high coat-collar and a long sharp nose. He shivered, remembering the ugly business before him.

'Where are the Spoonbills?' he asked.

'By now they will be close around Brightwell, ready to run to my whistle.'

'Are they armed?'

'With staves only. We are men of peace.'

'Suppose Norreys has a troop of Kingston's Horse for garri-son. Or even that he and Kyd and a servant or two have pistols. We are too evenly matched to administer justice in comfort.'

'Then we must use our wits,' was the answer. 'But a file or two of your Highland muskets would not be unwelcome.'

The wish was fulfilled even as it was uttered. As they swung round a corner of road, half a mile from Brightwell gates, they

had to rein in their horses hard to avoid a collision with a body of
mounted men. These were halted in a cluster, while by the light
of a lantern their leader made shift to examine a scrap of paper.
The sudden irruption set all the beasts plunging, and the lantern
went out in the confusion, but not before Alastair had caught
sight of him who had held it.

'God's mercy!' he cried. 'Charles Hay! Is it Tinnis himself?'

'You have my name,' a voice answered, 'and a tongue I have
heard before.'

Alastair laughed happily. 'Indeed you have heard it before, Mr
Charlie. In quarters and on parade, and at many a merry supper
in the Rue Margot. Your superior officer has a claim upon you.'

The lantern, being now relit, revealed a tall young man with
twenty troopers at his back, most of them large raw lads who
were not long from the plough tail. The leader's face was
flushed with pleasure. 'Where in God's name have you been
lurking, my dear sir?' he cried. 'I have looked for you at every
bivouac, for I longed to clap eyes again on a soldier of Lee's, after
so much undisciplined rabble.'

'The story will keep, Charles, and meantime I claim a service.
You are on patrol?'

'A patrol of Elcho's ordered to feel our way down this valley
and report at Derby town by breakfast. 'Tis a cursed difficult
affair riding these hills when there is no moon.'

'You have time and to spare before morn. Turn aside with me
here for a matter of two hours. You shall have a good supper to
cheer you, and will do your Prince a distinguished service. I
pledge my word for it.'

'Lead on,' said Mr Hay. 'I am back in Lee's again, and take my
orders from Captain Maclean.'

He cried to his men, and the troop wheeled behind him, where
he rode with Alastair and the Spainneach. 'Now tell me the ploy,'
he said. 'It should be a high matter to keep you away from Derby
this night, where they say the fountains are to run claret.'

'We go to do justice on a traitor,' said Alastair, and told him
the main lines of the story. Mr Hay whistled long and loud.

'You want us to escort the gentleman to Beelzebub's bosom,' he asked.

'I want you to escort him to the Prince.'

'Not the slightest use, I do assure you. His Highness has a singular passion for gentry of that persuasion. Yesterday Lord George's force brought in a black-hearted miscreant, by the name of Weir, caught red-handed no less, and a fellow we had been longing for months to get our irons on. Instead of a two or a bullet he gets a hand-shake from His Highness, and is bowed out of the camp with "Erring brother, go and sin no more." Too much damned magnanimity, say I, and it's not like we'll get much of it back from Cumberland. Take my advice, and hang him from the nearest oak, and then apologise to His Highness for being in too much of a loyal hurry.'

The gates of Brightwell to Alastair's surprise stood open, and in the faint light from a shuttered window of the lodge it seemed as if there had been much traffic.

'Where are your Spoonbills?' he asked the Spainneach.

'I do not know. In furze bush and broom bush and hazel thicket. But when I whistle, in ten seconds they will be at the door of Brightwell.'

The troopers were left in the dark of the paved court, with certain instructions. Accompanied by the Spainneach, Mr Hay and Mr Hay's troop sergeant, Alastair rode forward to the great door, and pulled the massive bell-rope. A tinkle sounded inside at an immense distance, and almost at the same moment the door was opened. There was a light within which revealed the ancient butler.

'We have business with Sir John Norreys.'

'Sir John awaits you,' said the man. 'But are there not others with you, sir?'

So the conspirators had summoned their friends, doubtless a troop of Kingston's Horse from down the water. A thought struck him.

'We are also appointed to meet a Scotch gentleman, Mr Kyd,' he said.

'Mr Kyd arrived some minutes ago,' was the answer, 'and is now repairing his toilet after his journey. Will you be pleased to enter?'

Alastair spoke in French to Mr Hay, who gave an order to his troop sergeant, who took the horses and fell back; and the three men passed through the outer portals into the gaunt gloomy hall, in which Alastair had shivered on his first visit. Tonight there was a change. A huge fire of logs roared up the chimney, and from a door ajar came a glimpse of firelight in another room, and the corner of a laden table. Miserly Brightwell was holding revel that night.

Hay flung himself on a settle and toasted his boots.

'Comfort,' he cried, 'after bleak and miry moors, and I have a glimpse of the supper you promised me. Sim Linton will hold the fort against any yokels on cart-horses that try to interrupt us. But what has become of your swarthy friend?'

The Spainneach had disappeared, and the two were alone. Kyd has his papers here, thought Alastair, and it were well to make certain of them first. Evidence should be collected before the court sat. It would seem that the staging of the play was in other hands than his, and what had been proposed as a feast would by an irony of destiny be turned into mourning. . . . And then he realised with a shock that Claudia was beneath this roof, an unwitting, unsuspecting dove in a nest of ravens. . . . But in a little the Duchess Kitty would be with her and she would be safe in Oxfordshire, and some day he would journey there. . . .

A figure was standing at the foot of the great staircase, a splendid figure, with a nobly laced coat and such ruffles as were rarely seen outside St James's. It wore a sword, but its carriage was not that of a soldier. It advanced into the circle of the firelight, and, seeing it was observed, it bowed and smiled graciously. Its face was that of a young man, with a long sharp nose.

'I bid you welcome, gentlemen,' it began, and then its eyes rested on Alastair. An instant and extreme terror flooded its face. It stopped abruptly, stumbled a step and then turned and ran.

Alastair was after the man like an arrow, but his feet slipped on the stone floor, and ere he had recovered himself Norreys had disappeared in the corridor which led to the back regions of the house. It was in gloom, but a lamp burned at the far end, and to this Alastair directed himself. But the place was a *cul-de-sac*, and he had to turn back and find a side-passage. The first led him into cellars, the second into the kitchen, where there seemed to be a strange to-do, but no sign of Norreys. At last he found the way to the back-yard, and rushed through an open door into a storm of rain. Surely the Spoonbills must have prevented the man's escape. But the Spoonbills had been nodding on that side of the house, for it was certain that Norreys had gone. No doubt he had kept a horse always ready saddled, and the sound of hooves could be heard growing faint on the turf of the park. Hatless and cloakless, Sir John had fled to his Whig friends in Nottinghamshire to claim reward and sanctuary.

Alastair's first impulse was there and then to ride the man down, with Hay's troopers and the Spoonbills alike on his trail. His hatred of him had flared up furiously, when the mean face in the firelight had broken in on his thoughts of Claudia. The fellow must be brought to justice, or the castle of fancy he had been building would tumble. But it was clear that Kyd must first be dealt with, and, bitterly unwilling, he allowed his inclinations to give place to his duty.

Kyd's papers! The thought struck him that Norreys might have carried them off, and sent him hurrying along the passages to the hall, where Mr Hay was still basking like a cat in the warmth. There, too, stood the Spainneach, looking like a panther in his lean dark shadowy grace.

'Mr Kyd is in his chamber, cleansing himself of the stains of travel and humming merrily. I mistrust the servants, Sir Sandy, so I have replaced them by our own folk. Where are the said servants, you ask? Shut up in various corners, very scared and docile. Likewise I have discovered Mr Kyd's travelling-bag. It is in strange wardenship. Come and see.'

The man, stepping lightly, led the way up a broad shallow staircase, to a room of which he noiselessly opened the door. The hospitable warmth downstairs had not penetrated to that cold chamber, for the air of it was like a tomb. On a table stood a saddlebag from which the contents had been spilled, and over these contents hung the two grey women whom Alastair had seen on his earlier visit. They caressed the papers as if they were misers fumbling banknotes, one lean and hawk-beaked, the other of a dropsical fatness.

'Sir Robert Leatham – fifty men and five hundred pounds – good pickings in that, sister. That makes the roll of Hereford complete. The fines will not be less than half a million pounds, and at two pounds per centum that is a sum of ten thousand – half to cousin John and half to him we know of. . . .'

The other was fingering the rings on a tally-stick.

'He favours you, Caroline, and between you there will be a rare fortune. Cousin Johnnie has promised me Brightwell, when our father leaves us, and I look to you to assist the conveyance. That is my price, remember. If you play me false, I will scratch your eyes out and curse him till he rots. Ay, and I will tell on him to that puling miss in the Green Chamber. . . . Does Johnnie sup to-night?'

'Ay, and departs early, for he is bound for the Duke of Richmond, but he we know of stays till the Duke comes hither. He's the great man, sister, and Johnnie but a boy. A clever dutiful boy, to be sure, with an old head on his young shoulders. I'll wager that when they both come to die there will be little difference between the fortunes of Sir John Norreys of Weston and Sir Robert Grosvenor of Eaton. The pity of it that he has set his heart on that baby-faced wench.'

'She brought him a fine estate, Caroline.'

'Pish! He thinks less of the good acres than her pink cheeks. I could scratch them till the bones were bare. . . . Read the Shropshire roll again, sister. How deep is Henry Talbot?'

The two witches, obscene, malevolent, furtive, bent over the papers as over a bubbling cauldron. Alastair stepped forward, choking down a strong disgust.

'I must beg your permission to remove these papers, mesdames. They are required for the conference to which Mr Kyd will presently descend.'

The women huddled together, stretching each an arm over the papers.

'Mr Kyd gave them into our charge,' they said in one voice.

'He releases you from that charge,' said Alastair. 'Permit me, madam,' and he laid a hand on the saddle-bag and began to refill it.

The women would have resisted had not the Spainneach stepped behind them and murmured something into the lean one's ear. Whatever it was, it caused her to draw back her protecting arm and bid her sister do likewise. Alastair bundled the papers into the bag, and left the room followed by two pairs of wolfish eyes. The Spainneach locked the door, and left the key on the outside. 'Best keep these wild cats fast in their cave,' he observed. 'There might have been a tussle over that treasure-trove, had I not remembered something I had heard of those grey ones long ago. Now I go to find the servant Edom.'

'When Kyd leaves his room see that the hall is empty. I will await him in the dining-room. When I ring, do you and Hay enter and join us. Make Edom wait at the meal with the servants you have provided.'

'It is a noble meal which is now cooking,' said the Spainneach. 'Even the miserly will spend themselves on a high occasion. It is the habit of Madame Norreys to sup in her room, and that room is at the far end of the house from us. She will not be disturbed if we grow merry.'

Alastair sat himself by the fire in the great vaulted dining-room and tore open the saddle-bag. He ran hastily through the papers, for he was looking for what he knew to be there, and it did not take him long to discard the irrelevant. Once or twice, as he found what he hoped and yet feared to find, an exclamation was wrung from him. He selected several documents and placed them in his breast, and re-read others with set lips and a knotted forehead. Then he looked into the fire and mused. . . .

Through the open door came the sound of a step on the paved floor of the hall, a heavy, assured, leisurely step. The young man kicked the saddle-bag under the table and stood erect by the hearth with an odd smile on his face. Grimness had left it, and a wry courtesy remained.

The Laird of Greyhouses was a gallant sight. Gone were the splashed boots and muddy breeches, and all that might recall the wintry roads. He was dressed as on that night at Cornbury when he had kept Sir Christopher Lacy company – in flowered waistcoat, and plum-coloured coat, and canary stockings, and buckled shoes that shone like well-water. He was humming a little tune as he entered, his eye bright and content, his heavy figure tautened and refined by hard travelling, his shapely face rosy as a winter's eve. It was the entrance of a great man to a company where he expects to be acclaimed, for there was self-consciousness in the primness of his mouth. He lifted his genial eyes and saw Alastair.

The man was a superb actor, for though Alastair was watching him like a hawk he could see no start of surprise, no flicker of disappointment or fear.

'Captain Maclean, upon my soul!' he cried. 'And who would have expected it? Man, I did not know you were acquaint here. But 'tis a joyful meeting, my dear sir, and I'm *felix opportunitate coenae* the day.' He held out a cordial hand, which the young man left unnoticed.

'I am happy to repay hospitality,' he said. 'You welcomed me some weeks back at a wayside inn, and it is my turn now to provide the entertainment. Let us sit down to supper, Mr Kyd. There are other guests,' and he stretched a hand to the bell-rope.

'I confess I was expecting a wheen more,' said Mr Kyd, and there was just the faintest quiver of his eyelids.

'Sir John Norreys begged to be excused. He was summoned into Nottinghamshire somewhat suddenly – so suddenly that I fear he will take a catarrh, for he has forgotten his hat and cloak. The ladies of the house are detained in their chamber, and the master, as we know, has been bed-ridden these many years. But there are others to take their place.' Again he stretched out his hand, but Kyd interrupted him.

'What is the meaning of it?' he asked in a low voice. 'What does this pleasantry betoken, Captain Maclean?'

'It betokens that *Menelaus* has come to Phaeacia to see his old crony *Alcinous*. The two will have much to say to each other, but they will regret that *Achilles* is not here to make it a three-handed crack.'

The mention of *Achilles* seemed to perturb the other. He narrowed his eyes, and into them came the shadow of that look which Alastair had surprised on the evening at the inn. Then he stepped to the table, filled a glass of claret and drank it off, while Alastair rang the bell.

The Spainneach entered with Hay on his heels. Kyd regarded them with puzzled eyes, as if striving to recapture a memory.

'I present to you Mr Charles Hay of Tinnis,' said Alastair, 'who commands a troop in His Highness's Lowland Horse. The other gentleman is of the Nameless Clan. Sit you down, sirs.'

Kyd obeyed, but his eyes were not on the food and wine, for he was thinking hard. He had a stout heart and had often faced peril, so he forced his mind to consider the situation's possibilities, when a weaker man would have been a-flutter. Would the horsemen he had asked for from Kingston arrive in time? – that was the main point. Beyond doubt they would, and meantime he would confuse this Highland jackanapes, who seemed to have stumbled on some damaging truths. But the appearance of Alastair, whom he had utterly written off from his list of obstacles, worried him in spite of all his robust philosophy. He made pretence to eat, but he only crumbled his bread and toyed with his meat, though he drank wine thirstily. The servants who moved about the room, too, perturbed him. There was his own man Edom acting as butler, but the others were strange folk, outlandishly dressed and with dark secret faces, and one, a trooper of Hay's, had a belt with pistols round his middle and that at his shoulder which might be a white cockade.

Alastair read his thoughts.

'I fear, sir, that your entertainment is not what you hoped, but I have done my best to provide a recompense. Since his Grace of Kingston could not send a garrison, I have brought Mr Hay's Scots. Since Sir John Norreys is summoned elsewhere, I have provided Mr Hay in his stead. And since the ladies upstairs cannot honour us, I have bidden another lady, who will shortly arrive.'

The news seemed to move Kyd to action. Hope from Kingston's horse was over, and the only chance lay in carrying matters with a high hand, and bluffing his opponent who must be largely in the dark. His plans had been too deep-laid to be discovered by a casual moss-trooper.

'Most considerate, I'm sure,' he said. 'But let's have an end of these riddles. I come here to a well-kenned house, expecting to meet an old friend, and find him mysteriously departed, and you in his place talking like an oracle. I venture to observe that it's strange conduct between gentlemen of the same nation. What's the meaning of it, sir?' He pushed back his chair, and looked squarely at the young man.

'The meaning of it is that Judas has come to judgment.'

Kyd laughed, with an excellent semblance of mirth, and indeed he felt relieved. This was a mere random general charge, for which he could readily invent a defence. 'Oh, sits the wind that airt? It's most extraordinary the way we of the honest party harbour suspicions. I've done it myself many's the time. Weel-a-weel, if I've to thole my assize, so be it. I've a quiet conscience and a good answer to any charge. But who is to sit in judgment?'

The man's composure was restored. He filled himself a glass of claret, held it to the light, and savoured its bouquet before he sipped.

As if in answer to his question the door opened to admit two new-comers. One was a small lady, with a black silk mask from her brow to her lips, so that no part of her face was visible. A velvet hood covered her hair, and her dress was hidden from sight by a long travelling-robe of fur. Behind her shambled a tall man, whose big hands strayed nervously to his dusty cravat and the threadbare lapels of his coat.

'Here is your judge,' said Alastair. 'Madam, will you sit in the seat of justice?'

He pulled forward a high-backed Restoration chair, and placed before it a footstool. Solemnly like a cardinal in conclave the little lady seated herself.

'Who is the prisoner?' she asked. 'And what bill does the Prince's attorney present against him?'

The servants had moved to the back of the room, and stood in the shadow like guards at attention. By a strange chance the place seemed to have borrowed the similitude of a court – Kyd at one end of a table with the guards behind him, Mr Johnson like a justice's clerk sprawling beside the lady's chair.

'His name, madam,' said Alastair, 'is Nicholas Kyd of Grey-houses in the Merse, the principle doer of his Grace of Queensberry, and likewise a noted Jacobite and a member of His Highness's Council.'

'And the charge?'

'That this Nicholas Kyd has for many months betrayed the secrets of his master, and while professing to work for the Cause has striven to defeat it by withholding vital information. Further, that the same Nicholas Kyd has sought for his own gain to bring about the ruin of divers honest gentlemen, by inducing them to pledge their support to His Highness and then handing such pledges to King George's Government.'

'Heard you ever such havers?' said Kyd boisterously. This was what he had hoped for, a wild general accusation, the same he had heard brought against Balhaldy and Traquair and a dozen others, but never substantiated. 'You'll have a difficulty in proving your case, Mr Attorney.'

Then Alastair told his tale from that hour when in the ale-house he met Kyd. He told of Kyd's advice to go by Flambury and his troubles there, of the message given him in error, of

Edom and his mission, of Sir John Norreys and his suspected
doings, of his own kidnapping and imprisonment and the
confession of Ben the Gypsy in the moorland farm.

'Your proofs, sir,' said the judge.

'They are here,' he replied, and drew from his breast a sheaf
of papers. 'There, madam, is the full account of the Duke of
Beaufort's purpose in Wales, written out and inscribed to the
Duke of Kingston, for transmission to Mr Pelham. There you
have another document narrating conversations with the trusting Jacobites of the Marches. There you have a letter from
Beaufort to his Prince, which would appear from its super-
scription to be directed afresh to the Duke of Cumberland.'

The lady looked at the papers shown her, knitted her brows
and returned them. She glanced at Kyd, whose face was set in a
mask which he strove to make impassive.

'Proceed with your second and graver charge, sir,' she said.

Alastair told of his conversation with General Oglethorpe and
of Kyd's visit to the General's room at midnight. He told of the two
hags upstairs who were in partnership. 'And for proof,' he cried,
'here are the rolls of three counties taken from the man's saddlebags, giving a list of the gentlemen who are liable to fines for their
political action, and noting the shares which will come to each of
the conspirators. Do you require further evidence, madam?'

The room had grown very still, and no one of the company
stirred, till Kyd brought his fist down on the table. His face had
whitened.

'What says the prisoner?' the lady asked.

'Lies, madam, devilish lies – and these papers a common
forgery. Some enemy – and God knows I have many – has put
them in my baggage.'

'You are acquainted with the handwriting, madam?' Alastair
asked.

She studied the papers again. 'I have seen it a thousand times.
It is a well-formed and capable style, clerkly and yet gentleman-
like. Nay, there can be no doubt. His hand wrote these lists and
superscriptions.'

Kyd's face from pallor flushed scarlet. 'God's curse, but am I to have my fame ruined by a play-acting wench! What daftness is this? What knows this hussy of my hand of write?'

'Do you deny the authorship, sir?' Alastair asked.

The man had lost his temper. 'I deny and affirm nothing before a court that has no sort of competence. I will answer to the Prince, when he calls for an answer, and I can promise a certain gentleman his kail through the reek on that day.'

'I should be happy to be proved in error. But if the papers should happen to be genuine you will admit, sir, that they bear an ugly complexion.'

'I'll admit nothing except that you're a bonny friend to lippen so readily to a clumsy fabrication. Ay, and you've the damned insolence to bring in a baggage from the roads to testify to my hand of write. You'll have to answer to me for that, my man.'

There was a low laugh from the mask. He had not recognised her, partly because of his discomposure and fear and partly because he had never dreamed of her presence in that country-side. When, therefore, she plucked the silk from her face and looked sternly down on him, he seemed suddenly to collapse like a pricked bladder. His stiff jaw dropped, his eyes stared, he made as if to speak and only stammered.

'Your face condemns you, sir,' she said gravely. 'I have seen your writing too often to mistake it, and I have lived long enough in the world to recognise the sudden confusion of crime in a man's eyes. I condemn you, sir, as guilty on both charges, and fouler and shamefuller were never proven.'

Kyd's defence was broken; but there was a resolute impudence in the man which made him still show fight. He looked obstinately at the others, and attempted a laugh; then at the Duchess, with an effrontery as of a fellow-conspirator.

'It seems we're both in an ugly place,' he said. 'You ken my secret, madam, which I had meant to impart to you when an occasion offered. Here's the two of us honest folks at the mercy of the wild Jacobites and wishing sore that the Duke of Kingston would make better speed up the water.'

'That is not my wish,' she said, with stony eyes.

It was those eyes which finally unnerved him.

'But, madam,' he cried, 'your Grace – you are of the Government party, the party I have served – I have letters from Mr Pelham . . . you winna suffer the rebels to take vengeance on me for loyalty to King George.'

'I am a Whig,' said she, 'and will not condemn you for political conduct, base though I must judge it. The Prince's Attorney must hale you to another court. You will take him to your master –' this to Alastair – 'and leave him to that tribunal.'

'With your assent, madam, I do not ask for judgment on the first charge, and I do not propose that he should go to the Prince. The penalty for his treason is death, and I am unwilling to saddle His Highness before he has won his throne with the duty of putting an end to a rascal.'

She nodded. 'I think you are wise, sir. But the second charge is the more heinous, for it offends not against the law of men's honour, but the law of human kindness and the law of God. There I find him the chief of sinners. What penalty do you ask for?'

'I ask that your Grace pronounce sentence of perpetual exile.'

'But where – and how?'

'It matters not, so long as it is forth of Britain.'

'But you cannot be eternally watching the ports.'

'Nay, but he will not come back. There is a brotherhood which has already aided me – your Grace knows nothing of them, but they know everything of your Grace. It is the brotherhood of Old England, and is sure as the judgment of God. To that charge we will commit him. They will see him forth of England, and they will make certain that he does not return.'

Kyd's face had lightened, as if he saw a prospect of avoiding the full rigours of the sentence. The Duchess marked it and frowned, but he misread her mood, which he thought one of displeasure at Alastair's plan. He adopted an air of humble candour.

'Hear me, your Grace,' he implored. 'It's a queer story mine, but a juster than you think. I'm not claiming to be a perfect character, and I'm not denying that I take a canny bit profit when I find it, like an eident body. The honest truth is that I don't care a plack for politics one side or the other, and it's nothing to me which king sits on the throne. My job's to be a trusty servant of His Grace, and no man can say that I'm not zealous in that cause. Ay, and there's another cause I'm sworn to, and that's Scotland. I'm like auld Lockhart o' Carnwath – my heart can hold just the one land at a time. I call God Almighty to witness that I never did ill to a kindly Scot, and if I've laboured to put a spoke in the Chevalier's coach-wheels, it's because him and his wild caterans are like to play hell with my puir auld country. Show me what is best for Scotland, and Nicholas Kyd will spend his last bodle and shed his last drop of blood to compass it.'

There was an odd earnestness, even a note of honesty, in the man's appeal, but it found no acceptance. The lady shivered.

'If you can get him abroad, sir,' she addressed Alastair, and her voice was hard as granite, 'I think I can promise you that he will not return. My arm is a weak woman's, but it strikes far. His services will be soon forgotten by Mr Pelham, but Kitty of Queensberry does not forget his offences. Though I live for fifty years more, I will make it my constant business to keep the rogue in exile.'

The man seemed to meditate. Doubtless he reflected that even the malice of a great lady could not keep him for ever out of the country. She might die, or her husband lose his power, and politics would be politics to a Whig Government. One of those who looked on divined his thoughts, for a soft voice spoke.

'I do not think that Greyhouses will ever again be a pleasant habitation for the gentleman. Has he forgotten the case of the Laird of Champertoun?'

Kyd started violently.

'Or the goodman of Heriotside?' The voice was gentle and soothing, but it seemed to wake acute terror in one hearer.

'Men die and their memories, but when all of us are dust the Bog-blitters will still cry on Lammermuir. I think that Mr Kyd has heard them before at Greyhouses. He will not desire to hear them again.'

The Spainneach had risen and stood beside Kyd, and from the back of the room two of the Spoonbills advanced like guardian shadows. The big man in the rich clothes had shrunk to a shapeless bundle in the chair, his face grey and his eyes hot and tragic. 'Not that,' he cried, 'don't banish me from my native land. I'll go anywhere you please in the bounds o'Scotland – to St Kilda, like Lady Grange, or to the wildest Hielands, but let me feel that I'm in my own country. I tell you my heart's buried aneath Scots heather. I'll die if you twine the Lammermuirs and me. Anything you like, my lady, but let me bide at home.'

He found only cold eyes and silence. Then he seemed to brace himself to self-command. His face was turned to the Duchess, and he sat up in his chair, settled his cravat, and with a shaking hand poured himself a glass of wine. His air was now ingratiating and sentimental, and he wiped a tear from his eye.

'*Nos patriae fines et dulcia liquimus arva*,' he said. 'I'll have to comfort myself with philosophy, for man's life is more howes than heights. Heigho, but I'll miss Scotland. I'm like the old ballad:

> "Happy the craw
> That biggs i' the Totten Shaw
> And drinks o' the Water of Dye,
> For nae mair may I." '

The words, the tone, the broken air gave to Alastair a moment of compunction. But in Mr Johnson they roused another feeling. Half raising himself from his chair, he shook his fist at the speaker.

'Sir,' he cried, 'you are worse than a rogue, you are a canting rogue. You would have driven twenty honest men into unmerited exile by your infamies and had no pity on them, but you crave pity for yourself when you are justly banished. I have sympathy with many kinds of rascal, but none with yours. Your crimes are the greater because you pretend to sensibility. With you, sir, patriotism is the last refuge of the scoundrel.'

Alastair picked the saddle-bag from below the table, and emptied its remaining contents in the fire.

'Except what I keep for His Highness's eye, let ashes be the fate of this treason. There is your baggage, sir. You may want it on your long journey.'

The hand that lifted it was Edom's.

'I'll get the other pockmantie ready, sir,' he said to Kyd in the grave tone of a good servant. 'Your horse is no just in the best fettle for the road, but I ride lichter nor you, and ye can take mine.'

'But you do not propose to continue in his service?' Alastair cried in astonishment. 'See, man, you have saved my life, and I will take charge of your fortunes.'

Edom halted at the door. 'I thank ye, sir, for your guidwill. But I was born at Greyhouses, and my faither and his faither afore him served the family. It's no a sma' thing like poalitics that'll gar a Kyd and a Lowrie take different roads.'

SIXTEEN

Bids Farewell to an English Lady

Duchess Kitty descended from her chair of justice and came to the fireside, where she let her furs slip from her and stood, a figure of white porcelain, warming her feet at the blaze.

'There was some word of a lady,' she said.

Johnson, too, had risen, and though the man's cheeks were gaunt with hunger he had no eye for the food on the table. His mind seemed to be in travail with difficult thoughts.

'The lady, madam,' he groaned. 'She is in her chamber, unsuspecting. Her husband should be here also. He may enter at any moment.'

'He has fled,' said Alastair. 'Fled, as I take it, to the Whig Dukes for his reward. The man is revealed at last, and his wife must disown him or be tainted by his guilt.'

The news seemed to affect Johnson painfully. He cast himself into a chair, which creaked under his weight, and covered his eyes with his hands.

'Why in God's name did you suffer it?' he asked fiercely of Alastair. 'I had another plan. . . . I would have brought the dog to repentance.'

'I will yet bring him to justice,' said Alastair grimly. 'I have a forewarning of it, and to-morrow or next week or next year he will stand up before my sword.'

The words gave no comfort to Johnson. He rolled his melancholy eyes and groaned again. ' 'Twill break her heart,' he lamented. 'She will know of his infamy – it cannot be hid from her. . . . Oh, why, why!'

Alastair spoke to the Duchess. 'You will tell Lady Norreys that her husband has gone to the Prince. No more. I will make certain that he does not return to Weston, though I have to drag him with my own hands out of Cumberland's closet. . . . Forgive me, madam, if I appear to command, but this is a tangled matter. Pray take her with you to Amesbury, and keep her out of Oxfordshire, till I send word that it is safe. She must not go to Weston or Chastlecote till she has the news of his death. I will contrive that he die, and 'tis for you to contrive that she thinks his death a hero's.'

The Duchess mused. 'You are a singular pair of gentlemen, and wondrous tender to the child's feelings. I can see you are both in love with her. Prithee lead me at once to this enchainer of hearts.'

The Spainneach's face appeared in the doorway, and his hand beckoned to Alastair.

'My lady's woman has descended and is distracted by the sight of strange servants. It seems her mistress desires Sir John's company, which was promised for this hour, and the maid will not return without a clear answer.'

'Say that he is detained,' said Alastair, 'and add that the Duchess of Queensberry begs the lady's permission to wait upon her.'

He turned to the two at the fireplace. 'Madam, 'tis time for your mission of charity.'

'Repeat me my lesson,' she said, standing before him as demure as a schoolgirl.

'You will inform the lady that Sir John Norreys has been summoned in great haste to join his Prince, and has left incontinent, trusting to her loyal heart to condone his seeming heartlessness. Say that he will find means to keep her informed of his welfare. Then press her to travel southward with you, pointing out to her that the war moves southward and she will be travelling the same way as Sir John.'

' 'Tis a parcel of lies,' said the Duchess, 'and I am a poor dissembler.'

Alastair shrugged his shoulders. 'The cause is good and your Grace is a finished actress, when you please.'

'But is it not cruel kindness?' she asked. 'Were it not better that she should know the truth of her husband, that she might grieve the less when she has news of his end, which I see writ plain in your eyes, sir?'

Johnson broke in. 'A thousand times no, madam. If she learns that her trust has been ill placed, her heart will break. She can bear sorrow but not shame. Believe me, I have studied that noble lady.'

'So be it. Have the goodness, Captain Maclean, to escort me to this paragon.'

Alastair gave her his arm, and, instructed by Johnson – who followed in the wake – conducted the Duchess up the first flight of the staircase to a broad gallery from which the main bed-rooms opened. At the end, where were Claudia's rooms, the maid, Mrs Peckover, stood with a lighted candle to receive them.

But suddenly they halted and stood motionless, listening. A voice was singing, the voice which had sung 'Diana' at the Sleeping Deer. The door must have been ajar, for the song rose clear in the corridor, sung low but with such a tension of feeling that every word and bar seemed to vibrate in the air. The Duchess, clinging to Alastair's arm, stood rigid as a statue. 'O Love,' the voice sang—

> 'O Love, they wrong thee much
>   That say thy sweet is bitter,
> When thy rich fruit is such
>   As nothing can be sweeter.
> Fair house of joy and bliss,
> Where truest treasure is,
>   I do adore thee.'

The voice hung on the lines for an instant in a tremor of passion. Then it continued to a falling close—

> 'I know thee what thou art,
> I serve thee with my heart,
>   And fall before thee.'

'I think you do well to be tender of her,' the Duchess whispered. 'Adieu! I will descend presently and report.'

The heavy hand of Johnson clutched his arm before he had reached the foot of the staircase.

'Did you hear that?' the tutor questioned savagely. 'She sings of love like an angel of God, and her love is betrayed.' He forced Alastair before him, and shut the door of the dining-room behind them. The candles still burned brightly amid the remains of supper, but the logs on the hearth had smouldered low.

Johnson was become the strangest of figures, his sallow face flushed, his eyes rolling like a man in a fit, and a nervousness like palsy affecting his hands and shoulders. But Alastair saw none of these things, for his attention was held by something masterful and noble in the man's face.

'Sit down, Alastair Maclean,' he said, 'and listen to one who loves you as a brother. Sir, we are both servants of one lady and that is a bond stricter than consanguinity. I am poor and diseased and disconsidered, but I have a duty laid upon me which comes direct from Omnipotence. Sir, I command you to examine into your heart.'

He laid a hand on the young man's arm, a hand that trembled violently.

'What are your intentions toward Sir John Norreys?'

'I mean to find him, and, when found, to fight with him and kill him.'

'For what reason?'

'Because he is a traitor to my Prince.'

'And yet you did not press for the death of the man Kyd, who was the principal whereas Sir John was but the tool. Come, sir, be honest with me; why is the extreme penalty decreed to the less guilty?'

Alastair did not answer at first. Then he said –

'Because Sir John Norreys is the husband of a lady to whom the knowledge of his true nature would be death.'

'That reply is nearer the truth, but still far from complete honesty.'

Alastair had a sudden flame of wrath. 'Do you accuse me of lying?' he asked angrily.

Johnson's face did not change. 'Sir, all men are liars,' he said. 'I strive to make you speak truth to your own soul. The death of Sir John is intended merely to save the lady from the pain of disgrace? On your honour, for no other purpose?'

Alastair did not reply. The other sank his harsh voice to a gentler and kindlier pitch, and the hand on the young man's arm from a menace became a caress.

'I will answer for you. You love the lady. Nay, I do not blame you, for all the world must love her. I love her most deeply, but not as you, for you love with hope, and look some day to make her yours. Therefore you would slay Sir John, and to yourself you say that 'tis to save her from shame, but before God, you know that 'tis to rid yourself of a rival.'

The man's eyes were compelling, and his utter honesty was like a fire that burned all shamefastness from the air. Alastair's silence was assent.

'Sir, a lover seeks above all things the good of his mistress. If indeed you love her – and it is honourable that you should – I implore you to consider further in the matter. We are agreed that it is necessary to save her from the shame of the knowledge of her husband's treason, for it is a proud lady who would feel disgrace sharper than death. If that were all, I would bid you god-speed, for Sir John's death would serve that purpose, and you and she are fit mates, being alike young and highly born. After the natural period of mourning was over, you might fairly look to espouse her. But ah, sir, that is not all.'

He got to his feet in his eagerness and stood above the young man, one hand splayed on the table, as he had stood that afternoon at the Sleeping Deer.

'Listen, sir. I have watched that child in her going out and coming in, in her joys and melancholies, in her every mood of caprice and earnestness – watched with the quick eye of one who is half lover, half parent. And I have formed most certain conclusions about that high nature. She trusts but once and that wholly; she will love but once, and that with a passion like a consuming fire. If she knew the truth about Sir John, she would never trust mankind again. On that we are agreed. But I go further, sir. If she lost him, she would never love another, but go inconsolable to her grave. It is the way of certain choice spirits.'

Alastair made a gesture of dissent.

'Sir, did you not hear her singing?' Johnson asked. 'Answer me, heard you ever such a joy of surrender in a mortal voice?'

Alastair could not deny it, for the passionate trilling was still in his ear.

'But your reasoning is flawed,' he said. 'Granted that my Lady Norreys has given her love once and for all; yet if Sir John remain alive she will presently discover his shame, and for the rest of her days be tormented with honour wounded through affection.'

'It need not be,' said Johnson, and his voice had sunk to the level of argument from the heights of appeal. 'I have studied both of them during the past weeks, and this is my conclusion. She has made a false image of him which she adores, but unless the falsity be proved to the world by some violent revelation she will not discover it. She is a happy self-deceiver, and to the end – unless forcibly enlightened – will take his common clay for gold. As for him – well, he is clay and not gunpowder. He has been moulded into infamy by a stronger man and by his ancestral greed – for, judging by the family here, his race is one of misers. But let him be sufficiently alarmed and shown where his interest lies, and he will relapse to the paths of decorum. Good he will never be, little he must always be, but he may also be respectable. He will not lose his halo in his lady's eyes and they may live out their time happily, and if God wills some portion of the mother's quality may descend to the children.'

The thought to Alastair was hideously repellent. To whitewash such a rogue and delude such a lady! Better surely a painful enlightenment than this deceit. He comforted himself with the reflection that it was impossible.

'But by this time Sir John Norreys is with his paymaster, and the mischief is done.'

'Not so,' said Johnson. 'Sir John does not ride to Kingston or to Richmond but to Cumberland himself, and he lies far in the south. He may yet be overtaken and dissuaded.'

'By whom?'

'By you, sir.'

Alastair laughed loud and bitterly.

'Are you mad, sir? I journey at once to the Prince's camp, for I have news for him that may determine his future conduct. Already I am late in starting. I must order my horse, and bid farewell to the ladies.' He moved to the door, and cried instructions to the Spainneach, who smoked a cigarro by the hall fire.

Johnson seized him by the lapels of his coat. 'I implore you, sir, by the mercy of God. Follow Sir John and persuade him, compel him, at the sword's point, if need be. The happiness of my darling child depends on it. If you do not go, I must go myself. The Prince's news can wait, for it will be only a few hours' delay at the most. What does it matter whether or not he be in London a day earlier, compared to the well-being of an immortal soul? I beseech you, sir, for the love of Christ Who redeemed us—'

'Tush, man, you are raving,' Alastair broke in, and moved to the half-open door. At that moment the Duchess's voice sounded on the stairs.

'Come up, sir,' she said. 'My lady will receive you before you go, and she bids you bring the other, the clumsy fellow whose name I know not.'

Duchess Kitty met him at the door of Claudia's chamber.

'Oh, my dear, she is the very archangel of angels, and of an innocence to make one weep. She will come with me to Amesbury. She dotes on her Sir John and will weary me, I fear, with her rhapsodies, but I am nobly complaisant and flatter her passion. I fear you stand no chance, sir. Her heart is wholly in the rogue's keeping. Enter, for she awaits you.'

In the dim panelled room lit by many candles and a leaping fire the figure of the girl sitting up in the great four-poster bed stood out with a startling brilliance. Madam Claudia was dressed to receive him, as she had been in the midnight colloquy at Flambury, in a furred bed-gown and a nightcap of lace and pink satin. But her brown eyes were no longer pools of dancing light. She held out a hand to Alastair with a little sigh.

'I rejoice that you are free from your t-troubles, sir,' she said. ' 'Twas a shameful charge, and I did not credit it, nor truly did Sir John. And justice, they tell me, has been done to the traitor! Sir John was deceived like the rest of you, and 'tis a cunning rogue that can hoodwink Sir John. You are at the end of your mission, sir, and can now engage in the honest business of war.'

'And for yourself, my lady?'

'I, too, take the road,' she said. 'You have heard of her G-grace's kindness. I am fortunate to travel in such g-gentle company. So it is farewell, sir. You ride this night to the Prince, who is at Derby? My dear Sir John has preceded you there. Oh, would that I could be with him!' And with a morsel of cambric she dried a rising tear.

'And you, Puffin,' she asked, catching sight of Johnson. 'Do you travel south with us?'

'Nay, madam, I go with Captain Maclean to the Prince's camp.'

'Bravo!' she cried. 'You have declared yourself at last. God prosper you, my gallant gentlemen. I will be there to cheer when you ride behind the Prince into London.'

Alastair was scarcely conscious of her words. He saw only her wild wet eyes, compared to which those of the pretty Duchess were like pebbles to stars. It was the child in her that overwhelmed him, the appealing child, trusting utterly with no thought but that all the world was well-disposed to her and her love. He had known many women in his time, though none had touched his cold fancy, but he had never before seen a woman's face transfigured with so innocent an exaltation. The sadness in it was only the anxiety of a soul that trembled for the perpetuation of an unbelievable joy. He was nothing to her, nor was any man except the one; the virgin garden of her heart was enclosed with impenetrable defences. The truth moved him not to irritation, but to pity and a protecting care. He could not mar a thing so rare, and if its foundations were rotten he would be in league to strengthen them. For the moment he was not the lover, but the guardian, who would perjure his soul to keep alive a childish paradise.

He raised her hand and kissed it. 'I am your very humble and devoted servant,' he said. And then she did a thing for which he was not prepared, for with a little cry she put her hands over her eyes and wept.

He hurried from the room without looking back. He had made a decision which he found was like a dry patch of ground in the midst of rising floods, for gathering from every corner of his soul were dark and unplumbed tides.

As he mounted, the Spainneach spoke: 'He has gone by Milford and the Ernshawbank. Likely he will sleep an hour or two at the Pegtop. You might find him there if you haste.'

Johnson's horse had also been brought, and its rider had some trouble in mounting.

'You will delay me, sir, if you insist on keeping me company,' said Alastair.

'I am a strong rider when I am once in the saddle,' said the other humbly. 'But why this hurry? You will be in Derby long ere daybreak.'

'I do not ride to Derby, but down the vale to overtake a certain gentleman.'

He heard Johnson mutter a fervent 'God be thanked' as he turned for a last look at the house. In an upper floor there was a glow of firelight and candlelight through the curtains of un-shuttered windows. There lay Claudia, stammering her gentle confidences to Duchess Kitty, but with her thoughts ranging the hill-roads in the wake of her worthless lover. And from one of those dark windows two grey beldams were peering into the night and trembling for the riches that were the price of their souls.

SEVENTEEN

Ordeal of Honour

The night was growing colder, and the moon in her first quarter was sinking among heavy woolpack clouds. The Spainneach's whisper had been enough for Alastair, who in his sojourn at the Sleeping Deer had made himself familiar with the neighbourhood, after the fashion of a campaigner who may soon have to fight in it. The road led them past the silent hostelry, and then left the vale and struck over a succession of low ridges to another, where a parallel stream of the hills broadened as it neared the lowlands. The men did not spare their horses, and, as the hooves clattered on the bare ribs of rock which crossed the track sparks like wildfire flew behind them.

Alastair's mood was as dark as the weather. The sight of Claudia, babbling of her lover, had for a moment converted him to Johnson's view. In a fine impulse of quixotry he had ridden from Brightwell, his purpose vague towards Sir John Norreys but determined in the service of the lady. If her love was pledged irrevocably to a knave and fool, then be it his business to keep the said knave from greater folly, and see that disillusion did not shatter a gentle heart. For a little he felt the glow of self-conscious worth, and the pleasant melancholy which is born of approving self-pity.

It did not last long. Visions of Claudia, dim-eyed, stammering, all russet and snow, returned to ravish his fancy, and the picture of a certain sharp-nosed gentleman to exacerbate his temper. Before God he could not surrender such a darling, he would be no party to flinging such a pearl before swine! His heart grew hot when he thought of Sir John, the mean visage and hedge-hog soul. To condone his infamy would be to sin against Heaven – to foster his lady's blind fondness the task of a pander. Let the truth be told and the devil be shamed, for a wounded heart was better than a slow decay.

Presently his mind had swung round to a new resolution. He would go straight to Derby to the Prince, which was his direct soldierly duty. He knew the road; the next left-hand turning would lead him there before morning. He was already weeks, months late; he dared not tarry another hour, for he alone knew the truth about the West, and that truth might determine the Prince's strategy. True, His Highness was at Derby now, and the Rubicon had been doubtless crossed, but in so great a matter no precaution could be omitted. At that very moment Lochiel, with his letter in his hand, might be looking in vain for the man who had named Derby as the trysting-place. . . . He would sweep southward with the Army to conquest, and then in their hour of triumph would root Sir John from his traitor's kennel. The man must fight on his challenge, and he had no doubt as to the issue of that fight.

But would he? Would he not disappear overseas, taking with him his wife under some false story? If she were deceived in one matter, she might be deceived in others. . . . No, by Heaven, there was no way of it but the one. The fox must be found before he reached his earth, and brought to account at a sword's point. Stone dead had no fellow.

The cross-roads lay before them where was the turning to Derby.

'There lies the Prince,' said Alastair, his head over his left shoulder. 'My duty is to ride forthwith thither. I could breakfast in the camp.'

Johnson, though lacking a riding-coat, had grown warm with the exercise, and both he and his mount were blowing.

'You would not falter in your most honourable resolve?' he puffed.

Alastair clapped spurs to his beast. 'No,' he said, 'I am resolved before all things to find Sir John Norreys. But when I find him I will kill him.'

He heard a gasp which was more than Mr Johnson's chronic shortness of breath. As he cantered forward the slower and heavier beast of his companion was forced alongside of him, and a hand clutched his arm.

'I beseech you, sir,' said a tragic voice, 'I pray you, in God's name, to turn aside to Derby.'

'I will first meet Sir John,' was the reply and the hand was shaken off.

'But he will be safe at your hands?'

'That is as God may direct,' said Alastair.

His resolution being now fixed, his spirits rose. He let thoughts of Claudia flush his mind with their sweet radiance. He pictured her as he had last seen her – the light from the candles making her slim white neck below the rosy nightcap take on the bloom of a peach, and the leaping flames of the hearth chequering the shadow of the bed-curtain. He saw her dim eyes, heard her melting voice, felt the warm vigour of her body as she cowered beside him in the dark of the Flambury galleries. Too young for wife, too old for child, but the ripe age for comrade – and such a comrade, for there was a boy's gallantry in her eyes and something of a child's confident fearlessness. He did not hear the groans of Mr Johnson pounding dismally behind him, or the shuddering cry of owls from the woods. The world was a quiet place to him where a soft voice was speaking, the thick darkness was all aglow with happy pictures. The man's soul was enraptured by his dreams. He found himself suddenly laughing to think how new and strange was this mood of his. Hitherto he had kept women at arms' length, and set his heart on policy and war, till he had earned the repute of one to be trusted and courted, but one already at thirty middle-aged. Lord! but there had been a melting of icebergs! And like a stab came the thought of yet another molten iceberg – Sir John – of the sharp nose and the high coat collar! Alastair cried out like a man in pain.

They rode into Milford half an hour after midnight. There was no light in any house, and the inn was a black wall. But the door of the yard was open, and a hostler, ascending to his bed in the hayloft, accepted a shilling for his news. A man had ridden through Milford that night. He had not seen him, but he had heard the clatter as he was bedding the post horses that had come in late from Marlock. How long ago? Not more than an hour, maybe less, and the fellow checked his memory with a string of minute proofs.

Alastair swung his horse's head back to the road. 'Courage, my friend,' he cried. 'We are gaining on him. We shall overtake him before morning.'

Again Johnson caught his arm. 'Bethink you, sir,' he stammered. 'You ride on an errand of murder.'

'Nay,' was the answer, 'of love.'

But the next miles were over roads like ploughlands, and the rain blew up from the south-west and set the teeth chattering of the cloakless Mr Johnson. The night was very dark and the road seemed to pass no villages, for not a light appeared in the wastes of wet ling and fern and plashing woods. The track could be discerned well enough, for it was the only possible route through the rugged land, and happily for the riders there were no crossways. No other traveller met them or was overtaken – which, thought Alastair, was natural, for with the Prince at Derby the flight of the timid would be to the south, and not north or west into the enemy's country.

Long before dawn he was far beyond the countryside of which he had any knowledge. He had been given Ernshawbank by the Spainneach as the second point to make for, and had assumed that there, if not before, he would fall in with Sir John. Yet when he came to a village about cockcrow, and learned from a sleepy carter that it was Ernshawbank, he did not find his quarry. But at the inn he had news of him. A man answering his description had knocked up the landlord two hours before, drunk a gill of brandy, eaten a crust, and bought for a guinea the said landlord's cocked grey beaver, new a month ago at Leek Fair. Two hours! The man was gaining on him! It appeared that he had ridden the path for lower Dovedale, as if he were making for Staffordshire and Trentside.

The two breakfasted at an ale house below Thorp Cloud, when a grey December morning was breaking over the leafless vale and the swollen waters of Dove. Their man had been seen, riding hard, with a face blue from cold and wet, and his fine clothes pitifully draggled with the rain. He had crossed the river, and was therefore bound for Staffordshire, and not Nottinghamshire, as Alastair had at first guessed. A minute's reflection convinced him of the reason. Sir John was specially concerned with cutting off the help coming to the Prince from the West, and therefore went to join those, like the Duke of Kingston, who were on that flank, rather than the army which lay between Derby and London. The reflection gave him acute uneasiness. Nottinghamshire was distant, so there was a chance to overtake the fugitive on the way. But, as it now was, any hour might see the man in sanctuary. The next village might hold a patrol of the Duke's. . . . He cut short the meal, which Mr Johnson had scarcely tasted, and the two were again on their weary beasts pounding up the steep lanes towards Ershalton and my lord Shrewsbury's great house.

The mist cleared, a wintry sun shone, and the sky was mottled with patches of watery blue. Mr Johnson's teeth began to chatter so violently that Alastair swung round and regarded him.

'You will without doubt catch an ague, sir,' he said, and at the next presentable inn he insisted on his toasting his smallclothes before the kitchen fire, drinking a jorum of hot rum, and borrowing a coat of the landlord's till his own was dry. For suddenly the panic of hurry was gone out of Alastair, and he saw this business as something predestined and ultimate. Fate was moving the pieces, and her iron fingers did not fumble. If it was written that he and Sir John should meet, then stronger powers than he would set the stage. He was amazed at his own calm.

The rum made his companion drowsy, and as they continued on the road he ceased to groan, and at the next halting-place did not stare at him with plaintive hang-dog eyes. As for Alastair he found that his mind had changed again and that all his resolution was fluid.

His hatred of the pursued was ebbing, indeed had almost vanished, for with the sense of fatality which was growing upon him he saw the man as no better than a pawn; a thing as impersonal as sticks and stones. All the actors of the piece – Kyd, Norreys, the Spoonbills, Edom, the sullen Johnson, grew in his picture small and stiff like marionettes, and Claudia alone had the warmth of life. Once more she filled the stage of his memory, but it was not the russet and pearl of her and her witching eyes that held him now, but a tragic muse who appealed from the brink of chasms. She implored his pity on all she loved, on the casket where she had hid her heart.

With a start he recognised that this casket was no other than Sir John Norreys.

He might shatter it and rescue the heart, but how would the precious thing fare in the shattering? Her eyes rose before him with their infinite surrender. Was Johnson right and was she of the race of women that give once in life and then utterly and for ever? If so, his errand was not to succour, but to slay. His sword would not cut the bonds of youth and innocence, it would pierce their heart.

He forced his mind to reconstruct the three occasions when she had faced him – not for his delectation, but to satisfy a new-born anxiety. He saw her at Flambury, a girl afire with zeal and daring, sexless as a child, and yet always in her sweet stumbling phrases harping on her dear Sir John. He saw her in the Brown Room at the Sleeping Deer, a tender muse of memories, but imperious towards dishonour, one whose slim grace might be brittle but would not bend. Last he saw her set up in the great bed at Brightwell, one arm round the neck of Duchess Kitty, the other stretched towards him in that woman's appeal which had held him from Derby and the path of duty.

There is that in hard riding and hard weather which refines a man's spirit, purging it of its grosser humours. The passion of the small hours had gone utterly from Alastair, and instead his soul was filled with a tempestuous affection, not of a lover but of a kinsman and protector. The child must at all costs be sheltered from sorrow, and if she pined for her toy it must be found for her, its cracks mended and its paint refurbished. His mood was now the same as Johnson's, his resolution the same. He felt an odd pleasure in this access of tenderness, but he was conscious, too, that the pleasure was like a thin drift of flowers over dark mires of longing and sorrow. For his world had been tumbled down, and all the castles he had built. He had always been homeless, but now he was a thousandfold more an outlaw, for the one thing on earth he desired was behind him and not before him, and he was fleeing from hope.

In the afternoon the rain descended again and the road passed over a wide heath, which had been blackened by some autumn fire so that the shores of its leaden pools were like charcoal, and skeleton coverts shook their charred branches in the wind. The scene was a desolation, but he viewed it with calm eyes, for a strange peace was creeping into his soul. He turned in the saddle, and saw six yards behind him Johnson jogging wearily along, his heavy shoulders bowed and his eyes fixed dully on his horse's neck. The man must be near the limits of his strength, he thought. . . . Once again he had one of his sudden premonitions. Sir John Norreys was close at hand, for he had not yet stopped for a meal and he had now been on the road for twelve hours. The conviction grew upon him, and made him urge his tired beast to a better pace. Somewhere just in front was the meeting-place where the ordeal was appointed which should decree the fate of two souls. . . .

The drizzle changed into half a gale, and scouring blasts shut out the landscape. There came a moment's clearing, and lo! before him lay a bare space in the heath, where another road entered from the west to join the highway. At their meeting, set in a grove of hornbeams, stood an inn.

It was a small place, ancient, long and low, and the signboard could not be read in the dim weather. But beneath it, new-painted, was an open eye. He checked his horse, and turned to the door, for he knew with utter certainty that he had reached his destination.

He dropped from the saddle, and since there was no stable-lad in sight, he tied the reins to a ring in the wall. Then he pushed open the door and descended a step into the inn kitchen. A man was busy about the hearth, a grizzled elderly fellow in leathern small-clothes. In front of the fire a fine coat hung drying on two chairs, and a pair of sodden boots steamed beside the log basket.

The inn-keeper looked up, and something in the quiet eyes and weather-worn face awoke in Alastair a recollection. He had not seen the face before, but he had seen its like.

'You have a guest?' he said.

The man did not answer, and Alastair knew that no word or deed of his would compel an answer, if the man were unwilling.

'You have the sign,' he said. 'I, too, am of the Spoonbills. I seek Master Midwinter.'

The inn-keeper straightened himself. 'He shall be found,' he said. 'What message do I carry?'

'Say that he to whom he promised help on Otmoor now claims it. And stay, there are two weary cattle outside. Have them fed and stabled.'

The man turned to go, but Alastair checked him.

'You have a guest?' he asked.

'He is now upstairs at food,' was the answer given readily. 'He feeds in his shirt, for he is all mucked and moiled with the roads.'

'I have business with him, I and my friend. Let us be alone till Master Midwinter comes.'

The man stood aside to let Johnson stumble in. Then the door was shut, and to Alastair's ear there was the turning of a key.

Johnson's great figure seemed broken with weariness. He staggered across the uneven stone floor, and rolled into a grandfather's chair which stood to the left of the fire. Then he caught sight of the coat drying in the glow and recognised it. Into his face, grey with fatigue, came a sudden panic. 'It is his,' he cried. 'He is here.' He lifted his head and seemed to listen like a stag at pause. Then he flung himself from the chair, and rushed on Alastair, who was staring abstractedly at the blaze. 'You will not harm him,' he cried. 'You will not break my lady's heart. Sooner, sir, I will choke you with my own hands.'

His voice was the scream of an animal in pain, his skin was livid, his eyes were hot coals. Alastair, taken by surprise, was all but swung off his feet by the fury of the assault. One great arm was round his waist, one hand was clutching his throat. The two staggered back, upsetting the chair before the fire; the hand at the throat was shaken off, and in a second they were at wrestling-grips in the centre of the floor.

Both men were weary, and one was lately recovered of a sickness. This latter, too, was the lighter, and for a moment Alastair found himself helpless in a grip which crushed in his sides and stopped his breath. But Johnson's passion was like the spouting of a volcano and soon died down. The fiery vigour went out of his clutch, but it remained a compelling thing, holding the young man a close prisoner.

The noise of the scuffle had alarmed the gentleman above. The stairs ran up in a steep flight direct from the kitchen, and as Alastair looked from below his antagonist's elbow, he saw a white face peer beneath the low roof of the stairway, and a little further down three-quarters of the length of a sword blade. He was exerting the power of his younger arms against the dead strength of Johnson, but all the while his eyes were held by this new apparition. It was something clad only in shirt and breeches and rough borrowed stockings, but the face was unmistakable and the haggard eyes.

The apparition descended another step, and now Alastair saw the hand which grasped the sword. Fear was in the man's face, and then a deeper terror, for he had recognised one of the combatants. There was perplexity there, too, for he was puzzled at the sight, and after that a spasm of hope. He hesitated for a second till he grasped the situation. Then he shouted something which may have been an encouragement to Johnson, and leaped the remaining steps on to the kitchen floor.

Johnson had not seen him, for his head was turned the other way and his sight and hearing were dimmed by his fury. The man in underclothes danced round the wrestlers, babbling strangely. 'Hold him!' he cried. 'Hold him, and I'll finish him!' His blade was shortened for a thrust, but the movement of the wrestlers frustrated him. He made a pass, but it only grazed the collar of Alastair's coat.

Then he found a better chance, and again his arm was shortened. A hot quiver went through Alastair's shoulder, for a rapier had pinked the flesh and had cut into the flapping pouch of Johnson's coat.

It may have been Alastair's cry, or the fierce shout of the man in underclothes, but Johnson awoke suddenly to what was happening. He saw a white face with fiery eyes, he saw the rapier drawn back for a new thrust with blood on its point. . . . With a shudder he loosened his grip and let Alastair go free.

'I have done murder,' he cried, and staggered across the floor till he fell against the dresser. His hands were at his eyes and he was shaken with a passion of sobbing.

The two remaining faced each other, one in his stocking-soles, dancing like a crazy thing in the glow of the wood-fire, triumph in his small eyes. Alastair, dazed and shaken, was striving to draw his blade, which, owing to the struggle, had become entangled in the skirts of his riding-coat. The other, awaking to the new position of affairs, pressed on him wildly till he gave ground. . . . And then he halted, for a blade had crossed his.

Both men had light travelling-swords, which in a well-matched duello should have met with the tinkle of thin ice in a glass. But now there was the jar and whine of metal harshly used, for the one lunged recklessly, and the other stood on a grim defensive, parrying with a straight arm a point as disorderly as wildfire. Sir John Norreys had the skill in fence of an ordinary English squire, learned from an Oxford *maître d'escrime* and polished by a lesson or two in Covent Garden – an art no better than ignorance when faced with one perfected by Gérard and d'Aubigny, and tested in twenty affairs against the best blades of France.

Alastair's wound was a mere scratch, and at this clearing of issues his wits had recovered and his strength returned. As he fought, his eyes did not leave the other's face. He saw its chalky pallor, where the freckles showed like the scars of smallpox, the sharp arrogant nose, the weak mouth with the mean lines around it, the quick, hard eyes now beginning to waver from their first fury. The man meant to kill him, and as he realised this, the atmosphere of the duello fled, and it was again the old combat *à outrance* of his clan – his left hand reached instinctively for the auxiliary dagger which should have hung at his belt. And then he laughed, for whatever his enemy's purposes, success was not likely to follow them.

The scene had to Alastair the spectral unreality of a dream. The kitchen was hushed save for the fall of ashes on the hearth, the strained sobbing of Johnson, and the rasp of the blades. The face of Sir John Norreys was a mirror in which he read his own predominance. The eyes lost their heat, the pupils contracted till they were two shining beads in the dead white of the skin, the wild lunging grew wilder, the breath came in short gasps. But the face was a mirror, too, in which he read something of the future. If his resolution to spare the man had not been already taken, it must now have become irrevocable. This was a child, a stripling, who confronted him, a mere amateur of vice, a thing which to slay would have been no better than common murder. Pity for the man, even a strange kindness stole into Alastair's soul. He wondered how he could ever have hated anything so crude and weak.

He smiled again, and at that smile all the terrors of death crowded into the other's face. He seemed to nerve himself for a last effort, steadied the fury of his lunges and aimed a more skilful thrust in tierce. Alastair had a mind to end the farce. His parry beat up the other's blade, and by an easy device of the schools he twitched the sword from his hand so that it clattered at Johnson's feet.

Sir John Norreys stood stock-still for an instant, his mouth working like a child about to weep. Then some share of manhood returned to him. He drew himself straight, swallowed what may have been a sob, and let his arms drop by his side.

'I am at your mercy,' he stammered. 'What do you purpose with me?'

Alastair returned his sword to its sheath. 'I purpose to save your life,' he said, 'and if God be merciful, your soul.'

He stripped off his riding-coat. 'Take this,' he said. 'It is wintry weather, and may serve till your own garments are dry. It is ill talking unclad, Sir John, and we have much to say to each other.'

Johnson had risen, and his face was heavy with an emotion which might have been sorrow or joy. He stood with arm upraised like a priest blessing his flock. 'Now to Angels and Archangels and all the Company of Heaven,' he cried, and then he stopped, for the door opened softly and closed again.

It was Midwinter that entered. His shoulders filled the doorway, and his eyes constrained all three to a tense silence. He walked to the fireplace, picking up Norreys's sword, which he bent into a half hoop against the jamb of the chimney. As his quiet gaze fell on the company it seemed to exercise a peaceful mastery which made the weapon in his hand a mere trinket.

'You have summoned me, Captain Maclean,' he said. 'I am here to make good my promise. Show me how I can serve you.'

'We are constituted a court of honour,' said Alastair. 'We seek your counsel.'

He turned to Norreys.

'You are not two months married, Sir John. How many years have you to your age?'

The man answered like an automaton. 'I am in my twenty-third,' he said. He was looking alternately to his antagonist and to Midwinter, still with the bewilderment of a dull child.

'Since when have you meddled in politics?'

'Since scarce two years.'

'You were drawn to the Prince's side – by what? Was it family tradition?'

'No, damme, my father was a Hanover man when he lived. I turned Jacobite to please Claudie. There was no welcome at Chastlecote unless a man wore the white rose.'

'And how came you into your recent business?'

' 'Twas Kyd's doing. . . . No, curse it, I won't shelter behind another, for I did it of my own free will. But 'twas Kyd showed me a way of improving my fortunes, for he knew I cared not a straw who had the governing of the land.'

'And you were happy in the service?'

The baronet's face had lost its childishness, and had grown sullen.

'I was content.' Then he broke out. 'Rot him, I was not content – not of late. I thought the Prince and his adventure was but a Scotch craziness. But now, with him in the heart of England I have been devilish anxious.'

'For your own safety? Or was there perhaps another reason?'

Sir John's pale face flushed. 'Let that be. Put it that I feared for my neck and my estate.'

Alastair turned smiling to the others. 'I begin to detect the rudiments of honesty ... I am going to unriddle your thoughts, Sir John. You were beginning to wonder how your wife would regard your courses. Had the Prince shipwrecked beyond the Border, she would never have known of them, and the Rising would have been between you only a sad pleasing memory. But now she must learn the truth, and you are afraid. Why? She is a lady of fortune, but you did not marry her for her fortune.'

'My God, no,' he cried. 'I loved her most damnably, and I ever shall.'

'And she loves you?'

The flush grew deeper. 'She is but a child. She has scarcely seen another man. I think she loves me.'

'So you have betrayed the Prince's cause, because it did not touch you deep and you favoured it only because of a lady's eyes. But the Prince looks like succeeding, Sir John. He is now south of Derby on the road to London, and his enemies do not abide him. What do you purpose in that event? Have you the purchase at his Court to get your misdoings overlooked?'

'I trusted to Kyd.'

'Vain trust. Last night, after you left us so hastily, Kyd was stripped to the bare bone.'

'Was he sent to the Prince?' the man asked sharply.

'No. We preferred to administer our own justice, as we will do with you. But he is gone into a long exile.'

'Is he dead? . . . You promised me my life.'

'He lives, as you shall live. Sir John, I will be frank with you. You are a youth whom vanity and greed have brought deep into the mire. I would get you out of it – not for your own sake, but for that of a lady whom you love, I think, and who most assuredly loves you. Your besetting sin is avarice. Well, let it be exercised upon your estates and not upon the fortunes of better men. I have a notion that you may grow with good luck into a very decent sort of man – not much of a fellow at heart, perhaps, but reputable and reputed – at any rate enough to satisfy the love-blinded eyes of your lady. Do you assent?'

The baronet reddened again at the contemptuous kindliness of Alastair's words.

'I have no choice,' he said gruffly.

'Then it is the sentence of this court that you retire to your estates and live there without moving outside your park pale.'

'Alone?'

'Alone. Your wife has gone into Wiltshire with her Grace of Queensberry. You will stay at Weston till she returns to you, and that date depends upon the posture of affairs in the country. You will give me your oath to meddle no more in politics. And for the safety of your person and the due observance of your promise you will be given an escort on your journey south.'

'Will you send Highlanders into Oxfordshire?' was the astonished question.

Midwinter answered. 'Nay, young sir, you will have the bodyguard of Old England.'

Sir John stared at Midwinter and saw something in that face which made him avert his gaze. He suddenly shivered, and a different look came into his eyes. 'You have been merciful to me, sirs,' he said, 'merciful beyond my deserts. I owe you more than I can repay.'

'You owe it to your wife, sir,' Alastair broke in. 'Cherish her dearly and let that be your atonement. . . . If you will take my advice, you will snatch a little sleep, for you have been mosstrooping for a round of the clock.'

As the baronet's bare shanks disappeared up the stairway Alastair turned wearily to the others. A haze seemed to cloud his eyes, and the crackle of logs on the hearth sounded in his ears like the noise of the sea.

'You were right,' he told Johnson. 'There's the makings of a sober husband in that man. No hero, but she may be trusted to gild her idol. I think she will be happy.'

'You have behaved as a good Christian should.' Mr Johnson was still shaking as if from the ague. 'Had I been in your case, I do not think I would have shown so just a mind.'

'Call it philosophy, which makes a man know what it is not in his power to gain,' Alastair laughed. 'I think I have learned the trick of it from you.'

He swayed and caught Midwinter's shoulder. 'Forgive me, old friend. I have been riding for forty hours, and have fought and argued in between, and before that I rose off a sick-bed. . . . But I must on to Derby. Get a fresh horse, my brave one.'

Midwinter drew him to an armchair, and seemed to fumble with his hands for a second or two at his brow. When Johnson looked again Alastair was asleep, while the other dressed roughly the hole in his shoulder made by Sir John's sword.

'*Festina lente*, Mr Johnson. I can provide fresh beasts, but not fresh legs for the riders. The pair of you will sleep for five hours and then sup, for Derby is a far cry and an ill road, and if you start as you are you will founder in the first slough.'

EIGHTEEN

In which Three Gentlemen Confess their Nakedness

Fresh horses were found, and at four in the morning, four hours before daylight in that murky weather, Alastair and Johnson left the inn. At the first cross-roads Midwinter joined them.

'Set your mind at ease about Sir John,' he said. 'He will travel securely to the Cherwell side, and none but the Spoonbills will know of his journey. I think you have read him right, sir, and that he is a prosy fellow who by accident has slipped into roguery and will return gladly to his natural rut. But in case you are mistaken, he will be overlooked by my people, for we are strong in that countryside. Be advised, sir, and ride gently, for you have no bodily strength to spare, and your master will not welcome a sick man.'

'Do you ride to Derby with us?' Alastair asked.

'I have business on that road and will convey you thus far,' was the answer.

It was a morning when the whole earth and sky seemed suffused in moisture. Fog strung its beads on their clothes, every hedgerow tree dripped clammily, the roads were knee-deep in mud, flood-water lay in leaden streaks in the hollows of flat fields, each sluggish brook was a torrent, and at intervals the air would distil into a drenching shower. Alastair's body was still weary, but his heart was lightened. He had finished now with dalliance and was back at his old trade; and for the moment the memory of Claudia made only a warm background to the hopes of a soldier. Little daggers of doubt stabbed his thoughts – he had sacrificed another day and night in his chase of Sir John, and the Prince had now been at Derby the better part of forty hours without that report which he had promised. But surely, he consoled himself, so slight a delay could matter nothing; an army which had marched triumphant to the heart of England, and had already caused the souls of its enemies to faint, could not falter when the goal was within sight. But the anxiety hung like a *malaise* about the fringes of his temper and caused him now and then to spur his horse fifty yards beyond his companion.

The road they travelled ran to Derby from the south-west, and its deep ruts showed the heavy traffic it had lately borne. By it coaches, waggons and every variety of pack and riding horse had carried the timid folks of Derbyshire into sanctuaries beyond the track of the Highland army. To-day the traffic had shrunk to an occasional horseman or a farmer's wife with panniers, and a jovial huntsman in red who, from his greeting, seemed thus early to have been powdering his wig. Already the country was settling down, thought Alastair, as folk learned of the Prince's clemency and good-will. . . . The army would not delay at Derby, but was probably now on the move southward. It would go by Loughborough and Leicester, but cavalry patrols might show themselves on the flank to the west. At any moment some of Elcho's or Pitsligo's horse, perhaps young Tinnis himself, might canter out of the mist.

He cried to Midwinter, asking whether it would not be better to assume that the Prince had left the town, and to turn more southward so as to cut in on his march.

'Derby is the wiser goal,' Midwinter answered. 'It is unlikely that His Highness himself will have gone, for he will travel with the rear-guard. In three hours you will see All Saints' spire.'

At eight they halted for food at a considerable village. It was Friday, and while the other two attacked a cold sirloin, Alastair broke his fast on a crust, resisting the landlord's offer of carp or eels from the Trent on the ground that they would take too long to dress. Then to pass the time while the others finished their meal he wandered into the street, and stopped by the church door. The place was open, and he entered to find a service proceeding and a thin man in a black gown holding forth to an audience of women. No Jacobite this person, for his text was from the 18th chapter of Second Chronicles. 'Wilt thou go up with me to Ramoth-Gilead?' and the sermon figured the Prince as Ahab of Israel and Ramoth-Gilead as that (unspecified) spot where he was to meet his fate.

'A bold man the preacher,' thought Alastair, as he slipped out, 'to croak like a raven against a triumphing cause.' But it appeared there were other bold men in the place. He stopped opposite a tavern, from which came the sound of drunken mirth, and puzzled at its cause, when the day's work should be beginning. Then he reflected that with war in the next parish men's minds must be unsettled and their first disposition to stray towards ale-houses. Doubtless these honest fellows were celebrating the deliverance of England.

But the words, thickly uttered, which disentangled themselves from the tavern were other than he had expected:

> 'George is magnanimous,
> Subjects unanimous,
> Peace to us bring.'

ran the ditty, and the chorus called on God to save the usurper. He stood halted in a perplexity which was half anger, for he had a notion to give these louts the flat of his sword for their treason. Then someone started an air he knew too well:

> 'O Brother Sawney, hear you the news?
> Twang 'em, we'll bang 'em and
>   Hang 'em up all.
> An army's just coming without any shoes,
> Twang 'em, we'll bang 'em, and
>   Hang 'em up all.'

It was that accursed air 'Lilibulero' which had drummed His Highness's grandfather out of England. Surely the ale-house company must be a patrol of Kingston's or Richmond's, that

had got perilously becalmed thus far north. He walked to the
window and cast a glance inside. No, they were heavy red-faced
yokels, the men-folk of the village. He had a second of con-
sternation at the immensity of the task of changing this leaden
England.

As they advanced the roads were better peopled, market folk
for the most part returning from Derby, and now and then
parties of young men who cried news to women who hung at
the corners where farm tracks debouched from the highway. In
all these folk there was an air of expectancy and tension natural
in a land on the confines of war. The three travellers bettered
their pace. 'In an hour,' Midwinter told them, 'we reach the
Ashbourne road and so descend on Derby from the north.' As
the minutes passed, Alastair's excitement grew till he had hard
work to conform his speed to that of his companions. He longed
to hasten on – not from anxiety, for that had left him, but from a
passion to see his Prince again, to be with comrades-in-arms, to
share in the triumph of these days of marvel. Somewhere in
Derby His Highness would now be kneeling at mass; he longed
to be at his side in that sacrament of dedication.

Then as they topped a ridge in a sudden clearing of the
weather a noble spire rose some miles ahead, and around it in
the flat of a wide valley hung the low wisps of smoke which
betokened human dwellings. It did not need Midwinter's cry of
'All Saints' to tell Alastair that he was looking at the place which
held his master and the hope of the Cause. By tacit consent the
three men spurred their beasts, and rode into a village, the long
street of which ran north and south. ' 'Tis the high road from
Ashbourne to Derby,' said Midwinter. 'To the right, sirs, unless
you are for Manchester and Scotland.'

But there was that about the village which made each pull on
his bridle rein. It was as still as a churchyard. Every house door
was closed, and at the little windows could be seen white faces
and timid eyes. The inn door had been smashed and the panes
in its front windows, and a cask in the middle of the street still
trickled beer from its spigot. It might have been the night after a

fair, but instead it was broad daylight, and the after-taste was less of revelry than of panic.

The three men slowly and silently moved down the street, and the heart of one of them was the prey of a leaping terror. Scared eyes, like those of rabbits in a snare, were watching them from the windows. In the inn-yard there was no sign of a soul, except the village idiot who was playing ninepins with bottles. Midwinter hammered on a back door, but there was no answer. But as they turned again towards the street they were aware of a mottled face that watched them from a side window. Apparently the face was satisfied with their appearance, for the window was slightly opened and a voice cried 'Hist!' Alastair turned and saw a troubled fat countenance framed in the sash of a pantry casement.

'Be the salvages gone, gen'lemen?' the voice asked. 'The murderin' heathen has blooded my best cow to make their beastly porridge.'

'We have but now arrived,' said Alastair. 'We are for Derby. Pray, sir, what pestilence has stricken this place?'

'For Derby,' said the man. 'Ye'll find a comfortable town, giving thanks to Almighty God and cleansin' the lousiness of its habitation. What pestilence, says you? A pestilence, verily, good sir, for since cockcrow the rebel army has been meltin' away northwards like the hosts o' Sennacherib before the blast of the Lord. Horse and foot and coaches, and the spawn o' Rome himself in the midst o' them. Not but what he be a personable young man, with his white face and pretty white wig, and his sad smile, and where he was the rebels marched like an army. But there was acres of breechless rabbledom at his heels that thieved like pyots. Be they all passed, think ye?'

The chill at Alastair's heart turned to ice.

'But the Prince is in Derby,' he stammered. 'He marches south.'

'Not so, young sir,' said the man. 'I dunno the why of it, but since cockcrow he and his rascality has been fleein' north. Old England's too warm for the vermin and they're hastin' back to their bogs.'

The head was suddenly withdrawn, since the man saw something which was still hid from the others. There was a sound of feet in the road, the soft tread which deer make when they are changing their pasture. From his place in the alley Alastair saw figures come into sight, a string of outlandish figures that without pause or word poured down the street. There were perhaps a score of them – barefoot Highlanders, their ragged kilts buckled high on their bodies, their legs blue with cold, their shirts unspeakably foul and tattered, their long hair matted into elf-locks. Each man carried plunder, one a kitchen clock slung on his back by a rope, another a brace of squalling hens, another some goodman's wraprascal. Their furtive eyes raked the houses, but they did not pause in the long loping trot with which of a moonlight night they had often slunk through the Lochaber passes. They wore the Macdonald tartan, and the familiar sight seemed to strip from Alastair's eyes the last film of illusion.

So that was the end of the long song. Gone the velvet and steel of a great crusade, the honourable hopes, the chivalry and the high adventure, and what was left was this furtive banditti slinking through the mud like the riff-raff of a fair. . . . It was too hideous to envisage, and the young man's mind was mercifully dulled after the first shattering certainty. Mechanically the three turned into the street.

The courage of the inhabitants was reviving. One or two men had shown themselves, and one fellow with a flageolet was starting a tune. Another took it up, and began to sing.

'O Brother Sawney, hear you the news?'

and presently several joined in the chorus of

'Twang 'em, we'll bang 'em, and
Hang 'em up all.'

'Follow me,' said Midwinter, and they followed him beyond the houses, and presently turned off into a path that ran among woods into the dale. In Alastair's ears the accursed tune rang like the voice of thousands, till it seemed that all England behind him was singing it, a scornful valedictory to folly.

He dismounted in a dream and found himself set by the hearth in the well-scrubbed kitchen of a woodland inn. Midwinter disappeared and returned with three tankards of home-brewed, which he distributed among them. No one spoke a word, Johnson sprawling on a chair with his chin on his breast and his eyes half-closed, while his left hand beat an aimless tattoo, Midwinter back in the shadows, and Alastair in the eye of the fire, unseeing and absorbed. The palsy was passing from the young man's mind, and he was enduring the bitterness of returning thought, like the pain of the blood flowing back to a frozen limb. No agony ever endured before in his life, not even the passion of disquiet when he had been prisoner in the hut and had overheard Sir John Norreys's talk, had so torn at the roots of his being.

For it was clear that on him and on him alone had the Cause shipwrecked. At some hour yesterday the fainthearts in the Council had won, and the tragic decision had been taken, the Prince protesting – he could see the bleached despair in his face and hear the hopeless pleading in his voice. He imagined Lochiel and others of the stalwarts pleading for a day's delay, delay which might bring the lost messenger, himself, with the proofs that would convince the doubters. All was over now, for a rebellion on the defensive was a rebellion lost. With London at their mercy, with Cumberland and the Whig Dukes virtually in flight, and a dumb England careless which master was hers, they had turned their back on victory and gone northward to chaos and defeat. And all because of their doubt of support, which was even then waiting in the West for their summons. Mr Nicholas Kyd had conquered in his downfall, and in his exile would chuckle over the discomfiture of his judges.

But it had been his own doing – his and none other's. Providence had provided an eleventh-hour chance, which he had refused. Had he ridden straight from Brightwell, he could have been with the Prince in the small hours of the morning,

time enough to rescind the crazy decision and set the army on
the road for Loughborough and St James's. But he had put his
duty behind him for a whim. Not a whim of pleasure – for he
had sacrificed his dearest hopes – but of another and a lesser
duty. A perverse duty, it seemed to him now, the service of a
woman rather than of his King. Great God, what a tangle was
life! He felt no bitterness against any mortal soul, not even
against the oafs who were now singing 'George is magnanimous'. He and he alone must bear the blame, since in a high
mission he had let his purpose be divided, and in a crisis had
lacked that singleness of aim which is the shining virtue of the
soldier. . . . His imagination, heated to fever point, made a
panorama of tragic scenes. He saw the Prince's young face thin
and haggard and drawn, looking with hopeless eyes into the
northern mists, a Pretender now for evermore, when he might
have been a King. He saw his comrades, condemned to lost
battles with death or exile at the end of them. He saw his clan,
which might have become great again, reduced to famished
vagrants, like the rabble of Macdonalds seen an hour ago
scurrying at the tail of the army. . . . That knot of caterans
was the true comment on the tragedy. Plunderers of old wives'
plenishing when they should have been a King's bodyguard in
the proud courts of palaces!

The picture maddened him with its bitter futility. He dropped
his head on his breast and cried like a heartbroken child. 'Ah,
my grief, my grief! I have betrayed my Prince and undone my
people. There is no comfort for me any more in the world.' At
the cry Johnson lifted his head, and stared with eyes not less
tragic than his own.

Midwinter had carried that day at his saddle-bow an oddly
shaped case which never left him. Back in the shadow he had
opened it and taken out his violin, and now drew from it the thin
fine notes which were the prelude to his playing. Alastair did not
notice the music for a little, but gradually familiar chords struck
in on his absorption and awoke their own memories. It was the
air of 'Diana,' which was twined with every crisis of the past

weeks. The delicate melody filled the place like a vapour, and to the young man brought not peace, but a different passion.

A passion of tenderness was in it, a wayward wounded beauty. Claudia's face again filled his vision, the one face that in all his life had brought love into his bustling soldierly moods and moved his heart to impulses which aforetime he would have thought incredible. Love had come to him and he had passed it by, but not without making sacrifice, for to the goddess he had offered his most cherished loyalties. Now it was all behind him – but by God, he did not, he would not regret it. He had taken the only way, and if it had pleased Fate to sport cruelly with him, that was no fault of his. He had sacrificed one loyalty to a more urgent, and with the thought bitterness went out of his soul. Would Lochiel, would the Prince blame him? Assuredly no. Tragedy had ensued, but the endeavour had been honest. He saw the ironic pattern of life spread out beneath him, as a man views a campaign from a mountain, and he came near to laughter – laughter with an undertone of tears.

Midwinter changed the tune, and the air was now that which he had played that night on Otmoor in the camp of the moormen.

> 'Three naked men we be,
> Stark aneath the blackthorn tree.'

He laid down his violin. 'I bade you call me to your aid, Alastair Maclean, if all else failed you and your pride miscarried. Maybe that moment has come. We in this place are three naked men.'

'I am bare to the bone,' said Alastair, 'I have given up my lady, and I have failed in duty to my Prince. I have no rag of pride left on me, nor ambition, nor hope.'

Johnson spoke. 'I am naked enough, but I had little to lose. I am a scholar and a Christian and, I trust, a gentleman, but I am bitter poor, and ill-favoured, and sore harassed by bodily affliction. Naked, ay, naked as when I came from the womb.'

Midwinter moved into the firelight, with a crooked smile on his broad face. 'We be three men in like case,' he said.

'Nakedness has its merits and its faults. A naked man travels fast and light, for he has nothing that he can lose, and his mind is free from cares, so that it is better swept and garnished for the reception of wisdom. But if he be naked he is also defenceless, and the shod feet of the world can hurt him. You have been sore trampled on, sirs. One has lost a lady whom he loved as a father, and the other a mistress and a Cause. Naturally your hearts are sore. Will you that I help in the healing of them? Will you join me in Old England, which is the refuge of battered men?'

Alastair looked up and gently shook his head. 'For me,' he said, 'I go up to Ramoth-Gilead, like the King of Israel I heard the parson speak of this morning. It is fated that I go there and it is fated that I fail. Having done so much to wreck the Cause, the least I can do is to stand by it to the end. I am convinced that the end is not far off, and if it be also the end of my days I am content.'

'And I,' said Johnson, 'have been minded since this morning to get me a sword and fight in His Highness's army.'

Alastair looked at the speaker with eyes half affectionate, half amused.

'Nay, that I do not permit. In Scotland we strive on our own ground and in our own quarrel, and I would involve no Englishman in what is condemned to defeat. You have not our sentiments, sir, and you shall not share our disasters. But I shall welcome your company to within sight of Ramoth-Gilead.'

'I offer the hospitality of Old England,' said Midwinter.

There was no answer and he went on –

'It is balm for the wearied, sirs, and a wondrous opiate for the unquiet. If you have lost all baggage, you retire to a world where baggage is unknown. If you seek wisdom, you will find it, and you will forget alike the lust of life and the dread of death.'

'Can you teach me to forget the fear of death?' Johnson asked sharply. 'Hark you, sir, I am a man of stout composition, for there is something gusty and gross in my humour which makes me careless of common fear. I will face an angry man, or mob, or beast with equanimity, even with joy. But the unknown terrors of death fill me, when I reflect on them, with the most painful forebodings. I conjecture, and my imagination wanders in labyrinths of dread. I most devoutly believe in the living God, and I stumblingly attempt to serve Him, but 'tis an awful thing to fall into His hand.'

'In Old England,' said Midwinter, 'they look on death as not less natural and kindly than the shut of evening. They lay down their heads on the breast of earth as a flower dies in the field.'

Johnson was looking with abstracted eyes to the misty woods beyond a lozenged window, and he replied like a man thinking his own thoughts aloud.

'The daedal earth!' he muttered. 'Poets, many poets, have sung of it, and I have had glimpses of it. . . . A sweet and strange thing when a man quits the servitude of society and goes to nurse with Gaea. I remember . . .'

Then a new reflection seemed to change his mood and bring him to his feet with his hands clenched.

'Tut, sir,' he cried, 'these are but brutish consolations. I can find that philosophy in pagan writers, and it has small comfort for a Christian. I thank you, but I have no part in your world of woods and mountains. I am better fitted for a civil life, and must needs return to London and bear the burden of it in a garret. But I am not yet persuaded as to that matter of taking arms. I have a notion that I am a good man of my hands.'

Midwinter's eyes were on Alastair, who smiled and shook his head.

'You offer me Old England, but I am of another race and land. I must follow the road of my fathers.'

'That is your answer?'

'Nay, it is not all my answer. Could you understand the Gaelic, or had I my fingers now on the chanter-reed, I could give it more fully. You in England must keep strictly to the high road, or flee to the woods – one or the other, for there is no third way. We of the Highlands carry the woods with us to the high roads of life. We are natives of both worlds, wherefore we need renounce neither. But my feet must tread the high road till my strength fails.'

'It was the answer I looked for,' said Midwinter, and he rose and slung his violin on his arm. 'Now we part, gentlemen, and it is not likely that we shall meet again. But nevertheless you are sealed of our brotherhood, for you are of the Naked Men, since the film has gone from your sight and you have both looked into your own hearts. You can never again fear mortal face or the tricks of fortune, for you are men indeed, and can confront your Maker with honest eyes. Farewell, brother.' He embraced Alastair and kissed him on the cheek, and held for a second Johnson's great hand in his greater. Then he left the room, and a minute later a horse's hooves drummed on the stones of the little yard.

For a little the two left behind sat in silence. Then Johnson spoke: 'My dear young lady should by this time be across Trent. I take it that she is safe from all perils of the road in Her Grace's carriage.' Then he took up a poker and stirred the logs. 'Clear eyes are for men an honourable possession, but they do not make for happiness. I pray God that those of my darling child may to the end of a long life be happily blinded.'

NINETEEN

Ramoth-Gilead

Three hours' hard riding should have brought them to the tail of the Highland army, but the horses were still in their stalls when the night fell. For, as he sat by the fire with Johnson, the latches of Alastair's strength were loosened and it fell from him. The clout on the head, the imperfect convalescence, the seasons of mental conflict and the many hours in the saddle had brought even his tough body to cracking-point. The room swam before his eyes, there was burning pain in his head, and dizziness and nausea made him collapse in his chair. Johnson and the hostess's son, a half-grown boy, carried him to bed, and all night he was in an ague – the return, perhaps, of the low fever which had followed his wound at Fontenoy. There was a buzzing in his brain which happily prevented thought, and next day, when the fever ebbed, he was so weak that his mind was content to be vacant. By such merciful interposition he escaped the bitterest pangs of reproach which would have followed his realisation of failure.

The first afternoon Johnson sat with him, giving him vinegar and water to sip, and changing the cool cloths on his brow. Alastair was drifting aimlessly on the tide of weakness, seeing faces – Claudia, Kitty of Queensberry, Cornbury, very notably the handsome periwigged head of the King's Solicitor – like the stone statues in a garden. They had no cognisance of him, and he did not wish to attract their notice, for they belonged to a world that had vanished, and concerned him less than the figures on a stage. By and by his consciousness became clearer, and he was aware of a heartbreak that enveloped him like an atmosphere, a great cloud of grief that must shadow his path for ever. And yet there were rifts in it where light as from a spring sky broke through, and he found himself melting at times in a sad tenderness. He had lost tragically, but he had learned that there was more to prize than he had dreamed.

Johnson, his face like a bishop's, sat at the bed foot, saying nothing, but gazing at the sick man with the eyes of an old friendly dog. When Alastair was able to drink the gruel the hostess produced, the tutor considered that he must assist his recovery by sprightly conversation. But the honest man's soul had been so harassed in the past days that he found it hard to be jocose. He sprawled in his wooden chair, and the window which faced him revealed sundry rents in his small-clothes and the immense shabbiness of his coat. Alastair on his bed watched the heavy pitted features, the blinking eyes, the perpetually twitching hands with a certainty that never in his days had he seen a man so uncouth or so wholly to be loved; and, as he looked, he seemed to discern that in the broad brow and the noble head which was also to be revered.

The young man's gaze having after the fashion of sick folk fixed itself upon one spot, Johnson became conscious of it, and looked down on his disreputable garments with distaste not unmixed with humour.

'My clothes are old and sorry,' he said. 'I lament the fact, sir, for I am no lover of negligence in dress. A wise man dare not go under-dressed till he is of consequence enough to forbear carrying the badge of his rank upon his back. That is not my case, and I would fain be more decent in my habiliments, which do not properly become even my modest situation in life. But I confess that at the moment I have but two guineas, given me by my dear young lady, and I have destined them for another purpose than haberdashery.'

What this purpose was appeared before the next evening. During the afternoon Johnson disappeared in company with the youth of the inn, and returned at the darkening with a face flushed and triumphant. Alastair, whose strength was reviving, was sitting up when the door opened to admit a deeply self-conscious figure.

It was Johnson in a second-hand riding-coat of blue camlet, cut somewhat in the military fashion, and in all likelihood once the property of some dashing yeoman. But that was only half of his new magnificence, for below the riding-coat, beneath his drab coat, and buckled above his waistcoat, was a great belt, and from the belt depended a long scabbard.

'I make you my compliments,' said Alastair. 'You have acquired a cloak.'

'Nay, sir, but I have acquired a better thing. I have got me a sword.'

He struggled with his skirts and after some difficulty drew from its sheath a heavy old-fashioned cut-and-thrust blade, of the broadsword type. With it he made a pass or two, and then brought it down in a sweep which narrowly missed the bedpost.

'Now am I armed against all enemies,' he cried, stamping his foot. 'If Polyphemus comes, have at his eye,' and he lunged towards the window.

The mingled solemnity and triumph of his air checked Alastair's laughter. 'This place is somewhat confined for sword-play,' he said. 'Put it up, and tell me where you discovered the relic.'

'I purchased it this very afternoon, through the good offices of the lad below. There was an honest or indifferent honest fellow in the neighbourhood who sold me cloak, belt and sword for three half-guineas. It is an excellent weapon, and I trust to you, sir, to give me a lesson or two in its use.'

He flung off the riding-coat, unbuckled the belt and sat himself in his accustomed chair.

'Two men are better than one on the roads,' he said, 'the more if both are armed. I would consult you, sir, on a point of honour. I have told you that I am reputably, though not highly born, and I have had a gentleman's education. I am confident that but for a single circumstance, no gentleman need scruple to cross swords with me or to draw his sword by my side. The single circumstance is this – I have reason to believe that a relative suffered death by hanging, though for what cause I do not know, since the man disappeared utterly and his end is only a matter of gossip. Yet I must take the supposition at its worst. Tell me, sir, does that unhappy connection in your view deprive me of the armigerous rights of a gentleman?'

This time Alastair did not forbear to smile.

'Why no, sir. In my own land the gallows is reckoned an ornament to a pedigree, and it has been the end of many a promising slip of my own house. Indeed it is not unlikely to be the end of me. But why do you ask the question?'

'Because I purpose to go with you to the wars.'

Johnson's face was as serious as a judge's, and his dull eyes had kindled with a kind of shamefaced ardour. The young man felt so strong a tide of affection rising in him for this uncouth crusader that he had to do violence to his own inclination in shaping his counsel.

'It cannot be, my dear sir,' he cried. 'I honour you, I love you, but I will not permit a futile sacrifice. Had England risen for our Prince, your aid would have been most heartily welcome, but now the war will be in Scotland, and I tell you it is as hopeless as a battle of a single kestrel against a mob of ravens. I fight in it, for that is my trade and duty; I have been bred to war, and it is the quarrel of my house and my race. But for you it is none of these things. You would be a stranger in a foreign strife. . . . Nay, sir, but you must listen to reason. You are a scholar and have your career to make in a far different world. God knows I would welcome your comradeship, for I respect your courage and I love your honest heart, but I cannot suffer you to ride to certain ruin. Gladly I accept your convoy, but you will stop short of Ramoth-Gilead.'

The other's face was a heavy mask of disappointment. 'I must be the judge of my own path,' he said sullenly.

'But you will be guided in that judgment by one who knows better than you the certainties of the road. It is no part of a man's duty to walk aimlessly to death.'

The last word seemed to make Johnson pause. But he recovered himself.

'I have counted the cost,' he said. 'I fear death, God knows, but not more than other men. I will be no stranger in your wars. I will change my name to MacIan, and be as fierce as any Highlander.'

'It cannot be. What you told Midwinter is the truth. If you are not fitted by nature for Old England, still less are you fitted for our wild long-memoried North. You will go back to London, Mr Johnson, and some day you will find fortune and happiness. You will marry some day . . .'

At the word Johnson's face grew very red, and he turned his eyes on the ground and rolled his head with an odd nervous motion.

'I have misled you,' he said. 'I have been married these ten years. My dear Tetty is now living in the vicinity of London. . . . I have not written to her for seven weeks. *Mea culpa! Mea maxima culpa!*'

He put his head in his hands and seemed to be absorbed in a passion of remorse.

'You must surely return to her,' said Alastair gently.

Johnson raised his head. 'I would not have you think that I had forgotten her. She has her own small fortune, which suffices for one, though scant enough for two. I earn so little that I am rather an encumbrance than an aid, and she is more prosperous in my absence.'

'Yet she must miss you, and if you fall she will be widowed.'

'True, true. I have no clearness in the matter. I will seek light in prayer and sleep.' He marched from the room, leaving his new accoutrements lying neglected in a corner.

Next day Alastair was sufficiently recovered to travel, and the two set out shortly after daylight. The woman of the inn, who had been instructed by Midwinter, had counsel to give. The Ashbourne road was too dangerous, for already the pursuit had begun and patrols of Government horse were on the trail of the Highlanders; two gentlemen such as they might be taken for the tail of the rebels and suffer accordingly. She advised that the road should be followed by Chesterfield and the east side of the county, which would avoid the high hills of the Peak and bring them to Manchester and the Lancashire levels by an easier if a longer route. It was agreed that the two should pass as master and man – Mr Andrew Watson, the coal-merchant of Newcastle, and his secretary.

The secretary, ere they started, drew his sword and fingered it lovingly. 'I must tell you,' he whispered to Alastair, 'that the reflections of the night have not shaken my purpose. I am still resolved to accompany you to the wars.'

But there was no gusto in his air. All that day among the shallow vales he hardly spoke, and now and then would groan lamentably. The weather was mist and driving rain, and the travellers' prospect was little beyond the puddles of the road and the wet glistening stone of the roadside dykes. That night they had risen into the hills, where the snow lay in the hollows and at the dyke-backs, and slept at a wretched hovel of a smithy on a bed of bracken. The smith, a fellow with a week's beard and redrimmed eyes, gave the news of the place. The Scots, he had heard, had passed Macclesfield the night before, and all day the militia, horsed by the local squires, had been scouting the moors picking up breechless stragglers. He did not appear to suspect his sullen visitors, who proclaimed their hurry to reach Manchester on an errand of trade.

Thereafter to both men the journey was a nightmare. In Manchester, where they slept a night, the mob was burning Charles in effigy and hiccuping 'George is magnanimous' – that mob which some weeks before had worn white favours and drunk damnation to Hanover. They saw a few miserable Highlanders, plucked from the tail of the army, in the hands of the town guard, and a mountebank in a booth had got himself up in a parody of a kilt and sang ribaldry to a screaming crowd. They heard, too, of the Government troops hard on the trail, Wade cutting in from the east by the hill roads, Cumberland hastening from the south, Bland's and Cobham's regiments already north of the town, mounted yeomen to guard the fords and bridges, and beacons blazing on every hill to raise the country.

'The Prince must halt and fight,' Alastair told his companion as they rode out of Manchester next morning. 'With this hell's pack after him he will be smothered unless he turn and tear them. Lord George will command the rear-guard, and I am positive he will stand at Preston. Ribble ford is the place. You may yet witness a battle, and have the chance of fleshing that blade of yours.'

But when they came to Preston – by circuitous ways, for they had to keep up the pretence of timid travellers, and the main road was too thick with alarums – they found the bridge held by dragoons. Here they were much catechised, and, having given Newcastle as their destination, were warned that the northern roads into Yorkshire were not for travellers and bidden go back to Manchester. The Prince, it seemed, was at Lancaster, and Lord George and the Glengarry men and the Appin Stewarts half-way between that town and Preston.

That night Alstair implored Johnson to return. 'We are on the edge of battle,' he told him, 'and I beseech you to keep away from what can only bring you ruin.' But the other was obstinate. 'I will see you at any rate on the eve of joining your friends,' he said, 'We have yet to reach Ramoth-Gilead.'

The Preston dragoons were too busy on their own affairs to give much heed to two prosaic travellers. Alastair and Johnson stole out of the town easily enough next morning, and making a wide circuit to the west joined the Lancaster road near Garstang. To their surprise the highway was almost deserted, and they rode into Lancaster without hindrance. There they found the town in a hubbub, windows shuttered, entries barricaded, the watch making timid patrols about the streets, and one half the people looking anxiously south, the other fearfully north to the Kendal road. The Prince had been there no later than yesterday, and the rear-guard had left at dawn. News had come that the Duke of Cumberland was recalled, because of a French landing, and there were some who said that now the Scots would turn south again and ravage their way to London.

The news, which he did not believe, encouraged Alastair to mend his pace. There had been some kind of check in the pursuit, and the Prince might yet cross the Border without a battle. He believed that this would be Lord George's aim, who knew his army and would not risk it, if he could, in a weary defensive action. The speed of march would therefore be increased, and he must quicken if he would catch them up. The two waited in Lancaster only to snatch a meal, and then set out by the Hornby road, intending to fetch a circuit towards Kendal, where it seemed likely the Prince would lie.

The afternoon was foggy and biting cold, so that Alastair looked for snow and called on Johnson to hurry before the storm broke. But the fall was delayed, and up to the darkening they rode in an icy haze through the confused foothills. The mountains were beginning again, the hills of bent and heather that he knew; the streams swirled in grey rockrimmed pools, the air had the sour, bleak, yet invigorating tang of his own country. But now he did not welcome it, for it was the earnest of defeat. He was returning after failure. Nay, he was leaving his heart buried in the soft South country, which once he had despised. A wild longing, the perversion of homesickness, filled him for the smoky brown champaigns and the mossy woodlands which now enshrined the jewel of Claudia. He had thought that regrets were put away for ever and that he had turned his eyes stonily to a cold future, but he had forgotten that he was young.

In the thick weather they came from the lanes into a broader high road, and suddenly found their progress stayed. A knot of troopers bade them halt, and unslung their muskets. They were fellows in green jackets, mounted on shaggy country horses, and they spoke with the accent of the Midlands. Alastair repeated his tale, and was informed that their orders were to let no man pass that road and to take any armed and mounted travellers before the General. He asked their regiment and was told that it was the Rangers, a corps of gentlemen volunteers. The men were cloddish but not unfriendly, and, suspecting that the corps was some raw levy of yokels commanded by some thickskulled squire, Alastair bowed to discretion and bade them show the way to the General's quarters.

But the moorland farmhouse to which they were led awoke his doubts. The sentries had the trimness of a headquarters guard, and the horses he had a glimpse of in the yard were not the screws or cart-horses of the ordinary yeoman. While they waited in the low-ceiled kitchen he had reached the conclusion that in the General he would find some regular officer of Wade's or Cumberland's command, and as he bowed his head to enter the parlour he had resolved on his line of conduct.

But he was not prepared for the sight of Oglethrope; grim, aquiline, neat as a Sunday burgess, who raised his head from a mass of papers, stared for a second and then smiled.

'You have brought me a friend, Roger,' he told the young lieutenant. 'These gentlemen will be quartered here this night, for the weather is too thick to travel further; likewise they will sup with me.'

When the young man had gone, he held out his hand to Alastair.

'We seem fated to cross each other's path, Mr Maclean.'

'I would present to you my friend, Mr Samuel Johnson, sir. This is General Oglethorpe.'

Johnson stared at him and then thrust forward a great hand.

'I am honoured, sir, deeply honoured. Every honest man has heard the name.' And he repeated:

> 'One, driven by strong benevolence of soul,
> 'Shall fly like Oglethrope from pole to pole.'

The General smiled. 'Mr Pope was over-kind to my modest deserts. But, gentlemen, I am in command of a part of His Majesty's forces, and at this moment we are in the region of war. I must request from you some account of your recent doings and your present purpose. Come forward to the fire, for it is wintry weather. And stay! Your Prince's steward has been scouring the country for cherry brandy, to which it seems

His Highness is partial. But all has not been taken.' He filled
two glasses from a decanter at his elbow.

Looking at the rugged face and the grave kindly eyes, Alastair
resolved that it was a case for a full confession. He told of his
doings at Brightwell after the meeting with Oglethorpe at the
Sleeping Deer, and of the fate of Mr Nicholas Kyd, but he made
no mention of Sir John Norreys. He told of his ride to Derby,
and what he had found on the Ashbourne road. It is possible
that there was a break in his voice, for Oglethorpe averted his
eyes and shook his head.

'I cannot profess to regret a failure which it is my duty to
ensure,' he said, 'but I can pity a brave man who sees his hopes
destroyed. And now, sir? What course do you shape?'

'I must pursue the poor remains of my duty. I go to join my
Prince.'

'And it is my business to prevent you!'

Alastair looked at him composedly. 'Nay, sir, I do not think
that such can be your duty. It might be Cumberland's or
Wade's, but not Oglethorpe's, for you can understand another
loyalty than your own, and I do not think you will interfere with
mine. I ask only to go back to my own country. I will give you my
word that I will not strike a blow in England.'

Again Oglethorpe smiled. 'You read my heart with some
confidence, sir. If I were to detain you, what would be the
charge? You have not yet taken arms against His Majesty. Of
your political doings I have no experience: to me you are a
gentleman travelling to Scotland, who has on one occasion
rendered good service to myself and so to His Majesty. That
is all which, as a soldier, I am concerned to know. You will have
quarters for the night, and tomorrow, if you desire it, continue
your journey. But I must stipulate that the road you follow is not
that of the Prince's march. You will not join his army till it is
north of Esk.'

Alastair bowed. 'I am content.'

'But your friend,' Oglethorpe continued. 'This Mr Samuel
Johnson who quotes so appositely the lines of Mr Pope. He is an

Englishman, and is in another case. I cannot permit Mr Johnson to cross the Border.'

'He purposes to keep me company,' said Alastair, 'till I have joined the Prince.'

'Nay, sir,' cried Johnson. 'You have been honest with us, and I will be honest with you. My desire is to join the Prince and fight by my friend's side.'

Oglethorpe looked at the strange figure, below the skirts of whose old brown coat peeped a scabbard. 'You seem,' he said, 'to have fulfilled the scriptural injunction "He that hath no sword, let him sell his garment and buy one." But, sir, it may not be. I would not part two friends before it is necessary, but you will give me your parole that you will not enter Scotland, or I must hold you prisoner and send you to Manchester.'

Johnson turned to Alastair and put a hand on his shoulder. 'It seems that Providence is on your side, my friend, and has intervened to separate us. That was your counsel, but it was never mine . . . . So be it, then.' He walked to the window and seemed to be in trouble with his dingy cravat.

Next morning when Oglethorpe's Rangers began their march towards Shap, the two travellers set out by an easterly road, forded the Lune and made for the Eden valley. The rains filled the streams and mosses, and their progress was slow, so that for days they were entangled among the high Cumbrian hills. News of the affair at Clifton, where Lord George beat off Cumberland's van and saved the retreat, came to them by a packman in a herd's sheiling on Cross Fell, and after that their journey was clear down the Eden, till the time came to avoid Carlisle and make straight across country for Esk. The last night they lay at an ale-house on the Lyneside, and Alastair counted thirty guineas from his purse.

'With this I think you may reach London,' he told Johnson, and when the latter expostulated, he bade him consider it a loan. 'If I fall, it is my bequest to you; and if I live, then we shall assuredly meet again and you can repay me. I would fain make it more, but money is likely to be a scarce commodity in yonder army.'

'You have a duty clear before you,' said the other dismally. 'For me, I have none such; I would I had. But I will seek no opiates in a life of barbarism. I am resolved to spend what days the Almighty may still allot me on the broad highway of humanity. When I have found my task I will adhere to it like a soldier.'

Next morning they rode to a ridge beneath which the swollen Esk poured through the haughlands. It was a day of flying squalls, and the great dales of Esk and Annan lay mottled with sun-gleams and purple shadows up to the dark hills, which, chequered with snow, defended the way to the north. Further down Alastair's quick eye noted a commotion on the river banks, and dark objects bobbing in the stream.

'See,' he cried, 'His Highness is crossing. We have steered skilfully, for I enter Scotland by his side.'

'Is that Scotland?' Johnson asked, his short-sighted eyes peering at the wide vista.

'Scotland it is, and somewhere over yon hills lies Ramoth-Gilead.'

Alastair's mind had in these last days won a certain peace, and now at the sight of the army something quickened in him that had been dead since the morning on the Ashbourne road. Youth was waking from its winter sleep. The world had become coloured again, barriers were down, roads ran into the future. Hazard seemed only hazard now and not despair. Suddenly came the sound of wild music, as the pipers struck up the air of 'Bundle and Go'. The strain rose far and faint and elfin, like a wandering wind, and put fire into his veins.

'That is the march for the road,' Alastair cried. 'Now I am for my own country.'

'And I for mine,' said Johnson, but there was no spring in his voice. He rubbed his eyes, peered in the direction of the music, and made as if to unbuckle his sword. Then he thought better of it. 'Nay, I will keep the thing to nurse my memory,' he said.

The two men joined hands; and Alastair, in his foreign fashion, kissed the other on the cheek. As they mounted, a shower enveloped them, and the landscape was blotted out, so that the two were isolated in a world of their own.

'We are naked men,' said Johnson. 'Each must go up to his own Ramoth-Gilead, but I would that yours and mine had been the same.'

Then he turned his horse and rode slowly southward into the rain.

Postscript

Thus far Mr Derwent's papers.

With the farewell on the Cumberland moor Alastair Maclean is lost to us in the mist. Of the nature of Ramoth-Gilead let history tell; it is too sad a tale for the romancer. But one is relieved to know that he did not fall at Culloden, or swing like so many on Haribee outside the walls of Carlisle. For the Editor has been so fortunate as to discover a further document, after a second search among Mr Derwent's archives, a document in the handwriting of Mr Samuel Johnson himself; and there seems to be the strongest presumption that it was addressed to Alastair at some town in France, for there is a mention of hospitality shown one Alan Maclean who had crossed the Channel with a message and was on the eve of returning. There is no super-scription, the letter begins 'My dear Sir', and the end is lost; but since it is headed 'Gough Square', and contains a reference to the writer's beginning work on his great dictionary, the date may be conjectured to be 1748. Unfortunately the paper is much torn and discoloured, and only one passage can be given with any certainty of correctness. I transcribe it as a memorial of a friendship which was to colour the thoughts of a great man to his dying day and which, we may be assured, left an impress no less indelible upon the mind of the young Highlander.

'. . . I send by your kinsman the second moiety of the loan which you made me at our last meeting, for I assume that, like so many of your race and politics now in France, you are somewhat in straits for money. I do assure you that I can well afford to make the repayment, for I have concluded a profitable arrangement with the booksellers for the publication of an English dictionary, and have already received a considerable sum in advance. . . .

'I will confess to you, my dear sir, that often in moments of leisure and in quiet places, my memory traverses our brief Odyssey, and I am moved again with fear and hope and the sadness of renunciation. You say, and I welcome your generosity, that from me you acquired something of philosophy; from you I am bound to reply that I learned weighty lessons in the conduct of our mortal life. You taught me that a man can be gay and yet most resolute, and that a Christian is not less capable of fortitude than an ancient Stoic. The recollection of that which we encountered together lives in me to warm my heart when it is cold, and to restore in dark seasons my trust in my fellow men. The end was a proof, if proof were wanted, of the vanity of human wishes, but sorrow does not imply failure, and my memory of it will not fade till the hour of death and the day of judgment. . . .

'I have been at some pains to collect from my friends in Oxford news of my lady—. You will rejoice to hear that she does well. Her husband, who has now a better name in the shire, is an ensample of marital decorum and treats her kindly, and she has been lately blessed with a male child. That, I am confident, is the tidings which you desire to hear, for your affection for that lady has long been purged of any taint of selfishness, and you can rejoice in her welfare as in that of a sister. But I do not forget that you have buried your heart in that monument to domestic felicity. Our Master did not place us in this world to win even honest happiness, but to shape and purify our immortal souls, and sorrow must be the companion of the noblest endeavour. Like the shepherd in Virgil you grew at last acquainted with Love, and found him a native of the rocks. . . .'